Synchronous

Robert Kersten

Second Edition
Printed in U.S.A.
ISBN 978-0-9915246-7-9

Cover Design by Robert Kersten.

www.multidimensionaltime.com

Acknowledgements

A special *thanks* to my wife Anita, for all her feedback, suggestions, and editing, that helped bring this story and my writing to a new level. To my daughter Ashlyn, whose gift with words and music have been an inspiration.

And to Time, my greatest teacher.

FACT:

Time is real.
Nobody has seen it, heard it, or touched it.
We see change in the world around us, we measure it, and call it time.

Space is real.
Nobody has seen it, heard it, or touched it.
We see objects in the world around us, we measure distances between them,
and call it space.

What we think and feel consciously appears real.
Nobody has ever directly seen, heard or touched their consciousness.
We measure consciousness by the manner in which we express ourselves and call these expressions our thoughts and emotions.

What we think about ourselves as humans with regards to time and space is about to change and you are about to find out how.

1.

Dr. Adamel, Skylar's Modern Physics professor, finishes his lecture with the statement, "One of you, the next generation physicists, could possibly unite gravity and quantum physics and in doing so unite all the theories that describe this universe."

Skylar stiffens as she thinks, *What about human consciousness and the creative thoughts that allow us to come up with these scientific theories in the first place? They aren't included in these theories. Our consciousness is just as real as the theories being taught in this physics program.*

Skylar looks at her classmate and friend, Brian, who is closing his notebook with a pleased look on his face. Skylar has tried unsuccessfully in the past to engage Brian, as well as other friends, students, and even the occasional professor, in a discussion about the definition of *everything* in physics being too narrow. More often than not, she was told the same story: Physics is not psychology, and will never be. The two are not related.

Skylar knows they are wrong. She also knows this isn't the first time that scientists have fallen into the trap of thinking they understand just about everything.

Skylar's attention snaps back to the classroom as Dr. Adamel says, "Remember, there will be a test on Monday covering the chapters on quantum physics, so I am sure you'll be busy this weekend. Our next adventure will be exploring the physics of solids. See you Monday."

Skylar slowly slips her notebook into her backpack. The familiar feeling of isolation washes over her; to avoid it, she turns to start a conversation with Brian. But Brian is already rushing for the door to get to his next class. She wishes that Bohdi was not so far away. He would immediately understand her frustration.

Skylar has a break between this class and her next. She decides to get a cup of coffee and heads to the university coffee shop. Along the way, she thinks about Max Planck. Planck was a student studying physics at a university in Europe at the end of the nineteenth century and came from a musical family who thought his talents would be better served as a musician. A prominent physics professor who taught at Planck's university discouraged his interest in physics by telling Max that everything that needed to be understood in physics was already known, except some small problem that he expected would soon be solved.

Planck was particularly intrigued with the idea that energy in the universe can never be created or destroyed, it can only change form. Starting with this theory, he attacked that small problem plaguing physics. Max worked on this theoretical problem for more than two decades, and finally managed to derive an equation that accurately predicted what was measured experimentally. Problem solved. But this solution had an issue. In order for Planck's theory to work, he had to include a term in his equation that limited energy to jumps as it increased or decreased, something that was unthinkable to the scientific community at the time. It was, if a car could only travel in incremental jumps of five miles per hour, and nothing in between. It could go five, ten or fifteen miles per hour, but never seven, or twelve. Max called these energy jumps *quanta*. Planck's Quantum Theory radically challenged everything physicists understood about nature, and humans' relationship to matter. His theory continues to do so even a hundred years later. So much for the late nineteenth century idea that they almost understood everything.

Skylar's phone pings with a text from home. She reads it as she walks and gets a little thrill of happiness at the thought that even her beloved phone is a result of Max Planck's revolutionary solution. Skylar knows that the current understanding of the world is just one revolutionary idea away from being blown wide open again. She believes that if the physics behind human consciousness can be determined, it could radically change the chaos created in our world, politically, socially and personally. Finding this new idea is her mission and it is the reason she chose physics as a major in college.

No matter how often she runs Planck's story through her mind, it always leaves her feeling hopeful.

2.

David and Jean Donaldson listen as their daughter's cell phone rings from the speaker on David's smartphone. David fiddles with the laces on his shoes, while Jean brushes the lint off her skirt to release nervous tension. They are calling Skylar at college, hoping she has some spare time this Saturday after her midday study group is done so they can share some unfortunate news with her. David looks at his watch again. Still 2:15 in the afternoon, same as the last time he looked. Skylar's study group should have ended by 2:00.

"Hi, Dad," Skylar answers.

"Hi, Skylar. Mom and I are both here. We have you on speaker. How are you?"

"Fine."

David sneaks a look at his wife. Jean stares back with her intense brown eyes as she mouths, *Everything is always fine.*

"Hi, Skylar, glad we could reach you," she says out loud.

"Mom, I got your voicemail earlier and planned to call you later. School is really busy right now. I have to be at the library at 3:00 to meet up with Brian to go over some class notes for our Modern Physics test on Monday." She sighs.

David and Jean hear the frustration in their daughter's voice. Skylar perks it up to sound more casual. "I'm walking back to the dorm to pick up some notes I left behind. Give me a second to find a spot where I can sit down and have some privacy."

"Okay."

Skylar turns away from the people running and walking along the paths that parallel the river near her dorm. The weather is cool for a late April day in Boston, but the sun occasionally peeks out from behind the fast-moving clouds. Some of the trees have buds now, and it won't be long before the leaves start growing. She's glad the rain finally stopped and the ground looks dry enough to sit on. She decides to play it safe and sits on a large root under an old oak.

Leaning back against the trunk, she asks her folks, "Okay, so what's up?"

"How's school going?" her father asks, curious about what is going on in his daughter's life.

"All right, but I feel like I'm trying to drink from a fire hose," Skylar says. "I feel out of balance, actually. I'm a conceptual person, and so much of my waking time is left-brain dominated because we process tons of information. I can do it, but it's taxing. I really am enjoying my elective Painting class. Anyway, how are you both doing?"

David decides to joke, "We're selling the house and sailing to the Caribbean."

"Yea, funny, Dad," Skylar shoots back.

David continues. "On a more serious note, as you know, the economy is struggling and so many towns are forced to make cutbacks."

"Don't tell me Mom's losing her job," Skylar interjects.

David looks at Jean and motions with his hands, signaling for her to step in. She struggles to keep her voice steady. "We recently found out that six teachers will be laid off at our school. Since I transferred there not long ago, and have little seniority, I'll be one of the teachers they have to let go."

David jumps in. "Since your mom's income covers your tuition and board, we want to talk to you about the option of transferring to Patterson University. It has lower tuition. I hate to say it, but to save the cost of boarding, you're going to need to move back home and commute."

David and Jean wanted to offer both their kids the opportunity to live at school, since they feel it is a valuable part of the college years. They had been able to do that with Celeste for her entire school career, but with no opportunities available for Jean at any of the schools within commuting distance of their home, they are forced to consider alternatives for Skylar.

"Uuuggghhhh!" Skylar regrets her groan as soon as it escapes. "Um, what I mean is, how are you taking it, Mom?"

David is impressed with his daughter's quick recovery.

"It's hard, sw—Skylar." She almost says "sweetie" but catches herself in time. "I love teaching, and the past year has been fun, but I will be okay."

Skylar thinks fast. She's okay with leaving the city, not just because of her recent breakup with Gordon. The past two college years have made it clear there are parts of being in the city she really enjoys, but if she's honest with herself, the overall environment isn't a good fit for her temperament. On the other hand, she's not sure living with her parents, at home, would be any better.

"You still there?" David asks.

Jean breaks the silence. "Gordon can come visit. He can stay in Celeste's bedroom. I'm sorry we haven't met him yet. He was away the last time we visited, as I recall."

"Um, Gordon and I broke up."

"I'm sorry to hear that, Skylar."

"Yeah, it sucks. But it was the right thing for us to do."

"May I ask why?" Jean asks with a note of hopefulness in her voice.

"For a number of reasons, Mom. Nothing earthshaking."

Jean's hope of finding out more about what is going on in her daughter's life is dashed. David hangs back, letting his wife try to drill for the information she desperately wants to hear from her daughter. Whenever Jean talks to their other daughter, Celeste, she is always happy to fill her mother in on everything she has been doing. If anything, Celeste shares too much, and Jean ends up worrying unnecessarily. For the past two years, though, she has barely known anything about Skylar's life.

"Hello?" her father checks, making sure they have not lost the connection.

"Yeah. I, uh, I'm okay with leaving the university, since I already know I need to make a change."

David waits for Skylar to continue, but there is silence. He decides to break the silence,

"Well, Skylar, we can talk more when you have time. We just wanted to give you some notice before you finish the semester, so you can let people know that, unless something radical happens, you won't be returning to Adams University in September."

David looks for a way to gracefully end the conversation.

Skylar speaks first. "I'm sorry you're losing your job, Mom. I think it sucks for you, for both of you . . . and yeah, for me too."

Relieved, David says, "Well, Skylar, sometimes life can be a bit of a suckfest."

Skylar laughs; she's never heard that word from her father.

"I agree wholeheartedly, Dad!"

David grins. Jean scowls at him. The English teacher in her will never be comfortable with such slang, even after raising two teenagers.

David thinks it would be wise to end the conversation on this good note, since it has gone better than expected. "So, do you have any other questions? Anything else we need to chat about?"

"Nope."

"Okay. If you need to talk, call us anytime."

"I know. Thanks, Dad. Thanks, Mom."

"We love you, Skylar," they say in unison.

Skylar grins. Even as a fiercely independent college student, she still likes to be told she is loved. "Love you both," she replies before breaking the connection. She checks her watch. She has twenty-five minutes to make it back to her dorm and then to the library. That's enough time to rest for a few minutes, so she tilts her head back until it rests on the tree trunk and looks up at the bare branches, focusing on their little buds. As she tries to relax, last night's dream forces its way past thoughts about school and spreads dread over her like a wet towel. She is rushing to the hospital with her father after the doctor called to say her mother's condition has changed dramatically, and she has only a few hours to live. They run through the corridors as her father struggles with his phone to get a hold of Celeste, who is flying in from the West Coast to be with them. They find room 343. A nurse, busy with the monitors, says the doctor will be in shortly. Skylar's father worries that his older daughter won't make it in time. The doctor arrives, and soon after he leaves, Skylar's mother takes her last breath. Skylar screams, "How is this possible!"

—which was when she woke up.

The dream really bothers her. She thinks back to the intense images that she sees when she focuses on her mother with her eyes closed in her deep meditative state. She calls the experience her Perception Reality. She shivers at the thought of it. The changes in her mother's field took her by surprise. Instead of the more vibrant colors she usually sees, her field had a dark-brown patch, something she had never seen before. Skylar realizes that her dream correlates to what she saw in the Perception Reality, and that her mother's health is the common thread. But her mother has no medical issues she is aware of and so she is confused. Her train of thought is interrupted as she realizes that she has to get moving to make it to the library in time.

3.

Skylar sits on top of a picnic bench in the quarry of her hometown of Northants, relishing a moment in the warmth of the sun. So far, the move home has been as it normally is during her summer breaks. But the real change will be felt by her in September, when she'll be going to a different university, and living at home again with her parents while at school. She loved the independence of being on her own at Adams University, of never having to explain or justify her choices.

"Where do you think everyone is?" Bohdi asks, sounding a bit perplexed.

"No idea." Skylar snaps her attention back to the present. She likes the sound of Bohdi's voice. He has a lower tone than most men and it is especially odd coming out of such a thin frame.

"Well, let me text Joe and Amelia," Skylar replies. She pulls up the bottom of her black, oversized shirt so she can get her phone out of the pocket of her bright-red shorts.

Bohdi looks at Skylar, his friend since they were twelve. Ever since they had their first classes together, he's admired her intelligence and spunk. She regularly spoke out in class, challenging teachers and ideas alike. He was quiet, preferring discussion with friends in informal settings. She was easily bored and applied herself to schoolwork only as she saw fit.

Her intelligence is hidden behind eccentric experimentation with hairstyles, coloring her brunette hair, and her love of changing her look—which makes her popular with the art and music crowd. The only thing she leaves untouched are her dark-brown eyes. Bohdi thinks she's good-looking but probably a bit too radical for the physics guys in her classes.

Skylar reports, "Okay, Joe says he's getting back late from an away soccer game, and if he makes it down, it'll likely be close to 9:00 or 10:00 p.m. He doesn't know if anyone else is going to show up, and he hasn't heard from Amelia."

The quarry is a popular hangout for the young people in Skylar's town during the warm summer afternoons. Those brave enough, and those who can be talked into it, sometimes dive off the high rock into the seemingly bottomless black pool of water below. There are stories of teenagers using rocks and ropes of a hundred feet or more to see if they could find a bottom, but, so far, no one has been successful. The trees rimming the quarry provide a refuge from the heat of the day, and during the long evenings, it's a nice place to be with friends, play music, tease one another, and gossip. The quarry is large enough that the college kids gather near the tall rocks, while the high school kids gather down by the rope swing.

A moment later, Skylar receives a text from Amelia. She reads it out loud to Bohdi. "A few others are meeting at the diner to grab a bite to eat. Do you want to join us?"

"No, I already had dinner, and it is so peaceful here, I hate to move," says Bohdi. "How about you?"

"Agree. Anyhow, I had sausage with cabbage and potatoes for dinner. Can you imagine that?" she says sarcastically without looking up as she texts a reply. Bohdi chuckles. Skylar's family eat that meal at least once a week, every week, every month of every year.

She finishes her text and looks up to see Bohdi lost in his own world, looking out at the water in the quarry.

"Earth to Bohdi," Skylar says after watching her friend fade into his memories for a minute. In her alto voice, she sings, "Ground control to Major Tom . . ."

"Yes, yes, I hear you."

"Hey, you're back!

"Speaking of being back," Bohdi says, feeling glad to be distracted from his thoughts, "I want to continue our conversation from last night. You told me you had a new insight into this Perception reality of yours. I am very curious what you have learned."

Bohdi grins as his left eyebrow peaks. "From what I remember you saying last night, before we got interrupted by friends, is that the two of us go to a movie theater. We each have on a set of special glasses. When we leave the theater, I mention how I really enjoyed the traveling portion of the movie, and you say, 'What traveling portion? The whole movie took place in the same town. They never went anywhere.' During our conversation afterward, it becomes obvious we saw two completely different movies in the same movie theater at the same time. Explain that to me."

Skylar jumps off the picnic table, her body unable to contain her energy of excitement about her idea, "Because—we know that a movie appears as a continuous reality, but in fact, it's just a series of static images that are shown fast enough that our brain interprets them as a continuous reality. So, as long as any movie projector provides static images moving at twenty-four or more images per second, we'll see that as continuous. But what if two movies are interwoven with each other—both at, say, seventy-two images per second, the same way that three-dimensional movies are shown now? The 3-D effect is based on two views, and the glasses you wear allow one slightly different version into one eye and another into the other eye. You're watching two slightly different versions of the same movie at once. Let's assume you're wearing glasses that aren't passive, but are actively triggered via a wireless network. Let's assume the two separate movies project simultaneously, a romantic comedy and an action thriller. The glasses and projector are designed so that when the romantic comedy images are on the screen, *your* glasses are blocked, and mine are transparent. When the action thriller images are on the screen, your glasses are transparent and *mine* are blocked. We both see a continuous movie at the same time, but they are really two totally different movies. Because of the way images are processed by our brain, we don't notice that half of our reality is being blocked out."

Bohdi nods his head, to signify he understands the concept.

Skylar continues, "The images of both movies together are projected at one hundred and forty-four images per second; our individual movies at half that. It's critical that the timing of the glasses to the movie projector stay the same. If it changes or drifts during the movie, we'll start to see snippets of the other movie, which is like getting a peek into another reality. If we both have control boxes that change the triggering of the glasses relative to the movie projector, we could, at our discretion, change which movie we see. You, with your electronics knowledge, know that is not hard to do. Let's say that at a zero shift in timing signals, the glasses would be tuned into the romantic comedy. At some shift, say a fraction of a second, the glasses would be tuned into the action thriller."

"That is very cool," Bohdi says. "To have a couple sit together and see two different movies. . . I think . . . of course, they'd have to have special earphones to hear the soundtracks separately." He wonders if the idea has practical merit. "Anyway, go on."

"True, with the earphones, that would work," she replies but eager to carry on. "In this situation you have two completely different realities going on, in the same space and at the same time. The only difference is the timing of the triggering for each pair of glasses. Okay, now let's stretch that idea. Imagine there are multiple realities going on at the same time in all locations, and that if you could actively change a parameter, you might see these completely different realities."

"Ah! Your Perception Reality! Is that what happens with you?"

Skylar shrugs. "I don't know. This is a simple example, but in my case, I'm not sure what parameters I'm changing to perceive a different reality. I just know what mental and emotional changes I need to make in order to shift into this reality. In my model, I use a timing signal—but that may not be the only component. But it's the best model I have so far."

She looks at one of her closest friends for almost a decade now as he looks down while drifting off in thought. He's grown a bit these past two years, and now he is just over six feet tall, like his father. He looks attractive now that he's let his hair grow into a mop of black curls that always looks unkempt. She isn't sure if he intentionally grows his hair long or if he is just lazy. She figures the latter, since he doesn't pay much attention to his appearance, other than always being shaved. He has a light olive skin, a mix of his Indian mother and white American father. He has blue-green eyes that make him look older and sometimes more melancholy than he is. He's like an old soul, born serious but getting more spontaneous as he ages. The fact that he marches to his own beat is something she has always admired about him.

"That might be how intuition works," Bohdi says suddenly, snapping Skylar out of her train of thought. Bohdi continues, "There might be another universe, like a multiverse, where we can tune into the information of all the possible outcomes to an event. Maybe intuition is just our insight into this other universe of the most probable outcome. Makes you wonder what might be going on right here all around us, without us knowing."

"Agree. In my Perception Reality," Skylar says to add insight into this model, "My location is where my focus of attention is. I have to have a measure of discipline with my thoughts and emotions in this reality, because where my attention goes, so goes my experience. In our regular world, your location is where your body is."

"Well, in that case, in your Perception Reality, I'd be on a roller-coaster ride with all my interests!" Bohdi laughs.

"Truthfully, that's how anyone would start, but you can't sustain that type of crazy ride over the long term, trust me, so you learn to slow down your thoughts and emotions. I know that is not so evident in me, the way I behave, but I only have these experiences when I am calm inside," she sighs and then asks, "So . . . do you think our eyes and other senses could work like the glasses in my example?"

Bohdi thinks for a minute, "I think it's more than our senses; I think it's our consciousness. It could involve the 'third eye,' the pineal gland in our forehead that eastern mystics say is used to see a different reality than our familiar physical reality. The biological structure of the third eye is like an inverted eye, with the vision receptors on the inside, which gives new meaning to the phrase *looking inward*. The reality part is more difficult to explain."

"Cool, I never heard the third eye described like that," Skylar replies, brushing her hair out of her eyes.

She is not completely surprised by this insight from Bohdi. He always had a strong philosophical bent to him and in high school was a bit of a mystic. He read many books on eastern mysticism that his mother recommended in order to help him understand himself and intuition. Bohdi began a meditation practice that he still continues to this day. Along with his philosophical nature, he has been taking electronic and mechanical things apart as long as she has known him, and with his mind and talent, there is nothing he cannot do or not understand technically. His plans when going to college were to study physics or engineering, but chose to switch to psychology after halfway through his second year since he became fascinated by the workings of the mind.

"Going back to the movie theater and the glasses," Skylar continues, "—it's critical to keep the timing between the movies accurate over a long period. As you well know, in electronics you commonly use a master clock, which all the devices share. If all the devices are triggered to a common master clock, then it's easy to keep the timing correct."

"Yeah, I've seen that effect when a device gets out of time," says Bohdi. "But where is the clock in our reality?"

Skylar shrugs. "That's a difficult question. But for this discussion, let's assume that there's a fundamental clock in nature that governs matter in two realities. If we could shift the *timing* of our reality relative to this master clock, then we would see, or experience, the other reality just like we would with the glasses. I think that our timing is fixed, so we are locked into an experience of a very specific reality, the one we're familiar with."

Bohdi, in his excitement, blurts out, "Remember that only four percent of matter is visible to us, the other ninety six percent is invisible. We only see a tiny portion of what comprises our universe."

"That idea still baffles me," Skylar says as she shakes her head. "We know so little of the universe around us. So, just like my movie example, it is not far-fetched to assume there are other realities occurring at exactly the same time in the same locations, but the inhabitants of those realities can't see our reality, because of the timing. They are locked exclusively into experiencing their own reality, or movie, as in this discussion. Maybe our relationship to some cosmic clock keeps us from seeing, or even detecting, all this other matter and probably other universes."

Skylar unconsciously wraps her shirt tightly around her, feeling uncomfortable with the idea of being watched. She has always had trouble with any alien movies and one of her greatest fears is that she might interact with a non-human in these Perception Reality experiences. "It's a bit creepy to think there could be other intelligent life-forms right around us, and we can't even perceive them."

"Likely, we're the other life-forms to them too, and maybe they can't see us—so the idea of us existing could creep *them* out?" Bohdi says with a laugh, showing no signs of concerns about other forms of life.

At that moment, Bohdi's girlfriend, Hannah, along with their friends Joann, Diane, and Amelia appear on the path heading toward them.

"What are you guys up to?" Hannah asks with an edge in her voice as she moves in close to Bohdi.

"Oh, just talking about spacetime," Bohdi says with a laugh.

"Well, it's a good thing I showed up to save you," Hannah responds quickly, eyeing Skylar.

4.

Hank Slidel, the leader of an elite team within the Chronos Consortium, moves his tall, athletic frame to the front of the class. He is delivering one of his standard introduction lectures to a new group of specialist-in-training. He has just told this team of three trainees that once they have completed this training program as Time Specialists, they will have knowledge of time that few people on the planet have.

He stares at them, letting that last statement sink in. He then continues, "As team of specialists, working under me, our team receives communications about specific people the Chronos Consortium feels are a threat to their necessary control over world events. The consortium knows that control through fear is crucial to making sure that the world does not descend into complete chaos. Our belief is that the strong leadership demonstrated in this organization is necessary to keep order in the world. Sometimes this means removing key individuals, or supporting other important individuals who can make the necessary actions happen to maintain control. You as specialists will be dealing with these key people, most of the time, disabling them in their current role." Hanks smiles. He likes that phrase, 'disabling them'.

"Our team is regularly given a list of individuals who are deemed disruptive to any objective of the extensive list of corporations under the Chronos Consortium's control. My team deals with the internal emotions and thoughts of these disruptive individuals, information they are able to extract from the individual's fields in time, which is a skill you will learn in this program. We also work closely with Paul Dremos, another elite leader of a team of agents, whose team gathers data that correlate to the external life circumstances of these same individuals.

"Our two teams have to work closely together, since the internal and external realities of these threats are often attacked at the same time. Paul's agents gather the information about the individuals' age, gender, locations, work and financial status, personal and family relationships, as well as any other information that could be important, or damaging. To get good information, Paul's agents almost always work undercover to infiltrate organizations or impersonate roles. In addition, Paul also has a special team of field agents whose task it is to get within close proximity of a target to scan their three-dimensional Time Field. This is done with a secret device called a Time Field Scanner, which you will also learn to use, but more importantly, learn to analyze the data from this device. The Time Field Scanner fits easily into an agent's pocket and records all the known three-dimensional time frequencies.

"Each Time Field Scanner is calibrated to a specific agent, so the agent's field is removed from the scanner data. New calibrations are done at least once a day to compensate for any modifications in an agent's field due to stress from physical or emotional changes, good and bad." Hank flips his PowerPoint presentation to a new slide, showing graphs and metrics.

"Technicians analyze scan data collected on a targeted person and pass the results on to us. You," Hank pauses, looking at each of the three trainees for any sign of lack of attention to what he is saying, "as part of my team will assesses metrics on mental IQ, emotional IQ, and spiritual IQ, as well as some physical conditions, from this data. This will give us a profile of the target's mental, emotional, and physical health. Our responsibility is to integrate this information of the target's inner state with the targets external for a complete history of this target and then input it all into a data metrics package."

Hank is not interested in taking questions. He has a message to deliver and is going to race through it quickly. He does this purposely to see who has the confidence to remember the information without writing it down, since that is too slow.

"The purpose of this data metrics package is so that our teams can undertake deconstruction missions, a strategy designed to create negative circumstances in a person's life that cause frustrations and failures, undermining the target's attempts at self-empowerment. In this deconstruction process, my team of specialists manipulates the Time Fields around an individual, to explore and exploit their weaknesses in thoughts and emotions and in the process create a feeling of emotional instability. This triggers a response from the amygdala, an ancient part of the brain that humans inherited from reptiles." He turns to the slide and with his laser pointer, highlights the amygdala in an image of the brain.

"This amygdala cannot handle complexity and when there is a perceived threat, it can overpower the newer part of the brain, the neocortex, which handles the more rationale and intricate thoughts. It is this amygdala hijacking that we excel at. Now we have come to understand that it is not just the amygdala that we hijack, but other parts of the brain as well. But we still call it amygdala hijacking.

"Paul's team excels at launching effective disinformation programs designed to discredit the targeted individual. The individuals begin to experience remarkable coincidences, much like the ones that initially helped them rise in power or rank, only now, events conspire to bring them down. The effect is designed to unnerve them, because they can't determine the origin of the unfortunate circumstances, or how these affairs play out. The targets quickly learn that their choice is either to stay within certain boundaries or be prepared for further consequences. Fundamentally, no human self-destructs without them absorbing some negative message based on fear, such as greed, envy, panic, or frustration about themselves as truth." Again, Hank stops his lecture. He stares into the eyes of each trainee, looking for signs of concern. He sees a flicker of fear in the eyes of one of the trainees.

"These shifts in the internal reality of a targeted human will cause them to undermine their own reality in three-dimensional space with what appear to be inopportune choices, events or accidents. When the deconstruction is done well, most targets in the face of these difficult internal and external experiences back off and disappear into the background.

"Because the three-dimensional time domain and its power are invisible to human senses, very few people know how to navigate it effectively. Indeed, the vast majority of humans have no clue of its existence, never mind its power. While every human unconsciously creates a reality in the three-dimensional time domain, without a conscious understanding of its impact, they have no idea how it supports or undermines their day-to-day reality in the space domain. If a person truly understands that what they think and feel, much less *intend,* manifests as a structure in the three-dimensional time domain, then they can make significant changes in their lives, and society as well, to the detriment of our necessary control. You, as I said before, are one of a very small elite group that will understand how this works."

Hank then flips to a summary slide.

Thoughts and emotions are energy.
Knowing is power.
Time is both.
In time, fear is the power that we control.

He reads the words out loud for emphasis, and then continues. "The Chronos Consortium's objective is to use the invisible fields in time so targeted people believe that the *thoughts in their minds* and the *feelings in their hearts* are their *own.* We can influence people this way because most do not think for themselves or question their own beliefs; they only think they do. It's easier to absorb ideas from others and from messages around them, making it easier in turn for us to step in and help mold their thoughts and beliefs. The most powerful way to do this is through fear."

Hank smiles. He knows there is a very real battle going on for the hearts and minds of people in the invisible dimensions of time. The consortium has had to step up their influence of select individual's thoughts and emotions to maintain their own social, economic and political objectives. Hank then turns off the projector and moves to the other side of the table at the front of the room. He stands closer to these three individuals sitting in the front row purposely to make them a bit uncomfortable.

He starts, now with a stern tone in his voice, "A handful of individuals, from many different cultures, have pierced the veil of time, each interpreting this domain within the context of their culture. These individuals talk about how we as humans are so much more than biological creatures, that what we experience internally really matters. Spiritual texts from the East speak of masters who describe a reality beyond everyday experience that allows for all sorts of things to be done that are impossible without an expanded understanding. The Chronos Consortium works to distort, quarantine, or destroy the masters' messages and if possible, render them ineffective, to minimize their impact.

"The *real concern* of the Chronos Consortium is that the principles of empowerment can be taught more effectively by someone who *does* understand the true scientific link between what humans create in three-dimensional space and what they create in three-dimensional time with their thoughts and feelings. With such knowledge, especially in our current culture that looks to science to explain our experience of reality, people could begin to grasp where the strength, and power, of the human character comes from in a whole new way. The masses might absorb these new ideas as part of their cultural truth and then use the knowledge to empower themselves, and their societies. This we have to stop if we see it happening."

"Our control of conscious creation in three-dimensional time has to be the *dominant* reality for all people. As long as the masses feel powerless about the circumstances surrounding them in the space domain, the Chronos Consortium's negative dominance can overcome the weak positive collective presence of humans in the three-dimensional time domain. We have a great deal of influence, and the know-how to use it."

"One of our techniques is to disseminate conflicting information in all media outlets, but particularly social media. Then, websites and blogs are generated to counter the very statements made earlier. We know if we do this constantly in quick succession, the very notion of what is true is undermined. People get so overwhelmed they give up trying to understand the issues, making it easier to influence them. But," he says with particular emphasis, "we cannot count on this as a long-term strategy. Fortunately, the consortium influences the members of government through whatever means necessary. This is crucial since these people are the ones that make the laws. Most of this real activity is hidden to the general public, even as the public is becoming more aware of the dark money that influences these legislators. This organization takes the mission statement of "leave no trace" very seriously.

Hank glances at the clock in the room. His twenty minutes are up, and he has to head out. He is about to send a text to Joe, the lead in charge of the training, when Joe bursts back through the classroom door.

"Good timing." He looks to the three trainees and says, "Glad to have met you. I will see you in a few days," and with that short goodbye, he heads out the door, his six-foot-seven frame moving fast. He takes great pride in his fitness and always measures himself internally against the younger members of his gym. He is fitter than most members who are twenty, even thirty, years his junior. He stops at a door with a dark glass window to check that his graying hair is still neatly combed.

The conference room is in another part of the building. It takes him almost three minutes of walking and climbing stairs to get there, about half the time it takes anyone else.

"Did everyone have a good weekend," he says warmly as he enters the room. His current team is clustered in a corner, talking. Upon hearing Hank, they immediately turn and, almost in unison, say, "Yes," as they move to their chairs. Hank did not schedule any work this past weekend, since his team has handled many weekend missions in the past six weeks, and he wants to conserve their energy.

"I just spent some time with a new batch of trainees. I hope that at least two of them make it through the training program so that in six months they can help relieve the pressure we are all under." Hank finds an open seat at the front of the conference table. "All right, then, let's get some work done!"

For forty minutes, Hank hears feedback on eleven individuals his team is working to deconstruct. Five are politicians and lawmakers, and the options for deconstructing them are numerous. The difficulty lies only in choosing which method to focus their attention on. The other six targets are involved in corporations ranging from finance and banking to international construction engineering, as well as political action groups. After hearing varying degrees of success with these targets, Hank briefs the team on three new targets. He dismisses the group, then heads to his weekly status meeting with his superiors. These meetings have been contentious lately, owing to the ever-increasing burden on an understaffed group.

5.

The front doorbell rings, and Bohdi tears down the stairs to answer the door. Skylar is there to pick him up. He opens the door, and she says cheerfully, "You ready?"

"I am."

"Let's go. We have to be there by two, which gives us only half an hour."

Bohdi locks the front door behind him as they head to Skylar's new car. Well, new to her. Her parents found a used car they hoped would last at least the two years of commuting she has to do without needing any major repairs. It is a small dark blue sedan. True to Skylar, she has named the car Shitty Shitty Bang Bang, because it occasionally backfired before her parents brought it to the shop and had it tuned up.

"What is this guy's name again, and who is he related to?" Bohdi asks as he climbs into the car.

"It's Bruce's uncle. Bruce is the new drummer in Lenny's band. I went to see them practice." When Skylar was introduced to Bruce by her friends, they introduced her as the resident Space Geek because she has all these crazy ideas about spacetime and this concept for special glasses. After the band practice, Bruce approached Skylar and asked her about her glasses concept. She briefly explained it to Bruce. He listened intently. After she was finished, he says, "I have someone you have to meet. He is an uncle of mine and he has invented some goggles which you would be fascinated by. My uncle says they see other states of matter."

Skylar continues, "His uncle's name is Dr. Victor Brown, and he's a retired physicist. Bruce wanted to come, but he couldn't make it. He figures I should have lots to talk about with his uncle and I figured it would be more fun if you came along."

"Well, I am intrigued. You with your glasses idea and now a Dr. Brown with his goggles. Should be interesting," Bohdi chuckles, "Seems like a real bit of synchronicity don't you think, you talking about your glasses and now two months later, we're going to see some goggles."

Skylar is amused by his comment. She is happy to be driving since Skylar enjoys adventure, but Bohdi's driving sometimes gives more of an adrenaline rush than she cares for. She's learned to make no comment, though; both her parents think her driving is a real adventure for them, so it is all a matter of perception.

Bruce told Skylar that he tried the goggles and saw interestingly colored shapes and joked that maybe his uncle "had a little too much fun in the 1960s, if you know what I mean." But Bruce corrected himself by saying that his uncle is actually a very smart guy, and a nice guy. He didn't mean to disparage him, and didn't want her to get the wrong impression.

Skylar is eager to know more about the goggles but also feels a bit nervous, for reasons she cannot figure out, and she is grateful for the quiet in the car.

Bohdi blurts, "Hey, do you have that Moonwalker CD in the car." *He clearly can read my thoughts*, Skylar thinks as she reaches over to grab the CD from the center console and inserts it into the player.

Moonwalker is a band Skylar likes; in fact, they're due to stop on their tour at a city nearby, and Skylar recently said she could get a bunch of tickets. Their friends are looking forward to it.

After about twenty minutes, Skylar flips on her turn indicator to take the next exit for the town of Bradford. They head off the exit ramp and as they come to a stop, Bohdi says, "You have to take a right here"

"Turn up the volume on your smartphone so I can hear the navigation," she asks, as she turns down the volume on the radio. They both listen to the navigation voice as it guides them toward Dr. Brown's house.

The neighborhood is typical for the small towns in the area, with houses on small plots of land grouped tightly together. Most were built over a hundred years ago, and still have the Victorian gingerbread on their facades and front porches. Some are neatly maintained, with small garden plots overflowing with flowers. Other houses look tired and a bit neglected, even more so today, with the dreary cloud-covered sky typical of a cool September day. As they approach the Browns' home, Skylar notes the well-kept flower gardens and freshly painted porch. On the porch sit two rocking chairs, and one rattan chair hanging from the porch ceiling. *Bit of an ex-hippie look to it,* Skylar thinks, not that she knows what that means or should look like—but it fits her idea of colorful, and a bit eclectic as a loved home should be.

They exit with a double slam of car doors, then walk down a small brick path to the entrance of the front porch. Skylar hurries to the door and rings the doorbell. They hear a dog bark a few times and then come running to the door. Human footsteps follow it. A woman opens the door. Skylar guesses she is in her seventies. She has long gray hair, pulled into a ponytail, and is wearing jeans and a flowery shirt. Her blue eyes have a kindness to them that immediately puts Skylar at ease.

She gives them a pleasant smile and says, "Come in. Ignore Princess, she's just excited to see people." She turns to the dog and says firmly, "Princess, go lie down in the kitchen." Princess, a black Labrador, turns around and walks to the kitchen. "And you're Skylar, the young woman I spoke to on the phone."

"That's right, and this is my friend Bohdi."

"I'm Annie, and I'm pleased to meet you both. Please, leave your shoes here near the front door, and then go left to the door down the hall and make yourselves comfortable. I will let Vic know you're here. Do you want anything to drink? I can offer water, homemade lemonade, or some herbal tea."

"I'll have some of your lemonade," Skylar replies.

"How about you, Bohdi?"

"Yes, please, lemonade is fine with me, as well."

They walk down the hall to a small, brightly lit room. It has two large windows, lots of potted flowers, a tan couch against one wall, and two comfortable brown chairs opposite the couch with Tibetan-looking blankets thrown over them. "I'll be there in a minute," Annie's voice says from down the hall. "If either of you need to use a bathroom, there's one on the left as you came in."

Skylar notes the oak floors, beautifully maintained. *I can see why she has people take off their shoes.* Bohdi and Skylar sit on the couch and look around the room. The walls sport paintings of the countryside, including one with a house in a meadow and another of flowers on the home's front porch.

Annie comes in carrying a tray with their drinks. "Vic will be here in a minute." They take their drinks and place them on coasters on the small side tables near the two chairs; Annie takes her glass of water to the couch.

Then Dr. Brown shuffles into the room, using his cane to balance himself. Skylar is surprised, having expected someone recently retired and full of vitality. Dr. Brown looks older than his wife. Although hunched over as he walks, he still has a full head of unruly white hair. He stops for a moment, looks at the two visitors and smiles.

"Hello, you must be Skylar and Bohdi."

Skylar sees a sparkle in the brown eyes underneath Dr. Brown's bushy white eyebrows. The intelligence communicated through those eyes is enhanced by his beige turtleneck sweater and brown corduroy pants, which make him look like the wise old professor she assumes he is.

Dr. Brown shuffles over to the couch where Annie is sitting, and pauses to put the glass he's holding in his left hand down on the side table. He then shuffles to the right side of the couch, eases himself down, and rests his cane against the arm of the couch. Dr. Brown suffers from bad back pain, and it has recently flared up, causing him additional pain.

"So, which one of you knows Bruce?" Dr. Brown asks.

Annie jumps in and says, "Skylar knows him."

"Oh, yes, I forgot." He turns to Skylar. "How do you know my nephew?"

"He is part of a band that my friends are in and I went to see them practice." She waits to see if Dr. Brown asks another question."

"Yes, somebody mentioned about him recently joining a new band," Dr. Brown says in a deadpan tone. "How did Bruce come to mention me?"

"My friends mentioned my ideas about a set of glasses that could allow people to see two different movies and my thoughts about an alternative reality to Bruce." She stops, looking for some response in Dr. Brown's eyes, sensing nothing out of the ordinary, she continues, "Bruce thought that I should talk to you because since he thought I would be interested in learning about your goggles."

Dr. Brown is very intrigued by this response, especially the mention of the glasses and alternative reality. But first he wants to learn more about these two young people.

Dr. Brown laughs. "Bruce thought you should speak to his wacky uncle. Are you a student, as well?"

"Yes. I'm studying physics at Patterson University in the undergraduate program."

"Very nice."

Dr. Brown turns to Bohdi. "And you, young man, you are in the same program?"

"No, same university, but I'm now studying psychology. I was studying physics but switched."

"How very interesting!"

"Um, Dr. Brown, what is your background?" Skylar asks.

"I am also a physicist. I have a PhD in Plasma Physics. My thesis was focused on plasma fusion reactions. I worked most of my life for a company that made nuclear magnetic resonance spectroscopy equipment."

"Skylar, how do you and Bohdi know each other?" Annie interjects.

"We've been friends since we were twelve, and graduated from the same high school, then went to different universities for two years, and now we're both at Patterson."

"That is really nice. Have you known Bruce long?" Annie probes.

"Just about two months."

"Bruce is a smart kid. He would start some interesting discussions when our families get together for holidays and birthdays. He's our favorite nephew."

Dr. Brown continues to ask Skylar and Bohdi about their family history and how long they have been in the area. After ten minutes, Dr. Brown feels comfortable enough with both Skylar and Bohdi to change the topic to the goggles he left back in his office.

"Tell me more about your glasses and this alternative reality of yours," he asks Skylar.

Skylar spends the next five minutes describing her concept about two different realities that are linked via some universal clock and how a set of movie glasses would allow people to view these two different universes.

"Well, I think you will find my goggles very enlightening," Dr. Brown says with a pleased look on his face. "So, what do you know of these goggles from Bruce?"

Skylar replies first. "Uh, not m-much, other than, well, Bruce said you can see different states of matter,"

"That is all I know," Bohdi quickly adds.

"What part of Bruce's description made you want to talk to me?" Dr. Brown's eyes are now showing intrigue as a smile forms.

Bohdi looks at Skylar, who says, "Well, . . . um, I . . . if your goggles allow someone to see different states of matter, I'd like to know more about that."

"Well, I'm glad to hear Bruce described it correctly, but not pleased that he mentioned it to others. But that is now history. I should preface this discussion with, *I believe* that another state of matter, other than the one we are familiar with, is made visible."

Skylar leans forward, barely able to contain her interest. "What do you use the goggles for?"

"I am trying to understand matter in a new way. The goggles give me a different view, and I am trying to integrate my findings into a new, or I should say, expanded theory."

"Have you been able to identify any new forms of matter?"

Dr. Brown shakes his head. "I'm not seeking new forms of matter, but to understand existing matter in a new way. The goggles make it possible to see this previously invisible matter."

He leans back to let the point sink in, then asks Skylar, "What is it that you see in this alternative reality of yours?"

Skylar squirms and clears her throat.

"Dr. Brown, what I am about to describe is not part of current physics. I am very interested in finding out how it does fit into physics, and I have some speculative ideas.

"I go into a deep meditative state, I see fields of color, sometimes brilliant colors with unusual dimension to them, some in the shape of an oval. These colors and shapes are associated with people I'm focusing on, but they also can represent places and events. I . . . I suspect that these fields of color are part of us, and of events, in another reality, or other dimensions. When I focus on the ovals, I receive nonverbal information specific to that individual. It might have to do with thoughts they have, or emotions they're feeling . . . or even physical conditions. It's hard to explain. I call it my Perception Reality, but that's just a label."

Skylar clams up, looking for a response from Dr. Brown before going any deeper.

Dr. Brown remains bright-eyed and calm. "Here is something to think about. Music is nothing but a beautiful mathematical ratio of frequencies. The notes are the foundation of music. Combinations of notes in specific mathematical ratios make up the chords. The chords are delivered to a beat. Notes, chords and beats are all based in time. Music is a complex mathematical composition of time that has the ability to affect us consciously on a very deep level. So, what does this say about our consciousness and time?"

Dr. Brown waits for that statement to sink in.

'Huh, I never thought of it in quite that way," Skylar says, intrigued by what has just been stated.

Dr. Brown then asks, "Do you think what you perceive has to do with time?"

"I'm . . . not sure what you are asking," Skylar says. "Like, perceiving the future?"

"No, not specifically. Based on your background, I am sure you have been introduced to the mathematical transforms developed by Fourier."

Dr. Brown waits for a response.

"Yes. I've only applied the Fourier transform to signals. But I'm familiar with how mathematical algorithms can represent the same measured signals in two different formats."

"Precisely. The Fourier transform of a chord played on a musical instrument would allow the scientist to say exactly which keys, or strings, were played. Now, have you worked with the Fourier mathematical transforms when they are applied to images, young lady?"

"No, I have not." She shoots a glance at Bohdi.

"No, me neither," he replies quickly.

Dr. Brown, eager to move the conversation along, continues. "The same mathematical technique can be used on images as well. If I took an image of you and then applied this mathematical algorithm to it, you would look like a strange blob, maybe not too different from the oval shape you describe. It is something you might consider. Both of you might want to go to the library and look up Optical Transformations. I suspect you might be surprised by what you see."

He moves forward in his seat again, rests his elbows on his thighs, and looks directly at Skylar. "What if a unique mathematical algorithm could convert space-based information, the familiar world around us, directly into information in three-dimensional time? That information would be based on frequencies, a time phenomenon. I think what you might be seeing is a unique frequency structure of information in three-dimensional time. Physics does not rule out more than one dimension of time." What if in multidimensional time, everything you think, you feel, you intend, is real? These thoughts, emotions, and intentions would be structures of energy in three-dimensional time."

Skylar thinks about it. "You mean that the information I receive from these oval shapes is stored in three-dimensional time?"

Dr. Brown pauses, giving Skylar a few moments to consider what he has just said. During the pause, Bohdi is fascinated by this idea that thoughts and emotions could be tied to time. Clearly, Dr. Brown has just detailed how her emotions triggered by music is tied to time.

Skylar thinks for a moment, then says, "If that is true, that would be tremendous. It would create a link between what we see in our physical world of three-dimensional space and what I witness in my Perception Reality, which you say might be correlated to time. I need to think about this some more."

"Well, before I bring my goggles out," says Dr. Brown. I need to say a few important things."

Skylar nods.

"The goggles I will show you were collaboratively developed by myself and a colleague who was also a dear friend. We have kept it very discreet for reasons I will not go into here. Other than Bruce, only a few people know about them. I will let you and Bohdi try them, but I need both of you to agree that you will not discuss anything you see today with anyone, unless you run it by me first. I especially do not want you to share this with your friends or professors. I was a bit alarmed initially that Bruce told you about them, until Annie mentioned that he did not share any specific details."

Skylar wants to look at Bohdi but Dr. Brown's unyielding gaze demands a response.

"Dr. Brown, if you're uncomfortable showing your goggles to us, I'm okay with that. I'm here mainly because of a conversation I had with Bohdi about Bruce." She swallows. "But I have no problem honoring your requirements."

"Yeah, no problem for me, either," Bohdi chimes in.

"Do you have a patent pending on the goggles?" Skylar asks, thinking that is the reason for the secrecy.

"No, my colleague and I did not want to reveal the structure of the goggles, as is required in a patent. The knowledge of how to construct them now rests only in me, since my colleague passed away five years ago."

"I'm sorry to hear that," Skylar says.

"Yes, it is a real loss. He and I shared some unusual ideas." He drops his gaze to regain his composure, then lifts his head. Skylar and Bohdi are the first people, outside of his family, that he's been able to discuss his technical interest with since his colleague died.

"All right, let me get the goggles." Dr. Brown grabs his cane, and grimaces with pain as he struggles to his feet. Skylar has to stifle an urge to help him, knowing that Dr. Brown probably needs to do this himself.

Annie turns to Bohdi and Skylar. "I'm so glad you both could come today. I really think he needs to find someone to share his ideas with. We are not getting any younger." She fakes a smile to cover up the concerns she is holding inside, but Skylar senses that she is hiding something.

"No problem," Skylar says.

"Happy to be here," Bohdi adds. "Can we help with anything?"

"No, that's all right. We'll be right back." Annie gets up and heads for the door with Dr. Brown.

Skylar and Bohdi use this moment to take a sip of lemonade from their glasses. Skylar looks at Bohdi and bugs her eyes. He does the same as they silently wonder where this encounter is going.

Annie comes back into the room and places a brown cardboard box on the side table next to where Dr. Brown was sitting. They can hear him shuffling up the hall toward them.

Dr. Brown enters the room with another cardboard box under his left arm. Annie takes it from him and puts it down next to the first box. Both boxes look aged, and their flaps well-worn from years of loading and unloading. Annie moves out of Dr. Brown's way, allowing him to move with the boxes. Dr. Brown reaches into the box he was carrying and pulls out what looks to Skylar like a set of modified scuba goggles without the nose piece. The normally transparent lenses have been replaced with a black material that has a frosted appearance on the surface and a gold sparkle inside. As Dr. Brown swings around to place the goggles on the couch, Skylar realizes that the sparkle comes from copper wires forming a repetitive hexagonal pattern in the black material.

"So, this is the part you wear," Dr. Brown says as he digs into the second carton and pulls out a black plastic box formed by two individual boxes, each about the size of a new smartphone box. They are taped together and have a belt clip mounted on the side. On top, three electrical connectors have wires going to each of the boxes. Dr. Brown puts this box combination next to the goggles on the couch. Bohdi presumes that the set of wires hanging from the goggles' right side will connect to the plastic boxes.

Dr. Brown withdraws another black box from the carton, this one wrapped with white tape. Bohdi is watching closely since building electronics has been a hobby of his since middle school.

"What states of matter do your goggles help a person to see?" Bohdi asks.

"Patience," Dr. Brown responds as he untangles the wires and connectors. "It's easier for me to have you wear the goggles, and then we can talk about what you see."

"Do you want some help there, Vic?" Annie asks.

"Yup, in a minute." He finishes untangling the connectors.

"Okay, Annie, can you hold these parts? Skylar, why don't you stand up and let's help you put on the goggles."

In a flash, Skylar is on her feet. She looks over at Bohdi, who stands up to get a closer look.

Annie moves toward Skylar as Dr. Brown says, "Okay, Skylar, face Annie. Annie, get the swim goggles on her first and then we can put the belt around her waist."

Annie puts a pair of ordinary swimming goggles on Skylar, then adds, "These swim goggles are for eye protection."

Skylar feels a twinge of anxiety, but curiosity overrules it as Annie grabs the black neoprene scuba goggles and adjusts the strap to a setting that should work for her head.

"There's a knob on the right side . . . here . . . with three settings." She points to a black knurled knob with a white line on it. "The settings are Plus, Minus, and One. The default setting is Minus."

"What do they stand for?" Skylar asks as Annie moves to her left side.

Annie ignores her. "Leave the goggles on your forehead until I have them hooked up, then you can pull them over your eyes and cover your ears."

Dr. Brown chimes in, "The settings represent the different states of matter. It is simpler to discuss this when you are using them." Dr. Brown feels a surge of concern ripple through his body. *I know showing these goggles with their complicated history to these young people is a risk, but my time is running out. I have to take this risk and find out if they are up to the task.*

Skylar is thrilled that they will be given the opportunity to use something so potentially fascinating. She can't wait to see what they might show her.

Annie then holds the front of the goggles with her right hand and pulls the strap with her left, slowly moving it over Skylar's head. "The strap might pull some of your hair. Let me know if it is uncomfortable in any way."

Skylar feels Annie place the goggles on her face, and she feels the strap on the back of her head. She flinches as the strap pulls her hair over her right ear.

Annie sees her flinch. "Give me second, and I will adjust them properly." Skylar feels her moving the strap around. "That okay now?"

"Yes, that is good."

"Okay, let's continue," Dr. Brown tells his wife. "Grab the microprocessor module."

Annie takes the black plastic box and mounts it to the belt she put on Skylar with a clip.

Bohdi watches her every move, fascinated by all the electronics.

"Now the battery supply box," Dr. Brown instructs Annie.

She attaches the battery box to Skylar's belt, then moves to her right side and hooks up the wires of the goggles to the microprocessor, and turns on the high-voltage generator and temperature control circuitry. She reaches to Skylar's left side to grab the wires from the battery supply and hooks them to the microprocessor box.

"Almost ready," Dr. Brown says as he makes sure that each of the headphone parts fits snugly over Skylar's ears. He then reaches over to the knob on the right side, and Skylar hears a click as Dr. Brown moves it. "You will see black until I get the microprocessor booted up."

Skylar feels a slight pressure on her right side as Dr. Brown pushes the microprocessor box's switch to on.

"Annie, why don't you move to Skylar's left and hold her upper arm? She might need someone to steady her.

"Give it about fifteen seconds," Dr. Brown says to Skylar, "and you should see us in the room. Let me know when you do."

The room falls silent as everyone waits for Skylar to reply.

Skylar looks intently into the blackness, waiting for something to appear.

"Okay, I see the room with Skylar and Annie!"

"All right, that's the Minus state. Now I'm changing to the One state. Tell me what you see."

Skylar can feel Dr. Brown adjust the knob on the goggles as he says, "Give it a few seconds."

"I see a soft white light, like fog, but it seems unusual. It has so much depth. Not like a fog where you see only a short distance. This light is . . . it's . . . hard to describe. It makes me feel emotional, somehow."

Skylar stops, because she is starting to feel vulnerable, knowing she is being observed by people she does not know. She closes her eyes. To her surprise, the white light persists. She also feels a sort of buzzing in her head, which seems to slowly move around inside her head. She ignores the sensation, keen on what she might see.

Dr. Brown, pleased with what he has heard about the white light, waits to see if Skylar has more to say. Skylar remains quiet, so Dr. Brown prompts, "Are you ready to try the next state?"

"Yes." Skylar opens her eyes, eager to see what appears next.

Again, she can feel Dr. Brown adjusting the knob.

"Give it a minute," he says. "Bohdi, why don't you move in front of Skylar, about six feet away? Annie, you come over here and hold Skylar's arm in case she loses her balance."

It only takes a few seconds before Skylar says, "Oh, wow!" She starts moving her head back and forth.

"What do you see?" Bohdi asks curiously.

"I see . . . a large oval field similar to what I see in Perception Reality! There's this brilliant green and beautiful red rose color. This is absolutely amazing. Incredible!"

"So, what you are seeing, you're familiar with?" Dr. Brown asks, a bit surprised.

"Mostly. I see shapes that are familiar. Not exactly the same, or the same intensity, but close enough. I see the familiar large oval that I associate with people, and the colors that generate feelings. I know Bohdi is in front of me now because I know what his structure in the Perception Reality looks like."

"Well! I am very pleased with your experience, Skylar. These goggles are meant for someone like you."

Skylar does not respond. She is too taken by everything she sees, awed that this view is available with a physical device.

Dr. Brown stays silent. He does not want to influence Skylar's experience.

Skylar looks around the room. She sees shapes and colors that she has never seen in her Perception Reality. What can all this mean?

She moves, and stumbles. Annie catches her arm and steadies her, saying, "Probably shouldn't move without me."

"It's hard to keep my balance when I move my head around too fast. It's amazing—wait until you try this, Bohdi."

Skylar goes quiet again. Annie looks over to Vic and gives him a smile. Annie is thrilled that Skylar is able to not only understand what they are showing her, but might well be able to take it to the next step.

"Let's give Bohdi a chance to try it," Dr. Brown says firmly. "You shouldn't wear it too long the first time."

"Okay." Skylar tries to sound upbeat, but she desperately wants more time. She feels Dr. Brown turn a switch on the goggles, and the goggles go back to the white fog state.

"I can't wait," Bohdi says excitedly.

Dr. Brown is very moved by what he has heard Skylar describe. He always wanted to get feedback from other users, especially younger users like Skylar and Bohdi. The fact that these two have a technical background causes him to play with some ideas in his head while he adjusts the goggle hardware so he can take it off Skylar.

"You're next," Dr. Brown says looking at Bohdi. "Annie, can you remove the goggles from Skylar? And Bohdi, you switch places with her."

As Dr. Brown sets the apparatus on Bohdi, Skylar asks, "Why are the headphones necessary? I didn't hear anything coming through the headphones when I was wearing the goggles."

"You would not hear anything since the sound is below what you can hear, but they are important. For now, just know they need to fit loosely over the ears so the person can easily hear what is going on around them."

Dr. Brown, Annie, and Skylar work to get Bohdi ready for his turn with the goggles.

"Ready?" Bohdi hears Dr. Brown ask him.

"Definitely!"

"Same process. Tell us when you see something. Skylar, hold Bohdi's arm like Annie did for you."

Dr. Brown asks Skylar to switch the goggles to One, then says, "Bohdi, tell us what you see."

"I see what Skylar was describing. A white light, like a mist. It feels so inviting. I feel lighter inside. Is it always white mist to people who use these goggles?"

"It seems so, but for some it has just a flat two-dimensional feel. For others, it is three-dimensional, and some describe an emotional content with it."

"I agree with the three-dimensional aspect and the feeling. But I can't describe what I'm feeling. I guess it's a sort of joy."

Dr. Brown bounces on his toes, his pains forgotten in his excitement. "You ready for the next state?"

"Yes, for sure!"

"Okay, Skylar, switch the goggles to the Plus setting."

Bohdi waits fifteen seconds.

Bohdi gasps. "Oh my! The room looks a bit psychedelic. I see colors and odd shapes everywhere. What is that large oval shape in front of me?"

"That's me," Annie says. Bohdi falls quiet, trying to absorb all he is seeing. After a minute, Annie motions for Skylar to swap places with her in front of Bohdi.

"One of the shapes, the oval, to my left just disappeared. Then another one appeared, but it looks different. Different color and different structure. Did you guys just switch on me?"

"We did. I just moved out of your field of view to your left," Annie replies. "Now you are looking at Skylar."

"That's you!" Bohdi exclaims. "This is what you see! Now I get what you were describing to me about Perception Reality."

Skylar is thrilled. She now has a way to share with him what she experiences. She can barely contain her joy, after feeling isolated for so long.

"Dr. Brown, this device is amazing. What inspired you to make it?" Skylar asks.

Dr. Brown is flush with pride but remains careful. "It's a long story that I don't want to get into right now. What is fantastic is that both of you see what I hoped you would see."

"Did Bruce see the same thing?"

"Not sure if it was the same, since he described it more of a light show than anything else."

"Get back into the field of view," Bohdi says to Skylar.

Skylar was investigating the side of the goggles. She moves in front of Bohdi again.

He studies what he sees until Dr. Brown says that the batteries are running low. "Bohdi, since this is your first time, I am going to switch you off now. I also want to sort out a few more details with both of you."

Skylar watches Dr. Brown power down the electronics, then disconnect each part and put everything on the side table.

"Why don't you sit back down?" Dr. Brown says to them both. He wants to talk to Annie and get her feedback. They have been partners in this mission, and he values her opinion, especially one so important as the next step he is going to propose.

He motions for Annie to come with him. "We'll be back in a moment." The couple walks down the hall and holds a whispered conversation just out of hearing range. Skylar and Bohdi exchange looks but dare not speak. Annie and Vic instantly agree. They know their time is running out, and that the technology has to survive the two of them, for the sake of the goggles, and the future of the next generation. They believe they have found an answer, but will proceed carefully.

When Annie and Vic return to the couch, Annie seems pleased. Dr. Brown looks at Skylar, and then at Bohdi. "Would the two of you be interested in taking these goggles and doing some experiments by yourselves for a limited time?"

"Definitely!" Skylar blurts, then blushes.

Bohdi says, "Yes, for sure!"

"Oh, I forgot," Dr. Brown says with a stern tone, "*always* use the goggles with a partner, so you can physically guide the one who is wearing the goggles. This will minimize any tripping hazard, and then you never have to worry about the possibility of breaking them. It is the way Annie and I do it. The goggles are pretty resilient, and the lenses would likely survive a drop, but should you trip and the lens material breaks, you must be careful in any cleanup. Do not get any of the chemicals in your eyes. It will not make you blind, but it will not be pleasant, either. If the lenses do break while you are wearing them, have your buddy assist you in removing them. Keep the swimming goggles on, and when you get a chance, wash your face and the swimming goggles with regular soap and cold water. Then take the swimming goggles off."

Dr. Brown waits for a response from the two of them. He purposely presented these concerns to see what response they have to his warning.

"Sounds good," Skylar says, too excited to worry about what Dr. Brown is saying.

"Okay with me," Bohdi says cautiously, a bit concerned about what the chemicals might be that require this formal procedure. I am familiar with precautions when using chemicals, so no issue there."

Dr. Brown nods. "Lastly, there are a couple of things I need to finish up before I can allow you to take them. Given that we do not have a patent, and there are some other complications, I need you both to sign a nondisclosure agreement. Are you willing to do that?”

“I think so,” says Skylar, “but I’m not sure what a nondisclosure agreement is.”

Bohdi nods.

Dr. Brown says, “It’s a legal form that binds you to not share, or show, any detail of these goggles with other people unless it is first cleared through me.”

Skylar shrugs. “No problem.”

He then looks at Bohdi, who responds, “Agreed. I am fine with that.” He struggles not to sound too excited.

“Good. In return, I want you to keep detailed notes of what you do and experience while you use them. We will communicate every month and discuss what you learn.”

“Definitely,” Skylar confirms.

“Not a problem. Maybe we can talk a little later about any format you want us to follow for note taking,” Bohdi responds.

“Where will you be keeping the goggles,” Dr. Brown asks.

Skylar looks at Bohdi. He replies quickly, “Has to be at your home.” Bohdi realized that his nosy, and annoying younger brother would be a constant problem.

“Yes, my home is where we will keep them,” she says, hoping to disguise any concerns she might be having. Secretly she wishes they had a neutral place, away from their parents. But she cannot imagine any place.

“For completion,” Dr. Brown states, “I want both your parents to sign the nondisclosure agreement, as well.

“Okay, we will do that,” Skylar stammers out. Bohdi is glad she responded because his response would have been laced with doubt.

Annie puts all the papers into a folder and hands it to them.

“Dr. and Ms. Brown, thank you so much for entrusting these amazing goggles to us. We are deeply honored you are doing this,” Skylar says with true gratitude.

Annie looks at Vic and they both smile. “We are so happy that you came today. I think the four of us have a lot of discussions ahead of us,” Dr. Brown says as he gets up from the couch, struggling with his cane.

Annie looks at Skylar, “I cannot tell you how happy I, and Dr. Brown, are that young people like you want to get involved and especially that a talented woman like yourself is getting involved. The world desperately needs the new point of view to technology and politics that we as females can give."

"Thank you, Annie," Skylar say a bit surprised by this compliment but very happy to hear it. She looks at Bohdi and makes a big smile. Bohdi chimes in, "I agree." Skylar would love to have more females to study and talk with.

Skylar and Bohdi get ready to follow the Browns out of the room. Before they leave, Dr. Brown repeats, "When you come back with the signed papers, I will go over more instructions for using the goggles and the occasional calibration."
Dr. Brown looks at Annie as they walk Skylar and Bohdi to the front door. He is thrilled that they very likely have found two technical people from the new generation to possibly entrust this important technology to. *Now it is possible, if all goes well, that future generations might benefit from this work. It will not be lost to humanity after my time on this Earth ends.*

6.

Jean and David work hard to follow the details about the goggles that Skylar and Bohdi describe. The story comes out in bits and pieces, as Skylar and Bohdi interrupt each other to add another bit they feel is important.

Jean locks in on the fact that special precautions are necessary if the goggles get broken. What if the user trips and the goggles break on their face?

Skylar explains that the user must wear swimming goggles underneath the scuba goggles to prevent any eye issues if that were to happen. She then moves on to discussing other fascinating features and possibilities the goggles present, figuring she has addressed her mother's concern.

But Jean presses the issue again, not satisfied so easily. "What will happen if this material gets in your eyes? Is it bad, like something burning them, or more serious?"

Skylar and Bohdi talk over each other again, saying that Dr. Brown said the chemicals will not blind you. It would just be unpleasant.

Bohdi reiterates the protective purpose of the swimming goggles, working to keep his impatience out of his voice.

Jean still struggles to understand and feels annoyed with herself. Why does she have to work so hard to follow this conversation? She has never struggled to stay tuned into a conversation. Pushing past her internal mental battle, she questions Skylar a third time.

"Skylar, again, what damage can this device do to your eyes? Is it really safe to use? All I hear is how amazing this device is and how it correlates to your Perception Reality experience. It seems to me that safety is the last thing on your mind."

"I *told* you, Mom. Dr. Brown uses the goggles himself, with the swimming goggles as a safety precaution. Do you think he would lend it out to me—to us—if he thought there might be some safety hazard?"

"But there *is* a hazard, he told you that. And I don't know if it's just as simple as you describe," she shoots back.

Skylar feels her mother's support slipping away, but also knows that her concerns are unfounded. "What about all those chemicals you use in the garden? You use eye protection and gloves all the time.

Some of those chemicals, you yourself have stated, should require a mask. Maybe this is just like that."

David, listening, wonders what is upsetting Jean so much. She is a stickler for details and protocol, but he hears something different in her voice. Normally, she's the patient one, not him. He's noticed a change in her behavior recently, and wonders if the loss of her job is affecting her more emotionally than she is letting on. He considers interjecting, but decides Jean has a right to get a better answer from Skylar than she is giving.

"Mom," Skylar says, trying not to sound exasperated, "I will ask him these questions. But let's assume he has not done any tests on his eyes to determine the effects. What if he says he knows there are no risks if we follow his protocol? What do you want to hear from him to satisfy your worries?"

"Get more details on what to do should those goggles break when you have them on. What if the chemicals get in your mouth? Those details are important."

David weighs in. "Skylar, why don't you call Dr. Brown and see what more he has to say. Then we can continue this discussion. Without more information, we can't consent to you using this device. Also, I want Bohdi's parents to consider everything carefully."

"If they say no, then we say no," Jean declares, grateful for David's assertion. Before this discussion of safety, she'd felt David pulled in by curiosity, when Skylar and Bohdi described their experiences with the goggles, and she had feared that they would disagree on how to handle it.

Skylar sees no way out. She sighs. She had hoped to call Dr. Brown and tell him that everyone had signed the agreement, and ask when she and Bohdi could pick up the goggles. She takes a deep breath and agrees to text Dr. Brown, disappointed that things are more complicated than she had hoped.

Bohdi stays quiet. He wants to talk to Skylar privately, but does not see an opportunity with Skylar and her parents involved in this conversation.

Skylar opens her pocketbook and takes out the yellow paper with Dr. Brown's phone number on it and she enters it into the encrypted link he provided. Dr. Brown had stated that he had trouble hearing on the phone, so wanted them to communicate via text, and had specifically told them to use this encrypted link only. Skylar thought it a bit odd, but she sees no reason not to use it.

She looks at Bohdi. "You have any questions you want me to ask Dr. Brown while I am talking to him?"

He wants to say yes, but fears that seeding unfounded doubts in front of Skylar's parents will hurt their case. Besides, they now have to convince his own parents, and that might have its own complications.

"Umm, no. Just let him know we still need to talk to my parents."

Bohdi sees Skylar's frustration in her body language as she texts Dr. Brown. Almost immediately, Jean turns to David and motions with her head for them to move into the kitchen.

While Skylar is composing a text for Dr. Brown, it occurs to Bohdi that in all the excitement of the day, he has not thought about what future implications this might have between he and Hannah. They are "on a break" since their last fight. He is exhausted with the dynamics between the two of them.

Today's events have moved quickly. They were only supposed to talk with Bruce's uncle. Now, if all these agreements are signed, they will have the goggles for themselves to experiment with. He will be coming over to Skylar's house regularly, and he will not be able to tell Hannah why. That is going to be an issue in the future if they decide to get back together. What he experienced today was unique and he suspects will take him down a path that is not going to be easy to backtrack on.

7.

"You have all the papers?" Bohdi asks Skylar as she gets into the passenger seat. They had arranged to be at Dr. Brown's at 2:00 p.m.

Skylar opens the folder on her lap. "Yup. But just to be sure, here are one, two, three, four, five, and six confidentiality agreements, with all those b-e-a-utiful signatures. And here's the second one, agreeing that the goggles stay at my house."

Skylar groans as they slip into traffic. "What a day yesterday was! I was completely exhausted when I went to bed, but I couldn't sleep for hours because I was so excited."

"Me too. I'm glad we went through the tough part with your parents first. Made dealing with my parents a lot easier."

Bohdi's mind drifts back to the phone call last night with Hannah. He told her he is breaking up the relationship for good. He thinks it is the best for both of them. Hannah immediately accused him of going out with Skylar. He told her Skylar was an old friend, nothing more. She told him there is nothing he could say that would convince her otherwise. In the conversation, he realized the decision to make the breakup final was correct, and there was nothing he could do or say that would convince Hannah otherwise.

"Dr. Brown hasn't said how long we can keep the goggles, but in his agreement, he asks us to commit to updating him on our activities every month. So," Skylar says emphatically, "it seems like we will have them for at least a month or two. What do you think?"

The question snaps Bohdi out of his sad train of thought, "I hope we have longer. I want to do so many experiments with those goggles."

"I can't wait until we get them to my house and try them again." She surprises herself with her strong response, realizing how true it is—she is more excited about this than she has ever been about anything.

****

Back at the house, Bohdi puts the boxes on the kitchen table and removes the battery pack to start recharging it. "Funny, Dr. Brown says that the goggles can only be used on batteries. He said the AC adds too much electrical noise. Interesting."

"When are your parents' due home?" Bohdi asks, hoping that it will not be too soon. He is glad that his parents are able to afford to have him live on campus. He likes coming home, but he is in charge of his schedule. He realizes that he will be coming home more often now that they have the goggles at Skylar's house.

Skylar looks at her phone. "In about an hour and a half, so we have some time to play."

Skylar joins him in taking each part out of the boxes carefully and laying them on the table. "We need to make a copy of these instructions, just in case we misplace them," she says as she organizes the papers.

Bohdi sends her an anxious look. "Do you have the calibration stone in that box?"

"Yes, right here. Bohdi, I want you to use the goggles first so I can repeat the start-up sequence."

"Fine with me. I'll make some coffee while we wait for the batteries to charge up.

While Skylar busies herself with their coffeemaker, Bohdi thumbs through the instruction manual. He closes it when Skylar comes back to the table with two mugs, and slides the manual over to her to peruse. She moves out of her chair so she can see the battery pack. One of the five green LEDs is lit. "Twenty percent." She is getting impatient. "How about we start when it's at eighty?"

"Sounds good." Bohdi likes how each connector is different, so it's not possible to connect them incorrectly.

Skylar verifies a few things in the pages of the crude instruction manual. It looks aged, but the pages do not have much wear on them. It looks to him like Dr. Brown has not given anyone else the goggles, unless this manual is a copy. She asks Bohdi some questions and the two of them scans the pages, making sure that they have the sequence correct and do not miss any initial settings.

After thirty minutes, Skylar moves out of her chair again to check the battery pack. "It's eighty percent. Let's go!"

They both get up from the table. Skylar repositions a kitchen chair and says, "Okay, sit here."

"Why?"

"Because I want to stand in front of you, and I can't do that and hold your arm as well."

"Good idea," Bohdi says, eager to get this process going.

Skylar puts the swimming goggles on him, followed by the goggles. Then she mounts the microprocessor and battery packs on his belt. Bohdi waits patiently as Skylar connects everything.

"Ready?" Skylar asks.

"I want you to stand in front of me."

"Okay, first let me get this fired up. Tell me when you see something."

Bohdi feels Skylar adjusting the goggles and the two packs on his belt. She moves in front of him once she finishes.

"I can see you now."

Skylar moves back to Bohdi. "All right, let me change the setting to One. Seems it has to go there before going to Plus. We have to stay at this setting for a minimum of fifteen seconds."

"I see that bright white fog again. It is so interesting! I wish I could move into it. It seems so real, so tangible. You know, it's odd to say this, but I feel a buzzing in my head. Nothing uncomfortable, but definitely there, moving around inside my head."

"I've felt the same thing. I'm thinking it's some frequency coming from the headphones, but outside our hearing range. I asked Dr. Brown about it, but he avoided a specific answer. Ready for the next setting?"

"I am."

Skylar turns the setting to Plus, moves in front of Bohdi, and waits.

"Move around," he says.

"Guess which way I am moving."

Bohdi hears her move and then sees it with the goggles. "To the left." He hears her move again and looks intently. "Still on the left."

"Well, you got the position right."

"So, this oval shape represents what part of you?"

"The images in these goggles are similar to the Perception Reality. The shape represents you, and the colors represent information relating to emotions. If I focus on one of these colors, information streams into my mind. Do you see different colors as part of the oval?"

"I do."

"Focus on one particular color and see what you sense."

"Well, . . . there's a blue that looks brighter than the rest."

Bohdi focuses his attention on this color. "It feels inquisitive. Curious, maybe. Like there's a need to understand . . . no, not quite that, a need to . . . to know. Yes, to know. The feeling is getting stronger. The words *to know* feels more . . . more powerful. That's you. The desire to know is a very powerful part of you. It brings you joy."

Skylar likes what she hears. "Do you see any other colors?"

He looks around and decides to pick a color that is not as vibrant. "There's a dull brown near the bottom."

Bohdi knows he picked up information about Skylar when he focused on the blue. He can feel it inside of himself, clear and strong. His mind jumps to the idea that these goggles can bring a whole new way to research psychology, but he pushes that thought away.

He shifts his focus to the brown and waits. Slowly, at first imperceptibly, a dread starts to infuse him. He becomes concerned.

"I am feeling anxious, like I don't have enough time," Bohdi says.

"What about?"

"I don't know, I just know I don't like what I am feeling very much."

"Okay, stay with it for a moment. Don't block it. Now ask a question in your mind, like, what is this feeling related to? Then vocalize the next image or feeling you get."

Bohdi does what is asked of him. A moment later he reports, "I see your mother. An image of your mother. What does that mean? You're afraid of your mother. No, that's not correct. Help me, Skylar."

"No, I want you to finish this exercise on your own," Skylar says firmly, pushing him to move past his logical brain that wants a sequence to everything.

"I don't want to. I feel a dread." He pauses. "All right, you are afraid . . . for . . . yes, for—your mother. Yes, that feels right. You are afraid *for* your mother."

He is quiet for a moment. "I don't feel anything else." But he does feel uncomfortable, for no reason he can figure out, and decides to move his head around, trying to absorb the strange shapes and colors he sees.

Skylar is again amazed at what can be seen through the goggles. What has taken her years of discipline and practice to understand in Perception Reality can be done easily with these goggles. She feels a twinge of jealousy over the ease with which others can access the same information, but it's overpowered by her need to know more. What she experiences in Perception Reality has more detail, and more information, than what she saw with the goggles the first time, but she is anxious to verify this and find the limits. The best thing, though, is that she can now share this experience with someone else.

"Skylar, move me over to the window," snaps her back into the moment.

She puts her hand on his elbow. "Okay, stand up slowly." She waits until he is on his feet. "Okay, move left a few steps. Now step forward. Keep moving, and I'll tell you when to stop."

Bohdi follows her instructions until she says, "Stop."

Once guided to the window, he looks around, trying to correlate his memory of the Donaldson's backyard with what he's seeing. He knows there is a large, healthy oak tree to his left. He sees bright colors where he expects this tree to be, but nothing that might resemble a tree.

"I wish I could see myself. That would be interesting."

"I agree."

"You said this is similar to what you see in your Perception Reality. I am really interested in knowing more."

"Well, similar, but not exactly the same. What you see is a good approximation of what I experience in that reality. I am really curious about what we can learn from these goggles."

They both hear a car doors slam.

"Hold on, Bohdi. Don't move." Skylar heads to the living room and looks out the front window.

"My parents are home early."

She runs back to Bohdi and grabs his arm.

He lifts his hands to his head. "Quick—get these off me! I don't want to be wearing them when your parents come in the door."

"Too late. There is no way we can power down properly and get the parts off of you in time. Just relax. I'm going to lead you back to the kitchen chair."

They hear the front door open. "Hello, anybody home?"

"Shit," Bohdi says quietly. Skylar feels his arm tense up.

"In the kitchen," Skylar replies.

David and Jean come around the corner.

"Oh my!" Jean exclaims. "What are you guys doing? Is that the device you picked up?"

"It is. Bohdi is trying it out first so I could get some experience hooking everything up."

"Umm, hi, Ms. Donaldson," Bohdi says sheepishly, turning his head toward Jean's voice.

"Nice new glasses you have," David quips.

"Thanks, they take a bit of getting used to." Bohdi relaxes a bit as the tension in the room subsides.

"I bet. Pretty tough to wear all day, as well." David smiles.

Bohdi can see the field around Ms. Donaldson expand and the colors change rapidly. The field and colors around Mr. Donaldson remain the same. He wonders if this reflects Ms. Donaldson's nervousness that he hears in her voice. He feels anxious about not being able to physically see them and is keen to get the goggles off for now.

Jean moves into the kitchen to grab two mugs as a way to get a moment to gather her thoughts.

"Tell me about this device," David says, peering at Bohdi. "I've been curious since you both explained it to me yesterday."

"Yes, tell us more," Jean adds, rejoining them.

"Probably the best thing is for you to try them." Skylar is disappointed she did not get a chance to try the goggles again before her parents came home, but she also wants to hear what her father has to say. "Let me get Bohdi powered down and unhooked, then I can hook up either one of you."

David looks at Jean. She motions for him to go first.

"Sounds good."

"Okay, Dad, you're next. Sit in this chair."

After Skylar gets her father set up, she says, "Tell me when you see me in front of you."

"Okay, I see you now."

"All right, that was the first setting. Now the second one, which is just temporary. But let me know what you experience."

"I see a white fog."

"Do you feel anything while viewing this white fog?"

"Nope."

"We have to stay on this setting for fifteen seconds."

"Why fifteen seconds?"

"Don't know. Those are the instructions."

"Am I supposed to experience something in particular?"

"No," Skylar answers carefully. "Okay, now to the third setting."

After a moment, David says, "Hey, that looks pretty psychedelic."

He moves his head all around. "I have no clue what I am looking at."

"Dad, don't get out of the chair without letting me know."

"Okay."

Skylar stays with her father in case he is distracted and decides to just get up and move. As she moves toward her father, she notices that her mother is standing back with a look of concern on her face. Skylar would like to make her feel more at ease and suddenly has an idea.

"Mom, move in front of Dad. Dad, hold your head still and just look forward. Let me know what you see."

Skylar waits a few seconds. "See anything different?"

"I guess. I see some funny shape. Could be an ellipse?"

"Well, that represents Mom. See what happens if she moves." Skylar motions for Jean to move to her father's right. "Do you see her move?"

"The image moved to my right. Did you move to the right, Honey?"

"I did."

"Do you see any colors associated with this shape?" Skylar presses, then holds her breath.

"I see some colors, but it's hard to distinguish more."

"Do you feel anything associated with what you are seeing? Focus on a particular color."

David is silent for some time. Skylar desperately wants to hear him say something.

Finally, David says, "Are you sure there's not a tiny camera in these goggles that is imaging what is in front of me and then processing the image into these shapes and colors? It seems to me that some fancy image processing is going on."

Skylar's mind briefly blanks in surprise. She manages to reply, "It is not image processing."

"How do you know that, Skylar? Did you ask Dr. Brown?"

"I did not."

"If you didn't ask, how do you know?"

Skylar struggles to find an appropriate reply. She recognizes that her father has switched into his engineer mindset, one she is familiar with. Then it hits her. "Because this is similar to what I see in my Perception Reality. That's how I know it is not all image processing. And the colors, they are the same as I see. How could he get the colors right?"

Bohdi, sitting down at the kitchen table so he is out of the way, can feel Skylar's emotions going up and down as Skylar tries to get her father to have the same experience that she and Bohdi had.

"What do you mean, get the colors right?" David says.

Skylar realizes that with her father's current train of thought, there is no way to get her point across. Then she has an idea. She moves over to the kitchen table and picks up a large notepad she left there. She puts it in front of the goggles her father is wearing, blocking the view of Jean. If there is a camera, then her father should see the shape associated with Jean disappear.

"Did you see a change?" she asks, holding her breath as she holds the notepad in front of the goggles.

"No, not really, slight change in contrast, but otherwise, no. What are you doing?"

"I…," then Skylar has a flash. Her father can still see her mother even with the board in front of the goggles. "Nothing," she says, I just grabbed a notepad because I want to make some notes. Her mother was not paying attention, so Skylar did not have to answer her questions. Now she has another perplexing issue. Those fields are not blocked by matter.

"Skylar, is this what you see in the Perception Reality you've been talking about for the past eight years?"

"Y..yes," she stammers, as her thought is broken by her father's question. "It is a pretty decent correlation. Not identical, but definitely has many of the same characteristics."

"It's pretty interesting," David says as he moves his head around. His technical mind is working overtime to make sense of what he is seeing, "You said Dr. Brown believes that what I'm seeing are different states of matter."

"Yes!"

"Does that mean you can now analyze elements in different ways than before?"

"I don't know. That's an interesting question. I would guess that should be true."

David goes quiet, trying to absorb everything he sees. Bohdi senses Skylar's satisfaction that she was able to assuage her father's skepticism. As Bohdi glances her way, she gives him a thumbs-up. He nods back. Jean catches this interaction between the two. She likes Bohdi and thinks he would be a good match for her daughter.

As David looks around, conversations he and Jean had with Skylar over the years about the Perception Reality come flooding back into his mind. In the beginning they were amused, thinking their younger daughter had an active imagination, not atypical for an eleven-year-old, although typically, children come up with these things when they are younger. But she spoke about her experiences with such clarity, such passion, that it was obvious she was not just making it up, but was experiencing something and relaying it to them. David and Jean witnessed her preparing for this experience and it looked like, after some meditation, she went into a trance-like state. Her face showed subtle signs of joy or concern, but that is all they could see from her outward appearance. Afterward, she spoke of amazing journeys into worlds of odd shapes and bright colors. They thought of having her evaluated, but kept on pushing it off since Skylar showed no other signs of concerning behavior.

David searched the Internet for help in understanding his daughter and found that other people described similar experiences they had with their deep meditation practices. David and Jean decided that Skylar had figured out how to do something similar on her own, and agreed that if they saw any unusual behavior in her, they would consider professional help. But that never happened. In the past four years, she has barely spoken of it. David is glad to finally see what his daughter tried to communicate to them when she was younger.

David says, "I am interested to see what you learn from these goggles. Jean, you want to try them on?"

Jean hesitates. "Maybe later. I'm ready for a coffee. Do the two of you need a fill-up?" She hears a unified yes from all both of them.

David considers pushing his wife to try the goggles but decides against it. They came home early because she was feeling exhausted, and he figures there will be a better time, possibly tomorrow.
Bohdi is excited after Skylar's spontaneous notebook experiment. *The goggles just verified that these fields of color are not blocked by physical materials*. That is a bit mind-blowing.

8.

Team Leader Paul Dremos heads out of his colleague's Hank Slidel's office. They have just completed aligning information on a particularly troublesome target. Paul is in a rush because he had a meeting with his agents, which he now cannot attend because this target has become a crisis, and this emergency meeting is now taking priority. But before he goes to this crisis meeting, an all-too-common event, he wants to touch base with his agents quickly since they're already waiting for him. As he hurries down the corridor, he winces in pain. His bad knee, injured playing football in college, is really acting up today. Paul was a big guy in college, packing 250 pounds on his six-foot-two frame. His weight the past five years has increased because he cannot find the time to exercise enough, and that exacerbates the problem with his knee.

He searches all the pockets of his tweed jacket, hoping he might have a spare painkiller left in one of them. No such luck. He wishes there was time to go back to his office and grab one. He needs it, not only for his knee, but also for the next few contentious meetings on his docket.

"Good morning," Paul says firmly as he enters the conference room where his four agents are assembled. Their conversations terminate immediately. Their leader doesn't tolerate a casual atmosphere; he's always pure business.

Paul steps to the head of the conference table and puts his laptop down. "All right, who hasn't read the background information I sent you about the list of new targets?" Nobody responds, and he nods sharply, pleased.

"Good. Unfortunately, I just learned I have to cut out of this meeting for another one, but I wanted to stop by and say that I have to add three more targets to your list. Please review this data on the secure server. I will use the update meeting tomorrow to listen to your plans for the targets you were going to discuss today. We will also discuss the tasks for the new targets and get owners for these new tasks. Please use the rest of this meeting time to put your ideas together."

After that, Paul picks up his laptop and heads out the door. He knows the team is frustrated with the lack of information on the targets they're assigned to, but that's the way the Chronos Consortium system is purposely designed. Data is compartmentalized, with each team provided a limited amount of information.

His team's objective is to make their targets feel victimized. It's the best way to reduce the level at which the targets unknowingly operate in multidimensional time. The Chronos Consortium has fine-tuned techniques to undermine each target's sense of personal power. If done correctly, the disempowerment becomes a self-fulfilling process.

Generally, with enough resources, most targets fall into the victim trap, since its power is so pervasive in the human experience. But some targets are rebels, born or instilled with strong ideals that empower them even in the most strenuous of circumstances. These are the most troubling ones for the Chronos Consortium, and are the source of Paul and the other team's headaches. In the past, it was possible to organize ways to eliminate these targets, while still adhering to the Highest Principle: *Leave no trace*. But these days, in the developed world at least, this is no longer an easy option. The Chronos Consortium teams' missions are harder and more time-consuming.

On the way to his next meeting, Paul dwells on Hank's recent remark about it being the tenth anniversary of the missing Time Information Field Scanner parts, the only ones ever lost. This purposeful dig from Hank rekindled an obsession with Paul over the parts, and a burning desire to uncover what became of them. They had nearly cost Paul his career at the Chronos Consortium.

Whoever organized the disappearance of the parts was very clever. That person had left the shell of the device in its plastic bag with all the paperwork so it looked like a proper scanner. A weight had been put inside to give the impression it was still a complete unit, rather than an inoperable and outdated scanner that was waiting for proper authorization for destruction. Due to the large bureaucracy that the Chronos Consortium has for managing these parts, it is not uncommon for them to sit on the shelf for a few weeks, waiting for authorization. This organized destruction is done at the same time for all departments in that sector of the Chronos Consortium. By the time the deception was discovered by the Chronos Consortium, they had no way to figure out when it had happened.

Every part of each Time Information Field Scanner is stamped with a serial number so they can be identified if they are found. Paul has a few suspects in mind, and one in particular, but he has no evidence to support his suspicions.

He is relieved that none of the secret technology has ever become public knowledge. This is still the Chronos Consortium's biggest fear. Even now, members wonder where the Time Information Field Scanner parts disappeared to and for what purpose. For the past ten years, this case has been used as the template for much stricter control, and it kills Paul that every new trainee eventually finds out he was the manager at the time of the theft. He desperately wants to recover the parts and clear a blemish on an otherwise stellar career.

9.

"All right, class, today we'll discuss a topic that's familiar to all of you, but we will take it to a new depth," Professor Chandler announces. "The topic is placebos. The word is derived from the Latin phrase *I shall please*, and hopefully I'll achieve that today in this class."

The students, including Bohdi, chuckle at the weak joke.

"Okay, Jane, what's a placebo?" Professor Chandler asks, looking at one of the few students sitting up front. She reaches back and adjusts the clip holding her long blonde hair as she waits for Jane to speak. Professor Chandler is dedicated to her field of psychology and expects the same attention from her students. She dresses like she is going to a job at a law firm or bank, not to teach a college class; it makes her look taller and more imposing.

Jane answers confidently: "It's a pill, usually sugar, I believe, given to a patient in clinical trials by pharmaceutical researchers to determine the effectiveness of their drugs. Those who receive the placebo are the control group."

"Very good," Professor Chandler says. "Anything more?"

"The tests are usually conducted as double-blind tests, so that even the researchers don't know which pill is the placebo, and which is the drug being tested," Jane adds.

"Let me interrupt you there. Why is it important to do a double-blind test?"

Jane continues, "In a study, researchers want to limit any influence the participants in the study might pick up, either consciously or otherwise, which might lead them to make assessments about what pill they're getting."

Professor Chandler paces in front of the class. "But why should researchers put this much effort into the study? I mean, either the pill works or it doesn't. Is that correct, Eric?"

She halts and glares at a student in the back of the classroom.

Eric, startled, says sheepishly, "I'm sorry, Professor Chandler, but I missed what Jane was saying."

"Of course, you missed it, since you were playing with your phone. Make a choice, Eric: Attend my class, or attend to your phone outside. Which will it be?"

Eric shoves his phone in his pocket. "Stay in class," he mumbles.

"Good choice."

"Anya, you want to add anything?"

Anya stiffens. "Uh . . . in studies on placebos, it's been found that there are many subtle and not-so-subtle influences determining the placebo's effectiveness." She hesitates, and the professor urges her to continue.

"The way a person administering the placebo is dressed and speaks changes the way the patient interprets their authority. For example, dressing and acting like a doctor, nurse, or any other medical professional makes the placebo more effective. The size and the color of the pill also makes a difference. The tone of voice and the environment have all been found to make a difference."

At this point, Bohdi, who has been sitting quietly in the middle of the classroom, pays close attention. He is thrilled to have been lucky enough to get this class.

"Very nice, Anya. Everything said so far is true. It's not as simple as just a chemical and biological interaction between placebo and participant. Also important is the attitude the participant or patient brings to the interaction. The more motivated they are for a recovery or healing, the more effective the placebo is. In some cases, the effect of a placebo has been staggering. Patients suffering from severe physical, mental, and emotional maladies have shown remarkable recoveries when placebos are administered in what the patient *perceives*"—she points to her head and pauses—"are conditions that lead to *belief or trust* in the medicine and the person administering the placebo. Side effects have also been reported by participants receiving the placebo. If the participant is told their placebo is a stimulant, it has that result; if it's labeled a relaxant, it has that effect. Same pill."

She grins. "Now, let me give you an example of how dramatic an effect belief has. A man comes to Joe's door and tells him that his mother has been in a bad accident. The person standing at the door is wearing a police uniform, and looks and sounds very authoritative. There's no reason to doubt that he is a policeman. Joe is rapidly interpreting data, consciously and unconsciously, to determine how to react. But in truth, this person could be a good actor dressed for the part. Joe has no way of knowing, at least at first. Once both conscious and unconscious decisions have been made by Joe that this is real, his body chemistry will change with the emotional state based on this decision. In a way, his body is waiting for him to assess the information, and if he determines it's real, certain emotional and chemical reactions occur in him. If he determines it's not true, a different chemical reaction occurs. In many ways, our physical, mental, and emotional states are determined by decisions constantly made by us, many on the unconscious level."

Professor Chandler pivots on her heel and resumes pacing at the front of the class. "Now, this is not exactly news. Take a sample of people and put them in a physically challenging situation. Some will see it as exciting and look forward to it; some will be nervous, others determined to override their fear of failure or embarrassment; and some will see it as unsafe and immediately look for a way out. Therefore, how you perceive a situation definitely is *not* absolute in nature."

Professor Chandler looks around the classroom, satisfied that all the students are focused on her.

"Let me give you two more examples. You're home for the summer, and your parents assign you to fix part of the wooden fence in the front yard. You're annoyed at the request. While performing the task, you miss a nail with the hammer and end up smashing your fingernail. You howl in pain. Now you're really annoyed. You didn't want to do this anyway, and *now* look what happened. Your state becomes one of suffering, and that state amplifies the physical pain you feel. You go inside and complain bitterly about what has happened and say you can't finish the work. Bandages and ointments are administered to stop bleeding and potential infections. The work stops, but the emotional state of annoyance continues, and the pain is reported as high."

She pauses for the class to digest the story. They are still paying attention, so she resumes.

"Let's flip the situation. You're inspired by a friend to build something together. During your project, the exact same thing happens. You hammer your fingernail. You howl in pain. You're now annoyed because you have to spend time away from the project to take care of this. You look for ways to get around it. Your howling has attracted one of your parents, who comes into the garage to see what has happened. You explain the situation. Well, they say, maybe you should stop and take care of your finger. You look at your finger, bleeding and pounding with pain. Your parent asks to look at it, but you're reluctant to show it, fearing they'll try to slow or, even worse, stop your progress. After all, your friend is counting on you to finish your part, and you're set on combining the parts into a larger whole tomorrow. Band-Aids and ointments are administered to stop bleeding and potential infections. Soon you go back to work, and, while lost in the project, you occasionally forget about the pain. You're hurting but not suffering, and the joy of working on the project takes your concentration away from your finger. You've made a conscious decision to not let it limit you.

"If you spoke to these people two days later, one would complain about their suffering, and the other would shrug and say it's a minor annoyance, not worth talking about. This difference in perspective has everything to do with your perception about the circumstances. There are two parts to this story: a physical objective event, and then an interpretation, or subjective part of the event.

"Second example: If someone makes a statement to you, you unconsciously and/or consciously decide how to respond to that remark. If you consider the statement an insult, you, on some level, decide to accept the insult and then decide what your response will be. It might not seem like you decide, but one person might accept the statement as an insult and respond with anger, and another might reject the insult and laugh it off, or feel sorry for the person who felt they needed to make such a statement. In every situation in your life, you're making decisions and responding to them, either allowing them to take away personal power or keeping your personal power.

"This is true with every experience in your life, including your personal history, as well as your interpretation of your family history. Talk to your brothers and sisters about your parents, the home you grew up in, and key events during your time at home. You'll hear similar and also very different stories. Some of the stories are so different, at times you might wonder if you have the same parents and lived in the same home. We have objective events and subjective interpretation. This comes together in placebo studies."

A student asks, "What happens if the participants are told after they get positive benefits from a pill that it was just a placebo?"

"In many cases the placebo effect disappears—but not always. It is a complicated situation." Professor Chandler pauses for a minute before she continues. "Let me finish on this note: Some cultures are more prone to having placebos work for certain ailments and not for others. Also, sham surgeries—that is, surgeries performed with all the fanfare of a regular surgery without any actual cutting involved—have also shown remarkable effects. We'll get into more specific examples in the next class. I should also say, it doesn't work on all people; and as far as I'm aware, there is no way to predict accurately whom placebos will or won't work on. But let's continue our discussion in the next class."

Bohdi picks up his books and slides them into his backpack. He leaves the classroom with a bounce in his step. This class had wiped away any of his lingering doubts about his decision to switch out of physics and into psychology. He still struggles with some guilt over his decision. His parents told him he can do anything he wants. But he did not realize how happy his mother was that he had chosen to become a physicist until the moment he told his parents he planned to change. He saw an unmistakable flash of disappointment in his mother's eyes. It was then that he realized that she said he could do anything, but she was secretly happy that he had chosen this field. His grandparents were very clear in their enthusiasm for their grandson's choice. In their mind, the best choices are to be a medical doctor, a scientist, an engineer and then all those other fields. Bohdi's mother had rebelled when she started college and chose to be a historian. As a history teacher, she is loved by her students because she had a very unique way of communicating history, constantly challenged her students to look for the past in the present, the only place it can exist anyway.

His mother Chandni Kearns had to deal with strong feedback from her parents once again. Bohdi knew that his grandparents loved him, but he could hear the conversation between his mother and his grandparents in his head, *Bohdi is now behaving like she did and that this is a repeat of the same behavior only one generation later.* Bohdi is not sure himself about all the components that drove him to this decision, but for today he has clarity, this is the right choice for him.

10.

"Uuuggghhh!"

Bohdi drags himself out from under the bedcover. He is still fully clothed because he was too tired to change at 4:00 this morning, when he went to bed. He just flopped onto the mattress and pulled the comforter over him.

He struggles to lift his exhausted body out of bed. He shuffles over to the coffee maker in his dorm room. "Cooooffeeee," he mumbles to himself, like some caffeine-craving zombie. He finds a can of dark roast and loads the coffeemaker. He hopes that soon the rich smell will fill the room and bring his consciousness back to life. He looks at the clock by his bed. *Wow, 10:30.* He missed a morning class and knows he cannot afford to miss his afternoon class. *Hurry up, coffee!*

When the coffee finishes brewing, Bohdi grabs the closest mug he can find. He pours himself a cup of coffee and then puts some coffee creamer powder in his coffee. He finds a packet of sugar, tears it open and pours it into his coffee.

As he returns to his desk, he reflects on his insights that were triggered by that discussion with Dr. Brown, where Dr. Brown hinted that what Skylar is seeing in her Perception Reality are energy structures based on frequency in three-dimensional time. Once Bohdi saw those images with the goggles, he knew he needed to understand this link between this technology and the psychological implications better.

Yesterday, after his Psychology class, Bohdi went to the university library and did additional research on Fourier transforms since he has more time in his school schedule than Skylar. He left with a pile of books and photocopies. After finishing his homework near midnight, he started reading and he could not stop until the early hours this morning. The pictures stunned him. Images of humans, after being processed by this mathematical algorithm, had a structure roughly similar to the shapes he saw when using the goggles and from what Skylar described, also what she sees in her Perception Reality. He cannot wait to show these to Skylar.

But there were clearly differences. The mathematically transformed images each had a bright point in the center, making them look star like, with nowhere near the detail he saw with the goggles. The images he saw with the goggles are much bigger, with much more detail. The images he's seen with Dr. Brown's goggles do not have the star like pattern, either, so they are not straightforward Fourier transforms. His experience with two years in the technical program has exposed him to these transforms, but he had never seen them applied to images.

But, to his amazement, the analogy of this mathematical algorithm by Fourier clearly shows how the same information can be represented in two completely different ways, and one of the ways is more in line with what he perceives normally with his eyes and the other similar to what can be seen in the goggles.

He wonders how to accomplish what Dr. Brown hinted at, that is, transforming a visible structure in three-dimensional space, like a human body, into an invisible and unrecognizable shape in three-dimensional time. The math in the textbooks cannot justify that. Bohdi realizes he and Skylar have much more work to do. He wonders if Dr. Brown already knows this technique. He sure seemed confident in what he was saying.

Bohdi suspects that he might, and wants to ask him more. Like, in the three dimensions of time, what does each axis mean? He knows that in three-dimensional space, one axis is for length, one for width, and one for height. These make up the dimensions of volume. How would that translate into time?

The one-dimensional time everyone knows goes from the past to the future. That would form one axis, but what could width and height in time correspond to? In three-dimensional time, all events would be captured in a huge time-volume just like the events in the cosmos are captured in the huge space-volume. Past, present, and future would all be there, available. Traveling in this volume of time would allow you to go to any event in time, past or future. Maybe, he thinks, the width and height axes of time are necessary to hold the information of every event for every person, every atom, every animal and plant for every moment. He's not sure how each moment corresponds to the unusual shapes positioned in the volume of time, but what is clear to him is that the mathematics Dr. Brown hinted at takes information of shape in three-dimensional space and changes it into a unique shape that exists in three-dimensional time.

No sooner does Bohdi adopt the idea that what he has witnessed with the goggles is based on three-dimensional time than he feels the next stage of confusion cloud his mind. If they receive information from the shapes in three-dimensional time, as Dr. Brown suggested and as he experienced with Skylar, and these unique shapes correlate with thoughts, emotions, and intentions, then shouldn't the reverse mathematics transform this invisible structured information in three-dimensional *time* back into visible structures in three-dimensional *space*? That would radically change psychology. No longer would it be like probing the inner workings of a human with clever questions, but direct insight would be possible into what people are thinking and feeling in a direct and scientific way.

If so, what shape in three-dimensional space would these structures transform into? The thoughts, emotions, and intentions, the components of human consciousness, have to have a corresponding structure in three-dimensional space. But where? Can we just not detect them because of limitations in our vision or equipment? If equipment could detect these structures, Bohdi is sure, then scientists would have already correlated the detected structures to human consciousness. They have to be either invisible or hidden in a form humans cannot yet understand. But why?

Unable to answer his own questions, he thinks to a question that his mother asked: "If I was asked to point to where time is in space, what would you say?"

Bohdi thought about it for a few minutes. It seemed that the only response has to be that time is everywhere. *It seems that in three-dimensional space, there's no place that time isn't. Even inside the atomic nucleus and out to other galaxies, time is always there. So a single dimension like time can be everywhere in three-dimensional space. In other words, time is distributed throughout all of space.*

Bohdi's mother smiled at his response. She would ask him these philosophical questions from time to time after her own musings about the ideas of an Indian author she was reading.

Bohdi had never thought of time in quite that way before. He used to think time was like an arrow, pointing from the present into the future in a state of constant change, each moment of now flying past. Now he understands that time is not an abstract measurement, but that people *live in time*. This one idea, that we live and experience life in time and that it is not some outside measurement is radically changing the way he looked at time, and humans.

Bohdi took that idea and began to ask his friends, "Where are you located in your body. They typically pointed to their chest, referencing their heart, the conceptual feeling part of themselves. Others pointed to their head. But when he asked them why, their answers were vague. They really didn't know how to capture something as distributed as their consciousness in one location in their body.

Bohdi recognizes that at moments like when he stubbed his toe—a not uncommon event for someone who does not like to wear shoes—his pain was a keen reminder that the toe was an intimate part of himself. As much as he would like to disown the stubbed toe, pain would not allow it.

Now, he realizes that if he takes the idea that *he* is in all parts of his body, including its trillions and trillions of cells, then his consciousness is distributed throughout all of his physical body. He also understands that he can live without fingers, or ears, or eyes, but cannot live without a brain or a heart. Clearly, he figures, some organs are more important than others in this consciousness game. But to be a human fully experiencing spacetime, is to be fully *in space* and *in time.*

A thought flashes in his mind: *If consciousness is distributed throughout our bodies, and everything we know is embedded in time, then maybe time and consciousness aren't just correlated, but our consciousness is also literally in time.*

A new appreciation for consciousness, and time, sweeps over him. Energy fills his being, leaving him feeling much, much larger than this physical body. The sensation triggers another thought: *Is consciousness limited to only being distributed throughout the structure of our body?* He understands that he owns his body, but innately, he knows he is more than his body. *What if consciousness has the property of quantum entanglement, where matter is linked independent of the distance in space?* Two particles, linked through quantum entanglement, *instantly* affect each other, no matter what the distance. What if time is the *link* between these particles? But can concepts in quantum physics be applied to humans, and human consciousness? If they can, then that might help explain the more controversial and confounding aspects of consciousness that are not limited to the body but seem to defy distances in three-dimensional space!

Bohdi shakes his head as these insights as questions pour into his mind. He scribbles his recent insights down on paper so he can organize them later. He now clearly sees himself in a whole new way. What he's seen in the goggles substantiates what he sees directly with a whole new level of confidence. Now he has images of mathematical transforms in textbooks to show Skylar that might be used as a template for how space and time link together. A true understanding for them might not be that far away. He feels his pulse quicken at the thought.

This evening he will put these new insights into a report, along with experiments that he and Skylar have done with the goggles, and propose to Skylar that they send them along to Dr. Brown. He texts Skylar and asks her to call him when she has a chance, saying that he has some cool stuff to share with her. He then switches to finish his homework for his afternoon class.

11.

Jean Donaldson spent Friday job hunting. Glad to be home, she opens the kitchen door and is pleasantly surprised. "Hi, Dear. I thought you'd still be at school. Glad to see you're home early." She puts her umbrella down, wet from the drenching October rain.

Skylar is taken aback by her mother's forgetfulness. Friday afternoons are her time off from school and work, and her mother had specifically asked for some one-on-one time with her this afternoon. Skylar was going to remind her, but she decides to just let it go. Skylar's still worried about her mother because her memory lapses are getting more common—and until now, her mother's memory has always been impeccable. She can't remember her getting things like this confused, even back when she was juggling work, parenting, and all the other things adults have to deal with.

"There's some coffee already made if you want some," she offers.

"Mmmm, smells divine. French Vanilla Roast? I *would* like some, but not now. I think I'm in the mood for some lemonade.

"I'll be right back." Ms. Donaldson steps out of the room to head to the bathroom.

Jean returns and goes to the refrigerator to fill her glass with lemonade. She sits in a chair next to Skylar. She is proud of who her younger daughter is becoming, but there are parts of her life she wants to understand better.

"Last weekend, when you were using the goggles, you mentioned a white light," she says. "Those words remind me of articles I've read about near-death experiences. Do you think there's a similarity between out-of-body and near-death experiences, where people talk of seeing or going to a white light, and this white light you see in the goggles?"

"Not sure, Mom. Good question. I could ask Bohdi, he seems to know more about those type of topics."

"I've been wondering ever since you had me try the goggles again this past weekend and asked me what I felt as I looked at the white fog." Jean gazes off into the distance, as if struggling to put words to her visual memory. "Well, I felt nothing. I just saw a white mist."

Skylar does not understand how the goggles can allow people to have such different experiences. Both she and Bohdi spoke of a calm feeling, a quiet joy that moved through their whole being in the short time they viewed the white fog on setting One. But both of Bohdi's parents felt nothing. How can that be? The goggles generate more questions the more she uses them.

"I don't know. Both Bohdi and I experience something I would describe as an inner joy. And I've spent up to three minutes with that setting. But you and Dad say the same thing."

"Do you think Bohdi is just saying what he thinks you want to hear?"

"No, it's not in Bohdi's nature to do that."

"You're right. Sorry I said that. These goggles are interesting, but I still want to understand what you experience with them. You two have spent so much time the past few weekends looking through them, and by your animated conversations, I can tell you are both excited. What am I missing?"

"I don't know, Mom. Bohdi and I need to communicate with Dr. Brown next weekend, since that's the four-week mark. I will ask him these questions."

Skylar notices her mom has that faraway look again. She wonders if she even heard her reply.

Then she says, "Are you going to get the goggles back?"

Skylar is confused. "Mom, not sure what you mean. I still have the goggles."

"Didn't you bring them back to . . ." She stops.

Skylar waits, then says, "To Dr. Brown," to break the awkwardness.

"Ohh, yes, Dr. Brown. Will he let you take them back?"

"No. He hasn't asked for them back." Skylar sees a look of confusion on her mother's face.

"Are you sure?"

"Yes. They're up in my room."

Her mother smiles and brushes the hair off Skylar's forehead. "Well, you seem to be enjoying them."

Skylar looks at her mother, a woman with a sharp mind and amazing memory, and wonders what is going on.

She finishes the last of her lemonade, then stands and places her empty glass in the sink.

"I've had a busy day. I'm tired and going to take a nap. I love you, Skylar."

"Love you too, Mom."

12.

Chronos Consortium's top manager, Hank Slidel, leans his tall, tired frame back in his chair after rereading the summary detailing targets written by another manager, Paul Dremos. Hank organized a meeting at 10:00 a.m. with Paul since he desperately wants additional help from Paul's agents, but he already has three-quarters of Paul's field agents doing background investigations for his own team. Hank has been pushing the organization to have these agents transferred to his own team, but the Chronos Consortium has consistently denied him. Hank admires the agents because they consistently do excellent undercover work. The Chronos Consortium insists on Paul controlling these agents for reasons that are not yet clear to Hank, which means Hank has to work within Paul's schedule and negotiate priorities with him.

He fiddles with Agent Tania Oster's research paper on his desk, which he received three days ago from an agent on his own team, Phil Harrison. Phil is one of the most technically competent specialists on Hank's team, so Hank cannot disregard this paper as easily as he might have, had it come from someone else. Phil spoke with real passion about Tania's work as a time engineer. He has never seen Phil so animated before, but after his first read of Tania's paper, he decided to get another opinion. He sent a copy to Paul and is still waiting for his feedback.

Tania's paper presents data on what she believes is a new mathematical and geometric ratio between the frequency patterns in the field scan data she has analyzed. Tania studied both music and music technology, so looking at patterns of recorded sound and understanding them is natural for her. This talent has helped her tremendously in her career. When the field agents came to the lab to talk about the data they'd acquired, Tania questioned them thoroughly about any circumstance that might have affected the field scan. Agents reported that the principal problem was interference from people walking within range of the target during the scan.

Tania already knows that interference is a problem. She sees it in the analysis from the data, which is why she presses each agent for more context, occasionally bordering on harassment. She asks them to describe in detail the people included in the field scans. From the agents' responses, she strongly suspects that when young people walk into the range of a field scan in progress, she sees a difference in the scan data.

In the world of power and influence, where many of the Chronos Consortium's targets work, getting a clear scan is the biggest challenge agents face. But the Time Frequency Lab has developed several good techniques to isolate target frequencies from others present during the scan.

Over the past few years, Tania has identified unusual geometric patterns of frequencies by correlating the agents' descriptions with analysis of the data. When she pressed agents for feedback, time and time again, she came to learn that the people walking into the scans were young interns, or new hires, running tasks for their boss, the target. She summarized the new frequency patterns and wrote her white paper with a clear warning in the conclusion: The treatments Hank's time specialists design, even with some generational tweaking, will not work as effectively on the new Time Information Fields of these younger targets. She suggested that time specialists, along with others in the Chronos Consortium, research techniques to couple into the new geometric patterns of frequencies.

Phil told Hank that he knew Tania well and they had often discussed her research. This bristled Hank a bit, since he has never been able to communicate well with Tania and doesn't understand why. Phil said that in the final analysis, Tania saw new geometric and mathematical frequency patterns unlike anything she or he has seen before. This is important because these ratios determine the critical effectiveness of the three-dimensional time broadcast frequency. If they get this wrong, in a worst-case scenario, the treatment could bounce off the distant three-dimensional fields without any effect on the target. In other situations, the coupling between the treatment and the target's field could be poor, reducing the treatment's efficiency. Tania stresses what many of the time specialists already know: That in order to maximize resonance with the frequencies in the target's personal three-dimensional Time Information Fields, the geometric structure needs to be determined accurately.

Hank's team knows that younger men and women are less affected by the frequency treatments, but the team has little experience with young people. Almost all their targets are over forty years old. Tania's description of a different field structure strikes Hank as a bit of a stretch. He also worries this project, if he were to push it, could compete for possible resources he is hoping to funnel into his Re-Imagination Project .

Tania told Phil she wants to get a more controlled sampling of young people. But Hank knows Paul would never agree to send one of his completely overworked agents to get experimental field scan data.

It annoys Tania that she did all this analysis and no one she talks to fully understands how the scan equipment works. Everything in this organization is so compartmentalized.

Hank reflects on the success his team has achieved using technology to surround a target with specially tailored, three-dimensional time frequencies designed to create instabilities in the target's mental and emotional state. His team needs to know accurately the composition of the target's frequency patterns of the Time Information Fields surrounding the target. Hank's team skillfully designs custom treatments that magnify the target's weaknesses. Their success rate is high for most of their targets, but there are no guarantees. Occasionally the treatment just doesn't work well on particular targets. The Chronos Consortium knows this and has assigned an engineer to investigate why. Hank is confident that, with more effort, they will nail the elusive.

He reflects on the fact that for eight decades treatments have been fine-tuned as generational shifts in attitudes are integrated into the larger societal three-dimensional Time Information Fields. Their scan technology is updated to accommodate these incremental shifts. Hank knows that the current treatments have been effective for almost twenty-five years. He is amazed at the specificity of each treatment. For a particular target with a history of infidelity, his team selected specific frequencies from the lower two frequency spectra. For a target who shows vulnerability to power issues revolving around money, status, and influence, they select frequencies from the next higher spectrum. For those susceptible to self-image or self-love issues, a combination of spectra is used. For a target who is not good at expressing and dealing with highly charged emotional issues, they are treated with frequencies that create intense emotional experiences that often causes confusion. The result is that the target begins to make a string of poor choices. If a target feels powerless in the face of their own emotional conditions, then the Chronos Consortium's job is well done. If the person feels victimized, the job is *very* well done. Often the feedback comes from Paul's agents working in close proximity to the target. If the effect of the treatment is not obvious, the Chronos Consortium takes follow-up field scans to verify the effectiveness. Poor results mean they have to adjust the treatments.

Hank looks at his watch, realizing he just wasted almost twenty minutes thinking about Tania's paper and his conversation with Phil. He heads to the conference room, eager to do some brainstorming with his team.

****

"Rachael will give us a summary of the plans her team put together," Hank says as he leans back from the conference table and turns to the front of the room. Rachael links her laptop to the presenter, then taps a few commands into the control in front of her. A large image of her presentation lights up on the wall of the conference room.

She runs through the details of her analysis of the target's Time Information Field data from the Time Frequency Lab and how this datum correlates to specific personal, financial, and career data that Paul's team accumulated on this target. She then defers to Phil, who has the task of presenting the effectiveness of the treatments on a model of the target's field.

Phil links his presenter to the holographic display in the center of the conference table. A few seconds later, a three-dimensional model of a middle-aged man appears. The physical model of this human is surrounded with a field modeled on the information from the Time Frequency Lab data. Every time this information is shown in the display, Phil swells with pride, since he developed the software to model three-dimensional time data. He moves the holographic image so people all around the room can see the structure.

"Our first treatment is designed to amplify emotional insecurities due to the target's financial problems." The team sees an oval field with color designating the different frequency components in the individual's field. The oval does not represent the whole spectrum of frequencies recorded because it contains too much data. Phil sets up frequency filters to only show a specific band of frequencies for clarity.

He stops the model's rotation, then moves his cursor to the treatment option in his display panel, selects the first option, and hits Run. The program computes all the interactions, and a few seconds later, renders a three-dimensional image that changes with time.

68

"You can see how effective this treatment is as distortions in the fields around the stomach area slowly build in strength. Now let me speed it up."

Phil uses the cursor to slide the Time Applied control to twenty-four hours. He waits for the program to recalculate the interactions. The field starts to oscillate. He repeats the process for forty-eight and then seventy-two hours. By seventy-two hours, the field shows strong chaotic oscillations.

"Typically, by this time, the individual feels out of control, potentially leading to a number of erratic choices and outcomes that could undermine their decision-making skills. I've looked at points farther in the future, where emotional amplification comes from conflicts within the individual. Recovery is not likely, given the estimated low emotional IQ of this target. If, by chance, this does not work as effectively as expected, we have a follow-up treatment."

Phil presses the Stop button in his program. Then he selects the second treatment option.

"This treatment, designed to impair his sharp intellect, will have less-efficient coupling into the individual, since he has strong confidence in his mental faculties. To overcome this strength, we would follow up with treatment number two only after we have shaken his confidence in himself. After he is shaken, the coupling of this second treatment into his field will be much stronger."

Phil hits Run again and goes through the same routine, this time faster.

"Okay," Hank says, happy with what he has seen. "Let's move to the next target. Looks like you guys have a handle on this one."

The team moves through the next two targets during the rest of the meeting. Hank is satisfied with their progress.

"In our next meeting, we'll evaluate the next targets on our list." The members nod slightly as he locks eyes with each of them. "See you on Thursday."

13.

It is Saturday afternoon, and Skylar catches her father while her mother is out with a friend. She's a bit hesitant. "Um, Dad, I wanted to run something by you."

"What's up, Skylar?"

David sits comfortably on the living room couch, reading technical papers from work; he looks especially relaxed in his blue jeans, green T-shirt, and tan socks. He looks more like an athlete than he actually is, and often jokes he does just enough exercise to justify sitting on the couch.

"Well . . ." Skylar looks away from her father's eyes, then forces her gaze back. David sits up straight and rests his papers on his legs.

"I know this might sound strange," Skylar continues, "but I noticed that Mom has been having some memory lapses and loses focus. A few times recently, she forgot what I said to her, or recalls memories out of sequence. You know Mom. She never forgets things like that. Her memory has always been impeccable. Is something going on?"

David sits up straight, realizing how worried his daughter is by her serious tone. "Well . . ." He looks away. "Your mother is experiencing exhaustion a lot lately, and it's probably from the stress of losing her job and trying to find another. She seems a bit depressed, too, since no job opportunities have come from all the effort she is putting in."

David says this to allay his daughter's concerns, as well as to hide his own. He hesitates, wondering how much he should share of his own observations. "I'm concerned about your mother as well. I'm sure once her job and our financial issues sort themselves out, she'll be back to normal. She's getting out and walking regularly to try to lift her mood, you know."

Skylar reluctantly says, "Mom has changes in the structures around her that make me feel a certain dread. I've confirmed this change with the goggles. I know you are intrigued by the goggles and have nowhere near the same confidence I do in what I'm seeing, but you have to believe me."

Skylar goes on to describe the growing dull-brown patch she sees in her mother's field.

David stiffens. "Skylar, you want me to believe your mother has a health issue based on some color that you've seen with those goggles?"

"Dad, try it yourself. I will tell you what to look for."

"Let's say I see this same dull-brown color. How am I going to communicate that to your mother? I have more interest in what you see in those goggles than she does, but I am certainly not ready to make the leap that she has a health issue based on the goggles."

"Not just the goggles, Dad, but also in Perception Reality."

David realizes he needs to take a new approach. As a parent, he wants to hear what Skylar has to say. "Okay, based on what you've seen, tell me, what do you think is wrong with Mom?"

Skylar shakes her head with a frown. "I don't know. I only know I've seen a real change, and when I view it, I feel dread." Skylar was about to tell her dad about her dream, but she stops, figuring that talk about goggles, alternative reality, and then a dream will not help make her case.

"Skylar, we both have a concern about Mom. But I am struggling to understand what it is you want me to do. You want me to tell your mother that she has some health, or other, concern? And what about a doctor, what information do we give him? There are certainly other reasons why I would suggest that your mother go to the doctor, but I am not convinced that what you are seeing in the goggles should be the basis for that decision."

Skylar can see the conversation is not going the way she'd hoped. She hadn't considered what it would take to convince her mother, never mind a doctor, about what she sees. She knows her father has a point, but it does nothing to alleviate her concern, which quickly turns to frustration.

"Forget it. I'm sorry I brought it up." She turns around and heads upstairs to her room.

"Skylar, hold on."

Skylar stops at the bottom of the stairs and turns around.

"I hear your concern," David says. "I am also concerned. I was just challenging you on how this insight you have can be used. Your mother will not react well to me, or you, saying she should see a doctor based on what you see in those goggles. That's the point I am trying to make. We, or I, need another approach. Let me think about what can be done. Okay?"

Skylar is not just frustrated with her father's questioning; she recognizes that her dad has a point. More, she is frustrated about sensing something is wrong and not knowing what it is, but also not being able to do anything about it.

"Okay, thanks."

Skylar heads to her room and settles into her favorite chair—the Blue Chair. It's an old living room fixture she grabbed before her parents threw it out. It takes up more space than it should in her room, with its huge armrests and big, soft pillows. It was a chair her father particularly liked, but her mother complained often that it didn't fit with the other furniture in the living room. David hung on to it for as long as he could, and Skylar jumped at the chance to have it for her own when she heard they were finally going to get rid of it. Her mother wasn't thrilled she wasn't going to see the last of it, but her father was amused. More than a decade later, it's still Skylar's favorite chair.

Skylar has thought through many problems in the Blue Chair, and today is no different. How can she convince her mother? She feels at a bit of a loss, but she is determined. There has to be a way. Maybe Bohdi has an idea. She sends him a text to see if he is available.

14.

The following day, David talks to Jean about the discussion he had with Skylar. His daughter's concern gave him the push he needed to address his own concerns with her. Skylar is at the school library, so David figures it is a good time to start this conversation with his wife.

"I don't need to see a doctor," Jean protests. "I don't understand why you're pressing me about this. Yes, I feel tired a lot, but it's probably because I feel a bit blue. Okay, maybe more than a *bit blue.* I'm depressed. But who *wouldn't* feel down about trying to find work in this tough economy? I'm frustrated, honey. I really liked my job, and now I'm in another job search."

"Maybe so, and I'm frustrated for you," David admits. "But Skylar mentioned yesterday she has also been worried about you."

"She did? What did she say?"

"That you don't seem to be your normal self."

"Is that based on what she is seeing in those goggles?" she shoots back. She has seen Skylar looking at her with the goggles on. Jean always inquires about what she sees, but she can feel her daughter is a bit evasive when she answers. She figured Skylar is learning and once she has figured things out, she will share it with her. Now she feels angry that she is hearing the feedback she was looking for through David, and her daughter didn't come to her.

"Yes, and no," he replies, trying to gather his thoughts. He was not planning to bring up the goggles, and is surprised Jean did so quickly.

"What is that supposed to mean?" she says, not meaning to sound so combative, but feeling out of sorts.

"Well, she noticed that you're having memory lapses, which is so unlike you. And . . . she's noticed something with those goggles that she's worried about."

"You know, ever since those goggles came into this house, they've dominated her time. She and Bohdi seem to spend every spare minute with them. Recently, I find myself talking more to my own daughter while she has those strange-looking things on than without. I don't like it! And now you are saying there's something wrong with me based on what the two of you are seeing? Are you also in on this goggle insight?" She barely recognizes herself in these responses. *What is going on with me?*

"No," David replies firmly. "Jean, forget the goggles for a moment."

David wants to bring the conversation back to real observations that he and Skylar have made. "Both Skylar and I have noticed that you are struggling with memory."

"You both think I have some sort of memory problem?"

"No, not at all," he replies softly, trying hard to keep the conversation going, but on a less negative note.

Jean turns her head and stares out the window. It is a sunny November Sunday morning. The sun streaming through the window brings some relief to a difficult discussion.

David can see she's working out something in her mind. He waits as she stares out the window.

She turns to him. "Okay, David. Truth be told, I don't feel like my normal self. Lately, I'm wondering if it's more than just depression. I feel like there's a fog starting to develop in my mind. It's taking more and more effort to remember everyday tasks, and more concentration to read or communicate ideas. It's making me pull into myself a bit, because I find communication . . . tiring. I honestly believe it will go away. In the meantime, it frustrates me." She looks at David with sadness in her eyes, then looks down at her feet. When she looks up again, he feels concern building in the air.

"David, while I was out walking this morning, I tripped over my own feet," she says. "I've never felt so clumsy."

She attempts to smile, but it doesn't work. David struggles to smile back in reassurance, but his concern is growing. He's already noticed that she asks him to drive more when they're together. Normally, she likes to do some of the driving. He is happy to take on more, figuring it's just one small way he can help her relax. But now pieces are starting to fit together.

"Jean, I want you to see a doctor," he says emphatically.

Tears roll down her cheeks. She says quietly, "I'm getting so clumsy I can't seem to walk, David. Today wasn't the first time I've fallen."

David moves close to his wife and puts his arm around her shoulders. He's sure now: She has to see a doctor. He repeats his request.

"But I don't want you and Skylar to worry something is wrong when it's just something stupid," she protests.

"Jean, tomorrow, we're going to call Dr. Jones. I'll go with you. Maybe it is depression. If so, she can help you."

Jean doesn't fight him. She's too tired to put up a fuss.

75

15.

"Okay, Dad, I'll do that," Skylar replies with some tension in her voice. "Yup, got it. No worries."

Skylar terminates the call.

"What was that about?" asks Bohdi. "I could see the colors in your field changing. It was interesting. Must be colors of frustration, since you sounded frustrated."

Skylar is indeed annoyed. With the concerns over her mother, this call with her father, and Bohdi watching her every move lately through those goggles and constantly asking her what she just thought or felt, this process is starting to irritate her. She stops herself before she says anything, realizing she now knows how her mother felt and why she snapped at her for viewing her so much.

"Oh, just my father being a parent. He thinks we spend too much time with the goggles. Both my parents are concerned. Dad says he needs help raking the leaves and would like me to do it this afternoon. I think it's just a ploy to get me out of the house."

Bohdi decides not to comment. Not only can he tell that this conversation was not what Skylar wanted to hear, he could see it. He's really getting to know what is Skylar's normal and what is not from viewing her through the goggles.

"Well, at least your father has convinced your mother to go see a doctor. Your conversation with him last week was likely the trigger for that discussion. You should feel good about that."

"I am glad. He said that our conversation gave him the push he needed to confront my mother. That's a relief."

Skylar's mind quickly switches back to the experiment she asked Bohdi to do before her father called. She suggested they view each other in a dark room and compare the effect with the light on and then off. Skylar was surprised to find that it did not affect the coloring of the images. When the lights were off, the color contrasts in these images were enhanced a small amount, but the rest was the same. Bohdi thought that the light from the room bled through the goggles in some small amount, affecting the contrast in this small way. Skylar agreed with him, as the information in the images did not change when the light was off. Bohdi makes some notes so they can report this to Dr. Brown.

Then Bohdi switches with Skylar, since he is keen to repeat the cardboard experiment she tried spontaneously with her father. He asks her to take the black cardboard sheet and hand it to him so he can hold it in front of the goggles with his free hand. He then moves it out of the way. He does this a few times to see if he notices any change.

"So, what I'm seeing is not blocked by the black board. This information, or energy, or whatever, goes through matter. That is still a crazy fact to me," Bohdi reports.

He asks her to take the cardboard and move it to block and unblock the goggles, not letting him know which position it is in. He cannot tell any difference between the two positions, same as before.

"That is kind of mind-blowing," Skylar replies. Bohdi reaches to the right side of the goggles and says, "I'm changing the setting to One. I will let you know if I see any changes."

Bohdi stares into the goggles. Skylar waits patiently as she moves the black board up and down.

"Same as before," he says. "A white fog. Nothing has changed?"

"Almost done, one last setting." They wait for the goggles to respond to the new setting. She moves the board aside, then back again. "I see the board blocking my vision when it is in front." A moment later: "I see the room when you pull it away. Okay, so for sure no image processing going on. But more importantly, we can see these fields of color through ordinary matter. That is mind-blowing."

Bohdi is still thinking about the fact that they can see through matter. He wonders if it is just that they can see through this board, or can they see through walls and doors, as well?

"Okay, let's expand on this experiment. I want to turn around, and then I want you to go behind the wall that separates the kitchen and the dining room." He reaches up and switches the goggles to One, counts off fifteen seconds, then switches to Plus mode. "Let me know when you are at that position."

Bohdi can see Skylar's fields in the Plus mode. Then he hears her yell, "What do you see now?"

"Same shape and coloring as before, but the contrast is lower. Are you behind the wall?"

"Yes."

She moves, asking Skylar each time what he sees. He confirms which way she moved and could tell when she moved and did not move. Since she was in socks, she knew he could not hear her move. Another experiment that negates any image processing.

Skylar then wonders, *Is the contrast lower because I am farther away, or because I am behind the wall?*

"I'm coming back and going to move you," she says as she counts her steps to approximate the distance between where she was standing and Bohdi is sitting. She then turns Bohdi ninety degrees so he is facing the opening between the kitchen and the living room. "Okay, I'm going to move back roughly the same distance as I was when I stood behind the kitchen wall. Let me know what you see."

Skylar counts the same number of steps as she walks away and stops, turns to Bohdi, and asks, "What do you see now?"

"The same as before. The contrast is a bit higher, maybe not as much as when you were behind the wall." Bohdi figures that maybe these fields of color are attenuated a bit when they go through matter, but that does not change the real mind-blowing issue, that ordinary matter does not block these fields of color. He desperately would like to get more objective answers so that what they are doing is more scientific. Unfortunately, his attempts at using a camera have been unsuccessful.

"You still here?" Skylar asks impatiently. Without being able to see his eyes, she has no idea if he is paying attention or not.

"Yeah." Bohdi snaps out of his train of thought. He was wondering if what they see with these goggles is the part of humans that survives after a physical death.

Skylar's mind is already moving on from the experiment they just did, and she says to him, "It's a pity we can't see ourselves, like we normally can in a mirror. I would love to see the three-dimensional Time Information Field of myself, instead of having you describe it to me."

"Just what I was thinking. We need to get data that is measurable, and repeatable, instead of anecdotal."

They complete the shutdown and take the goggles and headphones off Bohdi. "That reminds me," Bohdi says, ""I meant to mention—I did an experiment to try and capture an image on video when you could not get back here on time from school. I figured I would use the time to do a quick experiment. I set the goggles on a mount I improvised, which also held my smartphone. I then pointed the goggles, with my smartphone behind them, at that plant in the kitchen, the one with the colorful field in Plus mode. I took it down in case one of your parents came home and started asking questions."

Skylar breaks in, "Breaking the agreement, are we?"

"Shh, don't tell the guards," Bohdi shoots back. They both laugh.

"Anyway, I started the video recording on my phone, put it on this mount, put a black cloth over the back of the goggles and phone, and then moved in front of the goggles. I stayed a few minutes, did some movements, like running on the spot to get some energy going, and then went back to see what I could see. Nothing came out. I tried several times. Nothing! Clearly the goggles require your eyes and brain to see what is going on in the Plus mode. It's a drag that the goggles don't work with a camera. I was hoping we could do videos of ourselves. How cool would that be!"

"Totally cool. Let's try it again. Maybe we need to approach it in a different way," Skylar adds, keen to try out this new idea. "We could try it with your high-resolution digital camera."

Bohdi is amused that Skylar says this. He just happened to pack his high-resolution camera in his backpack this morning in the hopes of trying it. He goes to grab his backpack with his camera and the homemade mount in it. Upon returning, he adds, "Oh, I suspect that whatever signal is coming out of the earphones is interfacing with our brain in some way that either accentuates the effect or bypasses some filter in our brain. I can't figure it out yet." Bohdi's tone reflects his pensiveness. "Either the signal coming out of the headphones is subsonic, or it's ultrasonic, since we don't hear anything, but both you and I feel a buzz in our head. I suspect it could be subsonic, like the frequency of brainwaves. I need to measure that somehow without taking the headphones apart."

"Dr. Brown said the sound is below our hearing, so I assume it is subsonic. Luckily, it is not uncomfortable. I haven't felt any side effects from using the goggles, have you?"

"No," Bohdi says as he sets up his mount and camera.

Skylar and Bohdi spend the rest of the battery charge using the goggles to try to capture an image with a camera. They are unsuccessful.

Afterward, they go through their notes and work on summarizing their last month's activities into a report for Dr. Brown, excited to tell him about their new findings. Bohdi wants to see if they could fit more in, but Skylar suggests they capture what they have done and send it along. Dr. Brown did say every month, and this is their first report, so she wants to show how much they have already done. Bohdi suggests they leave the experiments with the camera out of this report because he wants more time to think about it.

Skylar types a summary into her phone, and then copies and pastes it into Dr. Brown's encrypted link. Not the most efficient way, but it's workable.

16.

Paul reviews his November staffing and mission list. He has three new agents going through the extensive certification process, which includes hands-on training with the Time Field Scanners. Paul figures he is still at least five agents short. He would like to shorten the Time Field Scanner certification process, because the new recruits are more technically savvy, but he knows from experience how seriously his managers take this training. It is one of the most important tasks an agent can do.

The Chronos Consortium strictly controls usage of their Time Field Scanners. Anyone caught using one without proper authorization is immediately fired. Getting good field scan data on targets is challenging. The device works optimally when the agent is within six feet of the target, and the target should be isolated from others by eight feet. When a target is close to others, multiple scans must be done, with attention to position and angle of the scanner to the target. In the lab, images are generated based on the GPS position data and the relative angle of the target to the agent for each scan. From this information, the frequencies associated with the target are pulled out from the data. The key components of the signal helps them discriminate between the target's signal and any other individual whose field is measured by the instrument because they happened to be in the field of view when the scan was done. Because of the additional signal processing, the resulting frequency data has lower resolution, but is better than no data at all.

Setting up agents to gather information and acquire Time Field scans is Paul's favorite part of his job. He enjoys brainstorming ideas with his small team on how to set up the sham IDs, personalities, and organizations. Paul has a number of front organizations that he uses regularly to legitimize agents. Money is never the limiting factor; the limitation is always qualified people.

In the past, agents have impersonated attendees at conferences, salesmen, members of corporations, all with the objective of getting close enough to the target to get a good field scan.

A Time Field scan only takes thirty seconds. The scanner is five inches long and one and a half inches in diameter. It has a black opaque glass exterior on the front end covered with a high-density hexagonal pattern. This end is pointed at the target from inside a jacket pocket, a bag, or accessory item. The back end of the scanner has a port to pull the data off and charge it.

Even though a complete scan only takes half a minute, the agents are always amazed by how challenging it is to do a scan free from any interference. Commonly, agents only have access to targets in meetings with lots of people around because these targets are busy people. Even if the conversation is one on one between the target and the agent, there are people waiting to converse with the target within the field of view of the scanner. Agents' most common request is to narrow the field of view of the scanner, but the engineers cannot do this without increasing the scanner's size. They feel the current performance is at the optimal trade-off of field of view and scanner size.

The agent can configure the scanner via his cell phone through a secure link. One option is to have the scan data immediately uploaded to a shared account via the agent's phone. The head of the Time Frequency Lab receives notification of the upload and immediately organizes engineers to begin processing the data.

17.

"Hi, Cathy." Jean seems happy to see her friend, but she wishes it wasn't a doctor's visit.

"Hello, Jean, how are you?"

Dr. Jones is surprised by Jean's demeanor; she instantly sees a change she can't quite put her finger on. She knows Jean not only as a patient, but also as a dynamic teacher, and they've been members of the same social circle for years. Jean and David sit in the two chairs opposite Dr. Jones.

"I'm struggling a bit," Jean says.

"I'm sorry we haven't connected lately, but my work and taking care of my eighty-seven-year-old mother have me flat out. How are Skylar and Celeste doing?"

They share brief stories about their children. Jean taught Cathy's son, Henry, when he was in high school and remembers him well. Then they get to the heart of the matter, and Jean repeats what she's shared with David: feeling like she has a fog enveloping her mind, and a loss of her normal emotional equilibrium. She's happy one moment, testy the next. She downplays what she considers to be a temporary problem with walking.

Dr. Jones listens attentively, her face unreadable. When Jean winds down, she says, "Jean, these problems could be due to any number of causes. When you fell while walking, did you hit your head?"

"No."

"Okay, good. First, I want to check for inflammation in your brain, since you were having problems before you fell. We will do a number of blood tests and some fluid checks. The tests will check for encephalitis or chronic meningitis. Both are treatable. Encephalitis, for example, is an inflammation of the brain that can cause the coordination symptoms you've described. Meningitis, which also can explain your symptoms, is an inflammation of the layers of tissue that cover the brain and spinal cord. It's a slowly developing inflammation, so it's easily caught and stopped. Again, both are treatable, and if we can catch them early, all the better."

She looks to see if Jean has any questions. Jean is listening intently but is waiting for more information.

Dr. Jones continues: "I'd like to do these tests so I can rule out possibilities. The diagnostic procedures include an MRI, along with collecting a sample of cerebrospinal fluid for diagnosis. That means you'll have to spend a few hours in the hospital."

"Hospital," comes out of Jean's mouth before she is even aware she is going to speak. She is surprised by how serious it sounds. "I thought I could just go to a lab. I wasn't expecting to have to go to a hospital."

David's heart sinks. A spinal tap? That's a more serious test than he envisioned.

When Jean glances at him, she can see the look on his face. "Okay, I'll do it," she says, turning back to her doctor. Heaving a sigh, she says, "How soon can this be done?"

18.

Larry Hanley, a retired employee of the Chronos Consortium, pulls into the driveway of a deceased colleague and friend, John Garrison. He walks up to the front door and knocks.

"Hi, Larry, come in. Glad it worked out that we were able to connect while I was in town," John Garrison's daughter, Jenn, says as she greets her father's friend from years ago. She closes the door quickly after him to keep out the cool November wind.

"Sorry for your recent loss of your mother. Your parents were wonderful friends." he replies as he walks into the foyer of the Garrison home, a place where he was once a frequent weekend visitor. He has not been inside for almost eight years.

"Thanks," Jenn replies, leading him to the basement door. She is eager to keep things moving. She still has a lot of packing to do before she can drop off these boxes before 6:00 p.m. so they can be shipped back to her home. She is flying home early Sunday morning.

"As I mentioned on the phone, my mother was my rock. Even though I lived almost two thousand miles away for over twenty-five years, we spoke daily on the phone. She was really lonely once Dad died, and her health limited her traveling."

Jenn leads Larry down to John's basement laboratory. It doesn't look the same to him. When he was a frequent guest in this lab, it was always meticulously kept. Now there are open boxes everywhere. He looks around for anything familiar. Other than the benches, there's not much.

"I apologize for the mess. I've had to use my father's lab for a storage place. My brother-in-law and nephews have been here and claimed many of his tools. But he has all this equipment that I have no idea what it is used for. I was hoping you would find a home for some of it before I call the auction house to come and clear out the house."

Jenn points to a corner of the basement. "Most of Dad's stuff is in those boxes with 'Lab' on them or on those blue shelves. Feel free to move stuff in the boxes. I'm just going to pack a few more things over here."

"Thanks, this is very kind of you."

"Well, I hope you find things of interest."

Larry spends about twenty minutes sorting through a number of the boxes on the blue shelves. He recognizes some ham radio electronics in many of them. He had long ago given all his equipment away to a local club. He grabs the next box and moves some parts around with his right hand. He freezes.

This cannot be what I think it is.

He goes in with both hands. *It is!*

He sees two more parts. *This cannot be. John Garrison would not do something like this.*

Larry looks up to see Jenn watching him.

"You okay? You look like you've seen a ghost."

Larry stands up. "Yes, just a bit light-headed from the bending over."

"Well, take your time. You want some water?"

"Yes, that would be great."

Jenn heads upstairs to get some water, and Larry quickly looks through the neighboring boxes. He does not find any identifiable parts other than the three in that one box. He knows these parts. He and John were on an engineering team that developed and built these devices.

I cannot believe John was involved in stealing those missing Time Information Field Scanner parts! I thought I knew the guy. And he had the technical knowledge to do something with them. Larry shudders at the thought. The Chronos Consortium would have fired him and then destroyed his ability to get any work. Ever. They will do anything to protect their technology. In the past, they would have organized to have him killed, but with all the media these days, that is much more difficult.

After a few minutes, he hears Jenn's footsteps on the steps leading down to the basement. He moves that one box and a few neighboring ones close together.

"Here you go. You look better already."

"Thanks. I found a few boxes with some interesting electronics in it. Let me look around a little bit more. Your father and I lost contact after we moved closer to our daughter. It's only three hours away, but funny how that can make a difference. Did your father have any other people he worked with?"

"Not that I know of. But I've been away from home for so long, and you were the one I remembered from when I did live here," Jenn replies as she works, wanting to end this conversation, since she still has so much to do.

Larry digs a bit more. "What was your father working on before he died?"

"No idea. Dad was very quiet about his lab stuff. He always wanted to talk about the grandchildren. Our family never shared much interest in his technical activities. Poor Dad," Jenn says with a note of sadness.

Then, just as quickly, she points to the far corner of the basement. "There are more electronics on those shelves if you're interested. Dad had his stuff in all sorts of places in this house, and my mother just left it there these last five years. She had more patience than I do."

It is clear to Larry that he is not going to get any useful information from Jenn. He goes over to the shelf and looks through every box carefully for any additional clues. He picks up another box so it will look like his time is well spent.

He comes back to the first box and puts the second one down. He asks hopefully, "Any other items you want me to look at? Your father was a creative guy."

Jenn looks up again. "Did you look on those lab benches? Might be something in those drawers. I haven't checked there."

"Okay, thanks," he says as nonchalantly as he can. He goes over to the benches and carefully opens each drawer. After ten minutes of looking as carefully as he can, he finds nothing of significance. He picks up a variable power supply from the bench to feign some interest.

He returns to his two boxes, puts the power supply in the second one, and says to Jenn. "I'll take these two boxes. I may have a friend interested in some of the other items. I will let you know."

Jenn looks up from her task of packing old family items. "Okay. I'm glad you found something you can use. You need help bringing them to your car?"

"No, the trips up and down the stairs will do me good."

"Okay. I leave tomorrow to go back home, and then I'll be back in ten days to finish up. I've organized with an auction house to clear out the house, so I can get it ready to put it on the market. There is so much still left to do," she says, sounding exasperated.

After Larry puts the boxes in his car, he goes down one last time to say goodbye, thanks Jenn, and make a mental note of the doors and windows in the house.

****

Agent Max reaches into his pocket to answer his ringing phone. The name Larry Hanley shows up. He quickly answers.

"Hi, Larry. How are you?"

"OK, I have some information you will be very interested in. I cannot share it here, but can we meet in person?"

"Hey, Larry, you caught me at a bad time, but I wanted to call you so I grabbed your call. Yes, I would like to get together for a couple of beers when I get back?"

"When do you get back?"

"In two days, so this Wednesday. I fly back Wednesday evening and then I have a commitment with the family for the weekend. Does the following Tuesday work for you?"

There is a silence.

"Larry, you there?"

"Yes, that works. Same place as before, around 7:00 p.m." "

Larry realizes he has already forgotten how it is to juggle a busy work and life schedule.

"Great. Thanks for calling. Sorry, I do have to go."

"See you next week!"

Larry really wishes Max was here and they could have organized a get-together tonight. He is not keen to have a week of being on his own with his knowledge. He has so much more time on his hands; in fact, some days it seems that all he has is time, with little to distract him. Life is nothing like when he was an agent and time was a premium. He starts to scheme on his drive back home about how to keep himself busy during this week of waiting. Already, his mind is fixating on John, someone he thought he knew.

19.

University Professor Dr. Jack Duncan's office is paneled with polished oak and has a wall of built-in bookshelves. The oak is a pleasing pale brown; he's glad it isn't the darker color of mahogany. Dark woods remind him of caskets. The two windows to the left of his desk overlook the grassy quadrangle at the center of the university campus. He's proud to be part of a growing trend of academic outsiders who possess a more business-minded approach to running colleges and universities.

The building his office is located in was built nearly a century ago, at a time when style and quality meant something. The office is an imposing room to all who enter, and Jack enjoys watching their reactions. It's a power thing, and he knows it. As much as possible, he tries to organize meetings in his office, which can accommodate up to twenty people comfortably. He feels more in control here, and free to intimidate people he senses are less inclined to stand up to him on his own turf.

Jack doesn't need this home advantage, since he's open to confronting anyone who gets in his way. He finds it more relaxing and, well, *fun*, to do it in his office. He enjoys seeing conflict in people's eyes and body language as they struggle with what to say, whether or not to say it, and the consequences of saying it.

He swings his chair around to the right and looks through an open door at a painting of the university's founder, John Patterson. Dr. Patterson was a researcher who, through his many patents, amassed a fortune. However, he wasn't especially motivated by material things. He and his wife had no children, but they prized education highly, so they funded the educations of their many nieces and nephews. After observing the results, he and his wife decided to start a college where young people could learn not only to think in terms of science, but also to learn a more philosophical approach to the sciences. His small college attracted a mostly independent-minded faculty who challenged students to investigate life critically, through the sciences in particular, and broadly through psychology and philosophy.

Forty years after the founding of the college, and soon after Dr. Patterson's death, a medical school was added to the growing collection of colleges that became Patterson University. It was the beginning of a systematic shift away from the balanced philosophical and critically based approach to one that favored critical-based thinking only.

When Jack became president, the atmosphere at Patterson was more focused on discussion, which he often found could turn into discourse and conflict. The approach left him frustrated, and he let people know that he considered it a waste of valuable time and financial resources. He could see where strong leadership would get things done much faster, simply by bypassing all the many rounds of discussion. He feels strongly that a business approach is needed, and sees it as his mission to get these *educators* thinking more like businesspeople than academics. He knows he needs to keep the Board of Trustees' confidence in him, as well, but he pushes the limits of both the Board and the faculty. However, Jack's success on the financial side of the university's business makes it difficult to justify getting rid of him.

Jack knows that universities that adopt a businesslike model tend to thrive. They receive more money for research and support well-paid professors, who regularly interface with business leaders. Many students end up working in leading medical institutions or influential positions in Fortune 500 companies. When he first joined the university, he chose the medical school as a starting point for realizing his vision. The frustrating part for visionaries like him is having to deal with academicians bent on derailing progress. What good is funding research if it doesn't have purpose in the business world? The obstructionists don't get it. But they just fuel Jack's determination to bring Patterson University in line with his vision.

It's odd, he thinks, *how it falls on so few very determined people to take the responsibility of managing for the good of all. What if people like me weren't willing to take on such risks? The world would be a mess, like the university is now—full of independent groups going in different directions.* Jack launched the same business initiative in the liberal arts colleges of the university as he did in the medical school. It resulted in immediate pushback from the faculty and students.

Dr. Suzanne Bradley and Dr. Henry Albates head the pushback. When they joined the faculty as young PhD graduates, they were thrilled to be a part of Patterson University and its ideals. Later, they became tenure-track professors, who watched economic and financial pressures cause the university to stray from its founder's ideals. They understand that running a university is a balancing act, but over the past few years, they've felt this balance tip too much in favor of business. Both professors, along with other faculty members and staff, have had to regularly challenge those in charge of running the university to try to keep its ideals intact. But their efforts have not worked well. Many of those who were part of raising these objections have either caved in under the pressure or left.

Determined to get the other colleges in the university in line with the progress made at the medical school, Jack has a renewed sense of purpose and energy.

He gets up to grab a bite to eat before he delivers an important speech. He received an invitation to speak on the role of business in education to a group of business professionals, politicians, and the media. He knows he has the support of the first two, but getting the media on board is more challenging. Jack has both media friends and enemies.

Mike Halden, who invited Jack to speak this evening, owns major interests in dozens of media outlets and is someone Jack has a keen interest in getting on his side. Jack intends to discuss his successes as well as strategies to change the mindset of Patterson faculty. He will also position the university's interests, and how he will manage the concerns about the risks.

He looks forward to the meeting. Through this group, he has met people who talk about the realities of life and feel it is their duty to manage events in *this world.* He checks the clock on the wall, then goes to the private restroom, reserved for the president and his guests. He buttons the top button of his white shirt and moves the knot of his red silk tie up to cover it, disliking the feel of a tight tie but needing it for appearance. He turns on the faucet, lightly wets both hands, and then runs them through his thinning brown hair to keep it neat. Then he rolls down his sleeves, buttons the cuffs, slips on his dark suit jacket, and straightens his frame. He still wishes he was five inches taller than his five-foot-six frame, but that has never stopped him. He heads out the door, keen to get there a bit early.

****

When Jack arrives, he hangs back at the rear of the hall, scanning the crowd for familiar faces. He sees the president of Chemtech, the executive who replaced him after he took on this position of university president, sitting at the table on the speaker's platform, talking to a group. The hall is alive with voices in discussion.

From the other side of the hall, Jack is recognized by someone he hasn't met yet—a man who, nonetheless, is integral to Jack's success. Chronos Consortium undercover recruiter, Edward Stagmier, heard one of Jack's early presentations several years ago about the biotechnology work at Chemtech, and recognized in him a driving ambition and hunger for power. Edward immediately tagged Jack as someone the Chronos Consortium could potentially use, or manipulate, to help in their future critical missions. Edward arranged to have Jack moved out of the lab and into management at Chemtech. It was a test. Through Edward's connections, projects were assigned to Jack, and Edward watched closely to see how Jack handled them. This is standard protocol for the Chronos Consortium, to learn whether they can trust candidates to execute key objectives "suggested" to them. The Chronos Consortium also uses corporations and think tanks as test beds for individuals with tremendous drive for power and/or material wealth, along with high intelligence. Their moral compass isn't important, as long as it can be aligned with the Chronos Consortium's objectives—which is often easy when enough money is offered.

Edward was recently told by his managers that there are some critical tasks on the horizon that need to be taken care of; therefore, they will soon need additional *qualified* people in the Chronos Consortium. They asked Edward if anyone he's monitoring is ready to be tasked with greater responsibilities in the coming year. Edward replied that he has one in mind but needs to give him one more task and watch how he responds before he can recommend him.

Edward encouraged a key person to introduce Jack to the university's Board of Trustees and push his credentials and accomplishments. This maneuvering got Jack into the position of president. Changing the direction of Patterson University would be an excellent test of his abilities. The Chronos Consortium spends large amounts of money to get the right kind of people into influential positions. They know the investment is necessary, since one mistake can wreak havoc on years of carefully planned work.

Edward believes that Jack has no idea why his fortunes have changed so quickly, and he will likely never know. No doubt Jack figures it's due to his drive to succeed. In part, this is true—but only in part. The Chronos Consortium can reshuffle events not just via the fortunes they control, but also via their manipulation of fields in three-dimensional time. They ensure that the individuals they put into key positions will carry out directions without questioning the intent. Jack and his kind simply know that each time they perform a task successfully, their lucky stars seem to align, with numerous benefits and opportunities continuing to come their way. This makes them feel like they're working with reality at a more sophisticated level, one where they're in charge of their fates—but that's a well-constructed illusion. What they don't know is that as they move into more influential circles, they trade financial gains for personal freedoms. The loss of freedom isn't immediately obvious to them. Indeed, it seems at first that their freedom is increasing. By the time they're completely hemmed in, however, it's too late for them to escape.

****

Jack is just about to drift toward the front of the room when he hears a voice from his right. "Jack, I'd like to introduce myself," says the cultured baritone. Jack turns to see a gray-haired gentleman in an expensive-looking suit; he lifts his eyebrow.

"I'm Edward Stagmier. I've heard a great deal about the good work you've done at Chemtech and now at Patterson."

They shake hands. "Well, thank you, Mr. Stagmier," Jack replies, quickly sizing up this tall, well-dressed individual.

"Call me Edward. I'm looking forward to your talk tonight. My associates and I are keenly searching for people like yourself. We feel the world is suffering a crisis of leadership, and we're looking for people who can be trusted to exercise good judgment and negotiate these rapidly changing times. It's certainly the responsibility of the few to organize the world for the many. At some point in the future, I would like to stop by Patterson and talk with you about this."

Jack is surprised but intrigued, and flattered enough to want to know more. He has heard the right words and feels in his element. These people can make things happen, he knows this intuitively. Now it's his turn to show what *he* can make happen, and he's up to the task.

20.

Skylar paces the floor in the hospital waiting room. She brought her mother here for tests because her father was scheduled to travel for work, and Jean had insisted he not cancel his trip over her. Besides, she said, Skylar had offered to take her. David was reluctant to push Jean on this issue, afraid she would cancel the tests altogether, so he relented, but reluctantly. Skylar promised to keep her Dad informed throughout the day.

The nurse had asked Skylar to go to the waiting room, where she has been pacing for an hour. She feels better when she is moving. Finally, the nurse pops her head into the waiting room. "Your mother has just finished her MRI. You can come in for a few minutes if you'd like. In about fifteen minutes, we'll start the spinal tap."

Skylar follows the nurse into her mother's room. The nurse works around Jean, adjusting her IV and preparing her lower back for the spinal tap. She finishes up and turns to Skylar. "The doctor will be here soon, and will ask you to step out while she does the procedure."

"Gladly." She's a bit embarrassed by how eagerly she responds.

"Skylar, you didn't have to come down just for these few minutes," her mother says, "but thanks for being here."

"No worries, Mom." They chat until the doctor arrives and asks her to leave.

The view from the waiting room is looking out onto a small quadrangle in the middle of the hospital. The few trees there have dropped all their leaves, and they look a little sad, especially on this first day of December. The grounds keeping crew has yet to come by and rake them up. Her mind drifts back to when she first noticed her mother having memory trouble, and then to her father's revelations after they visited the family physician. While she worries about the discomfort and complexity of the tests for encephalitis and meningitis, she knows both diseases are treatable. This eases her anxiety.

Images of her mother, witnessed in Perception Reality and with the goggles, flood her mind. Time and again, distortions in vitality and shape have appeared. *What do they mean?* The dread returns when she views these images, but she has no reference point to justify her concerns. If she, or Bohdi, can decode the information, maybe she can help her mother get better.

A voice breaks into her train of thought. "Skylar, you can go back in now."

The nurse heads back to her station, where a few other nurses are laughing together. Skylar envies their moment in time.

"How did the test go?" Skylar asks as she walks into her mother's room.

"I'm glad it's over. Now we wait for the doctor to tell us that everything is fine." She gazes at Skylar, her smile steady. "They want me to stay here for at least an hour before I can go home. The nurse says they want to make sure I'm okay, and some rest also helps to alleviate the possibility of getting a nasty headache."

Jean naps for forty-five minutes.

Skylar steps out into the hallway and calls her father, letting him know that the tests are done and they will be heading home within the hour.

Then Skylar calls Bohdi and is relieved that he is free to take the call.

The nurse returns and asks Jean how she feels.

"I'm fine."

"You're ready to go home, then?"

"Yes."

"All right, why don't we get you out of bed and see how you feel walking?"

Jean walks steadily down the hall and back.

****

Skylar and Jean reach the parking garage, and Skylar suddenly realizes that she wasn't paying attention when she parked the car, and now she doesn't remember what level the car is on. She curses under her breath.

Her mother says, "I believe you parked it on the blue level." She looks over at the parking garage wall, and sees that the floor above them is the blue level.

"Thanks, Mom. Glad *you* were paying attention. You wait here, and I'll get the car and pick you up."

Skylar heads off for the car, shaking her head. Here she is, worried about her mother's memory lapses, and she can't remember where she parked the car!

21.

"Dr. Bradley! Can I speak with you?" Bohdi calls out as Suzanne Bradley heads into the psychology building. Professor Bradley turns to see her student. She sees Bohdi with a young lady that somehow looks familiar. "Hi Bohdi. What is going on?" Before he answers, she turns to Skylar and says, "You look familiar."

Skylar recognizes Dr. Bradley but it has been just about six years since they saw each other last. "Hi Dr. Bradley, I'm Skylar Donaldson, David Donaldson's daughter."

"Skylar, what a pleasant surprise! I have not seen you since you were just starting high school.

"Yes, it has been a while."

"Are you visiting Patterson?"

"No, I transferred here this semester."

"Wonderful. You know, I have not spoken to your father in years either. I need to reach out to him."

Skylar was a bit nervous meeting a friend of her fathers after so many years. But in a few short exchanges, all the nervousness she felt disappeared.

Before Bohdi can take advantage of the short lull to ask her a question, she says, "Yes, I did manage to copy some papers on holography for you, Bohdi. If you would like to follow me to my office, I can give them to you before I teach my next class.*"*

Bohdi told Skylar about a lecture Dr. Bradley had given in one of her psychology classes about how the structure of memory relates to concepts in holography and quantum physics. Bohdi had asked his professor if she had any additional information so he could learn about more about human memory. Skylar figured it was a good opportunity to meet Dr. Bradley again, after so many years, so she joined up with Bohdi to get the papers.

Bohdi and Skylar work to keep up with Dr. Bradley. She is a casual dresser and always wears sneakers since she like to walk fast. She looks Scandinavian, tall, light-skinned, with very short blonde hair. If she were a student now, there would probably be purple highlights in her hair.

Dr. Bradley asks Skylar some questions to fill in the time since she saw her last. It does not take long before they are at her office.

As she hands Bohdi the papers, she comments, "Well from what I have learned, both of you will find these papers interesting."

"Agree, that is why we came to meet up with you together.

Dr. Bradley apologizes for the rush; she has a class a few buildings away, and needs to get there ASAP. She tells Skylar that it was great to see her again and to please not be a stranger. She would love to hear more about her life. Dr. Bradley figures any child of David Donaldson has to doing something unique.

Bohdi and Skylar head for the Student Union. As they go he shares with Skylar what he learned in this last class. Dr. Bradley, he says enthusiastically, discussed studies that indicate memories are stored holographically in the brain. In one study, rats were trained to negotiate a maze—then the researchers removed larger and larger portions of the rats' brains. The rats' ability to negotiate the maze slowly declined, but they never lost all of their memory. The details just eroded somewhat with each surgical removal, in much the same way a hologram loses its detail as more and more of the holographic imprint is cut off.

In studies of individuals who were involved in accidents, where portions of their brains were lost due to trauma, it was found that they usually didn't lose complete memories of portions of their lives. Dr. Bradley told the class that individuals lost particular details of their memories. Some researchers believe this supports the concept of a holographic model for memory, in which stored information is distributed over the entire brain, just as each portion of the hologram contains all the information, but the details become less intense as portions of the hologram become unusable or are removed.

But this doesn't explain all human memory, Dr. Bradley noted. The holographic model contradicts neurological studies, where specific portions of the brain were stimulated with electric probes, while the research subjects were awake. The brain doesn't have pain receptors, making general anesthesia unnecessary. The researcher found that by stimulating precise areas of the brain, specific physical responses and memory responses could be triggered, leading to the conclusion that memory must have both local *and* distributed or holographic properties.

Dr. Bradley discussed the properties of matter and gave the electron as an example, although the discussion applied to any subatomic particle. The theory of quantum mechanics, she said, describes matter as having both particle-like and wave-like properties. She explained how the double-slit experiment in physics highlighted this duality of matter. If a single electron is directed at two slits between it and a detector, each electron behaves as a wave. Dr. Bradley showed the pattern of light and dark bands measured by the detector, and that these patterns are a result of waves. The unusual part of this experiment is that the detected wave pattern is as if the single electron went through both slits at the same time. If one of the slits is covered up, and another single electron is directed at the open slit, the electron behaves as a particle—a completely different pattern. Here, the detector shows a pattern of detected electrons much like what would be expected if a bullet was shot through a slit. Most electrons are aligned to the middle of the slit, and the number of them detected falls off toward the edges of the slit. This quantum experiment demonstrates that the electron, or any other particle, can manifest as a wave or a particle, depending on how the experimenter sets up the apparatus. Matter has dual properties, Dr. Bradley said, so it could be postulated that memory also has both particle-like and wave-like properties.

As Bohdi shares the insights he is learning about consciousness from his classes with Skylar, she is amazed at how the particle-like and wave-like properties of quantum physics apply to consciousness. Bohdi likes to call these properties the local and nonlocal properties since he finds it easier to visualize, and she agrees it works better than particle-like and wave-like. She likes that the two of them share the insights they are learning in their respective programs. They both feel the overlap that both of them have between the technical and human consciousness is very powerful.

Both Skylar and Bohdi have about forty minutes before their next class, so they find a place in the Student Union, since it is too cold this December day to sit outside, and together write a report for Dr. Brown that is due. They had worked together taking notes on their continuing experiments of getting to know what is normal and abnormal in each other's fields of colors. Bohdi tells Skylar to include their unsuccessful experiments to use the cameras in their phones to capture images through the goggles. Skylar writes that the goal is to get objective results, instead of the subjective feedback they are forced to use. She states the obvious that it would make their investigation more scientific.

It pains Bohdi that they have to report they were not successful. He really thought they could make it work, but there seems to be more they have to learn about the goggles.

Bohdi tells Skylar he worries that this report is not as substantial as the first, since they had so much more to report the first time. Now that end-of-semester papers are due, and with finals and the holidays coming up, he doubts that they will get much done in the near future. He suggests that she add an explanation that they might not do much experimenting with the goggles until after the New Year because of school and holidays.

Skylar ends the report with a note that highlights how much they have learned so far and their appreciation for the opportunity they have to use the goggles. Skylar hands her laptop to Bohdi to do a quick read. He hands it back and tells her to send it.

Bohdi takes two of the four papers that Dr. Bradley gave him and passes them Skylar. They still have twenty minutes to scan these papers before their next classes.

22.

"What!" Paul exclaims after Max, his top agent, tells him about the three parts Larry Hanley gave to him from his friends John Garrison's home.

"Are you sure?"

"No doubt about it. It even has the right serial number on the parts."

"That son of a bitch! He was high on my list, but I could never come up with any evidence. Boy, I would have liked to nail that bastard."

"Where are the parts?"

"I have them in my office."

"Did you use the GPS locator to find these parts?" Paul asks before Max can follow up.

"We could not. Those parts were the outdated ones that don't have the GPS locator in them. I tell you, I think John knew exactly what he was doing. He knew those older parts would be harder for us to track down. If he had taken the new parts, we could pick up that they were in the house without entering it."

Max nods. "Not to add salt to our wound, it has been ten years now and I'm not sure the Time Frequency Lab even has one of those old detectors around anymore. They're probably all destroyed by now."

"Find out. And find out what it takes to build another one."

Paul paces rapidly back and forth behind his desk, getting more agitated with each insight Max is giving him. Each break-in requires a number of agents to scope out the property, watch for activity, and look for the right opportunity to go in. Luckily, they know the house is empty. Now they just have to worry about the neighbors and any alarm system that they'll have to disable.

Then it occurs to Paul, "Larry and John worked together"

"Yes, I believe so."

"Maybe he was in on this and this is a way of coming clean."

"Not Larry. I'm also friends with him. He is too dedicated to our missions."

"Mmm, I am not so sure."

Max feels a disappointment that his friend is being dragged into this, even by reference. "Paul, if Larry were involved, why wouldn't he trash the evidence instead of handing it over to me? Why come forward after ten years, knowing that it can only hurt him? No, Larry has nothing to come clean about. He found evidence and he is helping us."

"Probably right," Paul replies, realizing his emotions are getting the best of him. But he is not ready to take Larry off his suspect list. This issue has been festering inside of him for ten years, and now he has an opportunity to clear up the problem for good.

Forcing himself to display a calm he still doesn't feel, he tells Max, "Okay, our next step needs to be fast. You mentioned John's daughter is back at her home, but plans to fly to her parent's house next week for a final cleanup. That house is empty now, and there could be potential evidence still in it. We need to get in there before she comes back and lets the auction house take everything away."

"I agree."

"Okay, Max, organize that break-in."

"Okay. Larry suggested we focus on the rest of the house, since he already looked around John's basement lab carefully."

"Have our team recheck that area anyway. I want one of our guys to give me that information, not just take Larry's word for it. I want every last corner in that house looked over carefully. Sounds like we have the time to do a good inspection, so let's see if we can recover more of the missing parts."

"Got it. I will let you know what I have organized."

"No emails about this until I say so."

"Agreed."

Max turns and walks out of Paul's office in a hurry, since he is already late for his next meeting.

23.

The cold rain outside makes Skylar happy to be inside her warm home. She heads downstairs this Saturday morning to get some coffee.

"Wow, that smells good," she says to her mom as she shuffles into the kitchen.

"You're up early today," her parents say in unison.

"Yeah, nothing like the smell of bacon and eggs to disturb a good sleep." She grins.

Jean is happy Skylar is around, since she is the only family, from either side, left in the area. She smiles, thinking of Skylar and Celeste on the phone last night, when Celeste asked Skylar how her new roommates were. Skylar replied, while looking at her parents, "They don't hassle me much, except to call me a slacker for not cleaning up after myself. The food plan is really good, and it's usually cooked too. I could do worse." Jean realizes that the older her daughter gets, the more she sounds like her father, especially her sense of humor.

Jean feels something slide from her fingers. "Ah, shoot!" she exclaims as she looks down at the egg splattered on the floor.

"How clumsy of me. I dropped my favorite coffee mug a few days ago, and now this egg."

David, who is in the dining room setting the table, hurries into the kitchen. "I'll clean up."

"Don't be ridiculous," she snaps. "The way you're acting lately, I'm beginning to believe you think I'm helpless."

"Of course not, Jean. I just feel bad you're making breakfast for us, and you shouldn't have to clean up this mess."

"Okay, but really, I'll clean it up," she insists.

David decides he'd better let it go. He nods and heads back to finish setting the table.

Skylar feels the tension between her parents. There is something in her father's actions and in his face that makes her feel concerned. The moment passes. Skylar's attention locks on a photo of her parents mounted on the wall nearest the kitchen table. The picture shows the two of them at the top of a hill they had just hiked, with mountains and green valleys in the background. David, at six foot two, towers over his wife, who is just five foot four. His mostly gray and thinning hair emphasizes the pale skin of his European ancestry. He almost always wears a hat to protect his face from the sun, and in this photograph, it's a well-worn bright-blue baseball cap he picked up on one of their vacations. Jean has long, dark-brown hair that, in the picture, is braided into a thick ponytail down her back. Her olive skin reflects her Mediterranean ancestry. She looks like a person who loves to be outdoors, which she does. She has a big smile, and David sports an unusual grin, standard protocol for most of their photographs.

"Breakfast is ready," Jean say happily as Skylar and her father bounce out of the chairs to help put all the dishes on the table. The rain comes down heavily outside, making it even more cozy to sit here and let the morning roll by. They share small talk about the week and plans for the holiday weekend. Earlier in the week, the family agreed not to discuss, at least for a few days, the constant chaos, within and with other countries, that is being created by their government daily. They all need a break from the anxiety.

Skylar asks her father if he's heard anything about the meeting that had been scheduled earlier in the week between President Duncan and Professors Albates and Bradley.

"Oh, Professor Bradley told me it was canceled at the last minute. I'm concerned that their outspokenness about the ties President Duncan is forging between Chemtech and the university will get them fired. It seems that more than half the faculty support the professors' position, but maybe I'm seeing it from my own perspective."

Skylar reaches for her toast. "I forget how you know Professor Bradley. I met her the other day with Bohdi and she looks the same as I remember her. She is such a classy person, and so smart."

"You remind me to reach out to her. It has been about three years since we last spoke. I met her through a mutual friend. She called to ask if I could help with some equipment she needed for an experiment. She wanted her students to carry out some psychological tests and to measure some physical parameters, like heart rate, skin temperature, and so on, while the tests were being executed. She wanted to be able to pull all their data into one computer, so I helped her set up the electronics and did some programming to capture and present the data. She was happy with the results. She's one of the few professors left who still lives up to the mission set up by the founder. I'm sad to see the changes at the university over these last few years. It's been such a good school."

David catches himself, having momentarily forgotten that his daughter is a new student there. He gets up to make some more toast.

Jean looks straight at her daughter and wants to follow up on a topic Skylar shared with her parents last week, "On another note, I want to understand why you refer to life as a multidimensional game. This makes me wonder. Do you think we're all trapped in some kind of a game, and we have to find a way out of it? That sounds unhealthy."

Skylar knows that her mother is struggling with fears about her own life. "Yes, I've called it a game. But just like the sports or video games we play, they are a subset reality, within our larger reality."

"But you talk about it like it's some type of three-dimensional game you have to figure out how to escape from."

"Mom," Skylar responds patiently, "most people choose to follow an ideology—for example, a religion or political affiliation, or even an organized sport—and all these come with an established set of rules to define an experience, like soccer, or baseball. While the person participates in that game, they consciously, and unconsciously, accept certain rules. If it is an ideology, they accept certain values and beliefs. Do you understand what I mean?"

"Go on, I'm listening."

Skylar continues, hoping she can get her point across. Over the years she and Bohdi have had this conversation many times, so she is confident in her opinion. "One way to understand rules is to question them. This is certainly true for people with religious and political ideologies. If, at some future point, they may reject that ideology, they'll choose what rules they'll carry forward and which they'll reject. In a sport, when you finish the game and walk off the field, the rules of the game no longer apply to you. To me, it seems true of our general experience of life, which I believe is a reality we willingly jumped into, for reasons I'm still trying to figure out."

"But spending your time searching for a way out of life, like walking out of a game, is not healthy." Jean fidgets in her seat, ready to push the subject further until she hears something that makes her feel better. . . and Skylar now recognizes what her mother is trying to say.

"Mom, don't worry. I have a great life. It's not so much a way out as a way to decode the rules of our reality and understand it," she points out. "Once the rules are decoded, then I expect to experience reality in a whole new way, with a lot more internal freedom." She's just about to say, *it becomes a new game*, but catches herself. "Life has a different feeling."

Her mother stifles a sigh, but she continues anyway. "What I mean, Mom, is walking through a reality after completely understanding it isn't the same as trying to escape it; although I'll admit, at times, an easy escape option from what seems like a fair bit of insanity does appear appealing." She laughs.

"Hmmm. I still don't like it."

Skylar can see her mother is getting tired and looks for a way to end the conversation. "It's not that I recently adopted this idea, Mom. It's that my ideas about it are clearer. I'm more vocal about it now, so that's why it seems like a new idea." Skylar wants to introduce the red pill-blue pill concept of *The Matrix*, but figures that is not going to help this conversation. It might engage her father, but not her mother.

David finds the conversation interesting. He's never thought of life as a game with rules to be decoded. Until Skylar brought up the concept, he believed life has its mysteries, which need to be explored, yes, but not in a way like Skylar is explaining. He knows the younger generation thinks differently, since they spend hours playing complex three-dimensional games—not to mention having absorbed the influence of many science fiction novels and action films—so it's probably reasonable for them to view life in a different way.

David's still not sure if this is good or bad. He's come to respect Skylar for the way she questions life. Skylar's generation gives hope for the future.

David notices Jean's head flop down as she nods off. He quickly gets up to catch her, expecting she might fall off her seat. She wakes up suddenly, balances herself with her arm on her leg, and looks around. "Sorry, I must have dozed off. I am really tired. I think I'll go and lie down for a little bit."

She struggles to get to her feet, feeling a bit unsteady. David watches her closely, ready to spring into action if necessary. He does not offer to help unless she asks or is in real need. Jean hates feeling dependent and he understands.

24.

Agent Phil speed-walks to his boss's office. Phil is a runner, so he can walk fast, quite fast. Earlier, he received a secure message to come to Hank's office for an 8:00 p.m. meeting. He hopes his last presentation has changed Hank's mind, but why so late?

The front lobby is empty and quiet. Everyone has gone home. . . well, almost everyone. Walking down the hallway, he sees light coming from the open door of Hank's office. A moment later, he stops at the threshold; Hank looks up and waves him in.

The men share a moment of small talk. Hank has good relations with everyone on his team except Phil. There is always an underlying tension in their working relationship that Hank has never been able to get around, so any conversation with Phil needs extra attention.

"I called you in because I want a private word. I'm assigning you to a side project of investigating the field structures around the young people you and Tania are so convinced are different. Our discussion the other day convinced me I need to take some action."

Phil feels a glow of satisfaction.

Hank continues, "I'm working on Paul to get some field scanner agent time available to us, but so far he hasn't budged. Now, with Paco Reneau in charge of Tania's time in the lab, it will be even more difficult for her to do the analyses that this project needs. So, instead of sitting still, I want you and Tania to make the best assumptions you can about what is different in the fields of these young people she has identified. Then put those parameters into your model and try some of our treatments. See what you get. But the results cannot be publicized. It has to go through me."

He looks directly at Phil. "You okay with that?"

Phil is quiet. He wants to broadcast it to a wider audience within the Chronos Consortium. He has witnessed how information can disappear in this organization when it's presented to only one person, who might decide it's too risky to share, and he's not yet convinced that Hank is in favor of this project. This makes him a bit suspicious of Hank's motives.

"Why only you?" Phil struggles to keep his tone of voice neutral so it does not antagonize his boss. He is not afraid of Hank, but he needs him on his side if he is ever to get this project funded.

Hank knows he does not have a good enough answer for Phil, but in this case it is not that important, since without Hank's approval, Phil and Tania will get nothing done for their project. "I still have some fighting to do, but it's a good start. Can you make the time? You obviously have to finish your work on the other missions. I'll catch hell from my superiors if we bungle any of those critical cases, especially if it is due to a small project. In the meantime, I will work to get new personnel on our team, but that won't be soon enough. The pool of talent we have to draw on is small."

He stops to give Phil a chance to speak. Phil runs his hand through his hair. "We have to do this, so I'll fit it in."

"You agree that the results will only be presented to me, no other disclosure?" Hank pushes this point again, since he knows Phil wants a larger audience and resents reporting solely to him.

Phil hesitates. He wants to start this project, but wants Tania's opinion before he commits, since this is based on her data. "I want to talk to Tania."

"No, I want you to make the decision, since you will drive this project under my guidance. I have no authority over Tania because she is in a different department. You are on my team, so I want a binding answer from you—before you leave my office tonight."

Hank waits. He's clear in his mind. If Phil doesn't agree, he won't support his research. Hank is not about to risk a project that could jeopardize his reputation as an effective manager who does not create messes that others have to clean up. He has seen too many research projects balloon into messes. Hank just wants to move this project along far enough to justify shutting it down. His goal is to make sure his own secret project, which also needs critical resources, is funded. He thinks it is a better bet for the Chronos Consortium than Tania and Phil's project.

Phil squirms. *Tania will be mad at Hank for putting this constraint on the project. She does not like him. And I'm sure that any additional demands that either of us makes to broadcast this message beyond Hank will not work.*

Hank is patient. He knows if he gets Phil's word, he will honor it in spite of his current internal struggle.

After a long pause, Phil looks directly at Hank. "I agree."

He reluctantly sees this offer as their only opportunity to move the project forward, and hopes, with Hank showing interest, it won't be overshadowed by other priorities.

"Okay, good," Hanks says. "This is just between you, Tania, and me. Make that very clear to her."

"Okay," Phil replies. He is ready to leave.

"Anything else you want to talk about?"

"Yes. Make sure you get the resources so we can do this job," Phil says with some heat as he heads for the door. He wishes he could feel better about Hank's offer, but he worries that good ideas like theirs will get lost in all the conflicting interests.

Hank feels better. Soon he will have the information he needs to justify ignoring Phil and Tania's project, and focus on his main goal: getting his Re-Imagination Project funded.

****

In another part of the building, Paul is discussing the results of the break-in to the Garrisons' house with Agent Max. Max told Paul that no additional information or pieces were found. The only item of interest was a dusty photograph under a box on a shelf, showing John Garrison and some other guy. The picture was clearly taken in John's basement lab, so the other man might be someone who worked with John.

Paul states the obvious, that the other person must be identified. He won't rest until it is clear that every clue has been uncovered, and right now, there could be someone out there who knows crucial information, or has the other pieces of the missing scanner. Paul is determined to close this case completely.

25.

Jenn, John Garrison's daughter, looks at her ringing phone. She is expecting the auction house to return a call, but is not sure what number they might be calling back on. She answers, hoping it will be them, and she will be able to get things wrapped up soon.

"Hello, is this Jenn?" the voice inquires.

"Yes," she replies and waits expectantly.

"I am Annie Brown. I was friends with your mother. My husband and I were away when your mother passed away, and the funeral happened before we were able to get back. I am very sorry we missed it. I wanted to convey my sympathies. I really enjoyed her company and wanted to see if there is anything we can do to help. I know you live far away."

"Oh, yes, I do remember your name being mentioned. Mom really appreciated you helping her out after Dad died, when she could no longer drive. It's nice to finally talk with you. My sister and I are deeply grateful for what you did for our mother. Thank you."

"It was my pleasure. How are you doing?" Annie asks.

"Okay. I'm at my parents' house now, trying to clear up before the auction house comes. It's really difficult to go through their stuff, and some of ours. It brings back so many memories. My sister has been here and helped out quite a bit, as well. I also had Larry over for some of Dad's stuff. You know Larry Hanley, right?"

There is a moment of silence.

"Maybe the Hanleys were my parents' friends before you knew them," Jenn adds, realizing that the Browns might never have met the Hanleys.

"I've heard his name mentioned, but we never met," Annie says, quickly recovering from her surprise at hearing Larry's name.

"Anyway, I am reaching out to anyone I know to find a home for my parent's stuff before everything is auctioned off. Just seems a pity," Jenn says, sounding overwhelmed.

"Do you need any help?" Annie asks.

"No, I'm almost done. Is your husband technical?"

"Yes, he is. You need something repaired?"

"No, but he might be interested in some of my father's stuff from his lab."

"Oh, that is so nice of you. I'll mention that to him. Our basement is already overflowing with stuff, but he always manages to get more in there. If he is interested, we'll call back tonight. That is very nice of you to offer. Anyway, I don't want to take any more of your time. I just wanted to say I really enjoyed your mother's company. Sorry again that we could not make the funeral."

"That's fine. I'm glad you called. Again, thanks for everything you did for Mom."

"It was my pleasure. Take care."

After the call, Annie's heart is beating fast. She heads downstairs, her legs still wobbly from the news, to tell Vic.

"Vic," she says as she approaches, wanting to make sure she doesn't startle him as he sits at his lab bench, absorbed in his task. "I was just talking to John's daughter, Jenn, and she mentioned that she had invited Larry Hanley over to her father's lab to see if there is anything he might find useful before she calls the auction house."

"Oh no!" Vic blurts out, immediately looking panicked.

"I thought you would say that. Do you think Larry would have found anything in John's lab?"

"I'm not sure. I'm pretty clear what John had in his lab just before he died, and the parts we didn't use for the goggles weren't there."

Vic breathes a sigh of relief that Larry doesn't know about him. Larry had already moved away by the time he and John had started working together, and John was emphatic that Vic have no association with him, for his own benefit. John did everything he could to distance himself from his previous colleague, so he could do what he considered his most important work in the secrecy critical for its success. The goggles are the product of the work that John and Vic did together.

"Jenn did ask if you were technical. I said yes, and she extended the same invitation to you to go through her father's lab stuff. Are you interested?"

"Problem is, those parts are not in his lab. He likely had them in another part of the house. That's where I would like to look, but I can't just go looking through their whole house. Now that Larry has been there, I'll never know if he found anything or not."

He pauses to think. "Maybe Jenn found those parts in her father's closet, dresser drawer, or sock drawer. Who knows. I can imagine you collecting all the stuff I have all over this house and putting it all down here in my lab after I die." He lets out a deep sigh. "I don't have a good feeling about this. He was a bit of a pack rat."

"Maybe you should think about what you have in your basement lab, and your office, that should be taken care of before it's too late," Annie says anxiously. The conversation is upsetting her.

"Let me think about whether I should go over to John's house or not. Since Larry has already been there, it is much more complicated. I'm sure if anything was found, that house is now being watched. From what John told me of Larry, he is somebody who knows these parts well, and he's dedicated to the mission of the Chronos Consortium. That makes him very dangerous. This is not a good turn of events."

Annie leaves her husband to think about the situation. She goes upstairs to make some tea, hoping to calm her nerves. She had hoped that John's death would have permanently severed any possible links between them and the Chronos Consortium. The next generation needs all the help they can get to combat the thought control that is becoming so pervasive in the world.

26.

Skylar hears a ding on her phone. She sees a text message from Dr. Harry Smith, Eye Specialist. This is Skylar's cover name for Dr. Brown on his encrypted link and contact list. Dr. Brown had requested they not use his real name in their address book.

Hi. I need to talk to you and Bohdi. Can you meet this Friday evening about 7:00? I know the holidays are right around the corner, but this is very important. Please contact me as soon as you can.

Skylar feels panicky. The November report she and Bohdi sent to Dr. Brown was the weakest, and she fears that she and Bohdi might lose the goggles if Dr. Brown feels they haven't made enough progress. They also sent it a week late, so now it is mid December.

Hi, she texts back, followed by, *I can do it, but I need to check with Bohdi.*

Okay. But please try to get him to cancel any conflicts and make it. It will not be easy for me to reschedule this meeting. I expect we will need three to four hours for discussion.

Skylar is surprised by this last bit of information. It cannot take Dr. Brown that long to tell her and Bohdi that he wants the goggles back.

Okay, as soon as I hear from Bohdi I will let you know.

Dr. Brown texts back, I will send the address where we can meet.

The text messages stop. Skylar immediately texts Bohdi to see if he's available.

When she sees the address come through from Dr. Brown, she wonders whose home it is. She feels less panicked, since there is no mention of bringing the goggles. In fact, she wonders if Dr. Brown saying he needs three to four hours might mean he is ready to share more with them.

****

On Friday evening, Dr. Brown is in the dining room at the home of one of their friends. The Browns are looking after their dog and two cats for three days while they are away. Dr. Brown seized the opportunity to meet Skylar and Bohdi at this out-of-the-way location. He gets down to business as soon as they arrive, stating that he and

Annie are very happy with the work both of them have been doing with the goggles. "You both have validated the confidence we have in you."

He then tells them he has some health issues that are driving him and Annie to extend an offer. "Would you, Skylar, and you, Bohdi, want to be entrusted as the next guardians of this goggles technology?"

Both of them light up, but before they can speak, Dr. Brown puts up his hand to signify they should pause.

"Before you answer, I need to add some additional information. This technology, as you have already experienced, can help humans see that what they think and feel is real. We believe that this understanding is crucial to a better future for mankind, if we are ever going to take control of our future again. But I have to mention there is a dark side to this technology. My deceased partner, John, had a past experience with a very powerful group of corporations controlled by the Chronos Consortium. That is where he learned about the basics of a unique technology. We used this technology secretly to create the goggles. If you research the Chronos Consortium, you will not find anything about them, because they are a group of layered companies. But make no mistake: They are all controlled by the umbrella of the Chronos Consortium. John said the Chronos Consortium has a technology that allows them to influence the thoughts and feelings of most targeted individuals. They could only make it work on one person at a time while he worked there, but John felt it is only a matter of time before they would develop new technology that could influence large groups of people. That is totally frightening."

"For sure!" Skylar blurts out. Bohdi nods in agreement.

"John wanted to develop these goggles to correct what he had been involved in. I helped him interface some of their technology into the goggles that you are now using. It took us four years to develop, and, unfortunately, he died a year later."

Bohdi asks during his pause, "How did he get their technology?"

"He organized the disappearance of a device that was slated for destruction. The Chronos Consortium could not figure out who did it, but they know that some of these pieces are out there," Dr. Brown says, a bit sheepishly.

Skylar winces. *We've been using technology that was built with stolen property.* This makes her uneasy.

"This fact makes it complicated. John figured that if people could see that what they think and feel is real, then they will pay attention to what goes on inside their head and heart. We believed—I still believe—that these goggles are the only way humans can fully appreciate that they need to own the state of their inner thoughts and emotions. If they are not paying attention, this sinister group will help them think and feel in a manner that allows the Chronos Consortium to control events in the world. It is most evident in politics. If we do not stop what they are doing, our world will become like the frightening one depicted in the novel *1984*.

"But, it is not as simple as just putting the goggles out there. Now that you know that they contain parts that belong to the Chronos Consortium, you better believe they'll come after anyone who has these parts. That's why we've worked in secrecy, and why the two of you will have to do the same if you choose to become guardians, for your safety and the future of what this technology can do. My hope is that these goggles will also allow you to develop technology that will counter what the Chronos Consortium has."

"Did your partner know Chronos Consortium uses their technology to influence thoughts and emotions?" Skylar asks, taken by the seriousness of this conversation.

"He was aware of it. He primarily worked on a detection device that measured the frequency content of a person's attitudes, the foundation of thoughts and feelings."

After a pause, Dr. Brown continues, "Since his death, my focus has been to optimize the goggles' sensitivity, so they can help people. You now have direct experience with the result of that work. You need to understand that this is a very serious responsibility. The Chronos Consortium does not know of this goggle technology, so they are not looking for it. But if they saw the goggles, they would quickly figure out that the device has some basis in their technology and will want to crush it. We have been very secretive about the goggles until recently, when we took the risk with you two, and my nephew Bruce. But he does not have the capability to be a guardian. Fortunately, he brought you to us, though, and that is a great service."

Skylar feels bad. She likes Bruce, but she has to agree that he does not have the ability to take on this much responsibility. Her attention goes back to Dr. Brown.

"Working in secret is paramount. As long as you do that, you should be fine, just like my partner and his wife, and Annie and I did. Should you make it public for some reason, you will attract the attention of the Chronos Consortium, and they will come after you with full force. But, if an opportunity presents itself where you think the benefits of going public outweigh the risks, then you should do it. Their goal is to remain secret, so if this technology becomes public, it must be in a way that forces them to come out into the daylight to refute it. You need to get a group on your side that has the power and influence to keep the goggles for the masses, not destroy them.

"As I said before, we never saw an opportunity in the time we had the goggles, and so we are thrilled we found the two of you as potential guardians to take over from us. Our time is running out, but this technology must go on. As you might have noticed, more and more people are not thinking for themselves, and this just makes the Chronos Consortium's control easier. You, the next generation with this technology, are our hope for a better future, our own future, not one concocted up by some consortium.

"I am going to the bathroom to give the two of you time to talk. When I come back, if you need more time, let me know. But I need a decision tonight."

He struggles to get up and limps out of the room. Dr. Brown is purposely putting pressure on them to decide because he knows that this is a responsibility you have to *know* whether you are ready to take on or not.

Bohdi looks at Skylar.

She stares back at with determination in her eyes, "I'm a bit spooked, but I am committed. We need a better view of who we are as humans. We are doing such a shitty job running this world. These goggles can give us a fresh perspective on how to clean up this mess. I think we have to say yes. We have to take on this responsibility, for a better future for us all."

"I agree on both points— the fact that this is alarming and the need to take on the responsibility. It's also a real honor that they have such trust in us."

"I can't believe it. When I first got the text from Dr. Brown, I had a flash of panic, thinking he wanted to take the goggles back. I certainly did not expect this! What do you think the next step is?" she asks quietly.

"We need to know more about the goggles. He has to give us more detailed information so we can duplicate them, or repair them if necessary."

Skylar and Bohdi listen intently for evidence of Dr. Brown coming back.

Dr. Brown hears nothing as he approaches. He feels that is good, since a clear decision has been made. He enters the dining room.

"So, have you made a decision?"

"Yes," they reply in unison.

"And . . . ?"

"We definitely want to be guardians of the goggles," Skylar says.

"Agreed," Bohdi quickly adds.

"Well, then, it's official, you are now the next guardians. I am thrilled. You have taken on this great responsibility to battle the looming thought control that will soon be everywhere. No time for a celebration, though, since there is a lot of work to do."

He rubs his palms together. "Okay, so let's move on to the next task."

He gives them each a notebook and pen, then opens the first of four folders. He goes over the design and build of the goggles in detail. He has sticky notes with instructions on the drawings. Everything is very well organized, with a document explaining all the steps to building the goggles. Bohdi notices there are no names on any of the drawings or documents, and there is a black mark where he thought a name should have been.

The more difficult and technical steps Dr. Brown goes over slowly. He tells them that securing the material is going to be their biggest challenge. Dr. Brown and his colleague struggled to find materials that duplicated the effect as well as the materials that John had brought with him. This is where the real technical challenge will be for the two of them. It will require knowledge of both physics and some chemistry to make a new design work. He will supply some funds to pay for these materials, and can provide remote support.

He opens the second folder. "Here are the notes I've been keeping about materials, some of which are used in the goggle construction. There are small vials of twenty-five element samples in one of those boxes." Then he points to a pair of boxes, about half a foot in each dimension, on the floor behind him. "There is also a spare set of lenses in that box with the white tape. They are the trickiest part to make, so be very careful with them. I recommend you make all the other parts first and use these completed lenses to make your first set of goggles, so you build confidence in what you're doing."

"What about the headphones, why are they necessary?" Skylar asks, figuring this time she will get an answer to his question.

"Ahh, yes. There are frequencies that start at 24 Hertz when you boot up the goggles in the 'Minus' mode, which is in the Beta brainwave ranges of brain activity. When you change the goggles to 'One' the frequency moves to 12 Hertz. This is in the Alpha brainwave range. That is why a minimum of 15 seconds is needed. The brain follows the frequencies through entrainment. I found out how to speed up this entrainment process. I have a paper in this folder on the subject that you should read. When you go to the 'Plus' mode, the frequency shifts to 6 Hertz, which is the Theta brainwave region. This frequency optimizes the brain's state to interpret the information seen in the 'Plus' mode." Dr. Brown is anxious to keep moving along with this information transfer, so he switches back to making the goggles.

"Then tackle the part of making the lenses last. I'm sorry there's no time for training, but I have confidence in you both. The other box has parts you will recognize from these drawings. Keep them hidden to prevent any questions. I also have two larger boxes with a special oven, small in size, and some other equipment I made that you'll need in order to make another set of lenses. Before you start, I have documented some experiments that you should carry out to teach yourself how to combine materials so you get the right outcome, based on my physical and goggle research data."

He flips a few pages, looking for the beginning of these notes. "What you should do is witness all twenty-five elements I have in those boxes, and make sure what you see matches my description. Then, fortunately for you, I found a technique that makes it easier to make the goggle lenses when you already have a set, because you can witness the sample after each preparation step and validate that it is done correctly with the goggles. Our first construction required equipment that would not be available to you, but with the goggles, it is not necessary.

"You will already be using the information of the other state of matter to build these goggles. This information is a great starting point to learn and experiment how the states of matter in space and time come together, and how to use this information to combine materials optimally for effects in three-dimensional time, not necessarily three-dimensional space. Go through these preparation steps carefully. Given both of your backgrounds, I'm sure you should have the skills to do this."

Skylar is not so sure. They have been at this for the better part of two and a half hours, and she is beginning to be overwhelmed by the details, but she is not going to ask for a break. This is too important. She will do whatever it takes to make this work.

They take a coffee break after finishing the second folder. Three hours have passed. Fifteen minutes later, they go over the details of the electronics in the third folder. An hour and a half later, they finish up. It is now past midnight.

Dr. Brown opens the fourth folder, which holds his copy of the documents they all signed. He tears them up into small pieces, since they are no longer necessary. The reports they have been sending are no longer needed. He then hands them an envelope that he says contains two items. First are plans of how he built a secret hiding place, for the goggles and related information, in his home along with $10,000 in cash for them to buy the necessary materials to replicate the goggles and build this secure hiding place. He says if more cash is needed, they should let him know.

He opens the envelope and takes out the plans. He shows each of them the drawing and mentions a few modifications that could be made. If they have any questions about what he gave them tonight, and he expects they will, they are to just continue using the encrypted link he had them install on their phones to ask questions and communicate any interesting work they are doing. He will delete any communication after he has read it and suggests they get into the habit of doing the same. He reminds them of what he has told them in the past. They absolutely should not use any other technology for communication that is not encrypted. Then he says, with a note of melancholy, that when either he or Annie dies, they are not to go to the funeral. The links between the Browns and the two of them will be severed after this evening, other than some encrypted messaging.

Skylar and Bohdi agree but feel unhappy at the thought of never seeing their new mentor again.

"But—" Skylar starts to say before Dr. Brown cuts her off.

"No exceptions. We know you are grateful, and that is enough. The future of this technology, and what you will do with it, are more important than our passing."

Skylar then asks if Dr. Brown or his previous colleague, John, had any technology that could change the Time Information Fields they see with the goggles. For instance, if someone had some frequency structure in the Time Information Field that was not good for them, and it is not correlating to their thoughts and feelings, is there a way to change it?

Dr. Brown replies no. If they did, both he and his colleague would have used it, since they both suffered from maladies that were visible with the goggles. "Maybe you two will be the ones to discover how to do that," he says.

He is exhausted, but satisfied. He neatly puts the four folders into a larger binder for Skylar and Bohdi to take, and they transfer the two boxes in the dining room and the two larger boxes in Dr. Brown's car. After another round of handshaking and thanks, the two of them head off to get something to eat. There is no way they could possibly go home and sleep after this evening.

They would like to go to the local twenty-four-hour diner, but they dare not leave the car with all the secret information and equipment. Bohdi suggests that they order some food to go and they eat it in the car so they do not leave this equipment unattended. While eating burritos at 1:30 in the morning, they agree not to tell their parents about what happened tonight. As Dr. Brown emphasized, they must work in secret. That means behaving as if everything is the same. Bohdi says he cannot store any boxes at his house. His mother is obsessive about everything in the house having its place and would immediately know if something changed, so it has to be kept at Skylar's house. She says she will find a temporary hiding place in her room until they have built a secure place since her parents almost never go in her room now to give her some measure of privacy now that she is living back home. Should their parents, out of curiosity, ask about the reports to Dr. Brown, they agree to say that he does not require them regularly anymore.

Their lives already reflect the guardianship they have taken on tonight.

27.

Tuesday morning, Jean and David sit quietly in Dr. Cathy Jones's waiting room. The doctor left a message on Jean's voicemail the day before, letting her know that the results of her tests were back, and she wanted to go over them in her office. The office is decorated for Christmas, which is just a week away. There's a small tree in the corner with fake gifts underneath, and Dr. Jones's receptionist, Sally, has strung Christmas lights along the top of the walls to create a festive ambiance.

Smiling, Sally tells them Dr. Jones will see them now. Dr. Jones is seated at her desk when they walk in. She half-rises, motioning for them to take the same seats they'd sat in the last time.

"Nice to see you both," she says.

Jean fidgets, removing her purse from her shoulder. "Nice to see you, Cathy. We're glad to hear the good results."

"Yes, the results show no brain inflammation or any spinal fluid issues. Also, no signs of Alzheimer's."

Jean, a bit stunned by this statement, says, "Aren't I too young for that to have even been on the spectrum?"

"Generally, but early-onset Alzheimer's isn't unheard of at our age, so I wanted to rule it out," Cathy replies as she looks at Jean. "Since we last spoke, has anything changed with you?"

"Nothing for the better. Actually, I. . . I fell down in the kitchen the other day. It seems so silly. I went to turn around, and just fell over because I couldn't coordinate my feet. I felt so stupid."

This is the confirmation Cathy needs to press on with the testing. She leans forward and rests both arms on her desk with her hands clasped. "Listen, I've contacted a colleague in San Francisco who specializes in difficult-to-diagnose neurological issues. I would like you to see him, but I realize that could be difficult. There's a similar specialist in Boston, closer to home, but she's on sabbatical for a few months. The specialist in California tells me there are a few tests that we can organize here at a local hospital, but he needs to find a group he can trust to execute them. He would like you to spend a few days at the hospital he works in, on the West Coast. I understand it's not an easy thing to organize on short notice."

Jean blinks rapidly as she tries to absorb this. "Cathy, do you have any idea what's going on with me? Why the urgency?"

"I don't know what's wrong, but you're clearly suffering from something we've not identified yet. I want an answer for you, so I'm going the extra mile. I'm sure it might seem a bit extreme from your point of view. Of course, it's your choice, but I want to give you the best options I can come up with."

David takes Jean's hand. "Honey, let's go to this doctor in California. He can conduct the tests with his own team. We can spend a few days vacationing, and even see Celeste while we're there. It'll be good for us to get away."

Cathy agrees it would be better for Jean to have the tests administrated directly by this specialist and his team, with a few days spent under his care. Jean reluctantly agrees, and Cathy looks relieved. She asks Jean if she might have had a blood transfusion she hadn't told Cathy about.

"Just the one when Celeste was born, but that was over two decades ago," Jean replies.

"I remember that. I just have to ask, just in case. Please let me know what you decide, and I'll coordinate with Dr. Flourentini out West." She hands Jean a slip of paper with the name, address, and office phone number on it.

****

Just after dinner, David and Jean tell their daughters, Skylar and Celeste who is on speaker phone, that their mother does not have meningitis, encephalitis, or Alzheimer's, but doctors still don't know what is causing the problems she has been having. Her doctor is looking into doing the next set of tests with specialists on the West Coast, who are experts in neurological issues. They are all hopeful that this round of tests will help them get some answers. They spend time chitchatting about what is going on in each other's lives, and lightening the mood.

After the call, Jean goes to bed. Skylar gets her books together to meet a classmate to prepare for her last final exam of the semester in two days. She does not want to leave, but she has no choice.

The house is quiet once Skylar leaves, but David's mind is working overtime to put together clues from Dr. Jones's questions today and his own observations. Blood transfusions, memory loss, physical coordination problems, exhaustion, and depression. He wants to know what is common about this set of symptoms.

David opens up his laptop. He reads more about encephalitis and meningitis and, like Dr. Jones, dismisses both as cause. He types in more search keywords, and another disease starts popping up: something called sporadic Creutzfeldt-Jakob disease, or sporadic CJD.

David reads that sporadic Creutzfeldt-Jakob disease is a rare and fatal degenerative disease associated with the central nervous system. It occurs in about one out of every million people, and typically affects adults about forty years of age, although younger and older people are not excluded. The next two lines alarm him: Its onset is characterized by failing memory, vague changes in behavior, and lack of coordination. Sufferers might also experience insomnia, depression, and unusual sensations.

David squirms in his seat. He continues reading. The symptoms progress to involuntary movements, blindness, and dementia within a few months. Most patients die within a year. There is no known cure. His heart pounds, and he feels lightheaded.

He leans back in his chair and rubs his hands through his hair, then stands up abruptly. Anxiety courses through his veins. He heads for the back door, desperate for open space and fresh air. In the backyard, though, all he does is walk around in circles, going over what he's just read and trying to come to terms with how much could possibly apply to Jean.

After ten minutes of walking, he feels better. He heads back inside to his laptop.

He researches the history of the disease, searching for clues that might give him some hope. A website talks of German neurologists, Hans Gerhard Creutzfeldt and Alfons Maria Jakob, who described this fatal neurodegenerative disease in 1920. It's caused by Transmissible Spongiform Encephalopathy, or TSE, a process that leaves the brain with sponge like holes. Sporadic Creutzfeldt-Jakob disease is the most common disease arising from TSEs.

"Oh, no!" he says under his breath. "That's just like mad cow disease!"

David reads that sporadic CJD is often misdiagnosed as Alzheimer's, but these misdiagnoses are usually made by primary care doctors, not neurologists. There's no single diagnostic test for sporadic CJD, but a series of tests can narrow down the diagnosis. Dread grips him again. Now he's certain this is exactly what Dr. Jones suspects. No question about it.

After a sleepless night, David makes an early-morning excuse about needing to go to the hardware store. From the car, he calls Dr. Jones. Sally answers and tells him that Dr. Jones is busy, but she can hear the urgency in David's voice. As Sally writes down David's cell number, she sees Dr. Jones and waves her over. She tells David she has to put him on hold for a minute. Sally relays that it is Mr. Donaldson and he sounds upset. Dr. Jones tells Sally she will answer the call in her office.

She closes her office door. She'd planned to call David and Jean today, anyway.

She picks up the call on hold. "Hi, David, what's up?"

David immediately relays details of what he has read and asks if sporadic Creutzfeldt-Jakob disease is possible in Jean.

Dr. Jones says firmly, "I have no evidence to confirm that possibility," but she realizes that David has done his research, and he now knows what she's concerned about.

"Look"—she taps her foot nervously on the floor—"I heard from Dr. Flourentini late yesterday. He would like to see Jean right after the New Year. He'll arrange for an evaluation then."

"Why not next week?" David asks with an edge of desperation in his voice.

"With Christmas falling during the week and people taking time off for the holidays, not everyone on the team will be present. It's better to make it after New Year's." She tells David to have Jean, or both of them, call her office tomorrow, when she should have all the details about the tests, and possible dates. David thanks Cathy for all her efforts.

He puts down the phone, feeling lost, but he shakes off the looming sadness and heads back home so he can look into flights to San Francisco.

Still feeling half numb after looking into flights, he does more research into the cause of sporadic CJD. The best theory is that an infection of a prion protein causes it to fold inappropriately. The presence of badly folded prions causes normal prions to spontaneously change shape into the infectious forms, in a sort of biological chain reaction. Infectious prions clump together, and it's these clumps that researchers believe cause the neurological damage observed in sporadic CJD patients.

The disease is hereditary in five to ten percent of the cases, so knowing family history is a good place to start. David is not aware of any of her family members who might have had the same symptoms he read about. But that does not mean they are not carriers. Many people who carry the mutant prion protein never manifest symptoms. CJD can be acquired through certain medical procedures, specifically relating to nervous or brain tissues. This does not fit Jean at all. The most common form is sporadic CJD. This accounts for eighty-five percent of the cases.

But what causes proteins to change shape in the first place? David finds out that bovine spongiform encephalopathy, or BSE, is the animal form of this protein malfunction, but there is no research that supports a link between BSE and any variant of CJD. Blood transfusions have been implicated in a few cases. But this ailment can also be hereditary. The website he is reading states that five to ten percent of sporadic CJD cases are due to genetic mutations passed down from parent to child. David finds this chilling, not only for Jean, but also for Celeste, who is pregnant.

****

David and Jean wait a day, until Skylar is finished with her last exam, before telling her the details of when and where Jean's next tests will be performed. Skylar wants to go to San Francisco with her parents, but her mother insists that she not spend any more days in the hospital with her. She wants her to spend this time with her friends during the semester break and take the opportunity to make some extra money. She argues that school will start soon enough. As far as she is concerned, it would be a better time to go to the West Coast as a family next summer, when they can visit Celeste, and the baby will have already been born.

Skylar refuses to back down. After some back and forth, her parents relent. David calls Celeste and gives her the exact dates, and asks if she can pick them up at the airport. He also asks for suggestions for hotels close to her apartment. Then he mentions that since they are going to be out there anyway, the thought is to stay for three extra days and spend some time as a family, relaxing and sightseeing. He asks her to schedule some things for the family after Jean gets out of the hospital. "Not too strenuous," he admonishes. "Let's make sure we're either driving or being driven around between stops. I'm not sure your mom can walk long distances like she used to."

"Don't worry, Dad. I'll take care of it."

****

Later that same evening, after her mother has gone to bed, Skylar tells her father that in a discussion with Dr. Brown, she asked if there was a way to *fix* something that you see in someone's field that was not there before. Dr. Brown answered that if he and his colleague did have such a technology, they would have already used it on themselves, since Dr. Brown is suffering from health issues that Ms. Brown saw developing in his field with the same goggles.

David reminds Skylar that no diagnosis has been made by the doctors yet. David hides his major concerns that the outcome might be dire. He tells Skylar that he really appreciates the efforts she is making to help her mom. He encourages her to keep trying, saying they have to try whatever they can.

28.

After their return from their West Coast trip, Skylar notices that her mother seems to have aged years in just a week. Ms. Donaldson tries to maintain a cheerful facade, as usual, but Skylar can tell she is shaken by the seriousness of the tests she is going through. Skylar sees her father drawn and quiet, and knows that he feels the situation is serious. Friday evening, Skylar finds herself alone in the house. Her parents had left yesterday to go up north to visit friends, stay over for two evenings, and then come back on Sunday. Both David and Jean think it will be good to keep busy while awaiting the test results.

The three days they spent touring San Francisco had been an excellent time for the entire family. But now Skylar's worries about what might happen to her mother have increased. It is getting the better of her. Before, there was so much activity; now, there's just silence. Normally a bit of silence is okay, but right now she feels the walls closing in on her. She thinks about how amazing it was that Dr. Brown entrusted her and Bohdi to be the guardians of the goggles, but she worries about what she should be doing to honor that. The holidays helped break up the constant concern that hangs heavy in the Donaldson home, and now they have to hope for good news from the tests. Skylar cannot shake her dread.

"I have to call Bohdi," she mutters to herself before going into the kitchen to make a sandwich. A few minutes later, the phone rings. Skylar notes the caller ID.

"Hi, I was just thinking about calling you."

"Well, sometimes you need to do more than just think, Miss Time Traveler. You need to use your phone. Oh, wait, I forgot—you just think about someone and they call you." He chuckles.

Bohdi wants to lighten the mood, but he can sense her sadness and just keeps talking, since he doesn't know what else to do. Skylar called him right after she heard about the tests, and what they were designed to assess. Bohdi has a bad feeling about Ms. Donaldson, as well, but he knows that if he gets too worried, then Skylar will have to switch gears and work to cheer him up.

"Hey, Skylar, my evening is freed up because a study group was canceled, so I thought I'd swing by for a cup of coffee this evening."

"You're beginning to worry too much about me," she jokes halfheartedly.

"Well, you are worth worrying over."

Skylar is not sure how to respond to that. "Yeah, that would be great," she says, sounding a little more like her ordinary self.

"I'll be right over," Bohdi replies, happy to be able to do something to help Skylar.

****

"Wow, it's so cold out today," Bohdi complains as he walks in the door. "I'm going to keep my jacket on for a few minutes until I warm up." He follows Skylar into the kitchen and sits down at the table.

He looks around as Skylar makes tea, and notices a piece of notebook paper lying on the table. His curiosity gets the better of him, especially since he can read the title without moving it: *A Thought about Time.*

"Can I read this?" he asks, before Skylar has time to think about what he's asking.

She glances over and grimaces. "Um, I'd rather you didn't. It's just some stupid idea of a poem about time."

"Oh, a poet, are we?" he teases.

"No, I was overwhelmed and needed something to occupy my mind. It's not very good."

"Let me read it." He pulls it closer to him.

Skylar looks up to object but Bohdi is already bent forward, reading. After a minute, he looks up. "I think it's worth reading out loud."

"Ohhhhh, no."

"Oh, yes. Shame on you for hiding this from your best friend." He clears his voice and reads dramatically:

A thought about time.

    In the hourglass pours sand

    On the clock move hands

    To transcend the hold of time

"Miss Skylar Donaldson, I do declare, what a surprise you have here. May I have tea instead of coffee, and some biscuits to lend an air of sophistication to this literary affair?" He smirks, pleased with his own efforts at rhyming.

"Oh, knock it off." Skylar turns pink.

Skylar knows her feelings for Bohdi have changed. She just about asks him a question, but Bohdi speaks before her. "What have you got planned for tomorrow?"

"Promise you won't make fun if I tell you?" she replies, reluctantly letting her question go unanswered.

"Okay, no comment from the peanut gallery." He takes off his winter coat and throws it over the back of the chair.

Skylar prepares a cup of tea, as a change from coffee, for Bohdi and herself and waits at the counter for the water to boil. "Well, while I was in San Francisco last week, I went into my Perception Reality and I noticed a difference. The background colors were noticeably changed. But I could also feel a difference not only in me, but also in each one of my family members. I found myself playing with the idea of investigating how the fields in time change by geographic locality. You could feel a difference—in the location, and in the people. I decided to set up an experiment with my Perception Reality now that I am back."

"On whom?"

"Not whom. On a geographical location. I suspect that each location is imprinted locally with the thoughts and emotions of all the people living in that location. "

"Well, where, then?"

Skylar brings her tea and some cookies to the kitchen table. As she sits down, she shares her idea. "There was a lot of waiting in the hospital, and while waiting, I had an insight that triggered this line of thinking. You know how you sit in certain classes and your mind drifts? You snap back and have no idea how much of the lecture you missed. You look around the class and can see others doing the same. It might be said we are in the same location in three-dimensional space, but in vastly different places in time, because our attention is on all sorts of topics other than the one being discussed in the class. Everyone is in a different 'place' in three-dimensional time but in the same place in three-dimensional space.

"On the flip side, if people in very different geographic locations in three-dimensional space are focused on the same event, like a huge televised sports event, where the attention of all those people is singularly on the same event and the distances between them appear to vanish. They are in the same 'place' in three-dimensional time, but vastly different places in three-dimensional space.

"This idea got me thinking. Now, in my understanding of my Perception Reality, every person is continuously transmitting their intentions, thoughts, feelings, and portions of their physical information, in what I now label multidimensional time after our visit with Dr. Brown. Instead of my usual terms of mental and emotional fields, from now on I'll call them Time Information Fields since we know they have information. In these Time Information Fields, like activates like—but in a resonant way. So, common thoughts and feelings interact together. It's like when people say, 'We resonate,' talking about how their ideas and thoughts seem to mesh with someone else's. I think this is literally true in the time dimensions."

"Seems picking up good, goooood vibrations is real," Bohdi sings.

"Absolutely! They're like the inner layers of an onion. So, the inner layers are your own Time Information Field, and your interaction with the Time Information Field generated by your family group. With each outer layer, there are properties associated with each Time Information Field. The local community has a Time Information Field generated by all those, past and present, who have focused their attention on this community and contribute to shaping its character. These properties are more easily available for those who live in them. I see the Time Information Fields as creating a feeling for a local area that people instinctively sense and identify as local culture. Often, I hear people say they love to go to a particular area because it makes them feel more creative, more energized, more relaxed, and so on. Of course, the opposite is true too. People avoid certain areas, are frustrated by them, and are happy to leave them for all sorts of reasons. But I believe homesickness comes from your field missing what you are most comfortable with, likely from a geographical and a family perspective. We all grow accustomed to certain 'atmosphere' of the surrounding fields, and when that changes, our system craves something familiar."

"Interesting. . ." Bohdi pauses, thinking over what she has just said. He then asks, "You believe local cultures have a collective Time Information Field that influences individuals' behavior unknowingly?"

"Yes."

Bohdi continues, "I can imagine certain cities might have great Time Information Fields, such that even people with poor intentions find themselves behaving outside their norm in a positive way. If that's true, then other cities could have people who are generally calm finding themselves frustrated or restless. I have felt that myself. You're saying this interaction skews the quality of life and is an active reality?"

Skylar sits up. "Precisely! Layered on the individual and family fields are Time Information Fields specific to local geographic area, like cities, states and nations. I suspect certain nationalities will interact more positively based on the content in these Time Information Fields."

"And," Bohdi interjects, "an Earth Time Information Field that captures all the thoughts and feelings of global citizens?"

"Yes, exactly!"

Skylar feels a surge of excitement that Bohdi understand this concept so readily.

"These Time Information Fields must also have some feedback mechanisms," Bohdi asserts, "so they can adapt and change the psychology of those living in this field. Could it be possible that, like in the circumstances we are currently facing in our country that the changes accelerate beyond what can be tolerated by a field, and that will either damage or break the patterns in these fields." Bohdi is applying what he has learned in his classes.

"Hmmm. . . maybe." This thought makes Skylar uncomfortable, that a community or civilization could break down collectively in its group mind. But it seems to fit.

Bohdi continues articulating his thoughts, "But. . . stretching a field to its limit might help to force change for the better, because those living in this field will feel the tension like we do and hopefully work to change it."

Skylar wants to expand on her idea, "I want to get back to the geographic effect: I think Time Information Fields correlate to any idea that generates emotion across the whole spectrum of life. I suspect that while there's always a geographic effect, ideas do transcend location and will primarily coalesce into Time Information Fields with common properties. Which means that thoughts travel long distances, possibly at the speed of light, which, for our circumstances on this planet, is pretty much instantaneous."

"Get out—you believe thoughts move at the speed of light!" Bohdi replies, amused.

"I said *possibly*. They might move even faster."

"Mmmm, I have to think about the implications of that." Bohdi says as he sips his cooling tea.

Skylar continues, "I think that's how fads work, Bohdi!"

He shakes his head, a bit confused. "Go on."

"It's clear that for young people, much of our attention is focused on what others are doing around us. In our local environment, a fad to wear certain clothing, listen to certain music, or talk in a particular way starts off with individuals in our social circle. At first it grows slowly, being absorbed by a school, then neighboring schools; then retail stores pick up on it and put their efforts into marketing to increase business, further accelerating trends. But at some point, these things go viral, and it's as if the level of attention in these Time Information Fields collects all the emotions relating to this idea and reaches a sort of critical mass, so that the idea, style, or behavior is easily accepted by a huge audience. Today, with our constant connectivity, that's easier to understand—but these things happened in past generations without the Internet, although probably at a slower pace."

"I totally agree!" Bohdi sets down his mug, "I easily envision it happening in consciousness first, where ideas or concepts struggle for so long—and then, all of a sudden, it becomes everyone's reality. Like a group mind. Using that concept, I would speculate that brave individuals who try to make social change understand that it is most difficult for the first one, or first few. Then there's always appears to be a tipping point, where the critical mass of emotions pushes a new idea forward or breaks it apart. I'd like to think that most new ideas are empowering, but I know from looking at our world, that's not true."

"Why do you say that?" Skylar says, looking perplexed.

"Well, people could polarize these Time Information Fields. From my studies in psychology, I understand powerful people use this group mind to control events through perception. "

Skylar immediately understands the reality of how perception controls people. She brings her attention quickly back to what Bohdi is saying.

"Politicians work hard to reach the hearts and minds of people, because if they get enough energy behind this perception, it can spread more easily independent of distance. Politicians, or anyone communicating with large groups of people, understand that perception often supersedes facts if presented persuasively enough. Structuring information that controls perception is the key to influencing people."

"I totally agree," Skylar adds. "But I think that's happening in music too. For instance, when we go and see a band play, the members of the band can feel the audience's response to them, and they respond to our energy. We feed off each other, and when they tell a room they've been a great audience, it is a scientific fact. From what we have just said, the Time Information Fields of the people in the audience come together to create an environment, invisible to us, that influences the audience and the band. Clearly, locality has an effect. Some venues create an atmosphere that both band and audience respond to positively."

"To keep going with that idea," Bohdi says, riding the wave of excitement, "There are also dynamics between band members. We call it chemistry, but if I replace the word *chemistry* with *Time Information Fields*, then it's obvious why some combinations of musicians work and others don't. As you mentioned earlier, if you are watching a live international sporting event on TV, you then start to resonant with the collective emotion of everyone else that is watching all over the world, probably due to the Time Information Field being generated by the emotion of the event. I can imagine that if fans feel a sense of panic or doom, on some level, it affects the players, if they let it. Any player who struggles with doubt will likely be affected the most."

"Yup, I agree with all of that." Skylar looks down at her mug. She looks up more perplexed, and says, "I want to get back to the previous idea of like activating like. I see that in people, both socially and politically, but I wonder about opposites attracting? I see that dynamic happening, too, and it seems particularly true between men and women." Skylar was about to say that she has seen it in her relationship with the guys she has dated.

"Mmmm, haven't thought about that," Bohdi contemplates. He stops to think and then suggests, "Okay, here my best shot in light of our current discussion. If in our familiar three-dimensional space, opposites attract—oppositely charged particles, north and south poles of a magnet, and, as you mentioned, males and females. What if in three-dimensional time it is as you said, like activates like, so at a deep level, common ideals and interests feed each other, through resonance."

He stops, waiting for a response from Skylar, but she looks at him, waiting for him to finish. "Here's an example that just flashed in my mind. Suppose you decided to start a blog focused on a political idea. You'd attract people who align with your ideals, and they could just as easily say they resonant with your ideas and positions. *But,* your blog will also attract readers with the opposite viewpoint, who want to refute your ideas and positions. Both would happen at the same time."

"True," she says, "I like your analogy. It certainly applies to the division we see in our society today. So, what makes one dynamic dominate over the other?"

Bohdi shrugs. "Since we live in spacetime, both happen at the same time, and maybe the amount of attention given to one over the other changes the balance of these two dynamics. The philosopher will say we can learn from both points of view. They would ask if we learn more from hot than cold, or up versus down. I'm not sure. That's a really good question."

"But," Skylar says, her voice rising in volume, "How many times do we as humans have to be burned by hot water, or fall on our faces, to figure out that there is an approach that is saner and less chaotic."

"Absolutely true," he yells in return.

Bohdi gives Skylar some time to continue, if she wants. He can feel himself starting to sink emotionally just thinking about the mess that is being generated in their country and can only imagine what is going on inside Skylar.

Skylar gets up from the kitchen table. "I need some hot water to warm my tea up." She smiles, though she is confused by what she feels inside. *What is real and what is just another response to the same patterns inside me?* She wonders. The uncertainty eats at her.

She then looks at Bohdi, and with a vulnerability in her voice tells him, "I have no idea how I would deal with all this without your support and friendship. I cannot think of a better person to help me with my family struggles as well as be on this grand adventure with. We have such interesting conversations. It would blow our friends' minds if they knew. Or more like they would think our minds are blown," she adds with a hint of sarcasm.

They laugh together. The laughter makes Skylar relax. She realizes that he often manages to make her feel more relaxed.

Skylar watches Bohdi as he slowly sips his tea. He is so different than the guys she has known. With Hannah out of his life, Skylar wants to ask Bohdi out on a date. But the possibility he might decline complicates things more than she may be ready for. It could make their friendship, which she desperately needs right now, uncomfortable. Their commitment as guardians could then become awkward, as well.

She shakes her head to clear it.

Bohdi sees her shake her head. "You okay?"

She realizes she was so lost in her train of thought she made an unconscious gesture and Bohdi sees it.

"Yes and no. So much is going on in our lives, it is hard to keep all the balls in the air at the same time."

To lighten the mood, Bohdi changes the topic to their common friends and what is going on in their lives.

****

Later that evening, after Bohdi had left, Skylar realizes that she has to ask the question on her mind. She grabs her phone and decides to send him a text.

"Would you go out on a date with me?"

She feels an instant relief, having put it out there. After a few minutes of silence, she starts to wonder if it was such a good idea. Before her mind can go down that rabbit hole, she hears her phone ding.

"Absolutely YES!!" is the reply.

29.

"Table for two?" the hostess asks Bohdi.

"Yes," he says, feeling a bit nervous.

He motions for Skylar to follow the hostess, and follows them both to a table in the back corner of the Thai restaurant. Skylar flows ahead of him in an indigo dress—*Skylar in a dress!* He hasn't seen her in one for years.

Once they're seated, a waiter comes to the table. "Hi, my name is Gamon, and I'll be your server tonight. Can I start you off with something to drink?"

Bohdi looks at Skylar. "You know what you want?"

"Yup, some green tea, please."

The waiter looks to Bohdi.

"Ummm. . ." He scans the drinks section of the menu. "I'll have the pineapple juice."

"Okay." With that, the waiter is gone.

Skylar looks around. "I was here once, many years ago, when it was the Pizza House. They've done a nice job remodeling the place."

They comment on the small candles set on each table, clever artwork on the walls, in bold red, orange, and yellow, and the small potted trees along the wall that separate the tables. LEDs wound around the stem and branches give a warm glow to the room.

"Nice job."

Bohdi laughs, chiding himself for feeling nervous. For goodness' sake, he's known Skylar for almost a decade! But something changes when your best friend asks you out on a date.

Skylar watches Bohdi page through the menu. He's so familiar, yet she feels like she's seeing him for the first time. The waiter returns with their beverages. Skylar says she needs a few more minutes.

She flips the menu pages, only partially attentive to the choices. She is feeling nervous. Last night, after she got the courage to finally asked him out, she expected she'd be relaxed and funny today, as she normally is around him. But seeing him dressed up smartly in long khakis, a green-and-white plaid shirt she suspects he borrowed from his father because it looks a tad big, and real dress shoes . . . has changed that.

"I'm going for the spicy chicken and broccoli," she says, closing the menu. "And a small bowl of Miso soup."

"Good choice. I'm getting the Massaman Curry with shrimp. And a couple of spring rolls."

Bohdi looks around to grab Gamon's attention. He is nowhere to be seen.

Skylar says, "I feel so much older this evening. You're wearing clothes that make you look like you're ready for a job, and I'm wearing a dress. I like it and I don't."

"I feel like an imposter," Bohdi says with a laugh, "And I could see your mother approved."

"Ohh, so you caught that too." Skylar's mother had dropped her jaw when she saw Bohdi at the door, then smiled. Even her father had a look of surprise on his face.

"Well, you caught all of us by surprise there. Let's not make a habit of this impostering." She smiles at him.

Before he can reply, they hear, "You ready to order?"

Startled, Skylar stammers, "Y-yes."

They give the waiter their order and he disappears.

Skylar shifts in her chair, "I will say I am very happy to be here with you."

"In fact, one of the things that held me back is," Skylar says as she looks tenderly at Bohdi, "I really need your friendship now. Add to that the fact that we are guardians together, I didn't want to risk screwing it up by asking you out and having you say no. That would be more than I could handle."

"You thought I might say no! Funny, that is what held me back too," Bohdi says as he reaches for her hand.

"You would have asked me out?" She inquires.

"Yes, but you have so much going on with your mother, and these goggles, I just did not want to screw things up as well. Seems we were both thinking the same way."

"Do you need more tea?" the waiter interrupts.

Skylar looks in her cup and sees it is half-full. "Sure."

"And you, sir?"

"No, I'm good."

Right behind Gamon comes another waiter with their dinners.

"That smells great," Skylar says as she grabs a spoon.

"Mind if I try?"

"Not at all. See if you like it."

"Spicy enough."

"No, not really. It has a nice flavor." She puts her chopsticks down and picks up the spoon at the side of her bowl.

As they eat their meals, the conversation drifts to what they want to do during the winter break.

Skylar then shifts the conversation to one of her favorite topics, the goggles. She mentions how she has thought a lot about the way information is encoded in colors when they use the goggles. Her Perception Reality and the goggles were the same, but why? What is it about colors that is so important? Yes, colors are frequencies, which are energy and information, but there has to be something more.

She tells Bohdi she wants to do experiments to determine if, and how, colors might affect the Time Information Fields they witness. She has found an Internet company that sells colored Mylar sheets, with a sheet showing the associated color frequencies for each color. She says maybe they can do the research with a balanced white light source. He suggests also buying small semiconductor lasers, like laser pointers, and see if there is anything about the phenomenon of a laser that is different from regular light source in these dimensions of time.

Bohdi suggests that he make a color wheel for her, so she can flip between the colors while she wears the goggles. If she wants to do some experiments, he can notch the edges so she can confirm which color is currently being illuminated. He can imagine that after flipping between two colors, it would be easy to get confused about which color is being used. Both think the process of coming out of Plus mode to Minus mode, to confirm colors, might be disruptive.

Skylar loves the idea, and is even more excited about getting these experiments going.

They get up to leave, putting on their winter coats to brave the January cold. Once outside, Skylar feels a wave of happiness overcome her and she reaches over to grab his hand. They decide to walk around town before going to the movies, and it feels easy and right to stroll along, hand in hand.

30.

Hank is glad to be sitting down. The skiing adventure he had this weekend left him with really sore leg muscles. It had been a while since the skiing conditions were that good, so once he got started, he didn't want to stop.

He looks around the room. All of his specialists are now paying attention. "I asked Phil to create a special presentation for us today. As you all have read Tania's paper, you know that she, along with Phil, have some real concerns about changes in the time frequency spectrum, or as Tania likes to call it, frequency patterning of younger people."

Phil tenses as he listens. He knows Hank is not behind this idea, he can hear it in his voice. Phil does not understand Hank's resistance.

"To try and have us assess their concerns, Phil and Tania have made some assumptions about the properties of these supposedly new fields, and will attempt a few of our treatments on them." Hank looks at Phil. "All yours."

Phil stands. "Based on Tania's observations, we put together a database from all the data she has gathered over the years, then, after doing an analysis on this data, selected common geometric and mathematic ratios between the frequencies in the field and compiled the results to model what we believe to be a young person field that will be a problem for us. We estimate the age of this person to be around twenty-five."

Phil's voice warms in pride. He admires Tania's intelligence and her commitment to her craft. "We then applied the analysis to a database of targets we have already dealt with as a team, and selected the common features of the youngest among them. Their average age is forty-eight years."

He turns to his computer. "I'll now run a simulation of what we normally expect to see when we apply treatments to the modeled forty-eight-year-old target."

A three-dimensional image of the target, with a modeled three-dimensional field structure, shows up in the holographic display on the table. "This model looks similar to many of the targets I have shown in the past. For completeness, let me run treatments One and Two on this field."

Phil selects the first of the two treatments. He is not showing them anything new, so he accelerates the Time Applied from twenty-four hours, to forty-eight then seventy-two hours. The field structure around the head by then is oscillating chaotically, as expected. He selects Stop in his program, selects the second treatment, and hits Run. Again, the field around the heart starts to oscillate chaotically after seventy-two hours. "I am showing you this because I want you to witness the contrast between the two fields. What you have seen is the baseline. Now let me show you what I predict will happen with the new fields from young people."

An image with a different three-dimensional field structure shows up in the holographic display. "The difference," Phil says, "was not dramatic visually, since the geometric and mathematical ratios do not show up as clearly in the three-dimensional model. I subtracted the two fields to highlight the differences. It is Tania's opinion that these structure differences correlate to higher emotional and spiritual IQs, which is a concern for us. But in order to *really* understand the differences, I will rerun the same two treatments on this new field structure."

Phil selects the first treatment option again and hits Run. The program recomputes all the interactions, and a few seconds later renders a three-dimensional image that again changes with time. "Look at how much less effective our treatments are. You can see the distortions in the fields are much weaker—the coupling of our treatments into this individual's field is much less efficient than in our previous targets. And with a strong recovery process by the individual—as I model here with a dampening factor—you can see that the three-dimensional time structure starts to recover from the treatment quickly. Obviously, everything occurs at a much faster speed in this demo, but in real life, Tania and I think the individual could recover in two to three days. Maybe less."

He waits for a few seconds for comments. After a pause, all the specialists start asking Phil questions.

Hank listens and wonders if he could be wrong. But he is not ready to concede his project to make room for this one. He will not let any project, even this one, divert possible future resources away from his Re-Imagination Project. He's been waiting long enough to restart his project, and more than ever, he is convinced the time is now.

****

I have all the parts for our secret hiding places, Bohdi texts Skylar via their encrypted link.

She replies: *Ready for Saturday. My parents are visiting a cousin and will be gone all Saturday afternoon and evening. Should be plenty of time.*

Skylar is happy that the hidden compartment in her desk is done, but it still needs the camera and cable access mounted. The fake back wall in the linen closet is a little trickier, and that is their next task. The fake panel is at the bottom of the linen closet below the last shelf. The closet shares a wall with her bedroom, so cabling access will be easy. There are just a few boxes with linens her mother stored in case of company. Skylar knows they can organize it so it looks exactly the same when anyone opens the door. Their plan is to just go for it and if her parents ever figure it out and are mad, Skylar will apologize. They both will be happy when all this is done properly and they have this technology secure.

The two of them need to thread the wires to the hidden cameras. Bohdi wishes he could use a wireless or Internet system as well, but it is not possible to install that without Skylar's parents' permission. Besides, he consoled himself, it is too easy to hack for anyone who is a professional.

They both think the idea Dr. Brown's implemented of having a camera in the secure place so you do not have to open it each time to check on the goggles is a good one. At times, it feels like their lives have become like *spy mystery or Bond* movie. They will not rest easy until they have the secure places finished.

31.

"Jean, I have a very difficult task here," Cathy says to her friend as she sits opposite her. Jean looks directly back, apprehensive because of the tone. After a pause, Cathy continues, "The specialists have diagnosed you as having something called sporadic Creutzfeldt-Jakob disease. Do you know what that is?"

"Never heard of it, but it sounds awful." She doesn't notice David's stricken expression.

"It is like mad cow disease. Maybe you remember all the news about that some time ago."

Jean looks to David, stunned, and then turns back to Cathy.

"But what does this mean for me? Are you saying my brain is going to look like a sponge? I remember seeing that on the news."

"It means that you'll start losing the functions that your brain controls, like motion, memory, speech." Cathy stops, finding it necessary to regain her composure.

"Am I going to die from this?"

Cathy takes a deep breath. Professionally, she holds back emotion before saying, "Yes. I'm afraid so, Jean."

"How much time do I have?" Jean's focus is locked on her physician.

"Maybe six months. Twelve at best."

David moves his chair closer and puts his arm around his wife. If he hadn't already done his research, he would be firing all sorts of questions at Cathy. But all these sleepless nights, running through what he's read over and over again, allowed him to somewhat come to terms with this potential outcome ahead of time. It was his hope that this would help him be able to aid Jean in the process of adjusting to the news herself, if the test results pointed to CJD.

Jean asks faintly, "How many of those months will I be able to communicate with my family and friends?"

"I don't know. It could be as much as six months."

"Six months! I only have a six months of quality life left?" Jean's voice is ragged, and the tears crowd her eyes.

David doesn't know what to say. He wants to comfort his wife, but words stick in his throat.

"Jean, we'll do all we can to keep you as well and comfortable as possible," Cathy says, her tone and expression soft. "You are a dynamic and engaged person. I can't believe it, myself. I've given this my full attention. I want it to be wrong."

Jean turns to David, wraps her arms around him, and starts to sob. Cathy apologizes and then leaves her office so they have some time alone.

****

After Celeste heard the news from her father, she called her doctor, desperate to spend time with her mother while she still could. She had miscarried her first pregnancy, and she imposed a no-flying rule on herself with this one, hoping to keep this baby safe. Her doctor allays her fears that flying might put her at risk of miscarrying again, and she is relieved knowing this isn't going to end up with her having to choose between time with her dying mother, and her unborn child. With a go-ahead from her doctor, David booked a flight for her to spend two weeks with them.

Skylar knows that sporadic CJD will probably kill her mother before the year's out. Initially, she felt numb. Over the next few days, numbness changed to anger and pain.

Witnessing the struggle her mother is facing, as well as suffering her own inner turmoil, stretches her strength to the limit. She continues to focus on her mother's health in her meditations, but she doesn't know what to do. The family encourages Jean to use every natural remedy they can get their hands on and every therapeutic approach they believe might help.

Skylar feels so helpless. Here she is a guardian of a technology that can help detect a problem, but not fix it. What use is that? Even if she quit school, what are the chances she could teach herself enough and invent a radical technology that would cure her mother in time? What use is being a guardian to this technology if it cannot even help those nearest and dearest to you?

She voices this frustration to Bohdi, glad she can talk to him about it. He says he understands what she is saying, but if they give up on the goggles, then there definitely will be no hope for the future. Skylar has to agree with him.

She walks regularly in the woods, often with Bohdi, to help ease her frustration and guilt. In spite of her best efforts to relieve tension, she begins to experience almost constant stomach pains. Her doctor suggests she change her diet, specifically that she should avoid coffee and dairy for now. This makes little difference. She knows the pain is more emotional, presenting as physical discomfort. She speaks to her dad about the pain her mother's situation is causing her, and talking about it helps both of them.

At times, Jean feels overwhelmed, angry, then depressed. Skylar and her father do their best to support Jean by listening to her thoughts about her situation. Jean struggles to fathom why this has happened to her, and to comprehend everything she has to deal with. When her mother articulates those thoughts, it resonates so closely with Skylar that she finds her initial reaction is to pull inside of herself because she does not know what to do with these intense feelings.

Skylar remembers a family a few streets over who have a dying child, maybe three or four years old, and feels grateful she, at least, has had her mother throughout the crucial periods of growing up. She remembers a student in high school who lost her father to cancer during their sophomore year and wonders how she must have dealt with that during her turbulent teenage years. She realizes that many families have struggles, some worse than her own. But knowing this still does nothing to dull her sadness.

32.

Paul looks at the secure message on his phone from Max.

We have positive identification on the person in photo with John Garrison. Name is Victor Brown. A little research on him shows that he has a PhD in plasma physics. Have not found any link to John yet beyond the photo.

Paul responds immediately: *Organize a mission on how to get inside his house to find out if there is information there that will help us.*

His phone dings again.

Okay. I will keep you posted.

33.

Skylar looks for room 603, her stomach tied in knots. She hears a voice behind her call, "Skylar? Skylar!"

She turns to see Bohdi's mother, Chandni Kearns, rushing toward her. "Oh, I'm so glad you came. Bohdi needs his best friend right now."

Ms. Kearns is shaking. Skylar wants to step back, knowing if she doesn't keep some distance she'll start shaking too. She's been chanting a peaceful mantra to herself the whole way over to the hospital to keep herself calmer. She's still trying to process what's happening to her mother—and Bohdi has a car accident.

She received a call from Ms. Kearns only an hour ago that Bohdi was being moved out of the emergency room and into critical care. The Kearns had elected to take one of the new private critical care rooms. Though she wanted to speed over there immediately, Skylar drove carefully, aware that she wasn't centered and needed the time to prepare herself for whatever might come next.

Ms. Kearns tells her the nurses are in Bohdi's room right now and need about two more minutes. "There's a waiting room just over there." She points to their left. "I have to go to the nurses' station; I'll be right back."

Skylar heads for the waiting room and stands staring out the window. Hospital visits are happening all too often, she thinks sourly. It seems like one crisis after another.

She has no details yet of this particular crisis. Ms. Kearns only told her there had been a bad car accident, Bohdi was in the hospital, and she urgently needed Skylar to come as soon as possible.

She's glad Ms. Kearns is with her. Both Bohdi's parents have always treated Skylar as one of their own. They're glad to see her when she shows up, and they always ask about how she's doing. Sometimes she enjoys the attention, and other times it makes her uncomfortable; even her own parents don't ask so many questions.

Ms. Kearns comes into the waiting area and puts a hand on Skylar's shoulder. "They might be done by now. Let's go check on Bohdi."

She follows Ms. Kearns to room 603, walking fast to keep up with her.

"Mr. Kearns is away, but is doing everything he can to fly home as soon as possible," she says, "Looks like he might be here around midnight."

They enter Bohdi's room, and Skylar stops short, thinking—hoping—they're in the wrong one. Bohdi's head is bandaged up, his face is badly swollen, and he's on a breathing machine. His left hand is bandaged. A nurse bustles around him organizing IVs and monitors.

"The doctors say Bohdi has internal bleeding"—Ms. Kearns wrings her hands—"and they're monitoring him closely. Do you know any details about the accident?"

"No, only what you told me on the phone."

Ms. Kearns tells her that a motorist driving by when Bohdi crashed stopped to call the police and gave them an eyewitness statement. He mentioned Bohdi was traveling fast, and passed him while he was going at the speed limit. During the night there had been freezing rain, so the assumption is that he hit a patch of black ice. He appeared to brake too late for a corner, lost control of the car, then skidded off the road and hit a boulder, flipping the car a few times, before ending up against a tree. The roof of the car had been pinning Bohdi down.

She mentions the police took Bohdi's phone and checked for information on recent activity. When Skylar sees an opportunity, she quickly checks her phone to make sure she hadn't received any texts or phone messages from Bohdi around the time of the accident on February 27th. She hadn't and was relieved. There was only one text message from earlier in that day, about how he felt so impatient with school and how it seemed less and less important. He wanted to spend more time on the goggles research and was frustrated with all the other obligations taking up so much of their time.

Ms. Kearns phone rings. She grabs her cell phone and walks out of the room.

Skylar steps closer to the bed and reaches for Bohdi's unbandaged right hand. She has heard that sometimes, when people are in comas, they are still aware of what's going on around them. Thinking Bohdi might know she is there, she attempts to conjure up something profound to say, but what comes out of her mouth is, "Hey, you knucklehead, you need to slow down a bit!"

She shakes her head, wondering where that thought came from, then tries to feel a response from him. Nothing. Not even a heart tug. *His body's here, but Bohdi sure isn't.* Her body visibly shakes as the emotions just start overcoming her.

After a few minutes, Skylar feels the pain subside and just stands there, her eyes glued to Bohdi, hoping for a sign of movement. Some sign of life.

"Where's his mother?" a voice asks.

The voice startles Skylar. She glances around and sees a nurse. "Uh, she stepped out to talk on her phone." The nurse leaves the room to find Ms. Kearns.

Skylar latches on to the idea of using the goggles to see what's going on with Bohdi. She's scared that she might lose him, knowing now that he's her true partner. What if he doesn't recover? She and Bohdi have access to incredible technology to witness what is happening to people's consciousness, but nothing to help fix it. Why? Clearly fixing people's situations cannot be simple, otherwise Dr. Brown and his colleague would have done it already. With her mother and now Skylar needing help, other solutions are needed. Maybe that's why the goggles came their way. But she needs Bohdi's help in this.

She hears Dr. Brown's voice in her head the evening he made them guardians, about working with the goggles in secret. But Dr. Brown also mentioned that if an opportunity presented itself to make the goggles public, then they had to weigh the risks against the rewards. Skylar is certain that bringing the goggles into the hospital does not meet those conditions, but too bad. Some risks have to be taken, and this is one of them. The goggles have not allowed her to prevent what is happening to her mother, but that won't stop her from using the technology she has at hand to try to assess what is going on inside Bohdi.

Then the thought hits her: She can keep it secret by using the goggles from Bohdi's hospital bathroom. They have already shown that using the goggles through doors and walls makes little difference. She feels the risks are worth it.

She hears Ms. Kearns approaching the room as she speaks with the nurse. Skylar sits down in the chair beside Bohdi's hospital bed and works out a plan.

****

The next day Skylar pulls up on the strap of her backpack as she walks down the hospital hallway past the nurses' station. She is nervous about what she might see.

She stops at the doorway when she sees a nurse in Bohdi's room. The nurse looks up and sees Skylar waiting. "Hi, I'll be just another minute. Come on in."

"Thanks." Skylar walks in, takes off her backpack, and puts it on the floor. "How is he doing?"

"No change since yesterday. I am almost done, then will be back in half an hour to check on his medication."

This little piece of information delights Skylar. She should be able to get everything done within that time.

The nurse finishes up and points to a chair in the corner. "You can pull that up close to him if you want."

"Thanks, I will."

As soon as the nurse is gone, Skylar heads to the bathroom, closes the door, and locks it. She hooked up all the wires except for the one from the battery pack before she came, so she can be fast in setting up.

She no sooner has the goggles on her head than she hears footsteps coming in her direction. She freezes; not because they might see her, but if it is a member of Bohdi's family, she cannot spend a half hour in the bathroom. She waits to see what happens. A few moments later, the footsteps stop, but not in Bohdi's room. Probably a visitor next door, since the nurses all have quiet shoes.

She realizes the anxiety about what she might see is getting the better of her now that she's actually here. She reaches down to her belt to turn the power supply on. Knowing she has a few moments before it is powered up, she takes slow breaths to quiet her heartbeat. She then leans against the sink so she does not bump into anything, and pulls the goggles over her head. She reaches to the side of them and turns the knob to the One setting.

She quietly counts the seconds: "one thousand one, one thousand two. . . one thousand fifteen," and then she switches the goggles to the Plus setting. Again, "one thousand one, one thousand two. . . one thousand fifteen."

She looks in Bohdi's direction and waits.

She sees barely anything, just a dim glow where she expects Bohdi to be in his hospital bed.

She focuses her eyes and sees a shape that is more like a tall, round rod, not the typical oval shape she's accustomed to. She sees none of the familiar vibrant colors that are normally around Bohdi. In fact, the few colors present are weak, so weak she has trouble telling them apart.

She hears footsteps again and listens carefully. The footsteps stop close to the room. Skylar can see an oval shape, with strong colors of red and brown. She hears a few more steps. They seem to be coming into Bohdi's room. She sees the red color balloon in shape and gain a bit of chaotic motion. *Who is this?* she wonders.

She hears more footsteps, then sees the brown color take over. There seem to be some sparks in this field. She quickly realizes she'd better make noise, otherwise it will seem creepy if she just emerges from the bathroom. She quickly switches to the One setting; then, after fifteen seconds, she flips it to the Minus setting. She reaches for the toilet and flushes it. Whoever is on the other side of the door will be startled by this sudden flush coming from the bathroom, but at least it will alert them to her presence. She waits a few seconds and turns on the sink faucet to hide the noise she makes while packing the goggles away. When she's done, she opens the door—and gets her own surprise.

"Hannah!"

"Skylar! What are you doing here?" Hannah snaps.

"I have the same question for you," Skylar says, quickly recovering from her surprise.

"I wanted to talk to Bohdi," Hannah fires back.

"You are not his girlfriend anymore. When are you going to get that message?"

Hannah's face flushes as she feels a surge of anger.".

Skylar puts her backpack down, signaling her intent to stay. She moves away from the bathroom, figuring she will give Hannah some room to leave.

Hannah no sooner turns to Skylar then a nurse walks into Bohdi's room and immediately feels the tension. She has seen Skylar every day, so she turns to Hannah and asks, "Are you family?"

"No, I am Skylar's girlfriend."

"Ex-girlfriend," Skylar shoots back.

"Any discussion is to be outside this room," the nurse says firmly. "This is a quiet zone, so you two need to leave, now."

Neither Hannah nor Skylar moves.

"Are we having trouble hearing?"

"No," they both say.

Skylar picks up her backpack and leaves, knowing that the nurse will make sure Hannah is not far behind. She figures she will go to the cafeteria, get something to eat, do some homework, and come back in a few hours. *And Hannah better not be there!*

34.

"The only item of interest we found in the Brown's home is a USB memory stick. It was in the bottom of a box with some electronic parts. Nothing related to the lost parts we are looking for," Max informs his boss over the phone.

"Okay. Anything useful on that memory stick?" Paul asks.

"We checked the few files, and one is a recent nondisclosure document between Dr. Brown and two other individuals, Skylar Donaldson and Bohdi Kearns, for a viewing device. No other details on this device. The date is relatively recent, just a little over five months ago. My initial inquiry reveals they are college kids. So, not sure where this is leading us." Max thinks again of all the memory sticks lying around his home, and realizes that he needs to clear up his own place. He hopes he can find them all.

Not surprising to Max, Paul assigns him the task of investigating who these two college kids are. Max states the obvious fact to his boss that this mission is not in crisis mode anymore, unlike some of the others they have to deal with. Paul already has every agent working overtime dealing with the other critical missions.

Max is pleased that they are college kids, because it takes the pressure off. He can tell that his boss's anxiety level over this case is starting to lower now that he has delivered this news.

35.

Skylar paces in at her home as she goes back and forth in her mind about whether she should text a note to Dr. Brown that Bohdi had been in an accident and was in the hospital in a coma, his condition very concerning. She wants to breach the no contact agreement, but decides to wait to do anything until after her visit today.

Skylar looks at her watch. *Maybe I'll wait a half hour more for traffic to die down before I head out to visit Bohdi.* She likes to visit him every day. Two days ago, she called his parents to let them know that everyone was working through midterm exams, and there were so many posts on Facebook wishing Bohdi a speedy recovery. His parents were pleased to hear that, and mentioned that, even with exams, they have bumped into a friend or two stopping by for a short visit with Bohdi.

Skylar asked them if the doctors have anything new to say about his condition and learned that his internal bleeding has stopped, so no immediate surgery is needed. She is grateful to hear that, but still wishes he would wake up.

****

Skylar enters the hospital, takes another elevator, and eventually walks down the sixth-floor hall, reading the room numbers. She stops for a minute when she reaches 603, takes a deep breath, releases it, then walks in. In just a week, Bohdi already looks much better. His face is less swollen, and there are fewer bandages on his hand.

Her inability to communicate with him and to see anything meaningful through the goggles has moved her to try her Perception Reality method. She moves the chair so it's right next to Bohdi, settles her inner equilibrium, and then lightly holds onto his hand. Immediately, wisecracks come to mind; she misses their teasing. Sternly, she tells herself, *This is not the time to let those thoughts be foremost in your mind.* She centers herself, waits. . . and is pleasantly surprised to receive a silent communication deep within.

I see you didn't bring the goggles this time. You would have seen more this time. You're right—I'm a real knucklehead. I'm so glad you're here!

Her first response is excitement, but she knows any spike in emotion can interfere with the link, so she allows it to pass through her. Bohdi's voice is clear and holds all his inflections and cheerful sarcasm, as if he was speaking aloud. *I can see how stupid I was with all my impatience, and am sorry I've causing you and my parents so much grief.*

She feels a quiet sense of joy and sends back: *I am so happy to hear from you. . . I was afraid I would lose my best friend. We need to get you back home. The most important thing here is to focus on you getting better.*

She waits, and in response hears, *This experience has given me tremendous insights. . . and I'm clear that I want to heal and get my life back. There are some important things we still have to do.*

Skylar feels her whole body relax in relief. Bohdi communicates: *I can feel your communication easily on this level, as well as my parents and all my friends. . . but you are the only one can hear me. I know that distance in space doesn't matter. If someone focuses their attention on me, no matter where they are in three-dimensional space, I receive them. I understand how time is dispersed throughout three-dimensional space in a whole new way and how we are linked to time.*

Uh-oh—I just saw an image that my parents are coming.

Skylar immediately re-centers herself in her body after that message and opens her eyes, just as Mr. and Ms. Kearns become audible in the hallway. She looks around the room to get oriented and readies herself. They walk in the door and simultaneously say, "Hi, Skylar, we're glad to see you here."

"Nice to see you both too."

"The doctors are watching for a response from Bohdi. Having you here is a real help, I'm sure," Ms. Kearns says, her round face full of worry.

"Bohdi's going to recover," Skylar declares. "I just know it."

The Kearns stop and look at her. Skylar is surprised by the strength of her own tone. She has no authority to speak with such assurance, but the experience she just had with Bohdi fills her with certainty. She hopes he'll remember this when he recovers.

"I-I can't think otherwise," Ms. Kearns says, not meeting her eyes. She moves over to Bohdi. Skylar gets up and offers her the chair she was sitting in. Mr. Kearns moves over to the other chair to put down the bag he is carrying. Skylar decides to say nothing more. She recognizes she's said enough for now and excuses herself to go home. She is too excited about what happened to be in a solemn environment. As she goes down to the ground floor in the elevator by herself, she yells out "*Yes!* He's coming back!"

36.

Skylar walks across campus to her car after a busy day at school. It is an unusually warm day for mid March. Her cell phone rings and sees it is Ms. Kearns.

She answers quickly. "Hello?"

"Skylar!" Ms. Kearns exclaims, almost out of breath. "The nurses called. Bohdi opened his eyes and is moving his feet and hands! He's responding! He's going to be okay! It's just like you told us two days ago!" Ms. Kearns starts to cry.

"That's wonderful"

Internally she says to Bohdi, *Keep up the good work! You are needed.*

"Skylar, I can't tell you how grateful Andy and I are for your support and friendship," Ms. Kearns says, her voice thick with emotion. "We feel you're part of our family. Bohdi is so blessed to have you in his life. I'm sure he's responding to you. I know in my heart, it's something you and he share. You've always been a good friend to him."

Skylar recognizes the moment in this conversation when Ms. Kearns recalls that her own family is dealing with her mother's fatal illness and wonders if this good news might make her feel bad. Right now, it doesn't. Ms. Kearns breaks the pause, "Umm, how is your mother doing?"

"Not well," she answers frankly. "Her condition is deteriorating so rapidly, we see changes every few days. It's very difficult."

"Oh, honey, I'm so sorry to hear that. I wish I could stop all this tragedy. If we can do anything to help, just ask."

"Thank you, I appreciate it. I'm just glad Bohdi is responding. That's one good thing to celebrate for now."

"Yes, it is, Skylar."

Skylar senses that Bohdi's mother doesn't know what to say next, or how to end this conversation, so she helps her. "Thanks so much for the call. It really brightens my day."

"Take care, Skylar."

"You too. I'll be over to see Bohdi right after classes."

37.

David enters the kitchen from the garage after running errands in town. He had asked Skylar to stay with her mother while he was out, and as he walks in, he trips over one of Skylar's shoes. He kicks it out of his way and grumbles. *Why does she always leave her shoes right in front of the door so we trip on them?* He heads to the dining room, where Skylar is sitting next to her mother as she sleeps in her bed. She is holding her hand, her eyes closed in meditation. David is surprised that Skylar wasn't disturbed by the clatter of the kicked shoe. He's seen Skylar spending time in meditation with her mother several times over the past two weeks as she sleeps and he knows Skylar is trying to help. David is touched by this, but at the same time, he worries about the effect Jean's illness is having on their daughter.

After fifteen minutes or so, Skylar opens her eyes. She keeps looking for a sign that she's made a clear connection with her mother and that she's responding to Skylar's attempts to help her, but it hasn't come. Skylar looks around and sees her father sitting on the living room couch.

"I heard you come in," she says tiredly, rising to join him.

"How are you doing?" David asks, as Skylar slumps into a chair.

Skylar shakes her head. "Eh, okay, I guess."

An awkward silence hangs between them; neither wants to explore this subject any further.

After a while, David asks, "How is Bohdi?"

"Much better. He is home and doing schoolwork remotely. He is doing well with the physical therapy he does every day.

"Hey, Dad, you and I need to get out for a couple of hours. Can we schedule some time?"

"Sure," her father replies in a pleased tone.

"I have to go to school this Sunday to meet some classmates, but I have Saturday off. How about then?"

Skylar knew before asking that Saturday would be the best option. Last week, her father arranged for a home health aide to come in two days a week for eight hours, since her mother's condition has deteriorated to the point where she needs constant care. David has taken a leave of absence from work to care for her most of the time.

She can no longer get out of bed or go to the bathroom alone. David now sleeps on the sofa, while his wife sleeps on a rented hospital bed in the dining room. Whenever he is in another room, he carries the receiver for a baby monitor he'd set up next to her bed. Skylar helps her father by filling in some afternoons when she's not in school so her father can get out for a few hours. This helps, but David needs regular time he can count on. He has it now, thanks to Sandy Brooks, the hospice volunteer who started last Saturday.

David spent the first morning with Sandy, showing her where things are in the house and Jean's preferences. He informed Sandy that they'd stopped giving her showers just two weeks ago because it was too difficult for them to get her up the stairs and back down again. Sponge baths in bed are now the only option.

David's response to Skylar's questions snaps her out of her thoughts. "How about we go kayaking?" he suggests. "Sandy will be here at 10:00, then I should be free to go."

"Okay, that sounds good."

****

On Saturday morning, David tells his daughter, "We'd better dress warmly, because the water's very cold, and if the wind's blowing, we'll be chilled very quickly. It is a bit early in the season to be out kayaking on the water, but I really need some fresh air."

They spent the forty-five-minute car ride to the boat launch talking about Jean, the difficulty of responding to such rapid changes in her physical condition, and the inevitability of her death. It now seems unlikely she'll make it to the projected six months, and even if she does, her quality of life is already awful, and will only get worse. David expects she will likely slip into a coma within the next two months because of the decline in her neural functioning. He mentions how he is happy that Celeste is coming back for another visit next week. She is due in a month and during a time like this he wishes more than ever that she lived closer.

Once out of the car, they agree to talk about other things. They bring the kayaks to the lake's edge. The sky is overcast with a light breeze. Skylar is glad they came prepared, because even though the breeze is light, it makes the air temperature chilly.

"Dad, is this the area you kayak with your friend Bill?"

"No. We usually like to go to the Green River. It's closer to home, so it is more convenient. But the river is likely to get us wet, so it's worth the extra half hour to come to the lake when the temperatures are still on the low side."

They set up the kayaks, and within a few minutes, push off from shore. Skylar stares at the lake bottom, watching herself move over the rocks visible a few feet below the surface. The trees sway gently in the wind. It all seems surreal and tranquil to Skylar. She feels separate from the world, more like a spectator than a participant.

"It's odd how we have such a relative sense of motion," she says. "Maybe it's necessary for life."

David perks up, glad to have something new to talk about, and shares some ideas he purposely explored recently, hoping to keep the lines of communication open with his daughter. "If you think about it, a person at the equator is spinning around Earth's axis at a thousand miles per hour, Earth orbits the Sun at sixty-seven thousand miles per hour, and our solar system rotates around the galactic center at just over half a million miles per hour. The galaxy is moving as well, at over a million miles per hour in *another* direction. And yet, all we are aware of is the slow drifting on the surface of this lake."

"Thankfully, we're oblivious to all this motion." Skylar is still watching the kayak's slow motion over the shallow lake bottom while listening to her father. She adds, "We could not survive if we were not."

David, happy that Skylar is listening, continues, "Even the word *universe* reflects it, derived from the Latin words *unus*, for one, and *versus*, to rotate. The foundation of the universe is rotation. It seems the whole universe is spinning, both on a macro and micro level. If you look at this water, these trees, and even inside our own physical bodies, there are particles spinning at extremely rapid rates. In the physical world, the idea of something *not* moving seems impossible— everything is in motion all the time. Even our eyes are in constant motion, in order to perceive the world around us. The only stillness in our lives comes when the motion, relative to something else in motion, is the same."

"I didn't know that Dad. Our eyes are in constant motion, huh." Skylar now understands what she admires in Bohdi. He is a lot like her father and her father always managed to make her feel smart and more emotionally tranquil. She also feels the same curiosity about the world around her that her father expressed all these years. It is why she chose to become a physicist.

They drift for a while, then David is ready to paddle faster, so he says, "C'mon, let's speed up." As they focus on their paddling, they fall into a silence for an hour, just listening to the sounds on the water. David slows down after a while and restarts the conversation. "There's an interesting relationship between spin and our definition of time. We take the length of time it takes for Earth to spin once around its axis, and we call it a day. We take the length it takes Earth to revolve around the Sun, and call it a year. Our concept of time is related to spin. But I think spin matters in much more significant ways. What interests me is the idea that time and rotation, or spin, are divided up by numbers relating to base twelve."

"Huh?" Skylar stops paddling, surprise at this sudden shift into a discussion about time coming from her father. He has her attention.

David continues. "A day is divided up by two times twelve, or twenty-four hours. The hour is divided five times twelve, or sixty minutes, and again with the minute, using five times twelve to get seconds. We break the year into twelve months. We also measure one rotation with twelve times thirty, or three hundred sixty degrees. It seems that twelve has real significance to us, since it's used to define our relative measurements of time and spin.

"Of course, this is also true for the fundamental measurement of distance, twelve inches to a foot. A yard is twelve multiplied by three. Grocers sell items by the dozen. A form of this twelve basis system dates back thousands of years. The Sumerians and Babylonians used a base-sixty number system, so they could account for the minutes, seconds, and angles in a circle. Pythagoras had a great affinity for the number twelve, ascribing it to the universe. The Egyptians predate this use of twelve as a basis for a numbering system."

"Why did they choose twelve, and not some other value? The metric system of base ten seems so much easier to keep track of," Skylar interjects.

"I believe there's a philosophical reason. Twelve has included in it the factors of one, two, three, four, and six. Many cultures believe one represents unity, the spirit, or God. Two represents duality, which is our physical reality. Up and down, left and right, hot and cold, love and hate, positive and negative, and so on. The number twelve has both one and two in it, which is one reason why Pythagoras chose it to represent our universe. Three, or the trinity, has all sorts of meanings in mythology, spirituality, and music. In music, the tonal ratios of three-to-two and three-to-one create harmonies that are pleasing to the human ear, and, I suppose, the heart. Three represents the triangle in geometry. It's a number representing creativity. Four is associated with the elements: Fire, Water, Air, and Earth. It represents the square or rectangle in geometry and so represents structure, stability. Six shows up often in nature, as in the six axes of snowflakes and in crystalline structure. All of these are part of twelve."

"That is so interesting. I have to share that with Bohdi. Dad, maybe you forgot, but Dr. Brown believes that the different matter we see with those goggles is in three-dimensional time. Seems that maybe it also has to do with spin as well."

"I had forgotten about that. That is something that will be very difficult to prove, if not impossible."

"Yes, agreed," Skylar says with a sigh. "But there is still so much to learn. Maybe the math of three-dimensional time might allow more insight into how it impacts matter in our three-dimensional space. I wonder how the equations in physics, or electrodynamics, are impacted by three-dimensional time?"

"Something to look into." David feels a sense of pride in who his daughter has become. He hoped to instill in her a curiosity about the world around her and he has witnessed in her a remarkable ability to ask the right questions and follow them up with her own style of investigation.

"Speaking of time, I think it's time to turn around. It'll take about an hour and a half to get back to the car from here," David says as he steers his kayak toward the opposite side of the lake. Skylar follows him, lost in her thoughts about time, and spin.

"Your grandfather and I used to come down to this part of the lake to fish. That was one of our spots," he says, pointing to a massive willow tree he and his father had sat under while fishing so many years ago. "You've already heard my fishing stories with my father. There were some peaceful times spent under that willow tree."

They spend the paddle back oscillating between quiet and small talk.

"There's the boat launch," David says as they come around the bend.

Once the kayaks are tied down on the roof rack, David turns to Skylar. "You hungry?"

"Absolutely."

"Then let's get something to eat on the way home. We'll get back just in time to relieve Sandy. I'm happy we got out today, Skylar. I needed some time with you."

"Me too, Dad. I needed it in a bad way, as well."

38.

"Who's that?" Bohdi yells as he bolts upright from a deep sleep, dazed. He tries to correlate the reality of the large, penetrating eyes he just witnessed a second ago. They are still visible, as if burned into his retinas for a short period. He peers around his room, lit by only his alarm clock, trying to clear up the confusion.

His digital clock shows 12:12 a.m.

He flops back on his pillows, heart racing. *What a dream! It was so real. Those eyes. Who do they belong to?*

It can't be a side effect of the medication. I stopped taking it a week ago. He wonders about the effect of the coma he was in. Since that accident he feels like a whole universe has opened up inside his mind. He is using all this time he has of staying physically still to investigate this new landscape in his mind. But what does that have to do with these eyes. He does not know.

39.

After his phone call with Edward Stagmier earlier this morning, Jack feels confident that there was just cause to fire Professor Henry Albates, and that his decision will stand up to any legal challenges. He was mildly concerned about the blistering conversation with members of the liberal arts faculty over this issue in a meeting two days ago, but then, yesterday, he felt vindicated after four professors from the business school told him he'd done the right thing in getting rid of faculty that cannot deal with the new way a university is being run. Jack realizes he needs to control the message around his controversial action.

As soon as Edward had hung up with Jack, he called a colleague at the Chronos Consortium and expressed his concern about Jack being too impatient. If not handled appropriately, he could create problems for this Chronos Consortium program. Edward wants to pull together a few people who can help contain any collateral damage that Jack might create with his impulsive action. First task is to release a news story that keeps a positive light on the changes at Patterson University.

Toward the end of the day, Jack's phone rings again. This time it is Mike Halden, owner of six local media outlets. He asks Jack to make some time in his busy schedule for an interview with his best business bureau news reporter, Jerry Chambers. Jerry will ask Jack about his strategic plan and the changes being made at Patterson University, including the firing of Albates. Jack is pleased to hear this, and impressed by how efficient Edward is that he could organize this so quickly. He wonders exactly who is part of the organization. Clearly, they are powerful people, since no matter what sector of the business world he needs help with, there's always someone available.

****

Earlier that day, longtime newspaper editor Foster Braklee received a call from his boss, Mike Halden, the owner of the paper Foster works for. Mike stated that he wanted Jerry Chambers to cover this assignment. Mike said he thought Jerry's previous work was excellent, and felt that this was a chance for the paper to get a good local story on what was happening at the university.

Foster agreed that Jerry was a good reporter, but in this case, he had somebody else in mind. He explained that Jerry needs to be kept in check. Recently his one-sided approach to stories has concerned Foster. He also feels Jerry has become too politically opinionated to be impartial. Foster half joked that Jerry would make a better opinion writer than reporter. If Jerry wants to continue to write strong opinions instead of stories, there are opinion pages in their newspaper that can use his content.

"Foster," the voice at the other end of the line said sternly, "I like the way Jerry does his job. I'm not trying to tell you how to run the paper, but I *strongly* suggest you consider Jerry for this assignment. This will be a very good story for us, given what's going on and how close to home it is."

Foster decided he'd better end the conversation before saying anything he might regret. "I hear what you're saying, Mike," he said cautiously, "and yes, Jerry has been a good reporter. I'm just not sure he's the best one for this assignment. I *will* consider Jerry and one other reporter as candidates, and make my decision based on their qualifications."

Both hang up, unhappy with the way the conversation went. But Foster is firm in his mind. He got into this business to report facts, and that's what he will do. . . until he is no longer allowed to.

40.

Professor Suzanne Bradley is furious when she hears that the university fired her colleague, Professor Henry Albates. They recently worked together writing articles and organizing a protest over the direction of the university. She admires his dedication to good governance both locally and nationally, as do many students.

She immediately calls Henry's cell phone, but only gets his voicemail. She leaves a brief message about how sorry she is to hear the news and asks him to call her. She wants to tell him to fight it, but knows it is unnecessary; she knows Henry well enough to know he'll fight. Suzanne is worried about him. Henry has a father who is in and out of the hospital with problems related to his lungs and kidneys. Henry's mother passed away three years before, so his father now lives with Henry's family. These burdens have hardened Henry's resolve to keep fighting for his time-consuming passion of good governance.

Suzanne wonders if his family and political issues have caused Henry to neglect some of his professional duties. He taught in the Government and Justice Department. She understands the conflict between responsibilities, but Suzanne and her husband have regular, and sometimes contentious, discussions about priorities and which risk might bring in the most productive result in their struggle to balance the needs of one of their children, who due to a physical challenge requires constant physical therapy, and their professional obligations. She thinks she can help Henry, if he is willing to listen. She knows him well enough to understand that he considers his political activities part of his job as professor of this department. He practices what he preaches. She is sure many students and faculty see it this way, but obviously there are others who do not. The politics really frustrates her at times.

****

Joe Glasstone texts Skylar: *Patterson fired Professor Albates! That really sucks!* Joe took two of Professor Albates's courses as electives and really enjoyed the classes and material. He admires this professor's outspoken call to action to hold the university administration accountable for their conflicting interests.

Joe knows Skylar will share his anger. He wants to do something about it and hopes that the students he knows will feel enough outrage that there could be a student protest, and he wants to be part of organizing it.

Skylar feels her phone vibrate. She is in her Thermodynamics class, and the professor is writing an equation on the board, so, very quickly, she slips the phone out of her pocket, reads the message, and looks up to see the professor turning around. The professor does not see Skylar reading her text, and she discreetly slips the phone back into her pocket. She cannot believe what she just read.

She wants to focus on a reply instead of class, but with discipline, she keeps her attention on the material the professor is presenting. After class, she finally gets the chance to reply, sharing her outrage and her support for a protest. She is just about to send it when she feels an internal resistance to pressing the Send button. Her gut is in a knot. She puts her phone back into her pocket and heads to her next class. Throughout the next class, her phone vibrates repeatedly, but she does not check it. She needs time to think.

Bohdi has been out of the hospital for two weeks, but is under strict instructions to take it easy. He is catching up on some of his missed schoolwork from home for now. Skylar does not want him to be upset about what's happening at Patterson, so she decides not to text him about the Professor Albates dilemma, but she suspects he will probably see it on Facebook. She stops by his house every day to see how he is doing and drop off class notes from friends and pick up completed assignments. There is no way he can sit quietly for a whole day. His facial swelling is gone, and he has a light bandage covering the stitches on the left side of his head. His left pinkie finger and ring finger are still bandaged and taped to a metal splint to prevent him from moving them. His surgeon said she was happy with how the operation to fix the bones in his left fingers went, but Bohdi has to keep them immobile.

Skylar receives a text from Bohdi, asking whether she has heard about Professor Albates. Skylar texts back a short note: *Aren't you supposed to be relaxing?*

She quickly gets a reply: *Who are you, my mother?* with a smiley face.

She laughs. He will be on his feet quicker than either his parents or the doctors expect.

As the day progresses, she finds herself rethinking what she's able to do. *I'd love to help organize a protest, but I'm barely keeping up with all that's going on in my own life.* Then a new thought occurs to her: *Maybe I can help outline an editorial that Amelia Harding could write? She's an excellent writer and very politically involved. I can drop by Bohdi's and keep him involved.*

She sends off a text to Amelia, Joe, and Bohdi, suggesting the idea.

Her phone dings a moment later with a text from Amelia: *Already working on a story. Let's talk.*

41.

Bohdi is back at school to complete the last month of the semester on campus. He wears a hat to cover the short hair around his scar on his head and still has the splint on his left fingers. He carefully monitors his activity level, but feels stronger every day. He asked Skylar to join him in an office visit he scheduled with Dr. Bradley to pick up more papers she had found for him.

As Dr. Bradley, Bohdi and Skylar walk to her office in the psychology department, she asks, "Have you had a chance to read the papers I gave you?"

"We both did," he replies as they enter her small office, which has barely enough room for a desk, a table, three chairs, and floor-to-ceiling bookshelves along one wall. A large window looks out to the lawn in front of the student union, and allows plenty of natural light into the room, making it a bright, pleasant place despite how cramped it is.

Skylar and Bohdi sit in the two chairs to the left side of her desk, as Dr. Bradley sits down in her desk chair.

"Thanks for taking the time to see us," Bohdi says. "We want to discuss perception and time, specifically the experiments relating to remote perception that you discussed in class."

"Precognitive remote perception," she says with a smile as she puts her pocketbook away," does raise some interesting questions. The idea that some people can see events happening in the future challenges our cherished ideas of free will and destiny".

Skylar thinks that if they were ever to raise the subject of the goggles with somebody, Dr. Bradley would be a good person. Bohdi wanted Skylar to meet Dr. Bradley again with the hope that Dr. Bradley might be someone they could reach out to. Skylar has a positive gut feeling about her. But today the goal is just to discuss the implications of these papers.

"I have no problem with remote perception," Bohdi replies. "But I wonder if the accuracy of remote perception is due to the fact the targets in the experiment already have a predefined plan to go to a particular place. They do not know it consciously yet, but all their past potentials are leading them to this place. Therefore, the people doing the remote vision can pick up these potentials and determine which future potentials are most likely to unfold. But that means a lot of what we do is predetermined by past actions, instead of present free will, if the people doing the remote vision can see what is going to happen days ahead of time that we have made no conscious decision on yet."

"Good point. How much of the future is free will, and how much is predetermined? I've asked this question myself, and still lack a clear answer," Dr. Bradley states as she looks at Skylar.

Skylar jumps in, "I know people could also tune into the probability that a person would end up at a museum or café, or whatever, based on their personal interests. It's not hard for me to predict where some of my friends might go in an unfamiliar city. It seems their perception is the summation of personal preferences leading to certain types of places being visited, and the potential of those places being available in that city. But what if the person was going to a café, which we knew they would likely do, and along the way they saw an amazing building, or artwork, or a park, and it pulls them away from their norm?

"What if all these situations are potentials? Then there's no situation that doesn't have *some* probability, even if it's very, very small," Skylar continues, "so it could be that a person doing the remote sensing is just tuning into the probabilities that are most likely because they might have the highest intensity of being detected remotely."

Dr. Bradley is thrilled with the direction the conversation taking. She was just about to respond when Skylar, enthusiasm bubbling over, carries on.

"What if someone had a technique that would allow a person to go into a mental state and perceive what could be called another reality, say, extra dimensions of time? All these probabilities could be read in time. In these dimensions of time, what we think and feel are real structures, like our brains and hearts are in three-dimensional space. It would mean that what we think and feel not only matters, but is matter in other dimensions of time. For instance, this individual might perceive a person represented as an oval field with various colors in specific places, where some of the colors are unique to a particular person and others are common to larger groups of people in these new dimensions of time."

Skylar wonders if in her enthusiasm she said too much and waits for a response from Dr. Bradley. A short silence breaks the conversation.

Dr. Bradley asks, "You think that emotions and thoughts are related to time. How?"

Bohdi decides to attempt to answer her question, "Skylar and I have learned that if you take a regular image of a person and apply a Fourier transform to it, the transformed image is nothing we recognize, but both representations have the same information, just in a different form. It's like your analogy about memory. You can have the same information, one in a particle form, which we relate to and is local, and another in a wave form, the distributed or nonlocal form. But for humans, what if the particle form is our physical body and the wave form is our human consciousness… one we identify in space and the other, which we cannot see, correlates to time?"

Dr. Bradley shuffles in her seat as she considers what Skylar and Bohdi are saying.

She is intrigued. "Just to clarify what you are both trying to say, you speculate that human consciousness is real in other dimensions of time?"

Skylar hesitates. She almost blurted out *Well, not me, but someone we know,* but she lets it go and replies, "Yes." Then: "What if there was a technique that takes the information of our thoughts and emotions inside us in this familiar three-dimensional space, and transforms it into real structures in three-dimensional time?"

Dr. Bradley's eyebrows arch. "You think that a mathematical transform of our human consciousness might be real in other dimensions of time?"

"Yes, that is what we think."

Bohdi then relates the discussion he had with his mother about how time was distributed everywhere in space. That idea triggered him to ask people where they are in their body. Bohdi found that people pointed mainly to their chest, some to their head and others had no idea. But what is clear, people do not point to an exact spot. So, human consciousness could be said to be everywhere in our bodies and maybe beyond, as well, just like time is everywhere in space. We certainly live *in* time and *in* space. Our *location* in space is easily defined, but our *location* in time is not. We can only describe ourselves to the passing of a measurement of time. But if time has extra dimensions, there can be locations in time, as well."

"Interesting. I never thought of it in quite that way, so in this speculative model of yours," she says looking at both of these two young people in her office, "in other dimensions of time our thoughts and feelings have real shapes. But in three-dimensional space, where time has only one dimension, and is everywhere, our thoughts and emotions are dispersed, so they are more difficult to be described and located."

"Absolutely!" Skylar says with more enthusiasm than she meant to. She quickly collects herself and continues, "Bohdi and I think of thoughts and emotions as Time Information Fields, which are dispersed in three-dimensional space. For instance, all the people living in a certain area, through their thoughts and emotions, would create a certain Time Information Field of human consciousness in that area. That Time Information Field would be described as the local culture of people living in that area. If people are drawn to an area for its cultural aspects, I would consider that to be more of a time phenomenon. If they're drawn because of its scenery, that would be more of a space phenomenon."

"Well, I think the two of you might be on to something with this idea about a relationship between human consciousness and time. Maybe you two should write a paper."

There is a pause in the conversation. Dr. Bradley senses their hesitation and decides to break the pause. "Bohdi and Skylar, I'd love to continue, but I have a commitment and need to leave in a few minutes. Write all of your ideas down?"

Skylar replies, "We are."

Dr. Bradley quickly follows up, "Good, I enjoyed this conversation. Call me when you're ready for a follow-up discussion. Hopefully next time you both can share some of the ideas you have written down". Dr. Bradley has no way of knowing how committed the two students who have visited her today are to what they are doing.

"Okay, we'll do that," Skylar replies.

"Thank you", Bohdi follows up with.

Skylar realizes that it's very unusual to be able to communicate with a professor like Dr. Bradley and as much as she would like to open up to her, the goggles have to stay a secret until both she and Bohdi have decided it is time.

42.

As Paul enters his office, Agent Max is already sitting in a chair opposite his desk. Paul closes the door and sits down.

Max begins right away, since they have little time. "I will start with Skylar Donaldson. She completed two years at Adams University and she is now enrolled in Patterson University. Her father, David, is an electrical engineer who does research at Aldran Scientific Instruments. Bohdi Kearns, her friend, is getting an undergraduate degree in Psychology at the same university as Skylar, Patterson. Seems he had the intention of getting a degree in Physics as well, but changed that to Psychology after two years in college. They both appear quite technical as well since we found her name on several blogs related to physics and his name on a number of blogs related to electronics.

"I have details in this report on the financial states of these people and other family members. There is nothing in their history that alerts me. The only unusual bit of information we discovered is that Skylar's mother is suffering from a fatal illness. Seems she will not be here long."

Paul immediately speaks up. "Everyone you mentioned has a technical degree or technical background. And Dr. Brown has a degree in physics, as well. Now, not unusual that people of science interface with others who are also scientists and engineers. But it makes me a bit suspicious, and downright uncomfortable."

Max adds, "I checked with people we know at Patterson University, and we could not find any project that Skylar and Bohdi are involved in, either under a professor or as an individual project. I was hoping to find something relating to a *detection device*." Max stops for a minute, then continues, "I wonder why there were not more details on the agreement? Seems odd."

"I just have to take the next step," Paul says firmly. "I cannot afford to leave any clue uncovered, and you have given me enough justification to send someone to scope out the properties of the families Kearns and Donaldson. But I have to be patient. The evidence is weak, and I cannot pull anyone from other projects.

"Okay, thanks, Max. I think we are near the end of this trail. It feels good to finally know where those parts went. I would have loved to nail that Garrison."

Max makes no comment. Paul suffered the most collateral damage from those lost scanner parts, and unfairly, in his eyes.

43.

Stanley Polanski, the reporter chosen by his boss, Foster Braklee, to cover the Patterson University developments for their newspaper, drives over to the president's building on this day in early May. The sky is overcast but the meteorologist promised sunshine later. Stanley hopes the sun will come out by lunchtime so he can eat outside.

He walks through the president's open door and sees Dr. Duncan's secretary busy at her desk. As he approaches, she looks up and smiles. "Oh, Mr. Polanski, Dr. Duncan will be with you in a few minutes." Her tone is businesslike. Stanley read that everyone calls the university president by his first name, Jack. He likes the informality, but for a first-time visitor, it is Dr. Duncan.

Stanley sits in one of the chairs opposite the secretary. Through his research, he learned her name is Jennifer Marchen. She has been employed by the university for twenty-six years, the last ten as assistant to the president. Stanley notes that her desk is organized, with many piles of papers stacked across it. He gets the idea she could find anything anyone asked for in seconds.

I wish I could do that. I haven't seen the surface of my desk in years! He chuckles to himself.

As he waits for the university president to appear, he reflects on the articles and other documentation he's been able to dig up about Dr. Duncan, including those published in the student newspaper. He's particularly impressed by a recent article written by a student named Amelia Harding, titled, "Who's Running the Show?" The young woman reported on the excessive influence of corporations in government and education. She discussed how lobbyists, associated with banking and finance, have not only influenced lawmakers by supporting their elections with major contributions, but also, the lobbyists arranged to have their very own wording inserted into the legislation backed by key lawmakers. In one finance bill, for example, two paragraphs of the bill were copied word for word from the lobbyists' "suggestions." The lawmakers supporting the legislation had twice the support from financial institutions as those who opposed it. She argued that, in a democracy, tension and conflict between business and government is healthy and, like grit producing the pearl in an oyster, society benefits from both working together to present the best ideas. But this critical dialogue isn't happening, she continued, and hasn't happened with transparency for decades. She wrote that in the same way the lawmakers are influenced, professors are putting their names and reputations behind papers, supporting outcomes favorable to corporations.

Amelia Harding recommended the establishment of an unbiased oversight committee to ensure that any conflict of interest is vetted. Stanley is impressed with the perspective and knowledge of this college student, and dropped the article on his boss's desk this morning, saying, "Here's a future reporter." Stanley's other sources of information come from searches in the local public library and the university's library. He's already put together a list of probing questions he plans to ask "Jack."

"Stanley, welcome." He looks up to see President Duncan standing there with a large smile, extending a hand.

They walk into Duncan's office, and Stanley is immediately impressed—just as he's supposed to be. There's no need for him to say anything; Jack has already read the look on his face.

Stanley likes to see fine architecture, and this office is a wonderful example; but he's not swayed that easily, surely not enough to affect his job as a reporter.

****

An hour later, the door to Jack's office opens, and Jack and Stanley walk out to Jennifer's desk. Jack says pleasantly, "Jennifer, can you point Stanley to his next appointment? When he's finished, he would like to arrange a wrap-up interview with me at the end of the day, so what do I have available?"

As she taps the commands into her computer keyboard, Jennifer thinks, *Hmmm, the interview probably didn't go the way Jack wanted.* She's a good reader of emotional states, and as much as Jack thinks he's hard to read, Jennifer can easily tell when things are going well and when they aren't. Stanley looks the same as when he went in, friendly and disheveled.

She checks Jack's schedule and says there's a slot available at 5:00. Jack nods and lies to Stanley. "I have to leave by 5:30, so I can't give you more than thirty minutes, Stanley. That okay?"

"That'll work."

Jennifer looks at Stanley and smiles. "Whom do you plan to interview next?"

"I actually have a pretty full day," he says happily. He has a list of eight names, but just gives her one. He will work things out on his own from there. No need to give out too much information, he thinks.

"Do you need help getting there?"

"Definitely. I have a map of the university and an address, but any help is greatly appreciated."

As she gives him directions, he jots down the recommendations. Before he flips his notebook shut, he asks, "Oh, one last thing. Where do you recommend I get lunch? I'd love to eat under one of the trees in the quadrangle."

"Oh, *The Jolt* is a good place for sandwiches and salads, and they have great coffee."

"Thanks. Sounds perfect." He heads off for a day filled with questions—and hopefully some answers.

****

A few days later, after reading the newspaper article, Jack can barely contain his fury. "If that's what Mike thinks is *a reporter* who can protect the best interests of the university, he is crazy!"

Jack thinks Stanley's write-up in the local paper wasted far too much copy presenting conflicting viewpoints—and the case Dr. Duncan made that Professor Albates neglected his responsibilities as a member of this university is nowhere near as clear as he presented it to Stanley. He knows people reading the article will get the impression that the university might be losing its vision, a reaction completely *opposite* of the one Jack has been trying to create.

It doesn't help that the day before, the university paper, *The Beat*, published a scathing article written by a student about the loss of academic integrity in the research being funded by Chemtech, discussing how the president of the university helped contribute to the loss of this integrity. The article listed several of Patterson University research programs in which researchers from other academic institutions have been questioned about their apparently biased conclusions toward Chemtech's interests. The article went on to list the professors at Patterson who challenged the lack of integrity, and Henry Albates was presented as the most vocal of this group. The article ended by asking whether Professor Albates's outspokenness might well be the real issue behind him being fired from his position.

Jack paces alongside his conference table. *This is a huge risk for me. Where the hell are all the people who said they would cover my back?* He fights back an impending dizziness, caused by the realization he doesn't have control of this situation. A rare panic attack overcomes him as he focuses on his complete lack of control.

He stops to lean against the conference table. He can't let anyone see him in this state. He's having trouble marshaling his thoughts and feelings. Situations like this open a valve inside him, and each time, the panic comes out with more force than the time before. *I can't go home right now and have Mary or the kids see me like this. What will they think? I need to make an excuse and go for a run. That always seems to help.*

44.

"Celeste, I'm so happy for you both!" David's heart fills with love for his oldest daughter as he hears her good news. He is grateful that she had time to recover from her trip back home for a week before she went into labor.

"Thanks, Dad. She's just beautiful. Dan and I decided to name her Regina Jean. We wanted her to have Mom's name as her middle name. Don't they sound nice together?" Celeste doesn't wait for her father's reply. "I can't wait for you to see her! As soon as we have things settled a bit, Dan and I will bring Regina to see you and Mom for a week or two."

"Terrific, Celeste. Do you want to speak to your mother? She's. . . having one of her better days." He's telling a white lie, but hopes this news might change the day for Jean.

"Can she deal with talking on the phone?"

"I'll put it on speaker, and we'll give it a shot. Give me a moment to go to her bed." He crosses to the corner of the dining room, where his wife lies. "Jean, it's Celeste on the phone!"

She looks at him blankly.

Just then Skylar comes in with her phone after having texted Dan to send her a picture of Celeste with Regina. She walks up to her mother. Jean switches her focus from David to Skylar. David can tell it's taking everything she has to process what they're trying to communicate to her. "Mom, here's a picture of Celeste with her new baby girl," Skylar says gently as she holds her phone out to her mother.

Jean looks at the picture, struggling to speak. Skylar thinks she hears something like *baby.* "Yes, it's a baby. It's Celeste's baby. You're a grandmother. Congratulations!"

Jean is quiet. Then she looks up at David and smiles.

"Celeste, Mom is smiling; she recognizes she's a grandmother!" Skylar says, hoping to make this a special moment for her sister.

Celeste says loudly, "Hi, Mom, it's me, Celeste. You're a grandmother now. Your granddaughter's name is Regina Jean."

Jean looks at the picture again. She looks back up at David, but this time in confusion. David has no idea what part she understands and what part she doesn't. "Celeste is a mother, and you're a grandmother," he repeats to her.

She turns back to Skylar, who puts the image on her phone screen back in front of her. Jean looks for a few seconds and then looks up at the wall. She continues to stare at the wall afterward.

"I think that's all the good news your mom can process for the moment," David tells Celeste. He motions to Skylar to take his phone and continue talking to Celeste while he takes care of Jean.

Skylar puts her phone in her pocket and takes her father's phone. She walks to the staircase, finishing the conversation with Celeste, hoping to ease the pain she thinks her sister must feel in this moment. She desperately doesn't want her sister to break down on her because she's not getting the response from her mother that she needs on such a special day. She's relieved when Celeste continues to talk about the baby, what she looks like, their dreams for her. She responds with short *uh-hums*, trying to imagine a new parent's feelings. Skylar listens patiently to her sister, then says, "You'll make great parents, I just know it. After all, you had Mom and Dad as role models."

Celeste tells Skylar she'll call back because a nurse just walked into the room and she needs to talk to her.

As soon as Skylar replies, "No problem," the line goes dead.

Skylar texts Bohdi to tell him the news, then goes to see whether her father needs help.

45.

Hank walks into his office and slams the door behind him. He is frustrated at the slow pace of change in this organization. He flops into his desk chair, exhausted from nonstop twelve-hour days. He has spent more than a year trying to get the funding to take his Re-Imagination Project to the next level. The top manager of the organization will not allow him to take any of his specialists away from the current workload, which all seem to be either in crisis mode or have critical status. The organization is hiring, but it takes years to bring a person up to the level of Hank's specialists, and the organization is having problems with higher-than-normal attrition rates. People are leaving, and in their exit interviews talking about burnout resulting from the workload.

He leans back and closes his eyes for a few minutes, working to slow the franticness he feels inside. As he slows down his tempo, he feels hunger starting to take over his body. The thought of food lifts his spirit. He slowly opens his eyes and looks over at the small refrigerator in the corner of his office. He takes another minute to summon up the energy to drag his exhausted body out of the chair and see what there might be in his refrigerator. He spots half a sandwich on the top shelf, left over from yesterday's lunch, which still looks edible, and a ginger ale in the door. Perfect. It is a cool day in early July. He opens his office window to let some of the summer breeze in.

Hank sits and eats in silence. As some energy comes back, his mind switches to his Re-Imagination Project. He leans over to his right and opens the bottom drawer of his desk and pulls out a green folder with papers neatly enclosed inside.

He picks up the paper labeled "Results of Idea Induction into Medium Groups of Fifty or More People" and feels pride start to replace exhaustion.

It was nearly two years ago that Hank wondered if it was possible to take the technology the Chronos Consortium uses to influence individuals and modify it to target larger audiences. The limitation of the current technology is that it requires specific frequency spectrum information about that particular individual target to maximize the effects. If the frequency spectrum is too broad because too many people's fields are included, the effectiveness drops dramatically. This is why the Chronos Consortium has to continuously put specialists into challenging situations to get the frequency of that individual isolated from everyone around them.

Hank has read the previous work done by other research groups within the Chronos Consortium, which demonstrates that when a broad frequency spectrum is applied to a group of fifty or more people, the emotional bias results they hope for from the group become only a little better than chance—an unacceptable situation for the Chronos Consortium. In spite of the poor initial results, Hank knows that if they are ever to get out from under their current workload, the Chronos Consortium needs a radically new approach.

The Chronos Consortium has branches in media, and they demonstrated to Hank's satisfaction that tailored messages to targeted groups works. The same message repeated over and over becomes the group's new truth. But this technique takes too much time in a fast-moving world.

Almost nine months ago, this July, Hank organized a few lunches with one of the older retired specialists, Jim Stewart. Jim spent the last five years traveling with his wife, visiting many of the places on their bucket list and seeing all the friends and relatives that they could. To fill his time at home, Jim also fixed, updated, and improved everything that could be done on their house. He was starting to get on his wife's nerves with his constant fixing. In addition, Jim found that he was bored, so he reached out to ex-colleagues about doing some part-time work on a project here and there. Hank heard of this and immediately contacted Jim, who has the technical expertise Hank needs. He offered Jim a deal to work as an independent, giving him more control over his schedule, which was an important aspect of the negotiations for Jim.

Jim was happy for a chance to be part of the technology group again. He knew the Chronos Consortium's technology well and was highly regarded and well-liked by the technicians in the Time Frequency Lab. Hank's relationship with these technicians was at best cordial, and some days spilled over into frustrated exchanges. Jim knew Hank well, his strengths and his weaknesses, and figured Hank needed him to make this project of his work. He leveraged this knowledge to bargain with Hank.

After Jim set up his limited liability company and all the nondisclosure documents were signed, Hank detailed his Re-

Imagination vision to him. The project's technical objective is to modify the current field generator technology by optimizing the number of frequencies to be broad enough to influence the thinking of a group of people, the size on the order of hundreds, possibly even thousands. The overall objective, Hank told him, is to get these people to react to a particular idea or policy. Jim asked why not get them to support instead of react to an idea or policy? Hank told him this was one of the points he felt would cause the experiments to succeed where the others have failed. The key part of the new bias treatment, using the modified broad frequency range, is to prime this group with a generalized frustration, predisposing them to *amygdala hijacking*; then, when this priming is accomplished, seed them with an idea. The seed message would come via social media, sent while the bias treatment was in progress, and the message would act to focus their frustration on a particular idea. The results would likely be an amplified frustration from the content of this message. To work, Hank suspected the social media message had to trigger fear in a large percentage of the targeted audience to really get the amygdala hijacking, coming from the ancient part of the brain, to perceive an existential crisis mode. This existential crisis mode, whether real or imagined, put the person's thinking into survival mode. In that state, the future is irrelevant to them, and the targeted audience will hopefully override their own cognitive processes and questioning. They are ready to react out of a fear for survival, but they do not consciously know this is why they are reacting so intensely to the information they are being seeded with. This is Hank's objective.

Jim read the reports on previous experiments that were done, which showed the results to be just slightly better than chance. He listened to Hank's idea about coordinating the bias field generation in alignment with the fear-based seeding, and was intrigued by the change in focus Hank was suggesting. He also understood Hank's hypothesis that the effects of the previously generated fields were only better than chance because there was no convergence point for the generalized frustration that developed. If a convergence point was successfully seeded, and willingly adopted into the minds of the people through their own subconscious, then the results of the generated bias fields would be dramatically improved. He liked the idea.

Hank described how the generated bias fields no longer needed the specificity that they had struggled with in the past. A broad bias influence would likely be enough. The seed message, sent via social media, would insinuate that some fundamental freedom is threatened by the actions taken by specific groups or individuals. Hank suspects that if the timing of the message in coordination with the bias fields, was good, then the message would bypass the higher cognitive functions of the brain and be willingly accepted into the subconscious of the targeted people. The only thing the targeted group would be aware of is a feeling of being under assault, owing to the actions of the parties mentioned in the messages. The amygdala-hijacked people would then be willing to fight any or all actions taken by the mentioned groups or individuals in the message.

Jim said that he suspected that this type of brainwashing would be more effective on a group already disposed to grievances, and the technique might backfire if applied to the wrong group. He outlined some of his history with generated field treatments on individuals, reminding Hank that those with stronger higher-cortex functioning became irritated with the bias treatments and tended to push harder in the opposite direction than the Chronos Consortium had intended. Jim suspected this might be true for the group as well, so the group traits needed to be looked at carefully. With this feedback, Hank's confidence in Jim soared, and he knew he had the right man for the project.

Hank felt the potential in his Re-Imagination Project was enormous and would give the Chronos Consortium a new paradigm to work with. The Chronos Consortium works from the top down, using individuals in key positions to influence events. These individuals, if charismatic enough, could influence thousands with the delivery of *their* ideas. But these people are hard to find, and even harder to keep in line. The Chronos Consortium's research has shown that these types of individuals often become enamored with their own power and are not always receptive to the "guidance" given to them by Chronos Consortium members. Hank wanted a way to bypass these characters and use technology to get the same influence. He told Jim he had several experiments in mind, and he wants to move from simple to complex quickly, to determine what works and what doesn't.

Once Jim took control of this project, Hank has seen substantial progress this last year. Research started simple, taking a single volunteer, and, unknown to him, scanning his field as the control. They then arranged for him to watch a movie in a room with a refrigerator in the corner, loaded with water and sodas, and sent him a treatment that made him thirsty. After five experiments, Jim and Hank clearly demonstrated that the longer the treatments were, the more the volunteer drank. They used video technology to continuously scan the volunteers' eyes, and used that information to determine the attention the volunteers gave to the movie. They knew that the depth of engagements into a movie would cause them to suppress their thirst. When they were not as engaged, they were much more inclined to follow subtle cues from their bodies.

The next set of experiments used a treatment known to induce leg cramps. Again, the duration of the treatments correlated with how much the volunteers moved their legs and how often they got up during the movie.

Normally, the experimental protocol would be to increase the number of people in small increments, but Hank and Jim wanted to take larger leaps in fewer experiments and figure out the key input variables as quickly as possible. They also had to repeat each step, preferably a minimum of three times, so they had to be smart about how they designed the experiments.

In the next set of experiments, they increased the volunteer group to ten people. The amount the volunteers drank was higher than the control group who had no treatments to trigger thirst, and each person in the group drank less by more than half when the experiment was done with just one person. Already, they were seeing a lowering of the effectiveness of these treatments. Jim knew that it would be more complicated to trace all the attention spans of ten people, so they stopped monitoring the attention span. As he argued with Hank, when they go to fifty or more volunteers, they would not be able to use the eye metric data, anyway, so better to start ignoring it with the group of ten and decide what other metrics they might be able to use.

When they got to the experiments with fifty people, the effects were barely more than the control group. By fifty people, the treatments had diminished to virtually no measurable effect.

Next, they laid out the seeding experiments. Volunteers were asked to fill out psychological profiling questions designed by Jim, which he analyzed afterward. He then organized the volunteers into groups with similar profiles. In these experiments, Jim found the evidence he was looking for. The treatments were more effective with people with certain profiles. Even for a group of two hundred people, the response to physical stimuli of thirst or leg cramps was over seventy-five percent positive for this group. That far exceeded any previous results. But so far these experiments just dealt with physical responses. They then had to make the leap to responses about ideas, and policies.

Jim had his research group put ads in local papers and social media, targeting certain geographical areas, looking for people willing to be paid to be part of a focus group. Again, each person was asked to fill out a profile questionnaire that Jim designed based on the insights gained from the previous experiments. These questions focused on the volunteers' views on social, religious, and political issues, along with questions specifically designed to determine the strength of those viewpoints. Jim sorted out the applicants based on an algorithm he'd designed.

It was the summary of these latest experiments from Jim that Hank now had on his desk. Jim told Hank he was confident it had the necessary data to move his project forward. Included in this report is a budget and timeline that Jim outlined for the next set of experiments, letting Hank know that he needed to hire additional support to organize them. Jim, true to his past experience, would keep all the key goals and technology hidden from the temporary hires who were necessary to carry out the experiments successfully.

46.

Skylar hurries down the hospital corridor with her dad, feeling sick. *This is just like my dream last year! Mom's room number is even the same.* In the past year, she'd come close to telling her dad about the disturbing dream more than once, but after her mother's diagnosis, it seemed irrelevant. *I wish I could wake up this time. I hope I wake up!*

David called Celeste from the house, telling her to come straight to the hospital. "We got a call from the doctor, and they said Mom is declining fast."

David's cell phone rings as he and Skylar walk down the corridor. Skylar hears Celeste's voice from her father's phone: "I'm heading toward the airport rental counter."

"Skip the rental car and take a taxi directly to the hospital. It'll save you at least an hour, and you don't have to worry about directions and driving."

"Okay, I'll do that. Hold a minute, Dad." Celeste looks around for directions to the taxis. She doesn't want to end the phone call, wanting and needing to stay connected with her family right now.

While her father is on the phone, Skylar tries to communicate with her mother. *Mom, I realize you probably know it on some level, but Celeste is on her way. Can you please, please, hang on for a little while longer? We should really be together as a family before you leave us.* Skylar doesn't want her to die before Celeste makes it, as she did in the dream. . . the *nightmare.*

"It's room 343. Call me if you need to. Skylar and I are heading toward the elevators and will be in the room with Mom in just a couple of minutes. Love you," David closes.

"Love you, Dad," Celeste returns.

David puts the cell phone back in his pocket. Just then, the ding of the elevator breaks the silence.

"Quick—let's grab that one," Skylar says. The doors open, and three nurses and two visitors pour out before Skylar and her father can enter the empty elevator. They stare up at the floor counter for a few seconds, each lost in their thoughts.

"Oh. We need to press the button," David says, and steps forward to press the number three. Worried, filled with anxiety and grief, he can hardly think straight. He looks to Skylar and sees the sadness in his daughter's eyes, and the tense expression on her face.

He reaches over and puts his arm around Skylar's shoulders. As a parent, his first impulse is to say, "It'll be okay." But that doesn't fit this moment, because things are *not* okay. Jean is dying, and it wasn't supposed to be this way for any of them.

David decides to say nothing. The elevator dings again. *So soon?* thinks Skylar. *I'm not ready to leave this elevator.* But she is out of it in a flash. David hastens to keep up with her.

David tries to center himself. He desperately wants the love of his life to live, but he most assuredly doesn't want her to suffer. Her body can no longer provide the life she deserves, so it's time for her to go, ready or not. He slows down and takes a few deep breaths. Skylar shoots ahead, not looking behind.

David speaks to Jean in his head as he lags behind Skylar. *I've spoken with Celeste, and she'll be here shortly. Please hang on long enough for her to arrive.* He cannot know that Skylar has already made the same silent request. *It would mean so much to Celeste to be able to say goodbye in person.*

"Dad, what are you doing?" Skylar calls back, her worry and impatience plain.

"Coming, Skylar."

Skylar walks over to her mother's hospital bed. She hears her mother struggling to breathe, immediately reaches for her free hand, and shivers when she feels how cold it is. She wants to pull her hand away, but she needs to feel her mother's presence.

47.

David puts his cell phone away after talking to Celeste, who is in a taxi on the way to the hospital. He is worried about bad traffic from the airport and how much that might delay her. He rubs his face with his hands, takes another deep, slow breath to try to find his center, and walks back into his wife's hospital room.

He sees Skylar on her phone, sending a text, probably to Bohdi.

A moment later, the doctor comes in. He's a short man, with neatly combed black hair and an athletically trim physique. He looks at David, and in a firm but quiet baritone, says, "Mr. Donaldson, your wife's condition is deteriorating quickly. I am sorry." He looks around and asks, "Are all your family members here?"

David blurts, "My other daughter's on her way. Hearing the desperation in David's voice, the doctor looks at Skylar and says, "Hopefully she'll be here soon. I'll leave you alone."

Skylar sinks down into a chair, her eyes closed. David knows she's working to communicate with her mother's spirit. She imagines Skylar isn't altogether ready to let go. Nobody is. . . but at least he and Jean had a full life together. Skylar longs for her mother to meet her future husband, see her get married, move into a home, and mostly, be a grandmother to her kids. None of that is possible now.

David stands at Jean's bedside and whispers softly into her ear, "Celeste will be here in a few minutes. We'll be together as a family."

A moment later, Celeste rushes into the room and into her father's arms. He gives her a big hug and assures her, "You made it in time." She moves back, looks at Skylar, and heads over to give her little sister a big hug. She then moves to her mother's side. She puts her hand gently on her mother's forehead as she starts to cry. She's been holding in all her emotions the entire journey from the West Coast, but now that she is with her family, she can't hold on anymore.

After a few minutes, Celeste whispers hoarsely, "Why, Mom? Why do you have to die? You've only seen pictures of your granddaughter. You never even got a chance to meet her, to hold her. It's so unfair. I can't understand it. I just don't understand."

Celeste gently strokes her mother's hand and tries not to react to its coldness, but Skylar can tell it rattles Celeste like it did her.

The room is quiet. All the equipment that held Jean to life is silent.

"Mom," Celeste says in a firm voice, "I know you can hear me. I'm so glad I made it here before you left. There's so much I want to share with you. I just became a mother! I need you to talk to, to help me. You have to do that from wherever you are, Mom. You have to let me know you're looking after us and looking after Regina Jean."

Celeste is quiet for a moment, then continues. "I'm sorry, Mom. I don't mean to put demands on you. I miss you already. Just let us know you're okay."

There's no response, and Celeste starts to cry again. Skylar moves up to hold her sister's arm, and David puts a hand on each of his children's shoulders.

For a brief time, they sit without speaking, unnerved by the death rattle in Jean's excruciatingly slow breathing. But none of them wants to leave. The long pause before the next intake of breath causes them each to hold their own breaths, making them feel a bit disoriented.

A nurse comes in quietly and checks Jean's vital signs. Skylar and Celeste move to the window and look outside. They see traffic on the street, people walking around. Celeste says, "It shouldn't be this sunny and bright. I would feel better if it was overcast and cold, like I feel."

"She's very close," the nurse says quietly. "Her blood pressure is very low."

She finishes her task then asks, "Do you need anything?"

David looks at his children, and they both shake their heads.

About an hour later, Jean stops breathing. The nurse comes in to check. She looks at David kindly and says, "I'm so sorry for your loss. Her doctor will be down in a few moments. Take all the time you need."

She quietly leaves.

Celeste moves closer to her mother, tears making shiny tracks down her face. "I miss you already, Mom."

Skylar says confidently, "Mom, I'll see you again."

Celeste looks up at her sister, a bit taken aback.

Hearts heavy, Skylar and Celeste go to the visiting area, while their father says his final goodbye to his wife of nearly thirty-five years, and waits for the doctor to confirm the time of death.

About ten minutes later, David comes to them in the private visiting room and asks whether they want to stay any longer. They both shake their heads numbly. They're ready to go, but not home: too many memories. Skylar asks if they can drive around for a while, maybe eat dinner in the car so they can have some privacy. She feels too vulnerable to sit in a restaurant.

They all agree.

48.

Hank is surprised by the secure message he receives on his phone from Paul:

Got two candidates for your Young Project. Name is Skylar Donaldson and Bohdi Kearns. Will talk later.

Hank wonders what these young people did to get the attention of the Chronos Consortium. He will find out soon enough.

Hank imagines that Phil will be happy to hear that Paul is willing to commit one of his agents to get data on one of the young people that he and Tania are obsessing over.

****

Paul is pleased with himself. He put off Hank's request for agent time to get a scan on a young target, until an idea struck him. If he proposes Skylar Donaldson and Bohdi Kearns as the candidates for Hank's Young Project, he can get the information he needs and justify the time and expense against Hank's budget.

He wants to follow every detail to the end on this search for where those parts went. He summited a request to have an agent sent out to do a scope of both properties and a scan of each of these people. He wants the assurance of a frequency scan on Skylar and Bohdi so if either one of them should become a problem in the future, he will have another option to keep them in line.

Paul reflects on his dinner with Edward Stagmier the previous night, when Edward shared his disappointment in one of the protégé he had high hopes for. Edward relayed to Paul how, due to the rash action of this protégé, quite a bit of negative media attention was generated, and the fallout was that he was forced to resign as university president. Now three years of hard work was lost. Edward now has to see if he can move him into another opportunity and wait at least a year to see whether he has learned from his mistake. If not, he has another protégé he is working with, and she shows great potential to be someone who can execute the control they need. He states that change in the world around them is happening so fast, it is more difficult to keep up. The evening leaves Paul feeling better about his own challenges.

49.

Jean had requested to be cremated; there will be a memorial service but no burial. She chose to have some of her ashes buried in a particular flower bed at their home, and the rest scattered in the wind from atop a mountain she and David regularly hiked. Celeste asks for some of her mother's ashes to take home with her; she wants to bury them in the garden of the house she will eventually buy.

The following morning, Celeste's husband, Dan, flies in with the baby. The whole family stays at the house. Celeste decided to bring Regina Jean to the funeral, since there will be relatives she won't probably see again for some time.

The family is surprised by how many people show up at the wake to pay their respects. Students who have taken Jean's English classes and many of the teachers and administrators she worked with offer their condolences. Luckily the weather turned out as predicted, a cloudless, warm summer day. Skylar is busy talking to relatives outside the chapel when she sees Bohdi coming toward her, wearing the same kakis and shirt he wore on their first dinner date. When he arrives at her side, she pulls him in so she can introduce him to Aunt Elizabeth and Uncle Jack. His presence makes her pain more bearable.

The Donaldson want to deal with Jean's death as a celebration of who she was and the light she brought into their lives. They hope that the attending family members and friends will understand, and by and large, they do. Having Regina around is a good diversion. Celeste knows her mother would find it fitting that at her funeral, attention is paid to new life, especially her own granddaughter.

They didn't book a restaurant for after the service. Instead, when the service ends, they invite those who want to share some time with the family to stop by the house, where a lunch buffet will be served. David's friends offered to cook some special dishes, and other friends dropped off food, as well. They set up rented tables in the backyard, under the oak tree. While Skylar and her family talk to people, Bohdi keeps the food coming out of the kitchen. He brings a plate over to Skylar, but she can't think of eating.

50.

Two months after her mother's death, her father asks, "What's going on?", hoping to help.

"Everything and nothing. I'm so distracted. I can't concentrate like I need to because I've got all these thoughts and emotions and, from my perspective, *nothing* positive is happening."

"Skylar, you're dealing with grief," David states calmly.

"Really, Dad? I hadn't noticed."

"Listen, you can be sarcastic. I understand you're struggling. I've organized a few sessions of grief counseling for you, as well as for Celeste in California. If you want it, I can give you a phone number. I spoke with Celeste yesterday, and she's planning to see the counselor out there. She figures a few conversations with a professional will probably help. You have the option, as well."

Skylar sighs deeply. " I'm sorry I was sarcastic. I just feel frustrated." Skylar looks down at the floor.

"Skylar, cut yourself some slack. You just lost your mother, and it's a very significant event on all levels: physically, mentally, emotionally, and spiritually. As you've pointed out, we're connected through more than just our DNA. I've learned from you that our family has a field that all of us in this family resonate with. Now there's a piece missing. It changes the dynamics, and while our unit reorganizes, we can't help but feel out of sorts. It'll stabilize to a new normal, but let's give ourselves some time to adjust.

He puts a hand on his daughter's shoulder. "Going through what our family lived through this past year is traumatic. Honor that, and be patient with yourself."

"I'll think about it, Dad," Skylar replies, feeling a little less alone.

51.

Skylar feels better after her talk with the counselor. Initially, she resisted her father's suggestion because. . . well, in the end, she didn't know why. She ran out of excuses, and her frustration just got worse. One morning, she tripped on one of her sneakers in her room getting ready for classes, and went to kick it out of the way with her bare foot, missed the boot, and hit the metal corner support of her bed with her small toe. She yelled in pain, but the yell wasn't just to express the physical pain. It included a full measure of spiritual pain that needed release.

While she was on the floor wincing, holding her toe with a sock to keep from bleeding all over the carpet, she realized she needed to take a more constructive approach to her grief. Soon after complaining to Bohdi, she placed a telephone call to the grief counselor.

She and Bohdi have begun their last year at the university. Skylar finds the demands of school and the wonderful time spent with Bohdi provide some relief and distraction from the pain she is feeling. Bohdi reminds her that next week it will be a year anniversary since they went to the Browns' home to see the goggles for the first time. They share how much they have learned, still have to learn, and how that fateful day changed their lives in ways they never could have foreseen. Skylar sees the past year in a better context, and it helps her become more centered again, and feel better in her skin.

****

Skylar is amazed at how radiant her mother looks. She struggles a bit to understand how she can look so radiant. Then she hears her mother communicate nonverbally to her.

Skylar, sweetie, what you feel now is the true love we feel for each other. In physical space, it is lessened by all the mental and emotional filters we have in place. But I want to let you know how loved I feel by you, and how brave you are to be doing the work you are doing.

Skylar, you're stronger than you know. The world is full of contradictory messages, and these realities have different requirements, making life very trying for an awakening individual to deal with. Should you choose to continue on this path, you along with Bohdi will find yourselves attracted to opportunities and worlds you can't yet imagine. With them will also come challenges—but ones you can deal with. I see you, my daughter, in the process of creating opportunities for yourself and where wisdom of both the Eastern and Western cultures blend, bringing insights to people, particularly younger people like yourself, who are more open to it. As for the apology you plan to give me, there is no need. I feel blessed by how hard you tried to find a solution for my illness.

Skylar winces, but she recognizes the truth in her mother's perspective. She is so overcome by the love she feels radiating from her mother that she does not want to interject by asking a question.

I'm deeply touched by your determination to help me during the time I was sick. From this perspective, I can see a solution wasn't possible. It was a biological inevitability, given my genetics. In the future, with a better understanding of frequencies, DNA, and the information in the time you both so passionately work to understand, solutions to this disease and so many others will be available. Pioneers like you and Bohdi can be a catalyst for new insight into the breakthroughs. So, please, let your disappointment go.

When you are ready, tell everyone, especially Dad, Celeste and Regina that I love them.

Skylar struggles in vain to formulate ask a question, when suddenly she wakes up from her dream.

"Uugghh. That was only a dream."
As she recounts what her mother said in the dream, warm tears of joy flow down her face.

52.

Agent Jared walks into his boss's office after receiving a message to stop by for a few minutes at 10:00 a.m. Paul stands up as Agent Jared enters. Jared sees that Agent Max is also invited to this meeting.

Paul turns to Jared and says sternly, "You are assigned to a new mission. Max has the pertinent details for you. The two of you need to set a time to meet and organize the mission details." Then Paul heads out of his office, leaving the two of them together.

Max stands up and hands a folder to Jared. "I have some time this afternoon at 2:00. Can you meet with me to go over the details of this case? I want to brief you before I meet with Paul tomorrow."

As Jared accepts the folder, he replies, "I have a conflict at 2:00—can we make it 3:00?"

"I can make time at 3:00. See you in my office then."

"Okay," Jared agrees halfheartedly.

****

Jared reviews the information in the folder that Max gave him, including the white paper that Agent Tania wrote. As Jared walks out of the building at lunchtime, he embraces the coolness of this October day and climbs into his truck. He has an hour for lunch and needs to get away for the whole of it. He feels uneasy, almost nauseated, and wonders what is wrong with him.

Jared took on this assignment with Paul's group after retiring from the military. The Chronos Consortium told him he would be involved in an elite group whose purpose is to carry out missions to take out strategic threats identified by the commanders of the Chronos Consortium. The benefits and pay being offered were tremendous, and Jared could not believe he would get paid that well to do what he was good at. He thought that life could not get any better than this.

He remembers a statement made to him when he was interviewing, that once you join this organization you can never dissociate from it. Just like the military. It is a part of who you are. At the time, he did not really pay attention to what that might mean. Now he understands that the information he's accumulated while being part of this elite group is very damaging. Although similar rules applied to his missions in the elite unit of the military, this group's rules have a different, more sinister feel.

Lately Jared has been questioning exactly what constitutes a threat. He is not clear on what threat some of the targets they have focused on lately could possibly represent, and when he reads the background of the latest concerns, two college-age kids, it raises all the doubts within him again. Then the white paper seems to suggest that the Chronos Consortium is planning to target young people as well. This case specifically has hit a resonant note, bringing back feelings from when he, too, was twenty-one. That's when he first considered joining the military—his only way out from a life of desperation. But growing up poor he realized that the material deprivation was not the worst of poverty, it was the other problems that it triggered that often were the real issues. His father, John, was an alcoholic who was not physically or emotionally available and could not hold a job when Jared was a teenager because his drinking had gotten so bad. In Jared's first month in high school, he came home one day and discovered a note in his room. His mother, Ellen, stated she could not stay anymore. She would be back to take him out of "this desperate hell hole." Jared surely hoped so; he loved his mother. She paid attention to him, fussed over him when he did not wear enough clothing to ward off the cold, and tried to keep food in the house, which was so much more than his father did.

He waited for her to return, but a year went by with no contact. He wondered if maybe she tried to call or come back, but was too afraid to confront his father. He never learned what happened to her, and like any situation with unknowns, the mind constructs all sorts of alternatives that can never be validated. Jared comforted himself by adopting the idea of his mother trying to return, but fearing his father too much. Jared also entertained the option of disappearing, like his mother, but he was registered in school, and authorities would be notified if he didn't turn up. Maybe his mother came to realize this, too, and so she stayed away.

Maybe this, maybe that. Uncertainty. It was everywhere in the world he lived in. It undermined what he could envision for his own life in the future. This constant uncertainty slowly ate away at his soul and caused his mind to imagine all sort of possible outcomes, many just pure conjectures. To survive, he learned to quarantine his anxieties, about situations inside and outside of him, and just move forward with life as it was presented to him on a day-to-day basis. Little did he know that the skill he developed to survive his upbringing would come in so handy when he was working missions for the elite military units. He developed a reputation for being very cool under pressure and being able to think his way out of situations where events were rapidly changing.

He graduated from high school and yearned for more out of life than he saw around him, but he could not visualize how to get it. With no money for college, he took a job on a road construction crew working at night. He earned enough money to pay for the room he rented and stayed afloat financially. The fact that he worked at night and tried to sleep during the day made him feel even more isolated. The isolation finally drove him to sign up for the military.

The military provided a refuge, and he flourished. He was a natural athlete, and the discipline kept him focused. He did not drink, since he despised what it did to his father and to those around him. He associated drinking with weakness and death. Five years after he joined the military, he was notified that his father had been found dead in his house. No surprise to learn he'd been drinking and the doctors suspected his heart gave out. There was no need for an autopsy since he had been so self-destructive for so long. Jared took leave to take care of the necessary matters, cleaning out the run-down house and organizing the sale of it, and then went back to the life that gave him purpose. The military's sense of purpose empowered him, and he enjoyed the camaraderie of the units he was assigned to, although the drinking and drug use within them constantly disturbed him.

By the time he was forty-two, he decided to retire from the military. He had been married for twelve years, and he and his wife, Joyce, enjoyed being parents to their son, Kevin, now nine. Jared had already interviewed with the Chronos Consortium before he retired, and they quickly came to an agreement on responsibilities and pay. He was now making more money than he ever dreamed possible.

He and Joyce bought a new home. They also bought a small boat they used for fun and fishing. The past decade, his life had become more than he could ever have visualized as a young man of twenty-one. It motivated him to, with his wife's help, track down his mother. Their reconciliation started slowly; a visit to her while they stayed at a nearby hotel. She reciprocated with a visit to his family for a weekend. He is happy to form some link between his son and mother, since Joyce's family is regularly involved in their lives.

His mind drifts back to the uneasiness inside him. What is it about this assignment that affects him so? He opens the windows on his truck. The cold breeze makes him feel better.

Reflecting on himself at twenty-one, he realizes it would not have taken much in the way of bad circumstances to break him. But these young people he's assigned to did not have the same circumstances. They seemed to have a normal family and are in college. Jared understood that at the same period in his life, he was constantly battling hopelessness. The battle was like a scourge inside him that ate away at any chance of happiness. Even a beautiful day could only lift him temporarily. He could tolerate physical pain more easily than the psychological pain from the internal battle that used to exhaust him. It would have been so easy to give up and give in, like his father had. But something deep inside could not give up hope.

Now, though, he's suffering a new psychological pain after two years of seeing what this elite Chronos Consortium group does to people. Some deserve it, others he is not so sure about. As a father, he can't help but wonder what type of a world the Chronos Consortium is creating for his son, and his son's generation. Is he helping or hurting Kevin's future? The benefit of working with the Chronos Consortium is far less clear now than it was when he joined them. He was recently approached by another employee member with similar conflicts. They spoke about the increasing corruption of ideals they've been seeing in the organization. But so many organizations are corrupt that it seems the new normal. They should know, having gathered information on so many powerful groups that use money and influence to keep people doing work that is sold as idealistic, but in reality, is corruption. The legislative branches of government have been bought for decades, the judicial branch is compromised, and the executive branch is practically quarantined. The member who spoke to Jared wants to break away from the Chronos Consortium, and get involved in work that creates a better future for their kids. But they both know it's not that simple. You do not just quit the Chronos Consortium.

Jared made no comments to his fellow member beyond his concern about his son's future, and his role as a father in that. But he recognizes that his uneasiness is undermining the clarity he has always been able to rely on. He knows it is only a matter of time before he walks away. What he has with his wife and son is more important than the financial reward for his assignments, especially if this current one indicates a new direction the Chronos Consortium is taking.

Jared reaches deep inside himself to his trait of quarantining troubles he cannot find a solution to. For now, his doubts about this mission will have to go into that space. The decision gives him relief, and some clarity returns. He takes a deep breath and slowly exhales. He cleans up the crumbs from his sandwich and starts his truck. Time to head back to work.

53.

David is quiet while his daughter describes her vivid communicating with her mother. It has been five months since her mother's death, and he has noticed that Skylar is now healing quickly from her grief. As he listens, he is thankful that Jean communicated in the manner she did since it is clear it has help Skylar in healing her grief.

Her father communicates that he wishes he could be farther along in recovering from his own grief, but he still struggles every day.

Skylar replies tenderly, hoping to comfort her father: "If this happened even a few years ago, I would have had a more difficult time. This last year was a breakthrough for me, and your support has been crucial."

"I'm truly proud of you, Skylar."

Skylar looks at her father, and David smiles. Skylar is glad to see her father smile again. It's been a long while.

****

Later that day, Skylar calls Bohdi, and they summarize their experiments with colors. Bohdi built the color wheel, which can be taken apart, so that Skylar could load up different colors. He notched the wheel so that she could easily tell with her fingers which position the wheel was in. He also built a box around the light source, since, in the first experiment, she burned her fingers while fumbling to find the color wheel with the goggles on.

Their research shows that the colors coming from the lamp could not be seen through the goggles in Plus mode. What can be seen with the goggles is the effect of these colors on the Time Information Fields around Bohdi. So, clearly the colors have a Time Information Field component. After some experiments, Skylar hypothesized that maybe the warm colors—red, orange, and yellow—added energy to Bohdi's field, expanding the diameter of the fields of colors around him. When he was feeling energetic, she tried the cooler colors, blue, indigo, and purple. These seem to reduce the diameter of the fields, and Bohdi reported feeling calmer. Green, the color that is the midpoint between these two sets of colors, seems to have the same calming effect. She wondered what happens when one is sick; what happens to the fields of color then, and what should be done, adding energy, or bringing in calm? So many questions still needed to be explored.

54.

Skylar's phone dings that she has an encrypted link message from a Ms. Smith while she's sitting at the student union.

Yesterday my husband had a fatal heart attack.

Skylar's stomach tenses up as she recognizes that Ms. Brown said her husband without stating his name.

"Oh no!" she says out loud, oblivious to all the student activity around her.

She texts back, *I am so sorry. Our sincerest condolences.*

She is busy typing a text to Bohdi when her phone bings showing the text with condolences that Bohdi just sent.

She waits. A minute later, another bing.

Thank you. Meeting the two of you brought a joy and purpose back into his life, and for that we are grateful. We are having a service but as we agreed, there is no need for you to come. I hope you understand.

Skylar puts her phone on her notebook. She feels at a loss for words. She desperately wants to do something to honor Dr. Brown, her mentor and hero.

She feels a distinct shift in the responsibility of what they are doing. The work they are doing with the goggles now seems more important than ever before.

Bohdi texts Skylar that they need to do their own personal honoring. She agrees. In some ways, the unique relationship they have had with Dr. Brown does not need to be publicly displayed.

He might not have his physical presence, but maybe he can help from the other side.

55.

Bohdi sits up in his bed. It is 3:33 am. This is the third time the same dream has occurred, although this time it ended with the message: *This will be the last time.* He interprets that to mean he needs to decide. But a decision about what?

After the second occurrence of the dream, he felt strongly that an invitation is present in the dreams. Those eyes seem to see right into him. It unnerves him a bit. Is this a trick his brain is playing on him after the coma? He believes it is not that. It is clear something significant changed him during the coma. He feels the truth of that in every cell of his body.

He will not be able to fall back to sleep this time. He lies back down and retraces his thoughts. Three times, the same dream. What is he missing? *Last time for what?*

Could this be the answer to a strong wish he articulated about meeting someone in the time dimensions after he watched Skylar communicate with her mother. He wonders if there is a being who can share ideas about how best to navigate these intriguing and confusing dimensions?

If this is a response to his wish, what an odd way to communicate! They surely could learn some lessons on how to communicate with humans. Bohdi laughs at the thought. It is more likely that we need to learn how to communicate with others.

He gets up and reaches for his notebook to write down his impressions. Seeing the impressions on paper gives him clarity. The dreams have been trying to get his attention, and it has now worked. He plans to respond.

56.

"Okay, just got an email from Dr. Bradley. She confirmed she can meet up with both of us again during her office hours next Tuesday at 11.

Skylar looks at Bohdi, "Well, this is a big step. Our first attempt at reaching out to someone about these goggles. I feel good about it but still have some nervousness."

"I agree. It is worth the risk, but there is always the possibility that it could not go well. And she is my professor. I still have to finish up the semester in her class if it goes bad. Awkward!"

"We could wait."

"No, I am in this program another semester and a half, so next week is just as good as next semester, or next year. We are going to have to take some leap of faith with anyone we reach out to anyway. Dr. Bradley seems like a really good fit. With her background and connections as a Professor in Psychology, she could be a great help."

"Yup!" he hears in reply.

****

Skylar's and Bohdi's feet are barely touching the ground after their visit with Dr. Bradley. Dr. Bradley was intrigued with the description of the goggles and its capabilities. They offered her an opportunity to try the goggles and she quickly accepted. Skylar let Dr. Bradley know that since there is no patent, she has to sign a nondisclosure agreement.

The next day, Skylar stops by Dr. Bradley's office and she signs the agreement. Next, they discuss a time and settle on 2:00 p.m. on Saturday as a good time for her to come over to Skylar's house and try the goggles.

57.

During the visit, Dr. Bradley asked insightful questions, being the psychologist and researcher that she is, to elicit different emotions from Skylar and Bohdi while viewing them with the goggles. She could see the changes happening in real time. Her nonstop questions about what the colors meant, about the color changes she saw, and about the shapes, made clear to Skylar and Bohdi that she is exactly the professional they need for their project.

Dr. Bradley certainly was not expecting this. She knew it would be interesting, given the conversations she had with Skylar and Bohdi, but here was a technology that could possibly revolutionize the way mental and emotional issues, and possibly illness, are diagnosed. It was just the type of disruptive approach she had been looking for in her career as a psychologist. She left the meeting knowing what her next step would be.

****

The Thursday after the meeting with Dr. Bradley, Bohdi is still feeling good about how well the previous Saturday went. This semester of his senior year he has no classes on Thursday afternoon, and he should be spending time on homework, but he feels what he's learning is just not reflected in his grades. But he has another task to do this afternoon: address the response he believes those eye dreams are asking for. He feels there is an opportunity to contact someone, but he is not sure whom. He sits in the chair in his room and does some breathing exercises to slow his heartbeat and go into a deep meditation.

He approaches this contact attempt the only way he knows, to go into a deep meditative state. Since his coma, the experiences of being a universal being have just been magnified as well as his confidence in what he is feeling. Once in a deep meditative state, he feels a distinct vibration in his mind that was not there before. Even the ringing in his ear's changes to a higher pitch. He then feels a strong shift in vibration in his heart and his head. In his inner vision, he perceives a brilliant indigo light about an inch in diameter. He watches as it slowly expands to what seems like the diameter of a car wheel, with gold and silver points of light emerging within the indigo. The light is brighter than anything he has witnessed before, but it does not hurt his inner eye to look into it. He sees a red ball at the bottom of the indigo oval and a bright purple on top. A golden rod runs through all of them.

As he gazes at the image, he feels a wave of energy move over him. The horizon inside his head expands rapidly until it feels like the whole universe is inside him and the image he was just looking at becomes a dot. His mind feels like a planetarium, with millions of stars. Everything he sees has the resolution of a space telescope. It has the feeling of expansion that he remembers when, as a young boy, he first saw the Milky Way stretched across the sky with amazing clarity.

He feels awed in the presence of such cosmic majesty, and at the same time, he also feels comfortable, as if it was his home.

He poses a question nonverbally, in the manner Skylar described to him: *Who are you?*

He waits for a nonverbal response.

The nonverbal response comes in his mind, firm and clear.

«Glad you accepted my invitation, as I accept yours now.»

Bohdi is surprised, and suddenly reticent. If this was a human interaction, he could make small talk to cover up his nervousness, but there is nowhere to hide what he is feeling in this inner world. Bohdi struggles to concentrate because he is distracted by the wonderful imagery.

He decides to be straightforward: *I am unsure of what I have accepted and am nervous since this is new to me.*

« This is a response to your expressed wish to know more about time.»

Are you a response to my wish to contact a being in three-dimensional time

«Correct. You do not yet understand the power of these intentions and wishes. Not only you, but more and more in your generation will come to know their power.»

I am struggling with a concern that this interaction might go in a direction I have not considered and might be trouble for me. How do I know you are trustworthy?

«*I can see your struggle, and it is understandable, given the human paradigm you are working with. As far as going in a direction you have not considered, is that not the reason you wish for this contact, to take you in a new direction you have not considered?*»

Well, . . . I guess so. I mean, yes, it is.

«*So, now we have only your apprehension to deal with. It is not unfounded.*»

You mean we are by nature fearful creatures.

«*You have a built-in fear as a safety precaution, like a respectable fear for certain situations with animals, people, and events. Without this, you would not learn to prevent unnecessary injuries and deaths. But a fear of the unknown, beyond what you see, hear, touch, is a huge inhibitor for many humans. There is so much reality beyond your senses and the capability of your matter to detect. What is clear is that you personally have a strong curiosity that overcomes your apprehensions.*»

I would like to start simple. Do you have a name?

«*For this communication, I have chosen the name that you can easily understand, Sullivan. It means 'dark eyes', actually, little dark eyes, but I liked this human name. My real name will not translate.*»

Bohdi thinks choosing a name with reference to dark eyes is fitting. *Where are you from?*

The imagery in his head changes. The view narrows and focuses on a particular star cluster. The image of bright stars is presented to him, with seven—or is it eight—stars that stand out more because of their brightness. He assumes this is where the being is from, but before he formats a question, he hears a statement.

«From a planet in the Pleiades star cluster. I am from a star in the cluster being presented to you that scientists on earth have labelled Atlas.»

One of the stars begins to pulsate, and Bohdi assumes this is the Atlas star. While he is again captured by the image, which has so much depth and detail, he has a more fundamental question that he wants to ask. *Why are you communicating with me?*

«Because you asked for it. And given your interests, we are intrigued by your request and decided to offer our communication in response. What you are not aware of is that deep-seated requests are received outside of your human paradigm. Those of us who feel we might be able to communicate, might decide to do so. But we want to accomplish this without interfering with the path of the human we are communicating with.»

What do you mean by interfere?

«I have concerns about the risk of introducing ideas that can cause problems for you. If we should change your path, due to our communication, in a way that might not be in your best interest as a human, then we, you and I, own that responsibility. You and I are tied until it is cleared. It is not that I am afraid, but I recognize this communication is not equal. I have technology and insight that gives me far more information about you and the circumstances in your life than you have of me. This means that you might give up your personal power, not consciously, but unconsciously. I will try to make sure this does not happen.

«An example might be when those from a country with superior technology come to a country that has little technology. The people in the country with little technology might feel inferior, and therefore give up their personal power unconsciously. Those who come from the more

developed country, to keep the interaction fair, need to be aware of this and have the integrity and discipline to tailor their actions because of the perceived inequality. In your history, that has not been the case; particularly in business interactions, this disparity has been taken advantage of. What people do not recognize, is that the universe comes from a source of complete balance. As beings in this universe, we need to honor that, even in our interactions. Should there be a situation that has disparity, it is the responsibility of those with the larger understanding to work to keep a balance.»

Bohdi's mind races to figure out what advantages this being has. Can it see all his thoughts and emotions? Can it know his whole history, possibly recorded in time? Is he, or she, monitoring what he's thinking? He feels naked, and strangely, for the moment, inferior. He struggles to organize his thoughts into a coherent response.

«Take your time. I will wait for your next question.»

Are you male or female? I assume since you chose the name Sullivan you are male.

«We do not have the binary polarization of male and female that you have on earth. It is more than I would like to get into in this conversation, so for now, you can think of me as the male polarity as you know it on Earth.»

Why have you chosen me out of all the much more qualified humans you could interact with?

«This discussion is happening because you sent out a desire for it to happen, and you have the ability to hear and understand me. Many humans send out the desire, but the communication fails for a number of reasons. Most often, it is because they are unable to hear or understand me in this nonverbal communication. I understand it is quite a challenge for most humans, who do not know which part is real and which part is made up by their minds. In order for this to work, it

requires quite a bit of understanding of yourself, as you have discovered. Your years of deep mediation have sensitized you to the ebbs and flows of your internal dialog. The intention you sent out is for a deeper understanding regarding the nature of time, time travel and beings that might live in time. Our communication can work since your current understanding of time is unique relative to what most humans understand about the spacetime they inhabit.»

Are you close to me right now, that is, to Earth, or are you still in the Pleiades star cluster, which I still see inside my mind?

«I am at our star and am communicating over vast distance in space with your field in the dimensions of time. To reach you, we have to code our communications so that they resonate with one of your local stars, known as your Sun. All communications to beings in your solar system are directed via your Sun. In order to communicate with you specifically, we have coded this interaction to resonate with your planet Earth's node as well as with your own Time Information Field. For ease of understanding, think of it like using an IP address when sending information to particular individual's device. The link is coded so that it goes through the air to a local tower, then via fiber cables and is finally transmitted back through the air to the correct cellular tower to get to the intended device. Our communication happens in the dimensions of time, so that the distance of space between us has no effect. In time, we are very close to each other. The communication is for all purposes instantaneous, much like your telecommunications, in spite of the very large distances in space between us.»

But how am I communicating with you? I am not doing any of this frequency coding.

«For now, it is easier to say that this is being done automatically for you, again much like your cellular conversations are automatically encoded appropriately to reach the person you desire to communicate with. No effort is required on your part to establish the link.»

« Your efforts to understand time have and will continue to serve you well. You and your friend are starting to understand that time correlates to your states of thoughts and emotions. What is not yet fully developed in the human is the circuitry to not only see, but also to more clearly understand information in the time dimensions. Both of your biological circuitry is more developed than those humans around you. As this biological circuitry develops more fully with each generation of humans, each generation will then have more access to the energy and power of the time dimensions. »

Bohdi's mind locks onto the correlation of time, energy, and power. *So, thoughts and emotions are energy and power in the dimensions of time?*

« Yes. Intuitively, humans are beginning to understand this about your thoughts and emotions. Look around your world and you can see plenty of impacts that you humans have on your world, all of which started as thoughts and were energized by emotions. In future, you will come to understand there is real physics behind your thoughts and emotions. Your thoughts have the ability, the power, to reach me and start this communication. Already, the technology you call the Internet, along with your cell-phone technology, has exposed beings on planet Earth to the idea of information being available everywhere, at any time. Take this concept to a much larger extent, much larger than your mind can currently envision, this is how the universe is. There is information everywhere in the universe, and this information is energy. There will come a time when you recognize that information is energy, but of a different form of energy than you are familiar with, and humans will learn the physics of how this type of energy becomes power in the dimensions of time. »

Bohdi feels his mind being stretched, and with each new insight, a wave of energy comes over him. He can't quite grasp that his thoughts can be so powerful. His curiosity is piqued to a degree he has never experienced before.

There is a pause in the communication. Bohdi takes this opportunity to ask a question. *Why is this biological circuit not currently as active in humans? Why is time invisible to us?*

«There will be many questions that are not easy to answer. You can accentuate the development of this biological circuitry through specific meditative or contemplative practices, which help to clarify your thoughts and emotions. I ask that I may focus this communication on some aspects of living and traveling in three-dimensional time, if you so desire.»

Yes, go ahead! flashes into Bohdi's mind before he can think to respond.

«We, my civilization, travel the dimensions of time and have done so for a long time. Our civilization is not the only one that does this. There are other stellar and galactic civilizations who are capable of time travel. The best analogy I can give you is that we travel in the dimensions of time like you travel in the dimensions of space. Each additional dimension adds so many more possibilities to time. Think of the huge opportunities going from two dimensions in space, a totally flat universe with no height, to a universe that includes the height in its three dimensions of space. Now consider three dimensions of time instead of one. There is more to time than the human mind can presently hold. That is not a judgment, just a statement of fact.

« My home, as I mentioned previously, is a star and I, we, primarily exist in what might be best described as three-dimensional time. In this time reality our star looks very different from its appearance in three-dimensional space. Contrary to your experience, velocity here is always faster than the speed of light. In three-dimensional space, your experience is that it takes energy to speed matter up. But in three-dimensional time it takes energy to slow matter down. A simple analogy would be that it takes energy to slow down the thoughts in your mind. The velocity in three-dimensional time can never go below the speed of light, just as it cannot exceed the speed of light in three-

dimensional space. Our technology makes communication over vast distances, like the one in three-dimensional space between our star and your planet, just as instantaneous as your phone communications are on earth.

«Each location in three-dimensional time has a unique set of frequencies associated with it, which allows someone in this time reality to identify where they are. The range of possible frequencies is much wider than what you recognize on Earth.

«I am going to use your radio and television as an analogy for how we transfer energy, which will help in the deeper discussion of transmitting and receiving information as well as a possible later discussion on our form of traveling in time. Remember, information is just a specific form of energy, so use energy and information interchangeably. In order to understand traveling in time, we must first discuss communicating in time.

«Your earth radios each have a specific carrier frequency which for this communication we will call the fundamental frequency. Each radio station mixes information in the form of music and discussions onto its assigned fundamental frequency. If you want to hear a program from that radio station, you have to tune your FM radio to its assigned fundamental frequency, for example of 99.1 megahertz, or just 99.1 as you commonly refer to it.»

«Each star and planet has its own fundamental frequency for traveling which is used for transmitting and receiving energy. This is also true for each human. Each of you has you own communication frequency. In order to send a message, the proper frequency encoding that must be done. First is the frequency related to the star, then frequency of the planet that is revolving around that star and then the frequency of the specific being you wish to communicate with. The reverse is done for transmitting. Every person, planet and star are both a main transmitter and a receiver of energy for their specific fundamental frequency. In the case of humans, all thoughts, emotions, states of being, all information is transmitted on their personal fundamental frequency. That energy is then encoded into the planetary transmission frequency that are transmitted to the local star, in your case, the one you call your

Sun. Your Sun star then encodes that transmission into its own fundamental frequency so that it is available to all other stars in the local galaxy, and so on. »

Every person on this planet has an identifiable frequency signature in time that you can pick up separate from the other billions of people?

«Correct.»

Bohdi witnesses a transformation of the imagery in his head from the cosmic image to one where Earth is suspended in isolation against a jet-black background. Earth starts to shrink in size until Bohdi can no longer see it. Then, as if in an explosion, the point bursts into a kaleidoscope of colors and fills his whole vision. As it fills his vision, an energy of joy washes over him. Just like an image of the cosmos, there are too many details to absorb. He notices that in the background of color, there are millions, possibly even billions, of tiny lights set up in an orderly spherical pattern.

«What you are witnessing is the transformation of your planet Earth from your familiar image of it in three-dimensional space to a somewhat limited representation of it in three-dimensional time for this communication. As you can see, in space Earth has a simpler structure, but in time, it is as if your planet is a whole galaxy unto itself. If you were able to see beyond the frequency spectrum you know, you could see the universe in this format of time. »

The tiny lights I am seeing, what do they represent?

«Each human currently on your planet. You see, in time, each human's presence is quite orderly, unlike in space, where they are scattered all over the surface of the planet and would be difficult to find. Each human has a distinct location in the dimensions of time.»

But how do you separate out all these billions of tiny lights that represent each human?

The spherical ball of lights in Bohdi's mind starts to change, and he feels transported through the matrix of lights to one in particular. As he is taken to this one particular point of bright white light, it appears larger in size. Like a fractal, as soon as he gets close to this point of light, it is transformed into a whole new light structure, just as the Atlas star was transformed from a point of light. Bohdi feels like the universe is like a Russian nesting doll, where one universe is embedded in another in a never-ending series. He looks intently and sees the light form has a structure in the shape of an oval. He recognizes the oval shape immediately and understands that this is the representation of a human.

« Your thought is correct. This is a fuller representation of a human in the dimensions of time, as you recognize from your previous experiences with the goggles.»

Is this a representation of me in the extra dimensions of time?

« It is not, and purposely so. It would be too much of a distraction from our current discussion. But it is a good representation of a human who has become self-aware. Let me continue. The frequencies coming from you, your planet, and your Sun carry information. Depending on how I filter and interpret the frequency content coming from your planet, I get different information. For example, in the previous radio analogy, if you tune in to a particular communication frequency, you can receive certain types of information in the form of music, news, or discussion. If you tune into other communication frequency content, you can receive images with audio content on that appropriate technology, which you call television. It is the same for me. I have access to technology that receives, and decodes, frequency content in a similar manner, like the example of your radio and television technology.»

The image in Bohdi's mind moves away from him and the billions of tiny lights reappear in its spherical form. As his point of view continues pulling away, he sees another structure come into view. All these light structures, spherical in shape and brilliant in their display of colors, are interconnected. There is one very large light structure to which all the other structures are connected. Bohdi sees this connection as a conduit between what he still recognizes as Earth as it is represented in time, and this large light structure. In Earth's time image, he sees this conduit going to a particular location, which he assumes, if the magnification were large enough, would resolve to one human. He is then brought closer to the conduit, and he sees these threads inside. It reminds him of a fiber optic bundle, which carries millions of communications. He intuitively understands it is a communication link.

What you are showing me is the link between our Sun and Earth?

«Correct. I have created a simplified image of how one human is connected to the main hub of your solar system, your Sun star. What you do not see is the link between your Sun star and my star. But you can imagine it easily enough. Continuing on with the discussion, once the frequency content we receive is decoded by our technology, it becomes just like music or a movie with your technology. It is a medium of information we can use to learn about the history, culture, and psychology of your individual and group consciousness. We can decode the information not only of one individual, but of the planet, the stars, and the galaxy. It is a tremendous amount of useful information. So, all of the billions of individuals on your planet, every last one, is encoded on the fundamental frequency of Earth and your Sun. Each of you is intimately connected to the planet in ways you have yet to discover. This last part might be difficult for you to imagine, but a very large number of frequencies associated with each and every human are easily put on each fundamental frequency of your planet.»

Bohdi wonders what information is available in this connection he has with planet Earth. *How is the communication frequency of each individual set up?*

«It is set up upon your birth as unique frequency signature. Now, when you set up an intention, this sets up a band of frequencies, and the degree of passion for your topic sets up the strength of those frequencies. The frequencies of your intention are mixed with your fundamental

frequency. This is true for all your thoughts and emotions. Let's go back to the analogy of the radio technology you use. The frequencies of your thoughts and emotions are like the frequencies of the music mixed in with the fundamental frequency of that particular radio station. For instance, this music might have multiple singers and a symphony of musicians. This music can then be broadcast to listeners far and wide in space. A listener, skilled in the art of music, can deduct information about the skill of the musicians from the broadcasted music.

«Now imagine if, with that same musical message being broadcast, the emotional, mental, and spiritual characteristics of each and every member of the symphony could also be discerned at the time that they were playing that music piece. That is a good analogy of our technology. In order to determine the emotional, mental, and spiritual characteristics of any one member on a particular planet, the technical know-how of the complex frequency filtering and decoding is necessary.»

If a musician is having a bad day emotionally, that can be detected by you? Bohdi asks.

«Correct. We can determine if they are playing with joy or are struggling with some troubling emotions, independent of the quality of their physical musical skills.»

But that means everything you think and feel is constantly available for everyone to detect and monitor.

«Precisely.»

And all these thoughts and emotions, even my intentions, are embedded in planetary-based frequencies? Poor Earth!

«Your humor is appreciated. Let us explain your statement. To detect a set of attributes, we filtered frequencies based on your Sun, your planet Earth, and individual human structural frequencies with specific characteristics that are of importance to me. In this case, I could

determine personal characteristics of you, like integrity, receptivity, strength of character, perseverance, and also an understanding of time. All this information can be known from the frequencies you broadcast.

«Many beings intend for a communication to happen, but few are able to hear, or understand, what is being sent to them. For me, the critical component for this communication is the intent and comprehension of you, the person who desires this communication. What you think and feel about yourself is very important in three-dimensional time, and these attributes are part of your transmitting signal.»

Mmmm. It is humbling, and a bit concerning, to think that what I think and feel can be picked up so far in the universe.

« Yes, indeed. If more humans understood this, they might clean up some of what they allow to go on in their minds and hearts. In your three-dimensional Time Information Field, as your friend and you have labelled it, is a transmitter and receiver capable of processing all this information. It does so continuously. As humans, you continually broadcast frequencies with the information about what you are thinking and feeling. With the appropriate technology, not only your biological status, but also your emotional, mental, and spiritual status can be accurately determined as it appears in this time reality.

«The challenge for beings of Earth is not in the receiving of the information that the frequencies represent, but in recognizing and interpreting the information correctly. You receive this information unconsciously and continuously from three-dimensional time, but it is lost due to many factors. As I have already stated, some of the reasons is that the biological circuitry is not well developed enough for humans to take the information from these Time Information Fields and bring it, without distortion, into human consciousness. All the necessary equipment is there, and in the future this will be possible. You have the ability to hear this information correctly, a trait that will be more common in humans in the future.»

*How is it that I understand your nonverbal communication in English,
only one of hundreds of languages we humans have? Are you
formatting it that way?*

«*I am formatting our nonverbal communication in your language.
If I did not do this, the information would be too difficult to
understand. Anticipating the question about how I learned English, the
information about the structure of your language is in the Time
Information Fields of your Earth and in the Time Information Field of
your cultures. I can absorb the structure of your language, but that is
only one part. Using your language to communicate some of the details
of my experience can be challenging due to the limitations of your
vocabulary and experiences. For some of our communication, it may be
necessary to use a combination of language and impressions, as you
have noticed. There are humans who have the amazing ability to learn
languages in a matter of days. You can research this yourself. We can
do the same. I hope you enjoy the challenge of this communication as
much as I do.*»

*Can I learn and communicate in your language? Bohdi thinks how
wonderful it would be to have such a skill.*

«*You and I can learn any language. For the sake of expediency, it
is easier for me to learn your language. However, to have good
communication requires much more effort than just learning the
language. It requires a common experience, which is easy for humans to
share in the same culture and can get quite complicated with two
humans from very different cultures. Now add to this the added
complexity of our planetary differences.*

«*It is time to close this communication. You have already
experienced the effect of our interaction, which is the result of
information being energy since you experience energetically every piece
of information I am sharing with you. It is an immersed experience,
and because of this, the energy of the information needs to be monitored.*

222

I have modified the energy of this information, but it will still come as a boost to your system, as you experienced after our first communication. To explain what is happening, it might be easier to think of a transformer used in your electrical circuits. The transformer steps down the voltage outside of your home to a safe level that is usable in your homes. If this was not done, the voltages would be very dangerous to those living inside the home. This is also true with our communications. The energy of the information is transformed to a safer level, but content of the information means the energy is still higher than your normal energy state, so you experience this as a boost. With these high potentials now in your Time Information Fields, everything you think or feel will become more energized. If the interaction is too long, then it can cause some instabilities in your Time Information Fields. Since I can monitor the level of energy absorbed by your Time Information Fields during our discussion, I will determine the length of these communications. Exposing your body to water, in the form of a shower or pool, or walking in your yard in bare feet can also help keep you grounded.»

The beautiful image of the Pleiades star cluster shrinks as the imagery returns to the former cosmic grandeur he saw initially. Then, slowly, the imagery begins to dim. Bohdi starts to feel dread. The time went so quickly. He has so many more questions, but he can feel the energy of the communication waning.

How will I know when we should communicate?

«You will feel a deep stirring within you, much like you did the other night, but now it will be easily recognized since we have already communicated.»

Last question. Why did you appear to me in my dreams as a pair of eyes?

«Eyes provide a way to communicate. You can often tell a lot when you stare into someone's eyes. Also, as you will learn, and intuitively

understand, eyes do not just receive information, they transmit information as well. I created that format because I believed it would be the best way to connect with you. It appears to have worked. I will now close.»

With that, the energy of communication fades, but in its place, he feels a surge of excitement. The possibilities seem wide open. What more will he learn about three-dimensional time?

As the energy of excitement takes over Bohdi's body, he jumps up from the chair, his heart pounding. He races downstairs and walks outside. This September afternoon has a perfect temperature. He feels like yelling to the world that who we are is so much more than we know. He paces around the backyard, unable to be still because of the energy coursing through his veins. The opportunity to learn about these dimensions in time has just been blown wide open. He can barely keep a consistent thought because his mind jumps from idea to idea about what to ask the next time, what he can learn, what the implications of the communication will be.

He decides to call Skylar, but after ringing for a while, her voicemail picks up. He leaves an incoherent message with an ending to call him. Then he texts her.

He starts pacing like a wild animal, barely able to contain the energy. He realizes he was unable to string a sentence together coherently when he left the voicemail. He decides to go for a long walk to try to quench this strong energy running through his veins.

58.

Later the same evening, Bohdi has arranged to meet Skylar for a walk in an area of town where he figures they can talk with some privacy.

He reminds her of the eye dreams and explains the beginning of the communication with the being, who can travel in three-dimensional time.

"Get out of here, you really think you've communicated with an alien in three-dimensional time?" she shoots back.

"Well, I don't think *alien* is the right word. It has negative connotations. I prefer *a being*. But, yes, I definitely do."

Skylar is quiet for a moment. Her head is full of images from movies about aliens meeting humans, then invading them and then bursting out of them. She shudders at the thought and squirms. To lighten the conversation, she asks with some humor in her voice, "What is his name?"

Bohdi understands he is being setup, but answers, "He has chosen a name Sullivan for our communication."

"Sullivan, your ETBuddy has a name Sullivan. What kind of ET is that?"

Bohdi feels defensive, but works to come up with a counter remark, "A friendly one."

Skylar is not buying it. "How do you know you can trust this alien, this ETBuddy of yours?"

Bohdi bristles. He feels the *being* he is communicating with deserves more respect than that.

Skylar can see that he's not comfortable, but she is really struggling with her fear. "Let's call him ETBuddy for now."

"I'll go with that—for now." Bohdi wants to keep this discussion on a positive note.

"Okay. How do you know this ETBuddy of yours is not going to use you to get access to Earth? I mean, in so many of the movies I have seen, all these aliens . . . I mean, *beings*, start off nice, then turn really ugly and cause all sorts of problems for us humans."

Bohdi was going to say something, but she continues.

"Does he look reptilian, or does he look like us?'

"I don't know, Skylar. I've only had a visual impression of his eyes and his field, which I assume is his Time Information Field. His Time Information Field looks amazing. So bright and vital. A beautiful indigo blue with gold and silver in it. Also, there is a kindness I experience…"

Bohdi stops, realizing he is rambling on a bit.

"How will you know if you can trust this ETBuddy?" Her walking speeds up as the implications of what Bohdi is sharing starts to sink in. Bohdi keeps pace with her, grateful to have an outlet for this extra energy he feels inside, but disappointed by her reaction.

"How did you know it was your mother," he asks pointedly.

Skylar shoots him a glare, "That is totally different," she snaps back.

"Why?"

"Now you are starting to piss me off a bit. You are trying to tell me there is no difference between a communication in a vivid dream I had with my mother and this, this ETBuddy of yours!"

Bohdi instinctively reaches out for her arm, but she pulls back. She is not happy with this conversation.

"Skylar, I agree. I should not have compared the two. But I see it as an extension of what happened with your mother. I thought you would be excited. Think of what we can learn."

She looks at him with a stern look, "Think about what could go wrong!

Besides, I think this is a real diversion from where we should be putting or focus and energies, the development of the goggles. That to me is more important than what is going on here."

Bohdi immediately recognizes that what she has just said is a fair comment. This could easily be a distraction for him and they don't have loads of free time. But he also knows he is not going to stop this communication yet. There were three very lucid dreams that got him to this point. But he is struggling inside, in a way that he barely recognized himself. He tries to understand why he feels so upset.

A stressful silence drapes over the two of them with a cold and damp feeling as Bohdi and Skylar each withdraw into themselves trying to figure out where their limits should be.

After a long ten minutes of walking in silence, Bohdi feels his equilibrium return. He turns to Skylar and says, "What you are saying is fair. We do not have a lot of time and the goggles are a commitment we made. And true, this could well be a distraction. But I have to give it a few shots. It could also help us understand what we are doing. It could be a great help. So, I would like to propose that I try this communication a few times and if you and I agree it is a real distraction, I stop."

Skylar is still silent. She likes that he heard her about the distraction. But she wants this to stop now.

Bohdi reaches out to Skylar's hand.

She lets him hold her hand.

Bohdi proposes an idea, "How about you use the goggles to view me when I communicate with ETBuddy. You have enough history of viewing me to maybe develop some trust."

She recognizes this as a good idea. She softens in her stance. "If I see something that gives me a bad feeling, I'll let you know."

She moves in closer.

Finally, Bohdi stops. He holds her hand firmly as she tries to walk on.

He pulls her close to him. She lets him. As Bohdi wraps his arms around her, she rests her head on his chest. Bohdi feels the last vestiges of his tension drain away.

Skylar speaks softly, "I would say that I want you to stop, but I cannot. It's not who we are. But I am really concerned. If you are getting distracted, I am going to let you know. Or if this is causing changes in you that I am not comfortable with, I will say so."

"Okay, fair enough."

She pulls back, though Bohdi's arms prevent her from moving too far away. "If you screw this up and he and his buddies invade our planet, I will be really mad at you."

He laughs. "Okay, *then* you can be mad at me."

59.

"What is the purpose of this mission, and why the need for scans?" Agent Jared asks his boss, Paul, his voice sounding louder than he would like in this closed-door meeting.

"Skylar and Bohdi are now associated with stolen Chronos Consortium property," Paul replies sternly. He is in no mood to have a mission that nearly cost him his career be questioned by one of his agents.

"But the circumstances point to Dr. Brown as the recipient of stolen property. He is the link to John Garrison. Not Skylar or Bohdi!" Jared presses back with force. "And why the need for a scan of such a young person? I want a proper answer!"

Paul's explodes. "Under no circumstances—none—will you question me like that. Do you understand?"

Jared stays quiet. He has had officers far more fearsome bellow at him in the service and is not about to let Paul intimidate him. Paul had told him yesterday the scans were for a research project, and Jared does not buy it.

"Do you understand me?" Paul yells again. "It is your job to execute the missions we assign you, not to question the purpose of said missions."

Jared is not sure he will achieve his aim of getting an answer, but he wants to resist even more now, because of how Paul is behaving. But he knows he is outranked, so he locks eyes with Paul and says, "I do *not* understand, but I withdraw my question."

The reply stuns Paul, and he takes a second or two to formulate a response.

"Good. This meeting is over."

Jared slowly gets up from the chair on the other side of Paul's grand mahogany desk. He feels anger rising inside and hesitates to reconsider his reply. He is sick of the lies. The constant lies and cover-ups over the purpose of these missions.

Paul notices Jared's hesitation. His own anger becomes more forceful, and he is just about to let Jared know that he can be replaced when Jared continues rising to his feet, turns his back to Paul, and walks out.

It is the first time Jared has confronted his boss like this. He was hoping to get some information that might allow him to sleep better at night. Too many sleepless nights are starting to affect his emotional balance. He is also worried that he cannot quarantine the nagging feeling deep inside him. He desperately wants to understand what possible threat the targeted young people create to the financial and political structures that the Chronos Consortium uses to keep control over global chaos. These global organizations have trillions of dollars at their disposal, and these two are just college kids. Why does the Chronos Consortium need a scan? It makes no sense. Is he seeing an indication that the Chronos Consortium is willing to monitor anyone, possibly even his family . . . his own son . . . for unjustified reasons? Taking a scan of a young person, and giving the Chronos Consortium the potential to disrupt their emotional equilibrium, at such a turbulent time in their life, seems to Jared to be a serious action. The thought leaves him cold.

His stomach tightens as he drives to the Donaldson home on this pleasantly warm Saturday morning in October. He feels confused. *This is probably the easiest mission I've ever undertaken, yet it's the one that unnerves me the most.* He takes some cold comfort in the fact that the main goal of his assignment is to scope out the Donaldson property for a potential recovery mission. But the fact that he's also tasked with taking a frequency scan still bothers him. He does not believe the purpose of the scan data is for a research project that the Chronos Consortium is conducting on the field structures of young people. He figures it's a front for some other purpose, and he really wants to know why. He knows that many projects are cloaked in other motives so anyone without direct access to the mission cannot determine what the true intent is. One thing he's certain of, after seven years of working for Paul's group, is that the mission is not what Paul says it is.

For this assignment, he's been given the identity of George Mariazen with a phone, dummy address, and a website to support the constructed Global Endangered Species organization for which he is supposed to be getting donations for.

****

Bohdi sits next to Skylar at the dining room table. He has the goggles on and is watching Skylar as she struggles with her physics homework problems. They are spending a lazy Saturday afternoon together. Skylar's father had an invitation to go for a hike with a friend.

There is a knock at the door. Bohdi freezes. "Who could that be?" He immediately switches the goggles to the One setting. "Give me fifteen seconds," he says anxiously as he starts counting. Skylar moves to the front door and waits for Bohdi to switch to Minus mode and then pull the goggles off.

Once Bohdi has moved the goggles out of sight, Skylar opens the front door. She sees a stranger with a folder in her hand. "Can I help you?"

"Yes, my name is George Mariazen, and I represent Global Endangered Species, a nonprofit organization that seeks to protect species like the rhino, which is being hunted to extinction for its horn. I was hoping to talk to Skylar. Is she home?"

"Umm, that's me?"

"How are you today?"

"Okay."

Just then Bohdi appears at Skylar's right side.

"Hi, my name is George. Are you also part of this family?"

"No," he replies without directly answering this person's question.

George turns his attention back to Skylar. "Pleasant neighborhood you live in. You lived here long?"

"Yes. How can I help you?"

George goes into his speech about how Global Endangered Species is trying to get money to buy rhinos in Africa and bring them to sanctuaries protected by guards. The organization is looking for donations. He offers a certificate to show that the organization is registered.

"Umm, sounds like you have the wrong person. You probably want"—Skylar stops herself from saying her mother—"my father. I am a student, and I am broke, so I can't afford any donations right now."

Bohdi jumps in. "How do you get your names? Specifically, Skylar's."

George looks at his folder. "Seems like when you were at Patterson University, you signed a sheet to register your commitment to this cause. It looks like you did not, or I should say could not, donate money at that time, but you stated that you could be contacted in the future."

Skylar mentally scrambles to recall when this might have happened. Every day at the student union there were students trying to get other students involved in causes. She does not remember one asking for her address, but it could have happened. Typically, they wanted emails, not physical addresses. Maybe she was receptive to giving that information away. She can't remember, but doubts it. Too much has happened in her life to keep track of these details, so she lets it go.

"Could be, I really don't remember," she responds impatiently. Her upbringing would normally prompt her to invite George into the house, but she feels hesitant for reasons she can't put her finger on. Since it's a pleasant October day, she just lets George give more details about the organization's missions. She suddenly wonders why she and Bohdi are inside. It's too nice to let a fall day like this pass by.

Bohdi notices that George has put his left hand in his jacket pocket twice in the time they have been talking to him. He keeps expecting him to pull out a phone or some other object, but so far, nothing. He senses something fishy about this guy. He sure doesn't look like someone who is dedicated to endangered species. He looks like a former football player, with broad shoulders and a thick neck.

Jared is worried that the scans he's is taking of them both will not be as effective unless he can get one of them individually. He takes another scan again despite them being together, because he might not get a better chance.

He can see that Bohdi is focused on him, not the conversation. He decides the next time he will reach into his right pocket to pull out his phone and pretend to be looking at it and start the next scan remotely from his phone. He is glad that he has this option and makes sure he cannot see his phone screen. He already used his hidden camera to video the front and right side of the house, before he rang the doorbell. All he needs to do now is get a clean scan of each of them.

Bohdi has a knot in his stomach. He gets an idea, excuses himself and heads to the dining room.

George sees the opportunity he was looking for: Skylar by herself. Skylar continues to ask him questions, not sure why she feels annoyed about this whole interaction. She looks directly at George, "Why not catch us at the student union?"

"I also have a list of people in the town, most of whom are not students. I stopped by here because it was in the area. Many students are in the same financial situation as you, so students only make up a small portion of our contributions. But we like to get people involved when they are young." George smiles and shifts hands on his clipboard so he can put his left hand back into his pocket.

Bohdi sits down, moves the chair so that if he leans forward he can see Skylar's body in the space between the door and the doorjamb. He can also see the clipboard and the right arm of George's body. *Skylar, don't let that guy move!* he thinks as he puts the goggles on his head, waits for fifteen seconds, and then switches into Plus mode.

"Do you have a card I can have for future contact information?" Skylar asks. "I think this is a good cause, but I would like you to take my name off your list. If I have the cash to donate in the future, I'll contact your organization."

George is pleased. He now has an excuse to pretend to fumble through his pockets. He again reaches into his vest pocket to start another scan. Then, to continue the fake search, he reaches into his pants pockets. He only needs thirty seconds.

Bohdi leans forward enough to see the familiar outline of Skylar's field after the goggle startup sequence is completed. He has the sequence down to a science and can do it in less than 45 seconds.

"What the hell!" he almost yells out as he sees a white beam come from George's direction and spread itself into the field around Skylar. His instinct is to run to the door, but he cannot see any features of the house with the goggles in this mode, and he cannot reveal the goggles. He switches the goggles into One mode, pulls off the electronic boxes and heads to the front door.

George is passing the card to Skylar as he hears a noise, looks up, and sees Bohdi moving quickly to Skylar, his face showing alarm.

Skylar takes George's card as Bohdi pulls on her arm and says firmly, "You have a call from your father. He really needs to talk to you. Now."

Skylar sees the alarm in Bohdi's face, but before she can react, George asks, "Mind if I use the bathroom?"

"Uh, s-sure." Skylar is confused by the sudden change in events.

"Just a minute," Bohdi says firmly as he pulls Skylar back.

George knows he got enough time for a scan, but worries about the Bohdi's interference.

Bohdi closes the door so there is only an inch or so left open.

"What's going on!" Skylar asks in a hushed tone.

Bohdi puts his finger to his lips and continues pulling Skylar to the kitchen, safely out of listening range.

"That guy is not who he says he is!"

"Wha—"

Bohdi moves his hands to signify her to keep her voice down. "I saw a beam coming from his direction. He's doing something to your Time Information Field. Are you okay?"

"Yeah, just confused and annoyed."

"Stay here. I'll get rid of him."

Before Skylar can say anything, he is off to the front door.

"Sorry, we have a family issue to deal with, so we have to say goodbye. There is a public bathroom two miles in that direction, at the gas station. You probably passed it on your way here."

Jared is cool during his reply. He suspects Bohdi is not telling the truth, but he is in no position to call him on it. He planned to use the bathroom ploy to get video of the inside of the house.

He is about to work a new angle, but Bohdi cuts him short. "Sorry, I have to go. Good luck with your cause."

He steps back and closes the door. He is not going to let this dubious person in the house under any circumstance.

Skylar, stunned, moves to the living room window, where Bohdi is standing. Bohdi hears her and motions her to stay behind the door. He is standing in the corner of the window, behind the sheer curtain to hide his profile, watching George slowly leave.

George is standing at his car door, looking first up the street and then slowly down it. He is using his hidden camera to capture as much of the area as he can. Disappointed that this easy mission ended without an interior video of the house, Jared makes sure he has good video of the neighborhood in case they need extra time.

Then he gets into the car.

For somebody who needs to use the bathroom, he sure is moving slowly, Bohdi thinks.

He hears the car start. After it backs up slowly and then drives away, he turns to Skylar, who is anxiously waiting for an explanation.

"That guy is trouble. I swear, Skylar, he shot some beam at you, and it interfaced with your field. I've never seen anything like that in all the times we've used those goggles. I know how your field behaves in good and tense times. This was nothing like that."

"You saw *what*?"

"A beam. A beam of energy or something. It came from his direction and went directly into your field. Did you feel anything? Are you sure you're okay?"

"Well, I'm sort of edgy, but so much has just happened that might make me edgy even without the fact you saw this guy beaming me with something."

"Who has technology that interacts with our fields? That guy kept reaching into his vest pocket. Did you notice that?" Bohdi feels alarm rushing through his veins, and he's not going to try to hide it.

"Can't say it stood out, but my mind was still too lost in my homework to fully engage with this person."

"Well, I have a bad feeling about what happened."

"I agree it was a bit odd," Skylar says, then tries to lighten the mood. "Did you see the size of his neck? He looks like a football player, or a marine, not a granola type interested in saving rhinos."

Bohdi ignores him and shakes his head. "Something is going on. That guy is definitely *not* about saving rhinos."

60.

Agent Jared reflects on his report that he just sent to boss, Paul. He wrote it last night, but wanted a night to sleep on it. He is still able to justify the email in that it reported exactly what he was instructed to do. Get a scan of Skylar and Bohdi and scope out the property.

He did not report the odd behavior Bohdi had exhibited. It made him suspicious, and under other circumstances, he would detail that clearly in order to raise suspicions, but he did not trust the mission of these projects. He spoke with his wife about getting another job. If might require financial changes in their lives, but he has to make a change. His wife supported his decision, but his job search has not brought anything that he is excited about.

Jared feels a relief after hitting the Send button, and now wants to spend the rest of this Sunday with his family. Tomorrow he will start his search for a new life. He knows the Chronos Consortium can make his life very difficult, but he has lived through difficult times before and had no future. Now he has a future, with his wife and son, so the difficulties he will have to face will have a purpose. He also knows that he can make the Chronos Consortium's life difficult too, and is considering his options.

****

On Tuesday of the same week, Agent Tania reanalyzes the data she got from Agent Jared. She already called her colleague Agent Phil and asked him to come in. The result of the scan for their Young Project did not fit what she was expecting. There were even more fundamental changes in these field. Tania does not understand why this is so different. Could it be that these young people were an exception to the others that she has data on? She needs Phil's help to get information from Hank and Paul on these targets.

It is not just that these two have close to the highest combined emotional and spiritual IQs she has ever measured, but there are geometric ratios in the frequency data she has never seen before. What could this possibly mean? Did Jared get as clean a scan as he said he did? She is reluctant to send this data to Hank, since he will use it against them, saying their theory is incorrect, but she knows she is looking at something fundamentally new—she just does not know what yet.

61.

After Skylar and Bohdi gave Dr. Bradley that fascinating experience with the goggles, she placed a call to her friend Tom Williamson. He had recently reached out to her, looking to finance a project that would help open people's minds to a bigger view of who they are. He had read several Suzanne's articles and liked the way she approached her psychology with a bent toward the ideas that came out of the East. He and Suzanne had spent a number of evenings discussing over dinner what project she could set up. He understands Eastern philosophy very well and credits his happiness and his success to the mental and emotional practices that were a natural extension of his study. Along the way, he came to see that questioning your own beliefs, as troublesome as it can be sometimes, is eye-opening. Through this study, Tom learned that what you think regularly, of your life, of yourself, matters. He believes thought has a creative power, one he utilizes every day, but does not fully understand. He wants to bring this understanding to others, since he feels there is not enough critical thinking going on, which is why he reached out to Dr. Bradley.

Dr. Bradley knows she has found the project that Tom should get involved in. She plans to talk him into financing the development of the goggles to the next stage. She thought Skylar's insight about the next stage of development was very insightful. She knows that if she gets Tom to have the same experience she had with the goggles, he will throw not only his finances behind it, but also his great talent for organization. She spoke with Skylar and Bohdi about this call, given the nondisclosure she had signed with them, and they both said they trusted her judgement.

The call with Tom went as she expected. He expressed strong interest in what she described to him and asked that a meeting be setup as soon as possible.

****

Skylar and Bohdi meet Tom at Suzanne's home so he can try out the goggles. After the necessary paperwork, they explained the goggles to him in detail, the experiments they had carried out and what they had learned. Suzanne explained how she had used psychology-based questions with the two of them on her visit and saw changes in these fields of color in real time. Based on their experience with the Time Information Fields, she felt that a correlation between what is seen and what is felt is clearly there. It needs to be documented in a more rigorous fashion, preferably by someone like herself, who has expertise in the field of psychology. In addition, she wants to use EEG and other metrics to document emotional and mental arousal and correlate it to what is seen with the goggles. They showed Tom how the Time Information Fields can be seen even through matter. As Tom used the goggles and listened to what the three of them told him, he saw that this project exceeded what he had initially envisioned he might finance. He asks Skylar what her vision is for the goggles.

Skylar explains how it might be possible to incorporate this technology into a virtual reality headset. Virtual reality headsets are all the rage and already a hit in the market. The idea is to design the goggles to look like a virtual reality headset and then to incorporate the Time Information Field feature into the headsets, so it is an extra option that the other headsets on the market do not have. She figures that with some intensive technical effort, they can combine what can be physically seen in front of a person with the Time Information Field images.

Tom remembers Suzanne commenting about how a technology like this could revolutionize how people see their own mental and emotional patterns. It also has the potential to disrupt how people are diagnosed for mental and emotional issues. Tom loves the idea of a headset and says that they need to spend some time working out a strategic business plan. Skylar then fills Tom and Suzanne in on some of the history of the goggles, on Dr. Brown's work and wishes, and his comments about an organization called the Chronos Consortium. Skylar was pleased that both Tom and Suzanne were determined to undermine any organization, or situation, that hindered people's ability to think for themselves. Tom iterates that his mission is to help people understand that what they think matters, and that this is even more important, given the current political climate. This discussion galvanizes their commitment to the project, and the four of them decide they will get together soon to discuss more concrete details.

After Skylar and Bohdi leave Suzanne's home, they are beyond thrilled that they now have solid partners in their project. They wish that

Dr. Brown was still alive to be a part of this, or that they could share this news with Ms. Brown. In time, they hope they can.

62.

Hank has just spent a difficult hour in a meeting with top Chronos Consortium administrators right before lunch.

He paces the floor of his office, more convinced than ever that the Chronos Consortium needs his Re-Imagination Project. It is the way of the future. The need to keep scanning and targeting individuals is a technique of the past.

Hank opens the folder on his desk, which contains the analysis Jim did on the seeding experiments. Hank is thrilled with the results. Jim used his newly developed algorithm with the psychology tests to group people together, and then worked to find the right combinations of frequencies to optimize the bias. When that was combined with the right kind of message, the results exceeded expectations. They hinted that people are so reactive in response to the seeded messages that Jim suspects they might be coaxed into taking actions that might even undermine their own self-interests; that's how powerful Jim believes this combined bias field and seeding approach might be.

Jim states in the report that after the group grew to 120 people, the amount of energy required in the bias fields did not scale up proportionally at all. Less and less additional energy was required. It was as if a critical mass had been reached, and the people started affecting one another like a chain reaction. Jim also had cleverly done an experiment with thirty people in four locations. Since the bias field is designed to operate in *time,* distance in *space* is not a factor. Jim seeded the same message to all four locations. The results were identical. The technique worked independent of distance. With the modified technology, the Chronos Consortium could bias a group of people anywhere in the world, needing only to generate a critical threshold of energy and get the people to hear, or watch, the seeding messages. Jim laid out additional experiments that could be run and, with them, a budget for executing the proposed experiments.

Hank is thrilled all over again after reading the sentence about a group so influenced they might work unbeknownst to themselves against their own interests. Here, Jim has independently confirmed what Hank believes is possible: that they can move opinion in the masses to generate a push from the bottom up, and that it is about time. Jim's results prove a technique that the Chronos Consortium can use to more directly tap into the source of their power: people's fear.

Hank decides to use his lunch break to write an outline that he can present to his superiors, asking that the Chronos Consortium invest more in this new technique. He opens a document and titles it: "The Re-Imagination Project: Research, Results, and Future Implications."

Then he starts dumping into a document the key ideas in numbered points that he needs to communicate to get this project funded.

1. The past efforts of training single individuals to make key decisions for the Chronos Consortium have been successful, but it also represents single-point failures, and with the increased media attention, it is much more difficult to create all the necessary influences that the Chronos Consortium objectives require.
2. It is recognized that influencing larger groups of people with the technology the Chronos Consortium currently has is ineffective. Past research has demonstrated that these distributed fields, detuned to include more individuals, falls off in its effectiveness until in groups of fifty or more people, the results become only slightly better than random.
3. There is now new research carried out by myself and Jim Stewart that clearly demonstrates a unique and more effective technique. This technique uses modified Chronos Consortium technology to influence large groups of people toward particular seeded ideas and policies. The use of customized targeted bias fields and seeding techniques has created dramatically positive results.
4. Our experiments use custom bias designed fields, based on psychological profiling of specific groups, to prime the emotional level of fear and frustration in the targeted groups, putting the people into an artificial survival mode. This existential survival threat causes individuals to more effectively hijack the amygdala in the ancient part of the brain. As we well know, this bypasses the cognitive thought processes. Seeding messages are sent out on social media to

these individuals while they are in the existential survival mode. The seeding messages have proven very effective in converging this "group biased fear" in a particular direction. In order to work, the seed idea must have the following properties:

> 4.1. It must instill a fear that freedoms or rights are being taken away by a particular group or individual.
>
> 4.2. It must instill a mistrust in those who are responsible for execution of any possible policy that might take those threatened freedoms or rights away.
>
> 4.3. It must be applied regularly and in a variety of formats to achieve resonance across as broad a range as possible of targeted groups.

5. The technique has thus re-imagined for this group an emotional response that becomes a battle cry against the perceived threats mentioned in the seeded messages. Initial work in this area suggests that individuals not only willingly allow the messages in social media to become their battle cry, but also, they do this even when it is not in their self-interest to carry on the battle.

6. A key experiment demonstrates that at some point the strength of the generated fields becomes insignificant. A certain bias field strength will likely work as well on hundreds as on thousands, and possibly even millions, of individuals. What appears to happen is that at the subconscious level, resonances in time are so strong that the successive hijacking of the amygdala for additional people is done easily and requires no additional effort on the part of the Chronos Consortium. The hijacking reaches a critical mass and becomes self-sustaining.

7. What should also be stressed is that this bias influence on a group, before critical mass of influence is reached, cannot be continuous, since documented fatigue sets in, diminishing the effect. It must be done regularly, but with small periods of

downtime to prevent renormalization of the group's brain response.

8. The Re-Imagination Project represents the most significant technique that has been proposed to the Chronos Consortium to continue their influence. It addresses two of the critical issues currently faced by the organization:

    8.1. A continual staffing crisis in the last decades due to the high level of training necessary for individual specialists working on individual targets.

    8.2. The elimination of single-point failures when a target goes rogue, or an agent fails in their mission.

    8.3. A complementary bottoms-up approach to match the traditional top-down approach the Chronos Consortium has used in the past.

Hank stops there and revels in the glow of confidence that the future looks bright as he rides the success of his Re-Imagination Project to his own, as well as the Chronos Consortium's, success.

63.

Skylar still can't believe that Tom Williamson is willing to both finance the project and, as Suzanne Bradley told them, organize the business end of making the goggles. Suzanne is already starting to organize the psychology research she would like to do. She will use a second set of goggles that Skylar and Bohdi are finishing, with the spare set of lenses that Dr. Brown left them. Suzanne is thinking that, at the appropriate time, she will quit Patterson University. This makes it all so real. It excites Skylar and Bohdi, but also makes them feel nervous.

64.

Skylar looks at the clock, eager to get started since her father is away for the weekend. She expects Bohdi to be knocking at the door any minute, and together, they will build the Faraday cage that they want to add for added safekeeping of the goggles. She and Bohdi have this strong gut feeling they needed to take more precautionary actions.

Soon she hears a knock at the door. He is barely in the door, before she asks, "Let's see those copper plates."

Bohdi kisses her, and then goes to the kitchen, where he puts the box, with all the parts in it, on the floor and pulls out one of the twelve-inch by twenty-four-inch copper sheets.

"Are you planning to glue this to the walls inside the linen closet hiding place? Won't that stink for a while?"

"Sure would! That's why I'm not gluing. I'm going to drill little holes and mount them with screws to the walls, underneath the shelf and the floor. Then I will use one of the drilled holes to put a small bolt and nut into it and connect all the sheets with the ground wire."

He reaches in the box and pulls out a spool of thin stranded copper wire. "Should be easy to do. I also bought this conductive tape, which I'll use to tape all the joints between the copper sheets."

"I pulled the cover to the cable connector in my room and unplugged it in the basement. Once we have the rod in the ground, we can run the copper wire through the basement door and connect it to the cable."

"Your idea was great. Saves trying to figure out how to hide the grounding wire to your bedroom window in some other way," Bohdi complements Skylar.

He adds, "I figure we'll have to pull off the floor molding in your room and hide this grounding wire behind it.

"Let's get it done," Skylar says as she picks up one of the copper sheets, eager to create this additional security for the goggles.

Bohdi and Skylar spend the afternoon making the Faraday cage. Once done, they revel in the satisfaction that the goggles are now as secure as they can make them. The two head out for a couple of beers and pizza to celebrate.

65.

It has been three weeks since Bohdi had his first communication with ETBuddy. He has been working to temper his enthusiasm, since it is impacting his ability to concentrate on his schoolwork. The psychology and physics of what ETBuddy is implying in his communications gives new meaning to what he is learning at Patterson.

Waiting an extra week because of all of his commitments was challenging. He feels like he has ADD. His mind continually fluctuates between this reality and the ever more interesting ideas that have been communicated to him. He recognizes how distracted he is, but Skylar, thankfully, helps him stay focused through his last exam for the semester.

Skylar is finding herself more intrigued by this crazy adventure of Bohdi's after he told her about what he had learned in the first communication with ETBuddy. He asked her to use the goggles this time, but she declined and told him to go ahead without her and promised she would use the goggles next time. Bohdi plans to hold her to this promise.

Skylar reminded him that his current obsession with ETBuddy comes at the cost of goggles experiments. Bohdi recognized that what she said was true, but he needed another communication or two to get in his questions. He promised to slow down his pace after he and Skylar used the goggles during a communication. She gave him a kind, but surly, compliment on the way he is negotiating this. Bohdi did not deny it. He figured it would be better if she used the goggles during one of the communications sooner rather than later. He has no idea how long the communications may go on and he hopes that Skylar's experience with the goggles will erase what reservations she has left.

The house is quiet as Bohdi finds himself alone this Tuesday evening during the semester break. The holidays start in two days, and he knows there will not be any quiet time for two weeks or so. This is the perfect time for another communication with ETBuddy. He's been feeling ETBuddy's prompting, so settles down in the chair and glances at the clock—almost 7:00 p.m. He goes through his standard deep meditative practice and then waits for the communication to begin. The image he looks forward to, of ETBuddy, with his brilliant indigo oval, appears. Then it transforms into the spectacular universe inside his mind.

«Glad to communicate with you again.»

Bohdi does not feel as naked as he did before. He is who he is, and he is okay with that. *I am thrilled to have another opportunity to talk to you. I have more questions regarding traveling in spacetime. I am really curious about how it's done.*

«Do you have a specific question or just a general question?»

Mmmm, general spacetime travel in three-dimensional time probably is a good place to begin. He realizes that ETbuddy probably knows his questions, but he likes the format where he asks the questions.

«I am happy to oblige your curiosity. I will give you an analogy of what happens when we travel in spacetime. We have a material structure to travel in, which you might call a spaceship, and it is constructed in a particular way. We have carefully chosen the frequency content of the materials so there is harmony among them for a specific purpose. This is similar to a complex musical composition, like one created for an orchestra. All the frequencies are chosen specifically, along with their timing, and so on, to give a desired result. Let me use another analogy to explain why the frequency composition is so important for our spaceship and how it relates to time travel.»

Bohdi then hears a piece of music, softly at first, then louder. He recognizes it as Mozart. He remembers his mother playing this music for him when he was small, to lull him to sleep. Something about night music comes to mind, and that this piece was always the beginning, but that is all he remembers.

«This musical composition can be played in many different frequencies, or keys, as your musicians call it. One key is chosen by the creator of the music, because it brings the maximum desired effect. Now, if this same musical structure is played in a key that is beyond sound, that is, ultrasonic, you cannot hear it anymore, but the music composition is still there.»

He hears the music going up in pitch until he cannot hear it anymore. But even though he cannot hear it, he still remembers the notes, as if it was burned into his memory all those years ago.

«If you increased the key into the visible range, it is not identified as a musical structure anymore but possibly an interesting color arrangement. But a person versed in the art of frequency patterning could capture that light show, transform it back to the sound frequencies, and the musical composition would be back in a form that is easily recognizable as music.»

A light show begins to form in his mind. What surprises him is that the brightness of the colors, and the color change, seem to match the tempo of this music. He realizes this is the same piece of music from his childhood, but now in the form of light.

«Our material scientists and engineers build our materials using this principle of frequency shifting. As you are beginning to understand, in three-dimensional time all structures are composed of frequencies and therefore, resonances.

«Now, what if I took those frequency compositions, which are the structure of not only our vehicles, but our bodies—physically, emotionally, mentally, and spiritually, as well—and apply the same technique? This time, I transform the frequencies to a key that is beyond anything that your matter can detect. In other words, our physical presence cannot be seen by your eyes and is not detectable by any means you presently have on Earth. We become completely invisible.»

You can control if you are invisible to us or not?

«*Correct. Just as this piece of music disappears from your range of hearing, so I can come into your world undetected by any manner that you have available in your material world. I then can shift into a range of detection by your material world if I so choose, and just as easily disappear from detection.*»

But you mentioned before that you primarily live in three-dimensional time. What is the relationship between three-dimensional space, the world we see, and three-dimensional time, the world we cannot see?

«*This is a good question. Three-dimensional space and three-dimensional time are inverse of each other. In your familiar three-dimensional space, if you do not add energy to an object, its speed will naturally go to zero. In three-dimensional time, if you do not add energy to a 'time object', for lack of a better term, it will naturally move at much much faster than the speed of light. If you want to slow down this time object 'objects' speed, we have to add energy. You have theoretical particles your scientists call tachyons that have the same behavior. As mentioned before, the best analogy I can give to explain this is if you want to slow down the thoughts in your mind, you have to apply effort, or energy, to slow down the inner 'speed' of your mind. Hopefully this helps. Much more on this topic is far beyond this current conversation.*»

Interesting. I have to think about that. How do you travel in three-dimensional time?

«*Remember the radio example from our previous communication, where each star and planet has its own fundamental frequency. When you tune your radio to a particular radio station's fundamental frequency, you have a phenomenon call resonance. The radio station fundamental frequency and your radio's fundamental frequency are resonating together, and so the information from the radio station can now be detected and played to you.*

«Let's go back to where you are listening to a musical composition played in a concert hall. Your microphones and music-recording technology allow you to record this musical composition. Once this music is recorded, it can be sent anywhere in your world, easily and quickly. On the receiving end, you need technology to convert this recorded format back into the frequency structure, and with the use of a speaker, you can impress the local air mass with the same frequencies as the orchestra did at the concert hall air. You have now transported this music to a new location.»

So, this how you travel? Bohdi asks in his excitement.

«Similar, but not the same. I am using the music analogy to make it more understandable how the people and spaceship are transmitted. Remember the new location will be based on the fundamental frequencies encoded into the transmission, but the energy structure is what is transported, not the physical structure. Your traveling in three-dimensional space is similar to packing up the whole orchestra— musicians and instruments—into a vehicle and then transporting them in the vehicle to a new place. A slow and difficult process. In three-dimensional time, traveling involves converting what we are traveling in, and our bodies, back and forth between different structures, allowing for much faster traveling. »

An image of a sphere, with six human forms sitting inside, appears in Bohdi's mind. It looks like a simple representation of a spaceship.

«As a more accurate analogy is that the vehicle and all those on board are converted into a three-dimensional time structure, which in the previous example would be like the recorded form. An example of the transformation of the structure is the way the mathematical Fourier algorithms transforms an image of a three-dimensional space object into a frequency structure. This frequency structure does not look like anything like the image of the object did, but all the information necessary to reconstruct the object is in this new frequency structure.»

The image transforms into what looks to be a bright center light with lots of small light structures around this center light. This has no recognizable physical structure. Bohdi hears a single note loud and clear with a much quieter sounding arrangement of musical chords associated with the light pattern.

«This new frequency format is then vibrated from our present location in three-dimensional time to our destination in three-dimensional time. The new place can be thought of as a cosmic hub, somewhere else in the galaxy, or universe. Your Sun star is a cosmic hub, whereas your planet is a local hub. So first we travel to the star, on what could be described as galactic highways. Once we reach the star, then we travel on local roads, for lack of a better word, to the planet we are interested in. Moving around the planet would be like using the city road infrastructure.»

Bohdi hears a distant single note. He wishes he knew more about music to estimate what note it is.

«I tune the resonance of our three-dimensional time vehicle to the place I wish to go, the hub in this analogy. Since each hub has a unique resonance address, I just need to match this resonance. Think of two tuning forks. Put energy into one by hitting it, and the energy of this tuning is transferred to other tuning forks tuned to the same resonant frequency. The transit time in three-dimensional time is extremely fast. As stated before, it is always so much faster than the speed of light.»

Then the complex light shape begins to change. It slowly moves up in pitch. As the frequency of the key note of the light structure light comes closer to the frequency of the distant note, he hears a slow wobble in the intensity of the note, until all of a sudden, the ball of light disappears from view.

«Notice how quickly the form disappeared after hitting resonance with the fundamental frequency of the destination. There are some

features that need to be considered when navigating three-dimensional time.

«We have very detailed maps of the spacetime fields of the galaxy, as well as detectors used to measure the changes in this spacetime field. These maps are critical to knowing how to reconstruct our material structures back in three-dimensional space. Your travelers who travel on the water have to track weather phenomena as well as underwater structures such as rocks closely to prevent their vehicles from sinking. We also have to track anomalies in the spacetime fields in order to be able to adjust our frequency structure appropriately and avoid what you might call an accident. Sudden changes in speed, where the spacetime changes rapidly, can harm both vehicle and travelers. Think of what might happen if one of your airplanes suddenly flew into a space where the density of air was like that of water. It would tear the airplane apart.

«We only go much faster than the speed of light in well-mapped with uniform spacetime pathways, much like you can go faster along the relatively straight highway on your planet's surface compared to a small back road through mountains. In your solar system, this limits us to speeds that are slower than that of light, but for navigating around your solar system, that is just fine. It might only take us minutes to reach your planet from your central star. Even though we are a composite of three-dimensional time and three-dimensional space, as stated before we are undetectable by you and any instrument that you have.

«I should mention that passengers inside the spaceship do not experience the effects of this travel; much like with your airplanes, your passengers are not aware they are traveling at six hundred miles per hour. In your world, the passengers move about the airplane cabin with ease, as long as the speed remains constant. It is only when there are transitions in speed, when the place accelerates to take off or brakes after landing, that the motion becomes noticeable.

«Once we are close to our destination, for example your planet, we ramp down our speed again to much less than the speed of light, but still exceedingly fast by your standards. By working the frequency field structure of our craft carefully, we can remain undetectable by anyone on

Earth and can become visible in times that appear improbable by your current science.

«With our own technologies, it is possible to change the molecular frequencies of a transport vehicle, which you might call spaceship, and shift it from different combinations of three-dimensional space and three-dimensional time. When you change the frequency content of matter, as in previous examples, changing the key frequency around which matter is organized, you change the behavior of matter. This should give you a hint as to the relationship between what you see with your human eyes and what you see with those goggles.

«To finish up the time travel discussion, there are tremendous push-pull forces in the universe in the space and time dimensions. Much like your ocean currents and trade winds, these can be utilized for travel. But your ocean currents and trade winds are not necessarily optimized for travel, since the travelers, your sailing ships of the past utilizing these forces, often had to go out of their way to stay in the zone of these forces, whereas with the push-pull forces in the universe, travel is more direct. You know of one of these push-pull forces, you called it gravity, but there is a compensating force as well, one I will call levity. Our technology can be used to adjust the amount of gravity and levity forces applied to the space ship to control the speed and direction of a spaceship through three-dimensional time or three-dimensional space. »

Bohdi now sees an image of a large spherical shape matrix, made up of little points all equidistant from each other in spherical layers emanating out from the center of the sphere. The sphere fills up about half of his inner vision. Now the ball begins to expand, as if taking in a breath, and the distance between all the points of light expands equally in all directions. This expansion continues until the outer edge reaches the limits of his inner vision. Then, slowly, the points of light begin contracting, as if the sphere were letting out a breath. The process of expansion and contraction cycles three times.

So . . . if gravity is the pull force, levity is the push force?

«Yes. As mentioned before, relationship between space and time is reciprocal, so a pull force in multidimensional space is countered by a

push force in three-dimensional time. In three-dimensional time, the very structure of spacetime is contracting while in multidimensional space it can be expanding. The difference in amount of expansion and contraction is how much spacetime expands or contracts. The total amount of expansion and contraction throughout the universe always the same. Your scientists would say it is conserved. Your scientists postulate undetectable Dark Matter and Dark Energy to explain the state and expansion of the universe. It is because of behavior of matter in other dimensions of time that you are currently unfamiliar with. »

Then two identical spheres appear in his vision, one in red and one in blue, both occupying the same exact position. The points of the red sphere are rotated just a bit so that the red and blue points, all equidistant from each other, do not sit on top of each other. Then the blue sphere begins to contract, and immediately, the red sphere begins to expand, in an equal but opposite direction. This cycle of expansion and contraction repeats one more time.

ETBuddy waits for Bohdi to respond. *For every action, there is an equal and opposite reaction.*

«Correct. Adjusting the interaction of the spacecraft and its occupants to the push and pull of the local galaxy, or solar system, determines our direction and speed.»

So, three-dimensional space and three-dimensional time are working against each other.

«Not working against each other, but in cooperation with each other to maintain balance, a balance throughout all spacetime, a spacetime more expanded than you currently recognize. Always, there is balance. The spacetime universe comes from a place of balance, so balance is built into the very structure of the universe. This is true for humans as well, for all beings are embedded into space and time. Humans are about to discover that for themselves in the future and the work that you and your friend are doing is one very good step in that direction.»

Bohdi thinks it is likely a result of the local cultural Time Information Fields that he saw this relationship as working against each other and ETBuddy rephrased it as cooperation.

Our Sun is like the major airport or train station for our solar system? How is it that your ships are not burned up by the heat of it?

« Your Sun is the hub that I spoke of earlier, which we travel to in three-dimensional time, but I like your description better of your local star being a station. To address your question, your Sun has very different properties in three-dimensional time. The property of heat that you associate with your local star is a three-dimensional space property. In time, it has the inverse of the property of heat, that of a cooling effect. Previously, I gave you the image of Earth as it looks to you in space, and then showed you a form of Earth in time. »

Bohdi sees an image of the Sun. He feels the experience of heat emanating from this image. Then the image transforms itself into an image of a huge, colored sphere, with a matrix of small, bright-colored spheres that are so dense and complex he has trouble seeing any pattern. He notices the experience of heat has vanished. In fact, he now feels a cooling effect. The image transforms again, and he sees the familiar planets of our solar system all encompassed in this colored sphere representing the sun. He understands that in time, our solar system is within the influence of the sun. The planets transform into colored spheres, each much larger than its representation in three-dimensional space. It is now obvious how in the dimensions of time, all the information of these planets is interlinked. What impresses him is that all this empty space of the cosmos we think we understand is filled with frequency information. It is far from empty. His point of view moves into the white light, and then all of a sudden, he is back to the Sun, and our solar system, in three-dimensional space. Bohdi realizes that these two universes of space and time are nested within each other. Each is presented as a fractal within the other.

« The images I have just shown you, as you correctly surmised, is the best representation of your Sun and solar system that I can generate

for you to visualize what it looks like in three-dimensional time. You also now recognize that these two parts of the universe built inside each other.»

How can the goggles help us to move towards time travel.

« The goggles you and your friend currently use allow you to see the three-dimensional part. There are materials in this technology that are sensitive to the effects of matter in three-dimensional time, so allowing you to see what you could not see before. The goggles are limited, but they still introduce you to a whole other universe of matter.

« These goggles will help you identify new forms of materials since what you see in the Plus mode of these goggles is the basis of matter that is used to travel in the manner I have described to you. I hope this will give you a new appreciation for what it is that you are witnessing. In your future as humans, these goggles can help create a new science which will generate an entire new form of matter compared to your current understanding of matter.»

Do you always need to use a vehicle to travel in three-dimensional time?

«A very interesting question. The answer is no, but it is easier. We are digressing now, but I would like give a short answer to this question. The technologies we use for our spacetime vehicles stabilize the frequency structures and do all the frequency transformations, making it less far less work for us. There are elders, as you would label them, who have achieved a state of being where they can travel in three-dimensional time and three-dimensional space without vehicles. It is a technique, built into the universe, available to all of us, including you as humans. »

Bohdi feels the communication go quiet. He is glad. He needs a moment to absorb everything he has heard. In some ways it makes so much sense, but he still needs to absorb this information and formulate new questions.

« You wish to go on?»

You have given me a lot to think about, but I want to ask another question. Do you live exclusively in three-dimensional time, or do you have parts of your physical being in three-dimensional space?

«We go between the two, as we see fit, but our composite structure is geared more toward three-dimensional time because it allows us a greater flexibility of being.

«You have a physical body in three-dimensional space, but also energetic fields in three-dimensional time. You, with the use of the goggles, are seeing energetic fields in three-dimensional time. But, as humans, you have always felt them. Our experience of time allows us to utilize our bodies in both three-dimensional time and three-dimensional space. Each has its advantage based on what you choose to accomplish.»

An image of a familiar human form appears. Bohdi notices a slight sadness in the eyes and in the posture. Then the image transforms into the now-familiar three-dimensional time form. He sees that in one area, there is a significant color change. The three-dimensional form of the human transforms back to the familiar human image. Bohdi sees no change physically, but can see a change in the eyes and in posture. The posture is more erect, almost proud, and there is determination seen in the eyes.

«The transformation you witnessed shows how changing an attitude in time can be subtle in space. In time it can be easier to see, so more attention is paid to the effort to transform thoughts and emotions. As a being's attitude changes, so will their future, and this can be seen more clearly. In space, the unresolved issues of the heart and mind can be hidden from others, including from yourself.

«We have discovered, as you will also in your future, that coming from a place in three-dimensional time is a more creative place to live from.

«When working with matter from three-dimensional time, we can adjust the patterns that determine our structure more easily since these patterns are readily available to us. It is these patterns that are the templates used to generate the form of your matter, and your biology, in three-dimensional space.

«Your body is a good example, where your DNA has a large time component that holds the patterns of your biology. The smaller component of DNA, that your scientists recognize, cannot account for the complex shapes and patterns in your biology. This is true of the energy in your atomic matter, as well. The energy you label atomic energy comes from three-dimensional time. Also, in three-dimensional time, you can see gravity and magnetism in a whole new way.»

Bohdi is stunned. *You're saying that our DNA is, for the most part, of three-dimensional time?*

«Correct. For purposes of this conversation, let call it this component the Time-based DNA, the patterning component. The component you are familiar on earth would be the Space-based DNA, the component that executes the biochemistry in your biological form. The fields that are in three-dimensional time have patterns, or templates, and from these patterns the physical DNA generates the geometric physical biological forms you are familiar with. For example, your left and right arms have the same DNA and cellular structure, but different patterns to account for the left and right symmetry. The Time-based DNA information accounts for the correct symmetry.

«There is coupling between the Time-based DNA and the Space-based DNA portions of your DNA, much like electric and magnetic fields are coupled. A moving electric field generates a magnetic field and a moving magnetic field generates an electric field. That is why they are called electromagnetic waves.

« The Time-based DNA has many layers to it. For simplification in this discussion, I will divide these Time-based DNA layers into four. There is the personal layer that holds the patterns to your biology, the layer that has the mental and emotional patterns, the collective layer that *is impacted by societal changes and finally there is the cosmic layer, which currently is not active in most humans. Your Time-based DNA makes you humans multidimensional spacetime beings. As humans, you have not come to know that, which is understandable given your experience.*

«The first two layers determine the shape of you as a biological human and your mental and emotional tendencies. As you well know, you can have the same biological DNA as your siblings, but be very different in mental and emotional temperaments to them. This accounts for that. The collective layer is affected by the overall field of your society that you are born into, or as you and your friend call it, Time Information fields generated by your society. It might be hard to believe, but this patterns the Time component of the DNA of those who are born into it. So as the society changes, the change is imprinted into the dimensions of time, which is the same as saying the traits are imprinted into the Time-based DNA of the new generation. If a society can measure these fields, it will be clear what is being imprinted. With this knowledge comes a responsibility for the condition and the evolution of the overall societal Time Information Field generated by each society since it effects the behaviors of the new generations. When someone says this trait or place is part of my DNA, they speak more truth than they know.

«The cosmic layer is the most fantastic, and can also be the most troubling if not handled correctly. It is the layer that brings the most joy to any being as you transform into a participating multidimensional being of a wonderful universe. Some of you have had short experiences of this in deep meditation, reflections, or during near death experiences.

«Some of the patterns in Time based DNA are quite changeable, others require tremendous effort to change. These Time Information Fields connect your Time-based DNA to your thoughts, your attitudes, your emotions—essentially your character as a human. These fields in three-dimensional time are also affected by your geographical place, your national character, and so on. These attributes are also imprinted into your Time-based DNA. When someone says this trait or place is part of my DNA, they speak more truth than they know.»

If Time Information Fields are connected to DNA, can we see the patterns of Time-based DNA in three-dimensional time with the goggles?

«*Only in part. There are colors that are associated with the patterns of Time-based DNA, but you cannot see the full spectrum of frequencies with those goggles. As I mentioned before, you see only a coarse resolution of the Time Information Fields as you call them, but this is a giant leap, and a great start.*»

What you seem to imply is that evolution of a society is through its collective Time-based DNA changes?

«*Correct, but it is not just the Time-based DNA changes that are necessary. It must also be supported by education and example. As new individuals incarnate into human form, their Time Information Fields are imprinted with these Time-based patterns, which include changes that the society has made. Remember, the Time Information Fields are based on thoughts and emotions. Many of the expressed and unexpressed thoughts and emotions can be carried on by the next generations. In addition, generations come in with new Time-based DNA patterns that effect the way they see and interact with the world.*

«*Because of this new patterning in the Time Information Fields, the new generation will naturally resonate with these new ideas and work to introduce them into your world. Interestingly, it is the work that the previous generation has done within their own collective society that gives opportunity for new patterns for the next generation to be born into. Commonly, these new ideas from this younger generation can spark friction with a previous generation who have a different patterning of their fields, their collective Time-based DNA. The younger ones typically have brought about many of the needed changes in the past in your society and will do so even more in the future because they have dramatically new patterns within themselves that they are seeking to express.*

«Those fighting for, and against, any changes in the society can become upset, often expressing their frustrated energy as anger. Let's be clear: Anger is an appropriate emotion. But it is meant to be used as temporary fuel. It should not be a continuous source of emotional feelings. Remember, the new patterns can be viewed as good or bad, depending on your perspective.

«Your planet is undergoing a major change because people are not only desperate for change, they are also beginning to demand change. And it is about time. During this period, it is critical that people be clear about what attitude they are basing their actions on. There is a battle, unseen by humans, for their thoughts and emotions. These energies from thoughts and emotions are used by others to their advantage, and your disadvantage. This you can see easily in some of your structures, especially global business and financial entities that you as humans have allowed to be setup on your planet. There are battles over control of people's attitudes, as well as land and natural resources. Many of these manipulations are going on simultaneously, generating stress in these Time Information Fields, which are felt as internal stress and unease by humans all over the planet. Many have no idea why they feel this unease. The tension in these Time Information Fields are the source of the strong desire for change, particularly among the younger generation. There are those in the older generation who feel this tension and believe that if the changes that the new generations are stopped, it would relieve the tension within. But this is not true.

«The increased stress that you live in right now will not abate until the appropriate changes, made by humans, releases the tension. This is true for your society, as it is for each individual. In time, this period will be seen as the catalyst for many positive changes that are readily adopted by future generations. But we understand very well it is not easy to be the generations that have to live through this great stress.»

Bohdi falls silent to absorb the idea. *You have given me a lot to think about.*

« Yes, indeed. I would share two thoughts with you, if that is agreeable to you. »

Please go ahead.

« In closing, I would like to state that there are a number of organizations on your planet whose goal is to amplify the amount of fear in humans. When fear is high, humans are easier to manipulate because their cognitive reason is overshadowed by a fear of survival. The weakness of these organizations is that they always need to work in the dark. Their power does not come from light, but from the absence of light. In your world it appears that there are two polarities, light and dark, but in reality, there is only one polarity, that being light. Light is active, and since darkness is the lack of light, it is passive. For darkness to be effective, it has to suppress the light. These two polarities do not have the same power. This also seems true of love and fear. Fear is the lack of love, so love is the true active principal. Ultimately, there is more power in love and light and love and light are the same thing, so there is only love.

« Do not misunderstand me; just like there is power in fear and darkness. Many might argue that darkness has more power in your world, but this is an illusion. Granted, it's a very powerful illusion the way your reality is currently constructed, but ultimately the true source of power is love. Humans intuitively understand this.

The inside of Bohdi's mind goes totally blank, and a darkness envelopes him like a damp, cold towel. He feels a flash of fear ripple through him as an uneasiness about this darkness settles over him. Then a small spot of light appears, and it casts a weak glow. He can now just barely make out four walls, a window, and a door. He now recognizes that he is in a room. As he looks at the door, he can just barely make out that the door is ajar. He moves slowly to the door, walking carefully since he is unable to see the floor. At the door threshold, he feels this impulse to walk through the door. As he steps over the threshold, a brilliant gold light appears. He immediately understands what he is being shown. Even in total darkness, it only takes a tiny bit of light to help someone find their way out of the dark.

His mind immediately goes dark again, except this time, he sees a matrix of tiny lights dispersed through the darkness. Each tiny light, each with different intensities, casts a weak glow in its immediate vicinity. He watches as some of these lights stop shining, but then new ones appear. Some start to grow brighter, whereas other grow dimmer. This scenario of lights disappearing and then a new one appearing continues as the total number increases. This increased amount of light starts to brighten the scene, pushing back the emptiness of the darkness. Then an understanding is given to him. These points of lights represent humans, and although some of us give up our light, there are always others to take their place. He now understands, those who are in control fear the ever-increasing light because it takes away their cover of darkness.

«As a last note, your life experience on this planet is tied more closely to the galaxy than you currently understand, and some of your scientists are beginning to uncover this. Your Solar System is entering a small branch of one of the 4 major spiral arms of your Milky Way Galaxy.

«These Spiral Arm regions are places where there are more births and deaths of stars, and therefore, an area of much more Galactic Cosmic radiation. Your Sun plays a key role in how much of this Galactic Cosmic radiation reached the planets in your solar system, most importantly, to your planet Earth. The amount of Galactic Cosmic radiation reaching your planet's atmosphere is regulated by the magnetic activity of your Sun. As many scientists are aware of for centuries, your local star regularly has cycles of increased and decreased magnetic activity and this is tied to the regular reversal of the Sun's magnetic field roughly every 11 years. The Sun magnetic activity, aside from its polar magnetic reversal, also goes through a cycle regarding the maximum magnetic activity. Currently your local Sun's maximum activity is lower in each 11-year cycle, so on a larger time scale, your local star is quieting down.

«In times of decreased solar magnetic activity, there is less cosmic radiation coming from your Sun in the form of a Solar Wind which

deflects the amount of Galactic Cosmic Radiation that reaches your planet. This means more Galactic Cosmic radiation is reaching your atmosphere now and also in the future.

«Some of your scientists have found links between the measurements of Solar magnetic activity, the measurements of Galactic Cosmic radiation and the temperature of your oceans. They have validated these links for hundreds of millions of years through chemical analysis of fossils that were part of the oceans in your geological past.

«So, you now understand that you, your planet, your Solar System and your Milky Way galaxy are part of some very important universal cycles.

«Again, with regret, we must end this session to keep the balance. We also recommend any interaction with water to be a good balancer, so immersing your body in water will help you absorb the energy of this interaction. We have discussed many topics in this communication, and we are grateful that you have allowed us to share with you some concepts that are important in order to understand time a bit more and the work that you are doing.

«I must also state that this will be our last communication. I have given you plenty of information to consider about the dimensions of time and have truly enjoyed the opportunity you have given me to exchange these ideas with you. I have an important mission coming up and will need to prepare for it. I will say goodbye for now until we meet again.»

The communication goes quiet and the image of the lights in his mind disappears. As Bohdi opens his eyes, he feels a sense of confusion and sadness. He struggles to understand why ETBuddy closed this communication with a message that ETBuddy would no longer continue the communications because of some changed circumstances on his side.

This communication would be the last.

But he signed off with the statement, "until they meet again".

Did he mean that literally?

Did it mean at some time in the future, the communications would resume?

Bohdi sure hopes so.

But when? … after Bodhi passes away. That thought leaves him a bit cold.

To help ease the disappointment, he texts Skylar this news.

"What!" Skylar shoots back after she reads Bohdi's text.

Why? she texts again.

He responds, *ETBuddy said he has a mission that requires extensive preparation and that these communications had answered my initial inquiry about the dimensions of time.*

Before he can get his next sentence out, he gets a response.

That is unbelievable!

I felt we were just starting to get comfortable.

There is so much more to ask.

Bohdi cannot keep up with Skylar's texts. He waits for a pause, but another one comes in.

What does that mean, until we meet again?

He waits. No new texts, so he replies.

No idea. I am as confused as you.

She texts back, *How about meeting tonight?*

Bohdi looks at the time, 11:13 p.m.

He types, *Probably be easier tomorrow evening. I need to get all these thoughts on paper while they are still fresh in my head. That way I can communicate them coherently with you tomorrow.*

He waits. He can feel her struggle.

Then he gets a reply. *Okay, probably the better idea.*

Bohdi confirms, *Done. I will see you then. Love u.*

Bohdi hears his phone ding and reads, *Love u. Text me on how you are doing in case we need to change the time*

He texts back, *Okay, but I am keen to get all the new information I got tonight on paper and share it with you, so count on it being done unless something crazy happens.*

He gets a quick response. *Like what? This is not crazy enough?* with a smiley face.

Bohdi appreciates Skylar's shock at this news. It makes him feel better. He grabs a pad from his desk and begins writing all the information that ETBuddy about three-dimensional time and three-dimensional space.

After dumping all the ideas on paper over the next two hours, Bohdi reviews his summary. He is left with more questions than answers. He desperately wants more communication with ETBuddy. Why are we blind to so much critical information? What is the purpose of this blindfolding? Is this part of the game of life? Are we thrashing around in the dark trying to find our way out of some maze, and then we become enlightened? Is death the only escape from this silliness? He doubts it, since ETBuddy seems to have suggested there is a way out of the blindness. He would like some answers to these very perplexing questions. None will be forthcoming now.

66.

Bohdi and Skylar spent Saturday afternoon discussing all the fascinating ideas communicated by ETBuddy about time travel, and how a portion of our DNA that we cannot detect is linked to time. Their understanding of time has been forever changed. After hours of discussion, Skylar mentions how she has an obligation with her Dad and so has to head home. Bohdi mentions he some ideas on past, present and future that he needs to put on paper before discussing these with Skylar. She immediately asks him to meet her Sunday morning and he can share them with her. They agree on the Spontaneity Café.

****

Bohdi pulls into the Spontaneity parking lot. Even though it is early Sunday morning on a chilly November day, the place is already busy. There are bicycles out front, belonging to those who've decided to take advantage of the sunny but chilly May morning to get a bike ride in, and then reward themselves with great coffee and edibles.

He then opens the door, looks around, and sees Skylar sitting on one of the small couches in the far corner, separated a bit from the others. She already has a beverage in her hand and has her pocketbook in the place next to her to save a place for Bohdi. She sees him and waves.

"Hey, you were quick," he says. "You already have coffee?"

"You bet," she says as she reaches for the cup next to her and hands it to him.

Bohdi leans down and gives her a kiss. He likes her black T-shirt with a brightly colored text of her favorite statement from Einstein; *We cannot solve our problems with the same thinking we used when we created them.*

"You look nice this morning."

"Thanks." Skylar observes a glazed look in his eyes. "Didn't get much sleep last night?"

"No. I had trouble shutting down my mind."

"No doubt. After Friday's news from ETBuddy, that is not surprising. Did you finish getting all your thoughts about that paper down last night."

Bohdi sits down next to Skylar and pats his notepad, "I did."

She snuggles up to him, "OK, let's hear it."

Then she quickly interjects, "I had an idea about why ETBuddy terminated the communication."

Bohdi immediately perks up.

"Maybe ETBuddy is worried about communicating too much with neighbors. I mean, from a galactic point of view, we might count as neighbors. I figure we're the kind of neighbors the whole galactic neighborhood worries about. The ones most likely to blow themselves up!" Skylar says with a grin.

Bohdi fakes a grin. "Probably closer to the truth than anything else."

Skylar realizes that even this poor joke is not going to help Bohdi with his disappointment. "Sorry, bad joke, go on"

"Well, I remember reading this article about how scientists were investigating how humans respond to stimuli by measuring the time it takes for a touch stimulus to reach the brain as an electrical signal. They measured the time it took for a patient to respond by pressing a button, and the time it takes for the person to consciously become aware of the stimulus. The researchers reported it took one ten-thousandth of a second for the brain to respond, one-tenth of a second for a person to press the button, and half a second for them to consciously respond to the stimulus. In addition, the patients were only aware they had pressed the button in response to the stimulus a full four-tenths of a second after they had already done so."

Sounds like we're stuck in the past! That sucks." Skylar says this loud enough that one of the other coffee drinkers turns her head toward them.

Bohdi laughs. "Sort of true, at least the conscious part of ourselves we're most familiar with. But there is a part of us in the now and in the future, as well; we're just not as familiar with these parts of ourselves, for reasons that are not clear to me. Many people face the future with anxiety and find comfort in the past."

"Could be, but I always see the future as a brand-new opportunity. It odd to think of this half a second as the past?" Skylar states with a laugh, "but from physics I know what happens to matter in half a second? Millions or billions of events take place on an atomic scale."

Bohdi agrees, "I am coming to understand that it's a matter of perspective. For everyday human life, half a second seems meaningless, but it's the past, all right. It's at least four thousand times slower than the brain's response. That suggests there's plenty of time for our brains to process the information and filter what we've just sensed and then report consciously preprocessed information—and we're not aware of this preprocessing. There have been a lot of studies showing the statement 'believing is seeing' to be quite accurate. People often *recall* seeing an event that is colored by their beliefs. What we think of truth from memories is far more fluid than we think."

Bohdi asks Skylar a question. "Where does the past exist?"

She thinks for a few moments. "Well I suppose in our memories, which is mostly in our minds. I mean, photographs and videos are records of the past, but they only help to bring the past into the present."

"Now what about the future," Bohdi asks before Skylar goes to much into the past.

"Hmm, that seems to only exist in our minds. I mean, any book or image about the future is just a representation of what is in our minds"

"So….," Bohdi says slowly, " The past and the future exist primarily in the mind. The only real moment is the present. But the present is so fleeting that we as humans really struggle to stay in the present. Give it a thought, and it is gone and your are now in the past again, trying to recollect a thought about that present moment."

"Yup, stuck in the past," Skylar says sarcastically again, but much quieter.

"ETBuddy said there are parts of us in both the three-dimensional space and three-dimensional time. If I speculate that all the information of past and future events exist in three-dimensional time, that would be an incredible amount of information. ETBuddy mentions he can tap into information about just about anything and it appears he can absorb all the information around that person, or culture, or planet. There must be some type of membrane that limits us from accessing this information. ETBuddy says we have the capability, but it is just not active in us. So for all intents and purposes, it is like a blindfold, a membrane that filters this reality from our mind.

But here is what I think: in some ways, this membrane maintains our sanity."

"Now you really have my attention." Skylar leans in a little closer to him.

"Well, again just speculating, this membrane acts like a filter for us, filtering out information. If all information in time about all events in the universe were instantly available to us immediately, like right now, it would create chaos inside us, a form of insanity. Remember, information is energy. It seems our brain, in its current capacity, needs some structure to interpret it all this information." Bohdi has a sadness in his tone.

"Well, it seems to make some sense," she says, taking another sip of her coffee. "Remember the conversation we had at the lake, about the goggles and the two universes? A few months later, we end up with Dr. B's goggles." "You mentioned this synchronicity. But maybe synchronicity is just a matter of one of us reaching across this membrane and identifying the most probably of all the possible future outcomes in three-dimensional time. Synchronicity and intuition seem to be a lot more scientific that we think."

Bohdi is amused by Skylar referring to Dr. Brown as Dr.B. He responds, "Or do you think someone else created that synchronicity for us?"

"Don't know. Probably a bit of both. I can't take credit for Dr. B's goggles manifesting, but I can own the ideas about seeing two movies, or universes," Skylar replies.

Bohdi looks up from his notes, "I am not sure what part is from 'my mind' and what is not, after hearing ETBuddy say we are connected to the universe in ways we have yet to understand. We have this nonlocal part of us that is linked to all other parts of the universe, so are we just expressing in our local minds ideas that are already out there in the universe? These ideas might only appear as new insights to us because we are so identified with our local selves and have never allowed this information in."

Skylar feels light-headed. She sees symmetry in what they are both saying. The glasses idea she spoke of turned into a larger reality, and now they have achieved a deeper insight because of the goggles from Dr. B. She wonders if a part of her that is always on the other side of this membrane interfaced with the part of someone else on that side of the membrane. If that is true, that means synchronicity is something we are actively part of creating, not just something that is happening to us, as we normally think of it. Again, there appears to a real science behind it.

"This conversation raises all sorts of questions," Bohdi says, with a note of exasperation. "The questions always seem to outpace the insights we're getting. Doesn't it seem like we should know more about who we are? I mean, the whole of who we are, not just the incompatible bits and pieces we learn about ourselves?"

Skylar sits up, "What if being in the present is the way to access information in three-dimensional time."

"How so," Bohdi asks, totally intrigued.

Well . . . I can only conjecture that from a conscious point of view, but I'm not so sure from a materialistic or scientific point of view. Consciously, you avoid putting your attention on the past or the future. This is very difficult for our minds to do, since they want to be everywhere but the present. So our mind—our consciousness, that is, not our brains—is constantly distracting us with images or concerns of the past and or future, flipping between the two. If we are doing this, we are in our memories, not in the present."

She stops. Bohdi jumps in, "If I did not have a disciplined mind, my communication with ETBuddy would be a mess. My mind, if I let it, would latch on to something ETBuddy said, so I would be in the past, and I would miss what he is saying in the present. Then my mind will switch on me and conjecture what I might ask in the future relating to what he is saying, again missing what he is saying in the present. I have learned to listen, then questions either come effortlessly into my mind, or I use some silence to gather my thoughts and questions. But somewhere beyond, or inside, this distracted mind, there's a part that deals with all three time constructs—past, present, and future—in a more constructive way. That part probably is on the other side, the three-dimensional time side."

"Yup! That part about the mind jumping around, it says that in the book I'm reading now," Skylar replies. "The very same thing. They call it *the monkey mind* because it's constantly jumping around. Getting into the zone seems to be a good analogy of being in the *now*, where the experience of our time and the environment around us seems to disappear when you're not thinking about each moment—you're just being in the zone. I also think *being* is a key word here. Not *a* being." Skylar stops for effect, and smiles. "If you're doing something, it's probably focused in the past or future; if you're being, you're probably in the present, the *now*."

He smiles, "Correct." He is amused that he has started using this same reply that ETBuddy used.

Skylar laughs as she digs through her pocketbook for her phone. "Oh, and speaking of zones, what time is it? I've got some spacetime obligations coming up, and I don't want to be late again."

She grins, knowing that being late is a trait many around her find really annoying. *But better to be Skylar, late, than to be the late Skylar like Bohdi almost was.*

67.

Bohdi sent Skylar a note on the encrypted link. He needs to talk to her. He recommends a walk. When can he come over and pick her up?

Skylar recognizes that Bohdi wants to talk in private. She wonders what he has on his mind now.

It is Friday afternoon and Bohdi and Skylar plan to use a day this weekend to continue the work of getting another lens built. She is glad they have March vacation coming up in a few weeks and their plan is to use that time to complete the lens.

Skylar heads out as she sees Bohdi pull into her driveway. As she opens the passenger door, he asks her to leave her phone at home. She is just about to question him, when she sees the concern in his eyes. She quickly goes back inside and leaves it in her room.

Bohdi feels safe in his car because he checked on the Internet, and his car is old enough that it does not have a black box. Without a black box, there is no opportunity to hack into it and turn on a microphone. Once they are on the road, just for precaution, he turns up the radio and then says, "Our house was broken into!"

"No shit!" Skylar replies. "How do you know?

"Well, you know how obsessive-compulsive my mother is about everything having its place in the house? Yesterday, when they came back from visiting their friends, she started to notice lots of little things out of place, and as you know, we have a lot of little knickknacks. She asked if my father or I moved some of them. We both said we hadn't touched any of them. Then she looked in their bedroom to see if some of her jewelry is missing. Again, she noticed items were moved, but no jewelry missing. She is puzzled. My father checked all the windows and went into the basement to check the door and windows down there. He found no evidence of a break-in, but the dead bolt that is normally closed was open. Now my father is also suspicious. He knows that my mother is certain that an intruder has been in our home because too many items have been moved. My father wonders if someone broke into the house for quick cash items, but how did they get in, and why did they not take anything?

My mother suspects I did not lock one of the doors when I left. I initially fought that idea, then I realized it might be an easy out."

"What do you mean, 'easy out'?" Skylar asks, mystified.

"I did not leave a door unlocked. That shit of locking the door behind me has been drilled into me since I was, like, seven. But if they want to think I gave someone easy access to the house and then the person had to quickly leave before they had time to take anything of value, then I will go with that."

He asks Skylar if she's noticed anything out of place in her home.

"No, I never noticed anything."

Skylar wonders if she could tell. Since her mother passed, the house has become messier. All the surfaces downstairs have papers, books, mail and other items on them. She and her father keep saying they will pick it up, but neither of them has prioritized it. She doubts even if something was missing, it might take quite some time for either one of them to notice.

Bohdi parks the car in a shopping plaza parking lot and turns the engine off, but leaves the radio on.

"Have you checked recently if the goggles are still in our hiding place?"

"No, not since we used them last Saturday." Skylar feels alarm starting to build inside her.

"What about the information Dr. Brown gave us?"

"I have not looked at that for two weeks. When do you figure your house was broken into?"

"I figure it had to be yesterday or the day before. My parents were gone for a few days and they just got back yesterday. And as you know, I spent all of this week in my room on campus."

He smiles before adding, "And Wednesday night you were with me. So, it was a perfect opportunity for someone to go into our homes. Wasn't your father away for business some part of this week?"

"He was. Wednesday and Thursday night." Skylar feels even more uneasy. Then she counters, "But it is now common for my father to be away for work during the week. I am often on campus until very late during the week, so last week was not too different than other weeks at our house. But it was for your house. I wonder if they would do both houses at the same time, or one at a time."

"They could have broken into your house and we wouldn't know it, because we haven't checked the hiding places since," Bohdi replies, not hearing anything to quell his anxiety.

"Pity you didn't use wireless or Internet to have access to those two security cameras in the hiding places, so we could check easily. I think we need to go back and find out." Skylar looks at Bohdi, her increasing anxiety causing her to want to do something.

"Not yet," Bohdi answers. "How do we know the house isn't bugged? We need to figure out a plan of action."

Bohdi is grateful he did not use wireless or Internet technology for the two cameras. He figured they would be too easy to hack at the time, and he is even more convinced that was the right choice now. It is one less thing he needs to worry about now. There is no way whoever broke in would figure out where the cables are to access those two cameras. How fortunate for Dr. Brown to share the idea of setting up the secure hiding places with the cameras so it's not necessary to open up to determine if the goggles and information are still there.

"I think all this was triggered when that George guy visited your house about four, or was it five, months ago," Bohdi interrupts. "And. . . I think the request to go to the bathroom was a ploy to scope out your house. I feel it in every cell of my body. I asked you not to bring your phone just in case they were hacked. I left mine at home, too, just in case. There is so much they can do to trace what people say and where they are going."

Skylar looks at him. "You figure someone knows we are the new guardians?"

"I don't know. Dr. Brown and Annie were very careful. He said he was going to destroy any information he had, even those agreements we signed with him—we watched him tear them up ourselves, remember. And Annie told us, for our own safety, not to attend his funeral." Bohdi still feels disappointed they could not go and pay respect to a man he had come to admire very much.

"So, now we really are the guardians of this technology. This is for real," Skylar says, with a serious tone. "But I am committed. We are doing such a shitty job running this world. The goggles, along with our research, can give us a fresh perspective on how to clean up this mess. I have no regrets. But, I agree, the fact that we are discussing the security of the goggles sure makes it real!" We need a better understanding of who we are as humans."

"I agree," Bohdi says with a note of sadness.

Skylar looks around the car, making sure nothing in the parking lot has changed. "We need to find out if they broke into Dr. Brown's house. Maybe they found some information, maybe on his computer, or his phone about us. Just because you deleted it doesn't mean some of that information is not available. Maybe they're just checking to see if we have the stolen parts, or something related to them. I still feel we need to go to my house and check to see if the goggles are still there."

Bohdi responds with a heavy sigh. "If the goggles are gone, there is nothing we can do about it. I somehow doubt it. We have it set up pretty well, and even got some help from ETBuddy. But, I think after we've checked that the goggles and drawings are where they should be, we must be more careful. The house could be bugged, and I do not want to reveal how we check up on our hiding spots. Let's think about how we should move forward." Bohdi is quiet for a moment.

"Whatever is happening around us should not stop us," Bohdi says breaking the silence. Fortunately, we have Suzanne and Tom, who are really invested in taking these goggles to the next level."

He waits for a response from Skylar. She looks far away. Finally, she says, "I totally agree. There is only one option, and that is to continue moving forward. But. . . I do think it's a good idea to make sure that, for a while, someone is always at my home overnight. I would love to find a way that would tell us if my house was broken into. I know we discussed it before, and you think that these home security systems are too easily bypassed by professionals. But you are right: If you put a security system in your house, then we would have to let my father know, and that adds one more complication. Do you still think getting a security system with a camera and microphone will not be worth it?"

"I cannot believe any security system will present a challenge for a professional. But I can look into it again. For now, I suggest getting a confirmation that we still have the information and goggles, and move forward one step at a time."

****

Later that evening, while Bohdi is figuring out how to determine if the house is bugged, he remembers that his friend Jason, who works in the physics lab, had modified one of his old smartphones and removed the infrared filter. Jason uses it to image the infrared beams when he fixes remotes for TVs and stereos. Bohdi decides he will talk to Jason tomorrow and say that his father is having problems with one of their remotes, and ask if he can borrow the modified camera for an evening. He texts Skylar that he needs to meet with her. He is grateful they decided not to take any action that might reveal their hiding places for a few days.

A few days later, in the middle of the night, the alarm on Skylar's phone goes off. It is 3:00 a.m. She does not turn on any lights. She grabs the modified smartphone that Bohdi borrowed from Jason and checks around her room. She is looking for evidence of a hidden camera, specifically any infrared light source that would allow video to be taken at night without anyone knowing. She finds nothing in her bedroom. She is now ready to check the hiding places. The rest of the house can be checked later. She boots up her laptop, plugs the USB cable into the USB port in the back of her desk, and fires up the code she wrote to read the camera. She turns on the light source of the camera in the desk hiding place. She sighs in relief to see all the information still secure inside her desk. She unplugs the USB cable and then moves over to an AC outlet, where she has mounted an adapter plate that has two USB charging ports, as well as electrical outlets. They had secretly wired one of the USB charging ports as a connection to the camera in the hiding place in the linen closet, on the other side of the wall to her room. She plugs in her USB cable. She uses her laptop to turn that camera infrared light source on and verifies that the goggles and parts are visible. She wants to jump up and scream "Yes!" but does a silent air pump in the dark instead. The information and goggles are secure.

Skylar pulls out the USB cable and figures that she will check every day to make sure that the hiding places have not been breached from now on. She goes around the rest of the house, looking for a telltale infrared light source after that, but she sees no sign of any.

She sends an encrypted link message to Bohdi: *Cannot sleep. Watched a good movie that had a nice ending. See you later. Love you.* She is glad she did not have to text that she watched a terrible movie with a lousy ending.

Bohdi is awake. He hears the ding, sits up, and grabs his phone. He reads the text and flops back on his pillow. He feels a wave of relief push out the anxiety he has been holding these past few days.

Skylar would still love to communicate with Annie and find out if her house was broken into, but Bohdi told her that if Annie thought it necessary, she would reach out. They have heard nothing, so they need to move on. Skylar has to agree.

68.

Skylar receives a letter with the sent-to and return address that are both her home address. She is puzzled. She opens the envelope and finds a letter attached to some copied pages from what looks like a report.

> *Hi Skylar,*
>
> *You do not know me and, because of the work I do, will never meet me. I believe this attached report might be of interest to you. I am privy to information about an organization that has technology that can cause particular thoughts and emotions to be triggered in a targeted person. This technique is referred to as treatments in the report I have included with this letter. This technique [treatments] can cause major emotional distress in people, often resulting in them making poor decisions for themselves and those around them.*
>
> *This technology does not work well on everyone, as the attached report indicates. The report details concerns that some technical people, in that organization, have over the effectiveness of their technology on young people. All names and other reference have been taken out, but you might find the technical information in this report of interest. If so, consider the possibilities carefully.*
>
> *Sincerely,*
> *Incognito*

Skylar flips to the paper and reads about the technology that takes frequency scans of people. They have a process where they can analyze this scan data and determine all sorts of characteristic from it. Skylar is shaken by what she reads. There seems to be an organization that can do what ETBuddy spoke about, where fields in time are used to determine the mental, emotional, and spiritual qualities of a person. But it also alludes to this technology being used to undermine what people are thinking and feeling, to manipulate them.

She then realizes this is what Dr. B was referring to when he spoke of thought control. She wonders if the organization this guy, who she gives the name Incognito, is alluding to is the Chronos Consortium. A memory flashes through Skylar's head. It is of Bohdi racing to close the door and saying that he saw a beam coming from that guy at the door when he used the goggles. She wonders if that guy was doing the type of scan detailed in this paper. If so, somebody has the necessary information to make her a target. They might even have scanned Bohdi, as well. She feels a chill run down her spine.

Then another memory pops into her head. She remembers ETBuddy discussing beings who use Time Information Fields to manipulate others. She assumes that in a civilization like the one he is part of, this manipulation could be plainly evident since they live in three-dimensional time. If so, then maybe these beings would have to find a place in the universe where what they do cannot be seen, like humans who focus primarily on three-dimensional space. The information in this letter seems to suggest there is an organization here on Earth with a technology that can cause people to have thoughts and feelings that, as Incognito puts it, euphemistically, are not theirs and leads them to make poor decisions.

A sickening feeling settles over her. She finds a kitchen chair to sit on. These events appear to have a common thread. What Dr. B said, the communications with ETBuddy, the stranger at her door beaming her with something, and now this mysterious letter. Skylar realizes that humans can easily be manipulated, since not only can people not see what is happening to their thoughts and emotions, they also do not pay much attention to all that streams through their head and heart. Besides, these fields would be invisible. *Unless you had the. . . goggles*. All the pieces now fit together. If everything she now understands is real, this mission they are on has just gone cosmic. Maybe the communications with ETBuddy were intended to open their minds to these possibilities.

She grabs her phone and texts Bohdi on the encrypted link: *Need to meet. Just received important information. Let me know when, and pick me up in your car.*

She heads to her room with the letter and report and takes photos with her camera, not her cell phone, and then pulls the images off her camera and into her offline computer. She prints the photos of the letter and report, and then goes about the task of putting the original letter and report in the secure hiding place with the other information.

69.

The last semester of their senior year is a real challenge. Skylar and Bohdi are working every spare minute on developing the new set of goggles, and the time spent on this program is showing significant results. It takes every bit of discipline, and a large dose of regular parental nagging to do the minimum to get reasonable grades in school. If it were not for their parents, they would have taken the semester off, but they understood their parent's sacrifice and investment in their education, and so persevered through this grueling time.

****

A gentle May breeze occasionally blows as Skylar and Bohdi sit outside her father's home, enjoying the evening. The sun sits on the horizon. There's calm—internally and externally today—as both enjoy their desserts and watch the twilight of the day. Graduation was last week, and they are both glad school is over. They are now officially college graduates.

Skylar pokes Bohdi in the arm with her elbow. "Hey, remember a conversation from way back talking about how odd it would be if our senses were switched, like if we saw sound and heard light? Sort of like chromesthesia, where people associate sounds with colors, and photism, where colors are generated by sounds. The world would be a cacophony of sounds, since we'd hear the colors of everyone's clothes, the colors of the cars, houses, nature—everything around us. But it would be invisible until someone or something made a noise. Just think about how we would move around—it would be an enormous challenge."

"True. I never thought of it like that." Bohdi chuckles.

"It's a fun image to play around with. You would move around a quiet house by the sounds given off by the colors of the furniture and paint. The noise of the heating system would show up as a color. Probably a good picture of trying to negotiate other realities."

"Agreed," Bohdi replies, amused by the analogy.

They both slip into silence as they watch the sun disappear below the horizon.

Skylar's mind drifts back to how much her life has changed these past two years. She had to switch universities, and soon thereafter the goggles appeared in her life. She had no idea how much both her and Bohdi's lives would change after that fateful visit to the Browns almost two years ago. Then ETBuddy showed up and blew their minds with the information he communicated. Skylar realizes, at some point, an opportunity will come up where Bohdi might be able to share the experiences he had with ETBuddy with Suzanne and Tom. So much work needs to be done, but she clearly feels that she has found the beginning of an answer to the scientific structure of human consciousness. She understands people might find that disconcerting, but her reply would be that the precise mathematical structure of frequencies we call music can generate all sorts of beautiful and tender emotions in us. Just because something has a scientific structure does not mean it cannot be felt deeply by a human. She thought that when the moment arrived that she could answer this link between physics and human consciousness, there would be more fanfare. Instead, they are so busy, every day focused on the future, that she barely recognized that she found her answer to the challenge that her professor Dr. Adamel made in his Modern Physics class more than three years ago.

She is comforted by the fact that Tom Williamson just completed the necessary paperwork to form their private company, Bold Insights, to develop and mass produce the virtual reality goggles with the Time Information Field feature. Next week, she and Bohdi, along with Suzanne, will become the core full-time research and development group for this company. Suzanne already told the university she will not be teaching in the fall semester. She is taking a sabbatical, and plans to work full time for Bold Insights. The team decided to tell people, as a cover for their real purpose, that their goal is to develop a set of virtual reality goggles that does real-time spectroscopy. These goggles, they would say, can be used out in the field to identify crops that are not healthy. With Tom as the financier of this private company, they do not answer to anybody and they plan to keep their independence. Tom figures he can finance a three- to four-year commitment if they keep costs very lean. Everyone will take the minimum amount of salary they can afford so expenses can be kept low, and each will have ownership through shares in this company.

Now that this venture had structure, Skylar explained to her father what was transpiring with the goggles. She tried to keep quiet as long as possible, just in case something unexpected changed, and luckily nothing did. During her last semester of school, her father had been pestering her about what she was going to do after she graduated. Skylar kept telling him she was interested in graduate school, but felt she needed to take a year off and work. Her father asked about her chances for graduate school, given the recent slip in her grades and the competitiveness of getting into the programs. Skylar defensively replied that it was only one year out of four, and given the circumstances, the slip was totally justified. But Skylar knew her father's fundamental worry was her inability to articulate to him what she planned to do after school ended.

Skylar is still learning that in their business you only reveal what is necessary, when necessary. She was sorry to treat her dad this way, but she and Bohdi felt they had to answer to a higher calling that required them to be discreet about what they were doing. Bohdi used the same approach of thinking about graduate school with his parents, but, because of a challenging year, he told them he wanted to take a year off before going back to school.

Skylar still feels so grateful that the Browns entrusted the goggles to them, and that she and Bohdi decided to reach out to Suzanne. Now they have an opportunity to really effect the future, far beyond what either could have imagined.

She leans over to Bohdi. "I am sure Dr. B, wherever he might be, is pleased with how things have progressed with the goggle technology he made us guardians of."

"Little did we know what would happen when we went to visit him," Bohdi says jokingly. Bohdi knows that he is happy to share not only this moment with Skylar, but the rest of his life in this crazy adventure that life is taking them on.

70.

Edward Stagmier relaxes in this Chronos office. He is enjoying the feeling of victory. He has just returned from a meeting with Hank's agents, who briefed him on the latest results of almost a year's worth of work on a target Edward wanted taken care of.

The target is a politician who rose to powerful influence after a decade and half of Edward's careful coordination. This politician, Garry Lawrence, executed almost all of Edward's 'suggestions' and was able to get favorable legislation for so many of the Chronos's corporations in banking and finance as well as energy and materials, to name just a few. Garry's status rose significantly as he executed these 'suggestions'.

Then Garry started to go rogue. Edward suspects it was the influence of Garry's new wife, since it seemed to Edward that Garry started bucking Edwards 'suggestions' at around the time the two of them became serious. At first, Edward gave him some slack. When that did not work, Edward gave Garry suggestions with strong warnings of political consequences to his career. Garry chose to ignore Edward, feeling he had enough political capital to weather any issues that Edward might create for him.

Eventually Edward had enough. Nobody crosses him, especially after all he did for Garry. This guy needed to be brought down, and hard.

The agents already had plenty of scans on Garry, so they knew his emotional, mental and spiritual details well. The Chronos keeps key data on all of the people who they are manipulating behind the scenes, just in case these people think they can be successful without the Chronos Consortiums 'help'. They also have data on these people's spouses as well.

A year ago, after Garry was put on the target list by Edward, treatments were applied to not just Garry, but also his new wife. The goal was to cause problems in his career and simultaneous, if it all worked well, in his marriage.

Edward coordinated a program with other of Chrono's influencers to have Garry's integrity challenged for key congressional positions. He also arranged to have a mole in Garry's re-elections campaign. A key event happened when Edward found another politician who was willing to run against Garry. He now had a new recruit.

Since the treatments began, Garry has lost two key committee positions, his integrity was being question regularly and his campaign is now polling 15 points behind the new challenger in an election that is only a few weeks away. In addition, the mole reported that Garry is taking medication for his anxiety and he and his wife are fighting with each other regularly. The mole told Edward with some glee that Garry looked terrible, especially in his private moments sitting behind his desk.

In Edward's joy, is a feeling of relief. The Chrono's treatments have a high probability of effectiveness, but are not guaranteed. This slight uncertainty eats at Edward who hates loose ends. Now he knows their tactics have worked and success is imminent.

71.

Jared is watching *Technology Trends* while he catches up on some work on his laptop. He has the TV show on because it allows him to share ideas with his son about what is going on with technology in their world. The focus of the show is technology for young people. Although father and son usually watch it together, his wife and son are visiting her sister and brother-in-law and their kids. Jared has the day to get some work done.

****

Under Tom Williamson's organization and financial support, the project after a year and a half of intense work has a version of VR goggles that incorporates their goggle technology. Suzanne officially quit Patterson University and is in charge of the psychology research. Skylar and Bohdi have never been happier working around the clock.

Skylar is now standing in Tom's impressive entertainment room as the same *Technology Trends* show airs. Bohdi and Suzanne sit on the couch with Tom. The four of them had reached out to Annie Brown and invited her to join them. She declined but said she would definitely watch the show. She was surprised to hear that everything is moving so quickly. She reiterated that everything she and Vic had done was being validated by what Skylar and Bohdi are now doing. She cannot thank them enough.

Everyone in the room is feeling excited, with a tinge of nervousness. The pre-order sales of Real Dimension VR Goggles have taken off. Skylar, Bohdi, Suzanne, and Tom believe the show should be positive, but there is some worry that the content of what the goggles do will not be communicated effectively.

Their segment of the show begins, and everyone stops talking, eyes focused on the large flat-screen on the wall.

"And for our last segment, we have news on the newest and coolest set of virtual reality goggles with an unusual feature," the host says enthusiastically. "The maker of these goggles is Bold Insights. One of the special features of the goggles is that they allow you to see patterns of colors that one of their researchers, Dr. Suzanne Bradley, says correlate to human emotions. She says they used EEG, heart

285

rate variability, pupil dilation, skin conductance, and other parameters related to changes in emotional states and correlated them to the patterns seen through the goggles. We went to the company's website and found many papers that Dr. Bradley published on the correlation between what is seen with the goggles and people's emotions."

Jared cannot believe what he just heard. He slams his work laptop shut, reaches down, and grabs a notepad he has on the floor. He then grabs a mechanical pencil and writes down the names Bold Insights and Dr. Suzanne Bradley.

The hipster-looking host of the show says that one of their reporters, Joe Rezinski, who looks like he's probably one of the more veteran people on the show—that is, he might be thirty—spent time with Dr. Bradley, and she gave him an opportunity to try the goggles. The show then plays the segment with Joe trying on the goggles.

Jared feels that name, Dr. Suzanne Bradley, is familiar. But from where?

"Hi, this is Joe Rezinski with Dr. Suzanne Bradley, one of the people in charge of research at Bold Insights, the company that developed these unusual goggles that I am now wearing. She spent time with me going through the research they have done to correlate the measured metrics to core emotional states of the subjects. She showed me graphic images, done by a staff artist, since they cannot capture images on video. The rendered images show the same person feeling frustrated, happy, sad, having a good discussion, and having an argument. Suzanne explains what changes in the Time Information Field patterns of colors.

"Now, if you ask your significant other what is wrong, and they say nothing, you can put on these Real Dimension VR Goggles and see if they are telling the truth." Joe then jokes, "Seems when my girlfriend replies 'fine,' I can verify that. Of course, she can do the same to me. So, boys and girls, a whole new level of interacting with your significant other is coming your way."

Then it hits Jared. Patterson University. That's where Dr. Suzanne Bradley's name comes from. He immediately suppresses the urge to run and grab his private offline laptop, since he does not want to miss any of this program.

Suzanne explains to the audience, "Because you, the viewer, cannot see what Joe is seeing with the Real Dimension VR Goggles on, I will use the artist's rendering to help you visualize what he is looking at. We call the patterns of colors Time Information Fields. In three-dimensional time, consciousness is real, just like our brains and hearts are real in three-dimensional space. The Real Dimension VR Goggles allow the wearer to see three-dimensional matter, which, it turns out, includes our thoughts and emotions."

Then Joe adds, "Time to see what we think and feel!" He stops for a second, amused by his own statement, before continuing. "These goggles are opaque, so when you put them on, you cannot see a thing until they are booted up. Once they are operational, the room and people here are imaged on the inside of the goggle lenses. The lenses used to make these Time Information Fields viewable, do not transmit the light frequencies that our eyes use to see, so Bold Insights projects an image of what we normally see on the inside of the lenses."

Dr. Bradley explains, "A small camera takes the image of what is in front of you and overlays it with the image of the Time Information Fields. So, when you look at me, you see not only me as you normally would, but my Time Information Fields as patterns of colors. As you will see in the images, it is basically an elliptical shape with all these colors, some in circles and others in odd shapes." The show flips to one of the artist's renderings of a person standing and their Time Information Fields superimposed, just like what the goggles do.

Dr. Bradley continues, "Joe has looked at me, and to give him a sense of how it changes for different people, we have Skylar, one of our very creative researchers, to stand in front of Joe." Skylar moves to the same spot that Suzanne was standing in.

Jared just about falls off the couch after hearing that name, Skylar. He heard the term Time Information Fields and then they associated Time Information Fields to thoughts and emotions. Nobody else but the Chronos Consortium has technology to do and verify that. Every nerve in Jared's body is now on edge. Again, he uses all his discipline not to run to his office and grab his offline computer.

Joe sees the two of them switching places, then chimes in, "Interesting. Looking at Skylar, I see her with her Time Information Fields as a whole new pattern of colors and a different elliptical shape."

Suzanne jumps in to explain, "So Joe is seeing that each person has unique Time Information Fields, and that parts of the color patterns depend on your mental and emotional attitudes. The patterns associated with the long-term attitudes do not change much, but the short-term ones change rapidly."

"Well, Skylar, you look pretty colorful today," Joe says, looking to keep the show amusing for their audience.

"But. . . here is what is really interesting," Joe continues. "Naturally, I suspected the Real Dimension VR Goggles are doing image processing and then software is layering the Time Information Fields color patterns on top of the physical image of the person being looked at. I put this question to Dr. Bradley."

Suzanne answers, "To address the concern of image processing that Joe brought up, I asked Joe to keep looking at Skylar as I place a black cloth over his head." Once she finishes adjusting the black cloth over Joe's head, she asks, "What do you see, Joe?"

"The regular physical image of Skylar disappeared immediately, but the image of her cool Time Information Fields is still there," he answers with a tone of intrigue.

"Okay, now use your finger to point left or right to indicate the direction you want Skylar to move in. I am purposely not *asking* Joe to *tell* Skylar which way to move, because I wanted to eliminate any concern that voice recognition is being used."

The camera person focuses on Joe's hand so the viewer can see which direction he is pointing. Joe signals for Skylar to move left. Then right.

Suzanne asks Joe, "What do you see?"

"I see the image of the Time Information Fields moving in the direction that I am pointing. It follows my directions even with the black cloth over my head and the goggles."

"All right, let's try another experiment," Suzanne says. "First, I will remove the black cloth from your head. Joe, can you see Skylar's regular image and the image of Time Information Fields?"

"Yes."

"Skylar is going to walk through that door and behind that wall," Suzanne says, pointing to the white door that leads to a conference room. "Joe, let me know what you see."

Skylar walks toward the door, through the opening, and moves to her left so she is behind the wall, separating herself from the room Joe and Suzanne are in.

"Her physical image just disappeared, but I still see her Time Information Fields," Joe says. "Ha, I can see through walls!"
Suzanne explains that they conducted double-blind experiments, and the effect is real. "So, with these Real Dimension VR Goggles, you can see people's Time Information Fields through matter."

Joe quickly follows her statement with, "Pretty mind-blowing, right?" as he uses both hands to signify his head blowing up.

Then, just as quickly, he gets serious again. "Here is the other interesting thing. Remember I mentioned that the goggles don't work if you use a camera to try to record what you're seeing with them? The Real Dimension VR Goggles require your eyes, and brain, to see these interesting patterns of colors. I keep coming back to calling them patterns of colors, because that is what I am seeing.

"The goggles display colors in such a way that our eyes and brains see them in unique patterns. I have to admit, I find myself captivated by what I am seeing. I hope that in a future version of these goggles Bold Insights is able to use video to capture the patterns, since I would definitely like to see what I look like through the goggles."

In the next segment, Joe reappears, now with the goggles off, and looks into the camera. "I highly recommend people go to the Bold Insights website, read up on this really cool technology, and buy a pair of the Real Dimension VR Goggles. If you can't afford them, club in with a few of your friends and share. Hey, try playing the card games with these goggles. You can tell when the other player is excited about a card they just pulled from the deck." He laughs. "Bold Insights has many experiments and games that you can do with the goggles. Go to their website to download these. The goggles also work as regular VR goggles, so you can use them with your video games. I have already put in an order for my own.

"CEO of Bold Insights, Tom Williamson, hopes to bring the price down over time as they ramp up manufacturing and work to get process costs down. He told me that just by word of mouth, they have already sold out the next four months' production. With a new manufacturing partner coming online soon, they will be able to triple their output to meet what they expect to be an ever-increasing demand. So, give yourself a whole new look on life, literally! I will give you an update in the near future after I have experimented with mine."

Jared leaps off the couch and runs to his home office, opens his bottom drawer, and pulls out his laptop. He runs back to the living room. The host is talking about what they have lined up for next week.

After the show, Skylar, Bohdi, Suzanne, and Tom jump up in celebration. The show segment was everything they could have hoped for.

In the Browns' home, Annie is crying tears of joy. The loneliness she is struggling with is temporarily washed away as she just witnessed that their struggle had a purpose.

Jared flips open the laptop and fires it up. He watches the wireless button and makes sure it is orange. This laptop never goes online. He impatiently waits for it to boot up. "Come on . . . come on . . ." he says, trying to encourage the laptop to run faster.

As soon as the icons come up, he goes to the folder where he keeps all his information that could be damaging for the Chronos Consortium. He scrolls down to the Skylar Donaldson and Bohdi Kearns folder. Then he flips to the folder of the information Max gave him and that he compiled himself on the two of them. He looks for his document where he summarized all of their spheres of influence.

He finds it: Skylar Donaldson and Bohdi Kearns SOI.docx.

He looks at the date. *It was roughly a year ago that I visited Skylar's home as George Mariazen and took a scan of them.* A moment ago, he heard Skylar's name on a TV program associated with a technology he could not have envisioned. He is amazed at how much they have done in that short time period.

Jared still feels guilt over the incident, but that event was the tipping point inside him, and it had changed the course of his life. Now he feels he is helping to make things right. He believes he can do good by leaking out details about what is going on in the Chronos Consortium. It was about six months ago that he sent that letter to Skylar, hoping his intuition was right. This show sure confirmed that he did the right thing. He is glad, since the action he has taken this past year working against the Chronos Consortium is very dangerous, but no less stressful than being on the outside of the Chronos Consortium and looking over your shoulder all the time.

He opens the document and searches for Bradley. *There it is—Dr. Bradley is a psychology professor at Patterson University. I knew that name sounded familiar.* In the next section, she is listed as teaching one of the classes that Bohdi took.

Jared closes the lid of the laptop and puts it on the table. *So, Skylar and Bohdi had to have those missing time scanner parts, and clearly some very important knowledge, all along. I bet that John Garrison imparted his technical knowledge to Dr. Brown, and that the "viewing device" listed on the nondisclosure agreement probably was a generic description of those goggles, or an early prototype, that was handed off to Skylar and Bohdi. Boy, those two have been busy.*

Jared feels good that he has some small part in the success of the goggles. He is so glad he did not report Bohdi's unusual reaction during his visit. He had a gut feeling more was going on. Clearly, by making that trail go cold, he gave them time to develop this technology. Back then, he privately hoped they had some of the technology and that they would do something good with it, but they have exceeded his expectations. He hopes they took the information in his first letter seriously. He thinks that a follow-up letter might be needed.

Jared immediately starts to think who in his family, or friends, would be the right one to substitute-order a pair of goggles for him. It cannot be him. There is no way he wants his name linked in any way. He still has more disruptive work to do. He cannot wait to hear the fallout at the Chronos Consortium as news of these VR goggles spreads. He gets up to go get a beer to celebrate. He knows it will only be a few hours before his phone starts ringing with secure emails about escalated responses to this crisis. If these goggles go viral, it will only be a matter of time before people recognize that not everything they see in the Time Information Fields comes from their own thoughts and feelings. The cat is out of the bag, and unless the Chronos Consortium can come up with an approach to counter what people will see with these goggles, their ability to manipulate is on a one-way trip to the trash can of history.

72.

The next day, Jared is called to Paul's office. Jared walks in as Paul is texting something on his phone. Jared seats himself in one of the chairs and waits. A minute later, Paul looks up. Jared recognizes a fury in Paul's eyes he has never seen before.

"How did we fail in our mission to find those scanner parts?" Paul asks, barely able to contain his rage. He is looking for someone to blame for this failure.

Jared responds firmly, "You sent me to scope out the properties of Skylar Donaldson and Bohdi Kearns, and I did that. I also got a good Time Information Field scan of Skylar and a joint one of Skylar and Bohdi which allowed us to get information on both fields, as instructed. Phil and Tania were pleased with the quality of the scans. I was not able to get inside the house, but that is not unusual." Jared stops for a minute, because he can feel he is ready for a fight, but he collects his emotions. "I delivered on all the requirements assigned to me."

Jared feels particular satisfaction in Paul's crazed look. Jared can see that Paul is in an emotional free fall. His face is an awful pale white, the type of color someone would manifest right before they expected the floor beneath them to open up and swallow them whole. The analogy fits, because there is no way Paul will not be fired. The Chronos Consortium needs a target, and Paul will be it. Jared then has an insight. *Now you know what it feels like to be a target for the Chronos Consortium. Some cosmic justice here.*

As the day progresses, Jared watches as this branch of the Chronos Consortium descends into chaos. Emergency meetings are called. Jared is amused that two kids, in their early twenties are legitimately creating one of the bigger threats that could undermine the Chronos Consortium's power over people.

One of the people especially concerned is Hank. He is very concerned that the view that young people have effectively challenged the Chronos technology is bad news for his Re-Imagination project. Hank called a meeting with Agent Phil to try to convince him of his view.

Phil lets off some steam after Phil just finished a short, angry meeting with Hank. Jared has become a good listener and is really paying attention to what Phil is venting about. Phil recounts angrily, "He called me into his office, and I knew what he was going to say. His Re-Imagination Project. That's all he has been focused on these past years. I know it is ready to go, since it passed all the tests. Hank is now very concerned that some of the people he has staffed up for his project will be pulled to investigate young people's Time Information Fields. I think that is the right thing to do, and Hank knows very well how I feel. In our meeting, he reminded me that the results of the scan did not match our modeled data for young people, so any talk of starting that project up is based on a weak premise. I pushed back, saying the data was even stronger evidence that more research is needed,"

Jared has heard Hank argued that even if they eventually are successful in finding a new Time Information Field for young people, we are still left with a technique of only dealing with one person at a time, and the Chronos Consortium does not have the resources to deal with all the new threats one at a time. He feels that with his Re-Imagination Project, he can move whole groups of people and bring them in line with the policies beneficial to the Chronos Consortium. His is a proactive approach instead of the reactive process they currently use. The thought left Jared a bit cold.

Jared's attention shifts back to what Phil is saying. "But I still believe we should investigate these new Time Information Fields around young people. I asked Hank if he and Jim had included young groups in the tests they did. Hank answered specifically that they had not. I reminded him that he still might be vulnerable to this young effect. I could see the wheels turning in Hank's head to counter my remark. But there was nothing he could come up with. His groups were based on psychological profiling, which is suspect, given the parameters I suspect they were using are from the older demographics. I just sat back, because no matter what Hank says or does, after this fiasco, the time and money to get more data for our project will be coming, and real soon. And it is needed. Tania and I are worried that we are overlooking something important. We have already lost more than eighteen months of progress. Tania and I want to understand how that Time Information Field you took of that those two young people, could be so different. Are they outliers? We need more scans, and we are going to get them."

Jared can see and hear the satisfaction in Phil's voice. He thinks Phil is done talking, but he adds, "It was funny. As I left Hank's office, I had to stop just down the hall to respond to a text I received. While I was typing my reply, I heard a loud thud, like a flying object hitting a wall. Hank was not a happy man when I left."

Jared thinks Phil should be more cautious. He won a battle with Hank, and that is no easy feat. But Hank never rests, especially when he feels an oncoming fight, and he feels Hank has just amped up his battle mode.

73.

Skylar freezes. Here is another letter, with her as both the sender and the addressee. It has the same look as the one she received from Incognito a year and a half ago.

She walks upstairs to the spare bedroom that she and Bohdi use as a home office. Bohdi is finishing up his section of a document they will be sending to another new vendor to help manufacture their latest goggles.

"I think we just got another letter from Incognito. Want to read it together?"

He immediately stops what he is doing and leaps up from the chair.

Skylar hands him the unopened letter. She thinks for a minute. "We should use gloves as a precaution. Just to be safe. We have gone public with the goggles, and we just need to make sure we are not being targeted."

"Good idea. I will go and get some, and some breathing masks for us." Bohdi shoots out of the room.

Skylar puts the envelope down carefully on top of a bookshelf and goes to wash her hands.

When the two of them convene back in the office, they put on the gloves, the breathing masks, and goggles he brought back. They both head to the garage to open the envelope. They are nervous. The last letter had that eye-opening report, and it seemed that Incognito was trying to help them. But why, and who is this person? Is Incognito a mole inside the Chronos Consortium? The thought had occurred to them both.

Skylar opens the envelope with a blade. She pulls out the letter and slowly unfolds it. No powder or any contaminant is obvious. They both read:

To Skylar and Bohdi,

You are likely concerned about the nature of my letters. I ask nothing in return, other than you consider carefully the information I give to you. Congratulations on your new goggles. Given your success, here are my recommendations.

1. Your use of the term "Time Information Fields" by you and your colleagues at Bold Insights is very accurate. Well done.

2. Use the goggles to get a baseline of what is normal for you and those around you, especially individuals associated with your new goggle business.

3. Not everything you feel is directly related to you. As you, hopefully, understood from my last letter, there is technology available to an organization to generate effects that can impress on an individual specific thoughts and emotions. Typically, this results in emotional distress leading to impaired decision-making.

4. You and your associates have shaken this organization that developed and uses similar technology for thought control. This organization is likely where some of the technology used in your goggles originated. This organization will not confront you openly, but be assured, you are on their radar. They will go after you, not in a physical way, but you will be targeted. The details in this letter will let you know when you are being targeted. Know this, the technology does not work on everyone. Those with particularly high moral and ethical standards are not as affected by it. I suspect that you and your group will have this benefit, but you might still feel the effects impressed upon you. Follow the recommendations herein and you can learn how to counter this.

5. When you feel out of sorts, or bombarded with emotionally charged thoughts, for reasons that you cannot understand, document what you see through the goggles. See if you can determine common features in the fields of others when they are experiencing the same emotional distress. These common features during times of feeling bombarded can be the signature of Time Information Fields used to disrupt your thoughts and hijack your emotional balance and success.

6. Should you feel agitated or emotional distress, here are a few remedies, in order of effectiveness. Express vocally to someone what you are feeling. It takes the power away. Write down what you are feeling with as much detail as you can. The act of consciously trying to articulate what you are feeling in the moment counters the effect. Use meditation or lastly, try strenuous physical exercise.

7. Experiment with creating new technology that can generate the very Time Information Fields you and your colleagues are witnessing. I have no technical insight to pass on to you, but I know it is being done. Should you develop equipment capable of generating these fields, use two versions of the same equipment to see how the two generated Time Information Fields enhance or negate each other. You can use this technology to help people, but be aware, you can also cause them distress, if you are not careful.

8. With your goggles, you are giving people the opportunity to understand that what they feel and think is real, and hopefully, help them pay more attention to what goes on inside their heads and hearts. I applaud your creative marketing.

9. You have done well so far, but do not rest because those who wish to destroy your technology and intend to discredit your efforts will not rest. It is a battle that will escalate.

I wish you well.

Sincerely,
Incognito

Skylar immediately looks up when she is finished reading. "I bet the work we are doing with colors will help us. Colors have a Time Information Field signature, since we definitely see a change in our fields when we use colors, but we need to determine what is being enhanced or nullified."

"I agree," Bohdi says with a faraway look in his eyes.

"What is on your mind?" Skylar asks.

"We know this letter correlates well with what Dr. Brown told us about, the idea of the goggles being important for combating thought control. Incognito clearly knows what is going on, that we started this goggle technology with Chronos Consortium scanner parts, and what we are doing."

"The organization this guy is talking about must be the Chronos Consortium Dr. Brown spoke of," Skylar adds to confirm what she believes Bohdi is implying.

"I think so. But what if we are being set up by Incognito?" Bohdi says, flipping back to the first page of the letter.

"Could be." Skylar looks back at the letter. "But there is nothing being suggested in this letter that undermines our efforts. It seems all this information helps us, without giving away anything that we are doing."

"True. This sentence here that the technology does not work for everyone. It does not work as well on those with high moral and ethical standards. We should mention that to Dr. Bradley. See if we can figure out how to correlate what is in the field to these traits. It would help us sort out who is more vulnerable to these attacks."

"And you and I should pay attention, see if we can sort out when we are just out of sorts and when we feel an agitation impressed upon us. Could be tricky, but maybe what we see in our fields will make it more obvious."

"Definitely. Incognito suggests it is a battle, so we'd better be prepared for it."

"I still wonder if Incognito is George, the guy who showed up at our door," Skylar says, repeating her suspicion, as she has many times since the last letter.

Skylar likes the term *our door*. Skylar's father had taken a two-year assignment with a geologist to work on building new equipment that could be used in the field. David felt he needed a change, and this would require a temporary move on his part. Skylar said if Bohdi moved in, the two of them could cover all the costs of running the home. David agreed. He was happy that his daughter was involved in a serious relationship with Bohdi.

"Maybe," Bohdi says slowly. "He's the only person we have to suspect, so naturally, we gravitate toward thinking he is involved with this. But if he took a scan of me for the Chronos Consortium, why would he be helping us now?"

"I don't know. Likely we'll never know who Incognito is," Skylar says with concern.

"I am going to take a quick photocopy of this letter so we can bring it in to work tomorrow and show the others. For safekeeping, let's put this envelope and letter into our secure place with the other information," Bohdi says as he heads into the kitchen to get a plastic bag to seal the letter in.

74.

Skylar stops by Suzanne's office to see if she is free. Suzanne looks up from her laptop and waves her in. Their offices are still in the original building they started in. The fourth office down the hall, which was Tom's, is now used for a small conference room. The previous large conference room has become additional space for their research and development. Tom moved his office to the new lens manufacturing facility they opened recently.

Skylar steps in, closes the door, and sits in one of the chairs opposite Suzanne in her messy office. Skylar is tired and looking forward to going home.

"What's up?" Suzanne asks.

"Well, as you know, I am setting up the celebration of Bold Insights' three-year anniversary. I've been working on a slide show of how this company got started, how the first set of goggles went viral, and how that continues to support all the research we are doing. We now have fifteen people in our new manufacturing facility, making the critical lens components, and three vendors across the globe making the goggles for us.

"But there is no way I can talk about any of our current research and development to the rest of the company, and to our vendors, so the presentation is primarily focused on the history of the goggles and planned improvements, which are minor."

"I wish we could speed things up and get our next product launched," Suzanne replies. She shares Skylar's impatience to get the next product out to the public. "But we are a year or two away from doing that. It still amazes me how different the responsibility is for a product that just views the Time Information Fields, and another one that can actually change the Time Information Fields. Tom is very good for us because he constantly challenges us about liability. And he is right."

"I would love to talk about how we now have the technology to counteract what we know the Chronos Consortium is doing to control and manipulate with their technology. We have decoded, and countered, what they are doing, at least to the four of us. That is a huge achievement." Skylar feels pride swell inside her. The color experiments she started were the basis for this work.

Working with Bohdi as her subject and not finding a clear visual correlation between illuminated color and effect on his Time Information Fields while using the goggles, she continuously asked Bohdi to articulate what he was feeling. She documented his replies over time and found that the same color had one effect when he was feeling low on energy and another when he felt energetic. Out of this work emerged a pattern, a distinct correlation between color and its effect on human condition. Skylar summarized the data and showed it to Suzanne.

Suzanne listened carefully and immediately saw the potential in what Skylar and Bohdi had documented. Suzanne followed up by setting up scientific research that showed conclusively the correlation between color and its effects on human emotions. The three of them took their experiments to a new level and explored potentials for new therapeutic methods to deal with mental and emotional stress and illnesses. Suzanne started out evaluating student volunteers from local colleges and had them fill out a detailed psychological questionnaire on how they felt, physically, emotionally, and mentally. They assigned color combinations based on the initial data and gave them three treatments, all the while monitoring the volunteers with the goggles. After two years of work, they could make combinations of colors that targeted specific issues they saw in the Time Information Fields of individuals.

More than ninety percent of the people in the study group receiving these treatments were very pleased with the results. They reported feeling more balanced, which their Time Information Field images confirms. Many asked if they could purchase this technology and use it at home. In the control group, thirty percent of the people reported positive results. Suzanne knew that within the control group, where they did everything except turn on the color treatments, people would feel better because of the placebo effect. She knew from research that even patients given pills labeled as a "placebo" reported more pain relief than those who received no pill at all. She understands that an analysis of the true source of the efficacy of these treatments is complex.

But what is clear from their study is that so many of the subjects asked to purchase this equipment because they reported feeling better. The technique works.

After these successful experiments, Skylar, Bohdi and Suzanne took the "feeling bombarded" data, as they called it, and conducted a detailed analysis of the reported Time Information Field colors. They found common features in this data, and with their new knowledge, applied their understanding of how to change Time Information Fields to any one of the four of them who were feeling bombarded. The bombardment feeling went down significantly with just one treatment, and was gone after three treatments given three hours apart. They clearly had found an antidote to what they believed were the "treatments" that Incognito had referenced.

"You look worried," Skylar says, realizing she had drifted off during their conversation.

"Well, this whole social media phenomenon. It seems to me that people are actively undermining their own situations. It's almost as if the Chronos Consortium has figured out a way to influence people on a mass scale. I just feel a step behind. As soon as we worked out how to deal with their previous technique of bombarding individuals, they seem to have come up with a new method. It would be nice to know what is going on. Something very self-destructive is happening all around us, and I just cannot figure out how it is all being played out. It's as if people have temporarily lost their ability to think critically. Or maybe it is a permanent loss of critical thinking. That thought freaks me out even more."

"I do feel like there has been some major shift," Skylar says, "as if people are making irrational choices. But the work we've been doing with the new Time Information Field generators and how it helps people with psychological issues, that is awesome. We are still doing amazing work that will help many people."

Suzanne realizes that her recent concerns have been clouding her awareness of all the good work that is going on. She cannot wait to publish their findings and work with other colleagues who are open-minded enough to try the new technology. She hopes her research encourages researchers and practitioners to experiment with this new way to alleviate common issues, such as anxiety and depression. She is planning experiments in helping people with addiction and other self-destructive behaviors.

"Thanks. I'm glad you stopped by. You've picked me up from a dark place I have been stewing around in for a few hours," Suzanne says, looking less stressed already. "I am still impatient with the pace of progress, but it's good to appreciate what we have done so far."

"Glad to be of help. So, my reason for stopping by is to tell you that the anniversary slide show will be focused solely on the goggles, with information we can share with our vendors in other countries," Skylar says. "We can't present everything we are now doing, but we still have a lot to say."

"We do have a lot to be proud of," Suzanne responds, feeling better. "When you are happy with your first draft, send a copy to Tom, and me."

"Great. I will send it out tomorrow. Anyway, time for me to go."

Skylar is ready to spend a pleasant Friday evening at home with Bohdi. He left half an hour ago to stop by the hardware store before they closed. This weekend's project is fixing leaky faucets.

"Have a great weekend. And no bringing work home!"

"Easy to do. I have projects waiting for me at home," Skylar says with a laugh, as she happily heads out for the weekend.

75.

Seven years later, on the drive home from Bold Insights, Skylar is reflecting on the discussion she and Bohdi had about becoming parents. They decided it was a risk worth taking, even given everything that was happening in their lives. On looking back, she wonders how they could have doubted it. She loves the name they chose for their daughter, Kalani, since it means *the heavens* in Hawaiian. Now Kalani is five years old. How time flies.

Skylar wishes that each kid came with her own manual to help parents negotiate these complex relations, especially one for their five-year-old Kalani. She wonders how it is that her own parents were ever able to keep themselves together between work, parenting, and maintaining a relationship. When Skylar was a teenager, her mom told her, "Wait until you have kids and see how loving, concerned, and even fearful you become! You will not recognize yourself, both in a wonderful and not-so-wonderful way. It is the best and the hardest thing you will ever do."

Back then, Skylar ignored what her mom was saying to her. Her words were merely another parental platitude that parents espoused to justify their behavior. Skylar chuckles at her past teenage confidence, about how her version of the world was so much better and wiser than her poor lost parents. Since becoming a parent of such a precocious child, she misses her mother even more. She wishes she could call up her mother and just talk.

With Kalani, they have worked hard to figure out the dos and don'ts in raising her, and it is like nothing they could have imagined. Kalani is such a passionate girl. She can be sweet and endearing, but then has flashes of frustration when she cannot do a task. She seems hard on herself, and this worries Skylar. She thinks that at Kalani's age, life should just be a series of mysteries to be explored. But not for Kalani. She has no patience for the standard children's books. She loves any book with stars and galaxies. To keep her active, Skylar and Bohdi decided to enroll her in a private preschool, which Bohdi's parents and Skylar's Dad offered to pay for. The grandparents are so impressed by the stunning smarts of their grandchild that Bohdi and

Skylar have to tell them to curb their enthusiasm about their ideas for her future education.

As Skylar walks to the front door of their home, she feels a sense of pride. They bought her family home four years ago from her father. Their salaries had increased enough so they qualified for a mortgage. Little by little, they have been making personal updates to their home. She chuckles over how so many friends and family expect them to be multimillionaires, but that is not why they got into this work, and it is not what drives them. A better future is their mission, and the amount of money they spend on research substantiates this commitment. The company will always remain private, so no shares will ever be sold. The goal of Bold Insights is still to sell the goggles for a low enough price that more people can afford them in countries where they still are a huge expense.

She opens the front door slowly and peeks in to see if she can surprise anyone. Everything is quiet.

She goes upstairs quietly to peek into Kalani's bedroom. Kalani looks up.

"Mommy's home!" She drops her picture book on stars and runs to Skylar.

Skylar scoops her up into her arms and heads downstairs, asking Kalani questions about her day.

When she heads into the kitchen, she sees the back door open. She looks out and sees Bohdi with the back-door handle in pieces on a board. Bohdi gets up and moves toward his two ladies. After he hugs them both and gives Skylar a kiss, Skylar puts Kalani down. Their little girl immediately takes off back upstairs to her room.

"How did your day end?" Bohdi asks.

"Good. Glad to be home. And you, did you have a good afternoon with Kalani after you picked her up from school?"

"Yeah, great. I spent some time with her building a new spaceship with her LEGOs. It's funny, she has her book on stars open to the Pleiades star cluster and was asking me to read about them again. That kid's focus is a bit scary at times."

"The apple did not roll far from the tree," Skylar states, smirking at him.

"No, she is much more intense than I ever was," he says with a smile, knowing that statement is not going anywhere.

"What's for dinner?" Skylar is ready for food.

"We have some leftover fruit salad, and let's call for a pizza. We can eat out back on the grass, picnic-style. It's such a nice evening."

"Great idea. You want a glass of wine?" Skylar takes a glass for herself out of the kitchen cabinet and waits for Bohdi to respond, "We will celebrate the start of the weekend."

"Actually, I'll have a beer. I think there's only one left in the refrigerator, anyway."

Skylar and Bohdi sit at the kitchen table, taking a moment to enjoy their drinks. Just then Kalani bursts in with her favorite book. She puts it on the kitchen table and opens it to the Pleiades star cluster page. Bohdi smiles, expecting some nonverbal feedback from Skylar.

Kalani then steps back, puffs out her chest, and with authority, points to herself and declares, "I am ETBuddy." She looks at Bohdi, then Skylar, her eyes intense.

Bohdi chokes on the swig of beer he was taking. Skylar looks at Kalani and asks sweetly, "Where did you get that name, Kalani?"

Bohdi starts coughing.

"I am ETBuddy," she says emphatically, pointing again at herself.

"I like that name," Skylar replies, and looks to her husband for a reaction. He is still struggling to clear his throat.

Skylar continues, "Daddy likes that name too. Did you hear it somewhere?"

"No," Kalani replies. "I am ETBuddy. I knew Daddy and Mommy before I was Kalani."

She pauses, then adds, "I called myself Sullivan."

Bohdi snaps his head up and looks at his daughter. He feels a shiver go down his spine.

Kalani moves forward, points to the open page, and says, "That is my home." Then she snatches up her book and runs upstairs.

Skylar looks at Bodhi, and asks, "Did you ever mention that to her?"

"We haven't talked about ETBuddy in ages, probably before she was born. And we certainly have never mentioned or used the name Sullivan, ever."

All the hairs on Skylar's neck stand on end. She feels the full truth of what her daughter just said.

"Oh, shit," she says with alarm in her eyes. Leaning over, she quietly says to Bohdi, "We really are in trouble now. We've barely figured out how to parent her now and she is only five; what's going to happen later?"

Bohdi leans in and grins. "It will be interesting if she invites some of her *other playmates* to stop by."

"You're pretty funny," as she leans over to give him a kiss.

About the author

Robert Kersten is a physicist with a lifelong interest in space, time and human consciousness. His theories on these topics are available on his website *www.multidimensionaltime.com* in the form of white papers, a technical book on these subjects and links to his many *youtube* videos created to help those interested understand these fascinating topics.